Praise for the
New York Times bestselling
Belador series

WITCHLOCK

"Everything about this book from the villainess on the gorgeous cover to the very last page grabs you, sucks you in and won't let you go until panting and exhausted you read the very last page...Fans of Rachel Caine's Weather Warden series will enjoy this series. I surely do." ~~D. Antonio, In My Humble Opinion

"Every scene in WITCHLOCK is absolutely spellbinding...This remarkable author repeatedly leaves you wondering if there truly are happenings on earth of which we are not aware..." ~~Amelia, SingleTitles.com

"I LOVE THESE BOOKS! I wait impatiently for every book to come out and have never been disappointed. Thank you for continuing to allow me another world to escape to. :)" ~~Elizabeth, Reader

DEMON STORM

"..non-stop tense action, filled with twists, betrayals, danger, and a beautiful sensual romance. As always with Dianna Love, I was on the edge of my seat, unable to pull myself away." ~~Barb, The Reading Cafe

"...nonstop adventures overflowing with danger and heartfelt emotions. DEMON STORM leaves you breathless on countless occasions." ~~Amelia Richard, SingleTitles

"There is so much action in this book I feel like I've burned calories just reading it." ~~D Antonio, Goodreads

"...I have to thank Dianna for keeping this series true to the wonderful world, witty dialogue and compelling characters that I have loved since the first book." ~~Chris, Goodreads

RISE OF THE GRYPHON

"...It's been a very long time since I've felt this passionate about getting the next installment in a series. Even J. K. Rowling's Harry Potter books. It's a story you don't want to end and when it does, you can't help but scream out 'No! NO THEY DID NOT JUST DO THIS TO ME!! NO!!!!'" ~~Bryonna Nobles, Demons, Dreams and Dragon Wings

"...shocking developments and a whopper of an ending... and I may have exclaimed aloud more than once...Bottom line: I really kind of loved it." ~~Jen, Amazon Top 500 Reviewer

"I want more Feenix. I loved this book so much...If you have not read this series, once again, what are you waiting for?" ~~Barb, The Reading Cafe

"..fantastic continuation of the Belador series. The action starts on page one and blows you away to the very end." ~~Fresh Fiction

THE CURSE

"The Beladors series is beloved and intricate. It's surprising that such a diverse and incredible world has only three books out." ~~Jessie Potts, USA Today, Happy Ever After

"The precarious action and genuine emotion in THE CURSE will continuously leave the reader breathless...a mesmerizing urban fantasy story overflowing with heartfelt emotions and dramatically life-altering incidents." ~~Amelia Richards, Single Titles

"If you're looking for a series with an epic scope and intricate, bold characters, look no further than the Belador series...This new addition provides all the action and intrigue that readers have come to expect...a series to be savored by urban fantasy and paranormal romance fans alike." ~~Bridget, The Romance Reviews

ALTERANT

"There are SO many things in this series that I want to learn more about; there's no way I could list them all... have me on tenterhooks waiting for the third BELADOR book. As Evalle would say, 'Bring it on.'" ~~Lily, Romance Junkies Reviews

"An incredible heart-jolting roller-coaster ride...An action- packed adventure with an engrossing story line and characters you will grow to love." ~~ Mother/Gamer/Writer

"An intriguing series that has plenty of fascinating characters to ponder." ~~ Night Owl Reviews

BLOOD TRINITY

"BLOOD TRINITY is an ingenious urban fantasy with imaginative magical scenarios, characters who grab your every thought and more than a few unpredictable turns ...The paranormal action is instantaneous, while perilous suspense continuously escalates to grand proportions before the tension- filled and satisfying conclusion. The meticulous storyline of Book One in the Belador series will enthrall you during every compellingly entertaining scene." ~~Amelia Richard, Single Titles

"BLOOD TRINITY is a fantastic start to a new Urban Fantasy series. The VIPER organization and the world built ... are intriguing, but the characters populating that world are irresistible. I am finding it difficult to wait for the next book to find out what happens next in their lives." ~~Diana Trodahl, Fresh Fiction

"BLOOD TRINITY is without a doubt one of the best books I've read this year... a tale that shows just how awesome urban fantasy really can be, particularly as the genre is flooded with so many choices. If you love urban fantasy, don't miss out on BLOOD TRINITY. I can't wait to read the second book! Brilliantly done and highly recommended." ~~ Debbie, CK2s Kwips & Kritiques

ROGUE BELADOR

THE BELADOR SERIES

NEW YORK TIMES BESTSELLING AUTHOR

DIANNA LOVE

Cover Design and Interior format by The Killion Group
http://thekilliongroupinc.com

The Belador series is an ongoing story line, and this is the reading order:

Dedication

This book is for my Dianna Love Street Team who keep me sane while spending so many hours deep in the cave!
(Message from Dianna to the street team is at the end of the book.)

CHAPTER 1

Evalle muttered, "It's been thirty minutes and I don't see anything to kill." She hugged her leather motorcycle jacket tighter against the chilly night air and glanced over at Reece "Casper" Jordan.

"It's only been twenty minutes. Patience, Sunshine," Casper murmured.

"It's too cold for patience. And don't call me Sunshine." She had zero appreciation for January in Atlanta. The sun had set over five hours ago and the temperature had to be in the low thirties by now. Intermittent snow had started accumulating enough to leave footprints. Unlike the northeast corner of the country, this city saw little snow, and a one-inch dusting would empty stores of milk and bread.

The bread companies and dairies must have cut a deal with the gods of winter.

Huffing out a frosty breath, she announced, "I'm not hanging around all night and freezing."

He grinned.

She quirked a threatening eyebrow at the VIPER agent who loved to get under everyone's skin, but he was looking away and failed to notice. Plus, she wore special sunglasses and he couldn't see that well in the darkness anyway.

She could. Born with glowing neon-green eyes, she was capable of seeing in almost total darkness. It was one of the few benefits of being an Alterant, a half-blood Belador. But of all the strange preternaturals who belonged to the VIPER coalition, she'd never met another being exactly like her.

Sure, the other Alterants had bright-green eyes, but she knew of none who possessed her body's deadly reaction to the sun.

Casper had lifted his chin to stare into the night at the tops of trees in Candler Park.

She'd always felt at home in this section of town. It was close to Little

Five Points, where she ate at restaurants like The Vortex, a good place to chow down, and made an occasional stop at Psycho Sisters when she had a rare urge to shop.

Neither was an option tonight.

Not with a demon, or some other creature, stalking this vicinity. Evalle had fought a demon two months ago in Stone Mountain Park, up on the northeast side of metro Atlanta. Few had been sighted since then.

Maybe she and her sidekicks for tonight weren't actually hunting a demon. Might just be someone stealing dogs. She could see a report getting blown out of proportion until it changed from dognapping to an invisible force dragging dogs away.

That didn't sound like a demon in her book.

Tracking down a dog thief was a human law enforcement issue, but since VIPER also watched over humans, they'd assigned this to her, Casper, and Lucien Solis.

"Something doesn't feel right," Casper muttered. He'd just returned from scaling the tallest oak tree in this wooded section to view the area from a high point. Better him than her.

She liked her feet planted on solid ground.

But Casper had first shifted into his ghost form, then basically floated to the top. He'd once told her his ghost form couldn't actually fly, but he could levitate above anything solid, including tree limbs.

"I'm ready to go as soon as Lucien gets back," Evalle announced. She'd hiked all over this place and the nearby neighborhoods, hoping to catch whoever had been stealing domestic pets. "This is a crap assignment."

Inclining his head, Casper frowned. "Agreed. I don't see squat. Did you hear where the intel came from?"

A fair question, since she'd taken the call from her Belador superior then rounded up Casper and Lucien to join her. "Supposedly a troll reported seeing something dragging a pack of dogs into the park after midnight."

"Aw, hell. Might be a troll stealing the dogs. They eat about anything."

Eww. "I wouldn't point a finger at a troll right now if I were you. That's all it'd take to crank them up again after that mess with a warlock using trolls to power a spell to create fake demons."

"You're right. The trolls are still complaining that VIPER didn't do enough."

Since trolls weren't members of the coalition, they had an agreement with VIPER that allowed trolls to live in the city, as long as they didn't hunt here.

Translation: Don't kill humans.

Some trolls were good people, but as a race they were predators and not exactly at the bottom of the food chain.

With the exception of a rare few, humans had no idea nonhumans existed and cohabitated in this world, but if demons kept popping up, it wouldn't be long before that changed.

"This is bullshit," Casper grumbled. "I'm with you. I'm done with being a damn dogcatcher." He crossed his arms, then looked to his left as Lucien emerged from the darkness, seeming to do so without even disturbing the air around him.

The two men partnering with her tonight were from opposite ends of the spectrum.

Casper hailed from Texas. He had snakeskin boots and jeans to go with his southern drawl. He wasn't overly bulked up, but at six-two he took up plenty of space and filled out a denim jacket with a mile of shoulders. Standing with his legs apart, he looked ready for a showdown.

Lucien's black hair curled at the collar of his wool peacoat, just adding to the mysterious look of the Castilian who kept to himself. He spoke in a smooth voice, rich with his unusual accent. "I may have found something."

Evalle wanted to groan.

Casper did. "I didn't see a thing from up top. What'd you find?"

"I'm not sure yet. Every time I got close, *it* moved. I think whatever it is detects my power."

"And just what is that power?" Evalle asked, not expecting an answer since Lucien shared little with his teammates. Call her crabby, but cold weather brought out that side of her.

Snowflakes sifted through the air. Again.

Great. Just great.

Lucien studied her for a moment as if sizing up his reply. "When I first met you, I had no idea what an Alterant was, other than a half-blood

Belador. I know little more than that now."

She got what he was saying.

Back before she'd learned the ugly truth about the other half of her blood, Lucien had never hesitated to partner with her on a mission, even when other VIPER members balked. Also, he'd never questioned her background, as long as she wasn't a witch. "Point taken."

His lips quirked with a smile and he gave a slight nod.

If he'd shared that slight smile with a room full of single women, the next sound would have been panties hitting the floor. Thankfully, she had a natural immunity to his dark and sexy allure.

She had her own hot man at home. "Then what are we doing?"

Lucien turned to Casper. "Want to see if you can get close to whatever it is in your other form?"

She and Casper had been teamed up before in the past, too. She'd often wondered if that had been because neither of them fit into the usual nonhuman categories.

They were unknown, or *other*.

She'd graduated to *known* since she discovered that she carried the blood of two sworn preternatural enemies—Belador and the Medb coven. The cowboy, on the other hand, had gained his nonhuman status by accident. Years back, during a trip to Scotland to trace his family roots, Casper had been struck by lightning.

On the plus side, he'd survived the electrical charge.

On the not-sure-how-to-gauge-it side, he now shared his body with an ancient Highland warrior, and could morph into a shadowy image. When Casper decided to hide, he was harder to locate than a flea on a Saint Bernard.

There had to be more to his Scotland story, but when pressed for details he'd give his good-old-boy chuckle and say something like, "Ya'll don't have time for all that. Now, let me tell you about the rodeo I won in Houston ..."

Casper scrubbed a hand over his mouth. "I'll give it a try. This'll be my second time changing shape in less than an hour. I don't know how long my ethereal form will hold."

After Casper returned from his recon on top of the trees, it had taken him almost a full minute to shift back to human. He was vulnerable to attack during the change, and this one would be even slower.

Lucien said, "I understand. We'll stay close enough to cover you. Let me locate whatever it is again, and I'll give you a signal for which way to move. Don't engage unless you think your ghost form will scare it to death."

"Roger that." Casper lowered his arms, and his body slowly turned translucent.

Lifting her spelled dagger from where it had been tucked in the sheath at her side, Evalle nodded at Lucien. "I'll cover the rear. Lead the way."

She trailed far behind Lucien as he led them from the thick oak grove to the public pool she'd already searched once. Casper allowed his form to glimmer next to her.

Evalle gave him thumbs up that she had him in sight. Then his glimmer dimmed to the point that even her sensitive eyes were tested to see him as he moved ahead of her.

They kept their distance from Lucien to allow him a chance to locate the creature.

She glanced up at the unlit security lights. They'd been functioning when she'd hiked through here a half hour ago. She couldn't inform these two about that without speaking since neither one had the telepathic ability she shared with other Beladors, and all three of them knew to be silent at this point.

When Lucien reached the first corner of a one-story building connected to the pool by a fenced enclosure, he lifted a fist as the sign for them to stop. Without looking back, he signaled for Casper to move out to the right toward the pool.

Casper's translucent figure dissolved into the night.

Evalle moved in the same direction Lucien had gone, but she stepped very slowly. She amped up her Belador hearing until the silence became a shirring noise of snow falling and small creatures scampering around.

Then a crunching sound stopped her.

There wasn't enough snow on the ground yet to make that crispy noise.

She looked around to locate Lucien. He was out of sight again. How was she supposed to know if he'd made that sound or if something else had?

Lucien appeared far to her right and Casper's glimmer caught up to him. They raced off into the darkness.

Seriously? What the heck did Lucien want her to do? Working as a team meant communication, dammit.

Releasing a pent-up breath, she eased forward another step. Might as well give this place one last thorough look.

The sound of a door opening at the other end of the building turned her around. Had something drawn Lucien away, then it backtracked, thinking no one had stayed behind?

Evalle turned slowly, taking in the huge tree overhanging that end of the building, and crept up to the corner that was smothered in darkness.

She started to move around the corner but froze at a sound she couldn't identify. Sounded like someone had crossed a bullfrog with a cricket. The thing made a low, rumbling frog noise that ended in a smothered chirping. If not for powering up her hearing a moment ago, she would have missed it.

A flash of movement on top of the building drew her gaze upward.

The clouds had parted, and with a half-moon shining now, Casper's translucent form picked up just enough light for her to discern his outline. When had he returned?

He motioned that he was staying up top to keep an eye out.

At least one teammate kept her informed.

Evalle made it around the street-side end of the structure and stuck her neck out barely enough to look past the corner, then ducked right back.

Crap. Right around the corner, a door stood ajar.

That would be a clue, Sherlock.

Leaning out further this time to look inside the room, she counted at least eight dogs huddled in a tight group. Something invisible corralled them. There might actually be more than eight animals. It was so dark inside there that, even with her vision, she could only separate the light-colored ones.

Crud. So much for Casper's theory about being relegated to freakin' dogcatchers.

Something was holding those animals, but what? And what about that strange noise? If the gods were in a good mood, it was nothing more than a mutant bullfrog with no fear of freezing.

As she strained to see into the corners of the room, the animals became agitated and began moving around, howling and barking. The sound wasn't loud even to her ears. Weird. Their invisible constraint apparently also deadened the sound. Whatever held the dogs in place had muffled the noise to where no human security or maintenance person would hear it.

Checking over her shoulder and scanning the surrounding yard, she held her breath, listening for anything else.

Nothing. But the rest of the area was now pitch-dark. Even her exceptional night vision failed to penetrate it. What had happened to the moonlight? The clouds were still AWOL, so the moon should be right above her.

Heading around the corner, she'd made one step toward the door when the pack of animals backed away as far as they could, still huddled as a group.

Not one of them made a sound now.

That couldn't be good.

Hair stood up along her arms. She turned slowly to search around her again. A cold breeze ruffled her hair, but the chills racing up her spine were no longer driven by temperature.

She didn't see anything at first, but then her eyes focused on a dark shape *waaaaay* too close to her, blocking the moon. She looked up, up, up until she could make out just enough of a long snout shape, ten feet off the ground, to call that the head.

What *was* that thing? The rest of its body was just a dark blob.

So far, nothing that resembled any demon she'd ever seen.

It hadn't noticed her. Its head was tilted toward the roof, focused on something.

Could it see Casper?

She looked back around for Lucien. Still no sign of him, but she needed some room to deal with this sucker. Looking down, she could see where its feet had actually sunk into the frozen ground. It probably weighed as much as an elephant. She had no idea what she was up against. Backing up would give her a chance to size up her opponent and come up with a plan for fighting it.

This is what I get for complaining about being a dogcatcher.

The most she could do from this position would be to stab it in the side of the leg, which was pretty much guaranteed to piss off something this humongous. That would get her squashed by a foot she couldn't see to avoid.

She moved back toward the corner, taking a step, then another step, keeping her eyes on the creature. Another couple feet and she'd have some room to move.

Her next step dropped her foot into a hole as deep as her knee and just wide enough to trap her boot, jostling her backwards. She flailed her arms to keep from falling and breaking her leg. Once she caught her balance, she listened for any movement.

Had Sasquatch noticed?

Yanking her gaze straight up, she found two bright yellow eyes staring at her from the biggest horse head she'd ever seen. It was stuck on top of a giant, hunched-over human body.

Shock registered a moment before his huge hands lunged for her.

She shoved up a hit of kinetic power to block him.

He slapped the invisible force. Vibration jarred her teeth. Growling, he started beating both fists on her kinetic shield.

With only one foot for support, she was off balance and bending further back with each blow.

She yelled, "*Hey! Little help!*"

Casper was of no battle use as a ghost, but that didn't stop the cowboy from dropping to the ground. He began changing to his human form, slowly.

Thankfully, he made almost no noise while his body worked through the transition.

Besides, the monster was focused on her right now. It lifted a foot the size of a table and stomped her shield.

Her arms threatened to give out under the pressure. She shoved harder, calling on all her power to push back, but her arms started to shake with strain.

The thing weighed as much as a car.

Casper stopped changing in half-form and started shouting at the monster, drawing its attention.

"Casper, no!" she shouted.

Too late. Sasquatch swung away from pounding on Evalle's kinetics to go after Casper.

She had no way to stop the monster.
It would kill him.

CHAPTER 2

Evalle couldn't get traction from her awkward position to do anything more than throw a new kinetic hit at the creature determined to smash Casper.

She slapped a blast at its thick head, shoving the creature sideways. Its dark body flickered and the head came fully into view, complete with a bushy mane. Grayish-blue skin didn't look any more alien on Sasquatch than the wild-eyed horse head snapping at Casper. The hunched-up body was narrow and covered in a map of tight muscle. Tiny black pupils floated in its yellow eyes. The bottom half of its body kept fading in and out from a dark shadow form to reveal snippets of a human-like body.

Was it wearing a glamour?

Snow sucked up off the ground beside Evalle, and started spinning into a sphere the size of a laundry basket. The spiraling snow continued to take shape as it lifted higher and flattened out. In the next second, it turned into a thin horizontal disk five feet across, and made a high-pitched whine.

What. The. Hell?

She didn't have time to think about it. The monster jerked back around to her. She stabbed her hands down onto the hard ground, and shoved up, trying to free herself. Bones in her ankle were close to snapping.

Sasquatch kicked at her.

Dammit. She fought for balance and threw up a new kinetic wall, but it lacked the power of her first one. His kick jarred all the bones in her upper body.

A high-pitched whine screamed near her. She glanced around to find the snow disk spinning closer.

"Drop your kinetics, Evalle," Lucien ordered.

Was he kidding? She twisted further to see that, yes, Lucien controlled the snow Frisbee. "That all you've got?"

Lucien ignored her and moved his wheel higher in the air, just as the monster turned and drew back a fist to swing at Casper again.

"*Do it!*" Lucien demanded.

Evalle killed her shield and shouted, "*Hit the ground, Casper!*"

The cowboy dropped fast. His human form finished taking shape in mid-fall, just before he slammed the hard surface with a grunt of pain.

The bright, spinning disk shot upward and sliced across the creature's throat without any resistance.

Sasquatch froze, then reached up for his head as it tipped over and fell to the ground. His body tumbled next ... heading straight for Evalle.

She pushed up one more time, using what power she had left to block him from crushing her, but her arms wouldn't hold long. Blood spewed from his headless neck and splashed her through cracks in her kinetic wall. Warm liquid splattered her skin and clothes. Ick.

Soft howling and barking sounded from the side of the building as Casper got to his feet and shook his head. "Man, that body change screws with me." He took in the headless corpse. "Damn, son, you do that with snow?"

He got a quirked eyebrow from Lucien for that.

"You two want to make yourselves useful and get this thing off me?" she grumbled.

It took both Lucien and Casper to drag the body to one side.

She dropped her arms and sucked in deep breaths, waiting as Casper and Lucien dug a trough wide enough to free her boot. No small feat with the ground frozen. She accepted Casper's offer of a hand up and hissed at the sore ankle, but she could walk without limping.

"You're the only agent I know who could find a gopher hole while fighting a monster, Sunshine," he quipped.

She gave up correcting him on how to address her and said, "It's a talent. Anybody know what that thing is?"

Lucien studied the body. "I don't think it's a demon."

"Huh," Casper grunted. "What then?"

"With that hunched body shape and horse head, it might be a tikbalang from the Philippines." Lucien glanced toward the whining and yipping still coming from the back. "But I don't get why it was hoarding dogs instead of killing them, or what it's doing here. Something's not right about this."

As if anything was ever easy in their world?

Evalle glanced at the lifeless eyes staring up at the sky. The eyes were flat black now instead of yellow.

Mission accomplished, right? Why did Lucien have to make her think there was more to this than just life in the underworld of Atlanta's nonhuman community?

She wiped ick off anywhere she could. Storm was going to pitch a fit when she showed up bloody. "Do you think the Medb could have brought it in, or maybe made this thing?" she asked.

"They could," Lucien said, not committing to his answer. "But this doesn't fit for any of the covens, even the Medb. This took serious power to control, and I'm not seeing the reason for it even being here."

Casper added, "Yeah. Dog theft? What's with that?"

Lucien said, "No idea."

Evalle still liked her worst enemy as the culprit. "Maybe the Medb coven is behind this, and they just wanted to annoy VIPER because of the sanction. Create havoc. I don't know."

Lucien looked as if he considered that. "I forgot about the Medb getting sanctioned for that rogue warlock in November."

"Not all of them were sanctioned," Evalle clarified. "Just the queen and Cathbad. That doesn't mean those two wouldn't order their warlocks to find a creature like this and use it to screw with us."

Casper grunted. "It'd be same day, same shit for that coven. They probably sit around laughing about this, because you know they can scry damn near anything and they try constantly to watch this stuff."

Lucien and Evalle exchanged a look then raised their eyes to search around the area, as if they could see someone watching them via a scrying vessel.

Howls and barks grew louder from the room on the other side of the open door.

Lucien opened the door wide, exposing the animals that had moved forward again, but were still clustered too tightly to be free. He lifted his hands over the invisible enclosure and whispered something.

Evalle pushed loose strands of hair from her eyes, trying to make sense of all this. "What was the creature doing with all these ..."

"Watch out," Casper yelled, dancing sideways the second Lucien freed the dogs. Four-legged beasts shot out in all directions.

Lucien stepped out and looked around. "Guess that takes care of figuring out what to do with them."

"*Lucien!* Don't turn them loose. We need them for proof that our assignment's completed, and the local authorities can't get them back to the owners if we let them go."

Lucien spit out something angry, which she took to be a curse in Spanish, then raised his hands and did that whispering thing again.

Howling erupted in the distance and grew louder as the dogs ran back toward them.

The chain-link fence attached to one corner of the building circled a pool, then connected at the other side. A locked gate opened all by itself as the dogs ran straight for it. When the last one ran through, the gate shut and locked again.

"Satisfied?" Lucien asked.

"Yes, thank you." Evalle raked a hand over her head. She'd poke at Lucien's weird powers again, but right now she just wanted warm and clean. "We'll have our people inside Fulton County Animal Services come over as soon as we're done and pick them up."

That strange bullfrog grunting started up again, inside what Evalle had thought was now an empty room. A loud cricket chirp punctuated the weird noise, which could be heard easily now that the invisible enclosure no longer stifled the sound.

They all turned to look as a shaggy little critter stepped out of the room. It was the size and shape of a bichon frisé, but with salt-and-pepper hair and large owl eyes that were sunshine yellow. Really bright yellow.

If the eyes hadn't clued her in that this was not a recognized breed, then the unicorn horn sticking up four inches from its forehead would do it.

Lucien backed away.

Mr. Build-A-Monster-Killing-Saw-From-Snow retreated?

A little doggie thing bothered him? "What's the matter, Lucien?" she asked.

"I'm not getting near that thing."

Casper found this amusing too. "Why?"

"It's a witch's familiar. I want nothing to do with it."

The cowboy asked, "How do you know that's what it is?"

"I just do," Lucien said with finality, dismissing any future questions.

"White witch or dark witch?" Evalle asked.

"I don't know *that*."

Evalle took in the little critter's sad eyes. They reminded her of Feenix, her pet gargoyle, who was only two feet tall himself. She leaned over and called to it. "Come here, baby. Let's get you back to your owner."

The critter stood up on its stubby, thick hind legs. It waddled forward. Huh.

"Evalle, I don't think you un—" Lucien started.

That half-croaking, half-chirping, bullfrog noise started again. The fluffy critter stopped long enough to bare its fangs in Lucien's direction.

Lucien's dark expression warned that he would answer any challenge.

Evalle lifted a hand at the men. "Give me a minute." She patted her knee and the little doggie thing walked upright all the way to her, then leaped unexpectedly into her arms.

"Okay." She caught the animal, careful to stay clear of the horn. Smiling, she looked at Lucien and Casper. "See? No problem. We'll just take him, her, it to—"

Lucien was shaking his head. "There is no *we*. It's you."

She lost her smile and thought about baring *her* teeth. "I don't have any idea how to find its owner tonight, and I can't take this little guy home."

Casper suggested, "Give it to Sen and let him find it a home."

Lucien said, "Bad idea. The white witch council is having issues with VIPER. If that beast belongs to a white witch, handing it to Sen would light a powder keg of trouble."

Right.

Lucien and Rowan, a powerful witch, were chummy, even though he claimed to hate witches of any type. Actually, from what Evalle had seen the last time those two were within spitting distance of each other, steamy would be a more accurate description than chummy.

She told Lucien, "Then why don't you take this critter to Rowan and let her figure out who owns it?"

That seemed a perfect place to start looking for the owner, since Rowan led the white witch council.

"No. That's not my responsibility," Lucien stated.

The Castilian had always been a bit distant, but he'd never backed away from helping on any assignment in the past. Why now? Evalle shifted her heavy armful and said, "I thought you were friends with Rowan."

"We have an understanding, which includes me not dealing with her gaggle in any way. Besides, that creature being out on its own is a bad sign. Witches do not lose track of their familiars."

"Well, duh," Evalle smarted off. "We know it was dognapped or whatever."

"No. There's more to this, and I want no part of it."

What did he mean by 'more to this'? She'd ask, but he had a not-budging look on his face. "Fine." She turned to Casper. "Would you take this to Rowan?"

"Sure." He reached for the little unicorn mutt, but it bared its sharp fangs at him. Its jaw unhinged wide enough to snap off a person's head.

Casper snatched his hand back, then waved her off. "Nope, that one's all yours, Sunshine."

"How am I supposed to take this to Rowan?"

"I thought you drove Storm's Land Cruiser tonight."

Oh, that's right. I left my motorcycle at home. "I did bring his truck, but not to use for animal control," she argued. Weak, but that was all she had.

Casper shrugged. "Don't know what to tell you."

Should she take it home and call Rowan in the morning? Evalle envisioned this little terror around Feenix, who could be an even bigger terror. Plus, Storm would have to deal with the whole screwed-up menagerie. Her life was complicated enough.

She needed another option. "I can't take this home. I don't even know what it eats."

Lucien said, "Probably anything it wants, and I'm talking live food."

Not what she'd wanted to hear. "How did that tikbalang thing capture this familiar if he's that dangerous?"

Glancing around the dark room, Lucien speculated, "The familiar might have been hiding here if..." he hesitated, then shook off whatever he was going to say. "I don't know, but if someone with power was controlling the tikbalang, they might have sent it to capture the familiar. The tikbalang could've even brought the dogs to use as bait for the familiar, and shoved them in there when we showed up."

Evalle wanted to know what Lucien held back, but no one was pulling a word out of him if he didn't want to share.

"Why would anyone want a witch's familiar?" This from Casper.

Lucien shrugged. "I have no idea. Just throwing out possibilities for why it would be here with the dogs."

Evalle smiled at Casper. He'd been with her through a lot of missions, after all.

Casper crossed his arms. "No use wastin' those rare pearly whites on me, Sunshine. I don't have any majik mojo for containing that critter. You either take it with you or turn it loose."

Crud. If she turned this critter loose it might get lost forever *or* eat everything in its path. "Fine. If I'm stuck with this miniature land piranha, then you two can deal with Sen."

Sen served as the liaison between VIPER agents and their Tribunal, a ruling body of three deities who made decisions and passed judgment on nonhumans living in the human world. If humans had a clue what actually went on, they'd probably run screaming, which was why VIPER kept nonhuman activity hidden. Even Sen had to follow that rule.

He hated Evalle with a passion that she'd never understood, and she didn't like him any better because of it.

She wasn't alone in that club.

As a testament to just how much Lucien did not want any part of the witch's familiar, he nodded. "We'll handle this and Sen."

Casper added, "I'll get in touch with our people in animal control."

Evalle realized something else. "I don't have Rowan's new number. Maybe you could just call her..." Her voice trailed off as Lucien fished out his phone and punched in numbers.

Her phone played the default jingle.

While her phone continued repeating the jingle two more times before quieting, Lucien said, "Now you have her number."

She'd never seen Lucien so unwilling to touch something. In fact, Trey said that Lucien had once drawn a dark energy out of Rowan after a powerful Kujoo magician who answered to a Hindu god had found a way inside her mind. Rowan was one of the most powerful witches Evalle had ever seen, so anything capable of controlling her mind would have to be badass. Trey had been impressed by Lucien's abilities, and considering all that Trey had seen as a Belador warrior, it took a lot to impress him.

Evalle couldn't stand around and debate this any longer.

She told Lucien and Casper, "In that case, I'm off duty." She struck out for Storm's Land Cruiser parked two blocks away.

Should she just go home and see what Storm thought?

No. She was not bringing anything home that might shake the fragile truce Feenix and Storm had been working under for more than a month.

Feenix had stopped eating anything silver that belonged to Storm, and Storm had been using his majik to animate toys for her pet gargoyle.

Life was in balance most days.

She gave the shaggy critter another look and decided he was a male until she learned differently. "What am I going to do with you?"

The mutt-familiar showed his fangs, but made no sound.

She took that to mean he had no answers either.

With a little luck, this critter would belong to a white witch Rowan knew. Problem solved. If not, Evalle would have to report it to VIPER, which would then make it her duty as the Belador-Medb liaison to contact Queen Maeve to find out if it belonged to any of their coven members.

That would probably require being teleported to TÅμr Medb.

Wouldn't that be just what Queen Maeve wanted? To have Evalle trapped inside her kingdom?

By the time she reached Storm's truck, Evalle had come up with a second option that might save her from having to visit Rowan or deal with the Medb queen.

She put the mutt on the passenger seat and dug out her cell phone. She had Adrianna Lafontaine on speed dial. At one time, Evalle had wanted nothing to do with the Sterling witch, but that had been before they went through near-death experiences and got to know each other. Since then, they'd formed an unlikely friendship that had benefitted both of them in the recent past.

Adrianna answered, "Tell me you're not calling for anything witch related."

"That narrows our conversation to hello and goodbye."

Adrianna sighed audibly. "What do *you* need?"

"Stop sounding like I'm asking you to bloody your manicure."

"It wouldn't be the first time that happened with you."

Evalle let that dig pass. "What's got you so cranky?"

"I'm getting constant calls from VIPER agents asking about my Witchlock powers." Adrianna's voice changed to mocking. "*How does your new power work? Are you going to start a coven? Are you advising the new witch council? Will you be meeting with the dark covens?*" She took a breath. "I expect to hear from Oprah next."

Grinning, Evalle said, "It's tough to be a celebrity."

Had Adrianna just growled? The witch grumbled, "I even heard from the Sterlings this week."

"Really? What'd they want?"

"I have no idea. I disconnected the call immediately."

"Can't say I blame you for that." A lot of bad blood ran between Adrianna and her Sterling coven family. She'd disowned the lot of them, and for good reasons. Evalle could commiserate. The aunt who'd raised Evalle had kept her locked in a basement and knowingly allowed a man to abuse her as a teen.

To lighten the mood and get back to the problem at hand, Evalle said, "I didn't call for an interview or to ask about Witchlock. I have a lost familiar and just want to know if you could identify the specific witch who owns it."

"Probably not."

"I haven't even told you what it looks like, Adrianna."

"It wouldn't matter. The only way I'd know anyone's familiar was if I socialized with the witch, and we both know that doesn't happen."

There had been no emotion in Adrianna's words. She'd been raised a dark Sterling witch, but she didn't associate with either dark or white witches. That alone made her the best person to possess the ancient power of Witchlock, which could rule all witches. Rule a lot of other powerful beings as well.

Evalle had helped Adrianna fight Veronika, a crazy witch who had intended to use Witchlock to wipe out nonhumans who refused to serve her and force weaker witches to be her slaves.

Veronika lost that battle, and now resided in a cell beneath the mountain housing VIPER headquarters.

Evalle couldn't hide her disappointment. "So you can't help?"

"What're you doing with a witch's familiar anyhow?"

"It's not by choice." Evalle shared her night, including the snow-power disk that Lucien had used as a guillotine. "Here's the kicker. This little familiar might weigh fifteen pounds and doesn't even come to my knees. After killing the weird dog-thief monster, Lucien double-stepped away from this familiar as if it was a lethal disease."

"It might just be."

"Why?"

"If it belongs to a dark witch, the only way she'd allow anyone to touch her familiar would be if she were dead. As for white witches, it may be the same, but you'll have to ask Rowan to be sure. With the Medb coven infiltrating the city, it could belong to one of their group."

Evalle hoped not. "Any other time, I wouldn't lose sleep over one less Medb witch or warlock, but VIPER is actually sending agents out on security details for the Medb because the Medb are claiming harassment."

"You had to see that coming. The minute VIPER accepted the Medb into the coalition, the first strategic move I expected was something that would put all the non-Medb on defense, especially Beladors. VIPER should have anticipated these problems."

"Agreed, but this goes beyond harassment if one of theirs is dead," Evalle conceded.

"Exactly. If you show up with a familiar, and it belongs to the Medb, you'd better hope the witch died of natural circumstances or that you find the killer quickly. I'd start looking for a killer. If a witch or warlock died naturally, someone in the coven would know and would have come for the familiar, which means Queen Maeve can use this as grounds to demand restitution from the coalition."

Evalle made the leap to where Adrianna was headed. "Like handing over a gryphon."

"More like handing over *you*," Adrianna pointed out. "She wants any and all gryphons, but getting you would be a coup. Everyone knows you're on the top of Queen Maeve's wish list. A Tribunal might even suggest giving you to them as compensation."

True. "This timing sucks."

"I can't imagine it would ever be a good time to cross a powerful dark witch coven," Adrianna noted in a wry tone.

"Now is really bad, though. A Tribunal is supposed to finally vote on acknowledging the Alterant-gryphons as a free race this week, but I have a feeling it's been put off again. No one has confirmed the meeting. The deities are already jacked up about the constant conflict between Beladors and the Medb. If this familiar belongs to a Medb witch, things would turn far worse."

"True. How much time until the vote?"

"It's *supposed* to be tomorrow, but ..." Evalle shrugged. "The only ones with a vested interest in this vote are the gryphons. I have some degree of freedom and a life. When the vote doesn't happen, *I'm* the one who will have to tell them." *How am I going to do that, then return home to Atlanta with a clear conscience? I can't.*

"That's ... unfortunate," Adrianna consoled.

"Tell me about it. Every time Quinn asks Sen for information on the vote, Sen just smiles and shrugs. It's not like Macha will raise a fuss over it on our behalf." Still, Evalle had hoped for a quiet week leading up to the Tribunal meeting, just in case it did happen. Adrianna was right. Queen Maeve would turn this into an opportunity to go gryphon shopping.

At that point, it wouldn't be just Evalle's future at risk. There were the other gryphons to consider.

But beyond that, Storm, Tzader, and Quinn would get involved in a bloody way.

"Good luck," Adrianna offered. "I'll be interested in hearing how this turns out."

Me, too. "Thanks, I'll let you know." Evalle ended the call and glanced at the furry bundle in the passenger seat. Nothing to do now but contact Rowan. She texted a quick message to the witch, then cranked the engine to warm the cab while she waited for a reply. Nothing came back.

She drove away, determined to leave this little guy with someone tonight.

Evalle would rather have her fingernails ripped out one at a time than take this familiar to VIPER, but she'd end up hauled into a Tribunal meeting the second someone got wind that she'd failed to inform everyone of what she'd found.

She rubbed her head. No easy answers.

Not with her best friend and former Belador Maistir, Tzader, out of pocket at Treoir Castle. In Tzader's absence, her other best friend, Quinn, was doing his best to carry out the duties of Maistir over all North American Beladors. Added to that, Quinn was dealing with a boatload of personal grief over the death of the woman he'd loved in secret for years.

When Evalle pulled up to a stoplight, she turned to her silent companion. "So tell me, do you belong to a good witch or a bad witch?"

Big gold owl eyes looked up at her, clearly not getting the pop culture reference.

"Ho-kay. Plan B." Just as soon as she came up with one.

CHAPTER 3

Treoir Island in a hidden realm above the Irish Sea

Tzader Burke strode quickly through the halls of Treoir Castle, waving off one of the castle guards. He had no time for the man, not with Macha's ultimatum hanging over his head.

An hour.

The goddess had the patience of a gnat.

Mine is no better.

But Tzader would spend a lifetime finding a way to bring Brina's memories back and make her whole again. Macha had a one-track mind about Brina producing the next Treoir heir.

Granted, Macha had allowed him to leave the human realm and his position as the Belador Maistir to reside in Treoir for the past two months.

The goddess wanted results now and demanded proof of Brina's memory improvement.

Brina wasn't improving.

In fact, she continued to withdraw further into herself and, at this point, recognized very little around her.

Who would she be if her memories never returned?

Not the Belador warrior queen. Brina's presence on this island ensured Belador power. Macha had demanded Brina stay inside the warded castle as the best way to keep the only remaining Treoir alive, but the past four years of living inside the castle had taken a toll on Brina. Then she'd been attacked with Noirre majik.

She'd survived, but not without damage.

Her memories of life before the attack deteriorated each day.

What scared Tzader most of all was the possibility that his Brina, the valiant woman he loved, would cease to exist.

She kept regressing before his eyes, slowly losing the spark that made her the most amazing woman he'd ever known.

Macha cared only about having a second Treoir descendant as backup, to continue the bloodline for the Belador power base.

Tzader had a gut-deep feeling that Macha would get that heir one way or another, and he had an even deeper worry. Maybe Macha did not want him as Brina's husband.

Why? She knew he'd die for Brina. He'd already done so once. But the goddess had also known him long enough to understand that he'd put Brina first before anyone else.

He'd been gambling for the past month and the odds had dwindled with each day. Now, Macha had demanded that Tzader prove Brina could absolutely recognize him as the man she'd been committed to for the past four years.

If not, Tzader would no longer be allowed to remain here.

Without Tzader, Macha would pressure Brina into choosing a mate.

Would Macha compel Brina to take a *stranger* for a mate?

He shook off the disturbing thought. Macha had watched over the Treoir family for two thousand years. She had to feel something for Brina, even if Macha rarely showed emotion except when someone pissed her off. Macha might be angry once she realized what Tzader had done for the past month, but surely she wouldn't retaliate by misusing Brina.

He kept trying to convince himself of that as truth.

His gut didn't see it that way.

Didn't matter what anyone thought except Brina. She'd paid the price for being a Treoir, trapped in that castle for four years after her father and brothers were killed battling the Medb. As the last surviving Treoir, Brina had stepped up and accepted the responsibility for thousands of Belador warriors... a burden that no young woman should have to shoulder.

Macha owed her.

Brina had sacrificed long enough.

She deserved a life.

Tzader would give up his so that she would have one. He'd loved Brina from the first time he saw her smile, and would never love another.

Macha had better prepare herself for a battle if she tried to separate them.

Tzader had never walked away from a fight and wouldn't now, not without bloodshed.

His footsteps echoed through the hallway that led to Brina's sunroom. He rushed inside and fought a moment of panic when he didn't see her. "Where is she?"

Lanna Brasko looked up from where she sat on a window seat with her legs crossed. She wore a frown that cut deep worry lines into her smooth, teenage skin. "Brina is sleeping."

As he neared the deep window ledge, he could see Brina stretched out on the other side of the girl, her body engulfed by thick pillows. Lanna had been vigilant in watching over Tzader's warrior queen every minute he couldn't.

He squinted, thinking. "She just woke up three hours ago."

"Yes. She is ... very tired." Lanna glanced away when she made that comment.

What was the young woman not saying? No one knew exactly what powers Lanna possessed, but the eighteen-year-old had a crapload. Was that worried look because she had some inkling that Brina would not get better? Was the teen reluctant to tell Tzader the truth?

He didn't think Lanna had precognitive ability.

She was cousin to Vladimir Quinn, one of Tzader's closest friends, and had bonded with Brina when Lanna got caught in the Noirre majik attack on Brina two months ago. They'd ended up lost together in a different realm. Even with all the power those two females possessed, they hadn't been able to return to this realm on their own.

It had taken someone with demon blood.

Evalle's Skinwalker mate had drawn on the dark side of his blood and, with Evalle's help, brought them back.

Tzader had come so close to never seeing Brina again. She'd returned physically intact, but with corrupted recall. She still didn't remember that she and Tzader had been planning to marry for four years.

Lanna leaned forward. "What is wrong, Tzader?"

He glanced around the room. "Is the soundproof spell you created still in place?"

"Yes. I remove it now only when you are *both* asleep."

"Macha just said I have an hour to show her the progress Brina is making."

Lanna's eyes opened until white glowed around her blue irises. She shook her head, making the black tips of her blond curls fly around. "Brina is not ready. She is worse."

"I know that," he snapped then quickly apologized. "Sorry, Lanna." He ran a hand over his smooth head. "I think Macha is onto us."

"What do you mean?"

He gave her a look of *seriously?* "I think she suspects you're doing something to shield what's really going on. Macha isn't buying the phony conversations she hears Brina having with me when she walks in. If Macha had heard any of our arguments, she'd have busted me before now."

"Is not Brina's fault. She is frustrated, trying to remember simple things. It makes her angry. She cannot control her emotions." Then Lanna added, "Especially now."

Tzader had started to explain to Brina's little champion that he understood why she was irritable, but Lanna's last words stalled his brain. "Why is it especially harder for Brina now?"

Lanna's lips parted for her to speak but then she closed her mouth, looking confused. She tried again and her face showed the strain.

What the hell was wrong with Lanna? Tzader asked, "Are you okay?"

"Yes, I just ... forgot what I was going to say." Swallowing hard, Lanna asked, "What will we do?"

Whatever it took to protect Brina, but Tzader was no match for the Celtic goddess who ruled over all the Beladors, and he would not put this teenager at risk. "Macha wants me to bring Brina to the main atrium to state that she remembers all that we did as teens, and that I'm absolutely the man she wants to marry."

"You cannot do this to Brina," Lanna insisted, her hands fisted.

Brina moved and mumbled something.

Lanna whispered, "She is having *more* problems with memory. She says it also takes her longer to reach the dream-walking state."

Tzader wanted to ask how much worse her loss of memory could be, but in the preternatural world, that had the potential to be a dangerous question. "I've kept Macha off our backs as long as I can. She's no longer content with my telling her that I don't want to put Brina under pressure because I feel that will cause her to slide backwards." He swallowed and stared down. "But Macha thinks Brina knows who I am."

"Brina does."

"Not in this realm." He hated admitting this out loud. "Brina knows who I am as the man who comes here and talks to her each day. I *tell* her about her past, but she has yet to remember any of it on her own, or what I really mean to her."

"But in your dreams—"

"—her memory is fading there, too," Tzader finally admitted, the words twisting out of his gut. There was more to her deterioration than what played out on this realm, more than any of them had believed, and he had no idea how to combat it. He explained, "In fact, it's getting worse in the dream world. Brina is seeing ... things. I don't know if it's hallucinating for a moment, visions or ..."

"Or what?"

"Or if Brina is losing touch with reality." Dear goddess, that hurt to admit. He struggled for his next breath. She was slipping away from him, minute by minute.

Lanna's jaw dropped. "Why did you not tell me?"

Because he'd been living in a fool's paradise, enjoying the few times Brina still recognized him when they dream walked together.

He hadn't realized the significance of dream walking until Lanna explained that his meeting Brina in the dream realm was far more than *his* mind in control. He and Brina actually met in person during dreams. When they did, she remembered more while she was there.

Or she had at first.

Even those cherished moments of recognition were diminishing.

She hadn't recognized him last time until he'd caught her hand as she turned away. He clung to the optimism raised by that one touch like a man holding the last inch of a lifeline.

He cleared his throat. "I couldn't tell you because saying something out loud gives it life." *And I can't face losing her*, he finished silently. "If I take Brina to Macha right now, the goddess will know I've been misleading her for over a month."

"What will she do?"

"Based on what Macha has said and done up until now, I have a sick feeling she'll teleport me back to the human world and start parading men past Brina until one piques her interest."

"She must not do that to Brina. Or you," Lanna conceded. "You have been loyal to Macha for many years. She should help you and Brina."

At twenty-eight, Tzader had been Macha's North American Maistir for almost five years. He took over when his father died, but he'd been his father's second-in-command from the moment he'd turned nineteen. Pretty much his entire adult life.

That *should* count for something with Macha.

Lanna chewed on her lower lip. "You have not told me what we are going to do now."

Tzader owed this young woman for all she'd done to protect Brina and be her friend, and for helping him keep Macha at bay with the spell that shielded their conversations. "You said there was one more thing I could try with Brina in the dream world."

Standing and animating her hands as she spoke, Lanna whispered, "I also said you could be harmed, maybe even die, if she did not remember you when you both came out of the dream. You might both lose your memories. I am not sure of outcome."

"I'm out of options, Lanna. I won't be tossed out of Treoir without a way back to protect Brina."

"She would not want you to risk so much."

"If the day comes that Brina's memories all return, she would never forgive me if I failed to try everything possible. She would wonder how I could have truly loved her if I had not been willing to risk all and keep her out of a stranger's arms." If that day came to be, everyone would find out just how dangerous it was to piss off a woman who wielded ancient Treoir power.

"Macha would not really expect Brina to marry someone else, would she?" Lanna asked, in the voice of a teenager who couldn't imagine just how cold Macha could be.

At one time, Tzader would have asked the same question. "The goddess is ruthless when it comes to ensuring Belador power remains strong, and that won't happen if the Treoir dynasty ends with Brina. Macha wants the next generation of Treoirs started now, regardless of who fathers the child."

Over his dead body. No other man was touching the woman who belonged to him.

It might just end up over his dead body when the goddess figured out what he'd been hiding from her.

Lanna combed her fingers through her hair, getting upset, which would turn into a catastrophic problem if she brought on a thunderstorm. She'd caused one in the past.

Inside a building, no less.

Quinn had said his aunt, Lanna's mother, had vanished at one point nineteen years ago and returned pregnant, with no memory of the time she'd been gone. The origin of Lanna's powers was as unknown as the extent of what she could do.

"Lanna, calm down," Tzader said quietly. "No one is in danger yet."

"If you use this spell, you must hold Brina's hand as you return from the dream realm. If not, *you* may end up sleeping forever."

"I'm just going to have to make sure that doesn't happen."

"Did you bring a pen?"

"Yes." He handed the pen to her.

"Hold out your hand," she ordered, all business when it came to majik.

When he did, Lanna drew a series of Cyrillic symbols in a circle with each symbol connecting. She looked up at him. "I will cast the spell as I push you into deep sleep, while you hold her hand. When you both are ready to return here, you must hold Brina's same hand and repeat the chant as you leave the dream realm."

He nodded, listened to the chant, and ran it back through his mind.

Take these words to heart and mind
From when our souls were first entwined
For you I share my life and memory
Take what you need and set your mind free
We go forth as one, so hold my hand
Share my knowledge of when we began.

"Tzader?" Macha's angry voice rolled through the castle, shaking the walls.

Ah, shit. It hadn't been an hour, so why was the goddess calling him now? Didn't matter. He was out of time. Tzader said, "Step aside, Lanna."

When she did, Tzader stretched out next to Brina on the huge window seat and took her hand in his. Without opening her eyes, his beautiful warrior turned to him, the way she always did when her guard was down during sleep.

He turned to Lanna. "Put me under, fast."

Lanna hesitated.

Macha's voice called out, *"Tzader!"* The goddess would show up here if he didn't go to her.

Tzader said, "Do it now, Lanna! And tell Macha you put me under by *my* orders, and that I intend to meet her in an hour." He would not allow Lanna to take any blame for his actions. "Give me your word."

"You have my word. Close your eyes." Lanna lifted her hands above him and started chanting.

Power surged through the room in a rush so fast that Tzader felt Brina's gown ruffle then settle. His stomach churned with anxiety. He had one last hope of fixing this mess.

Hard chills shook him at the rapid change in his physical body, which loosened, stretched, and reformed as he entered the dream world where Brina waited. He heard Macha's voice once again, but it was distorted and losing volume.

He had to reach the dream realm and hope Lanna convinced Macha it would be unsafe to wake them while he was going under.

CHAPTER 4

"I'm coming for you," a raspy voice whispered through the air, shaking the dregs of sleep from her mind. She sat up, blinking to clear her vision, and stood to figure out what was going on.

Why am I outside with the woods nearby? Realization settled in as pieces began forming in her mind. She was in the dream world. Alone, except for the trees surrounding this peaceful clearing.

Who had spoken?

Wait. For that matter, who am I?

She closed her eyes, thinking hard. *'Tis a simple question, brain.* Nothing came to her. Her fingers curled into tight fists while she waited, until her head ached from thinking so hard. Slowly, one truth became clear.

She could recall nothing. *Where are my memories?* Glancing around again, she recognized this spot as part of the dream world she always visited. But that was all. She knew this feeling of searching for memories and struggling through the frustration.

Start simple. She'd come here for some reason. Why? Closing her eyes once more, she concentrated. Seconds ticked off as nothing came to her.

"I hate this!"

Her shout echoed briefly.

Then silence closed in on her once more.

What is wrong with me? She opened her eyes and forced herself to stay calm. As she unfolded her fingers and went to brush the hair away from her face, she noticed ink on her palm. She moved her hand for a better look.

'I am Brina' had been written in block letters.

Brina. *That's my name.* She knew that name. Her heart jumped at that gift and her mind perked up with that simple information. Images flashed by. Faces. Voices. Places. But nothing slowed down long enough to connect any pieces.

She must have imagined the whispered voice a moment ago, and now chuckled at herself as she thought it through.

I am Brina. This is the dream world. It bends to my will.

"Silly ninny. Some warrior you are," she chided herself.

Warrior? She cocked her head in question. Yes, that sounded right, and this dream world was a safe haven.

Her muscles relaxed a little.

It was coming back to her. She came here to reclaim her memories and had just gained one on her own. She'd been reared a warrior.

You can't escape your destiny, snarled inside Brina's mind this time.

She jerked around, searching for the owner of that eerie voice. Chills crawled up her spine.

Her vision blurred at the edges, then sharpened.

Fifty feet back, a shadow shaped like a person swept through the tall trees circling the clearing. She stood still in the ankle-deep grass. Her heartbeat raced.

Out of pure instinct, she called up a sword.

One appeared in midair right in front of her.

Grasping the hilt, she held the sword at ready and straightened her back, prepared for the threat. The feel of the balanced weapon steadied her pulse.

A memory formed in her mind. This sword had been crafted specifically for her. She recalled the day her da had gifted it to her.

She tightened her hold on the hilt in an effort to regain the memory and hold it. How bittersweet to have that memory return when so many others had abandoned her. That long ago day had been the last time she hugged her da before he and her brothers marched off to battle and never returned.

Her da had told her to be strong.

To protect the others.

She frowned. Who *were* the others?

Panic chipped away at her confidence. No. She would not lose the battle with her mind. Inhaling the fresh air deeply to calm herself further, she scanned the woods again. Nothing moved. Cotton-white clouds floated overhead through the blue skies. Leaves stirred, tossed gently by a breeze.

Where was the shadow that had moved within the trees?

Had she imagined the whole thing?

"Stop actin' like a scared rabbit," she muttered. "See? Nothin' moves in the woods. Keep a clear head, and all will be normal again. My memories will return and I'll..."

The wind whipped briskly across the carpet of grass now. Leaves chattered against each other in tall trees that suddenly swayed with one strong gust after another. The sky turned dark and ominous within a blink. Thunder rumbled, threatening to unload bloated clouds the color of pewter.

"As the last Treoir, you will pay for your family's sins," the creepy voice called through Brina's mind.

She gripped her sword tighter and searched for the enemy, but paused at that new slip of information that brought up a thought. Treoirs were powerful warriors who lived in a castle on an island.

That was good.

Was she really the last one?

Not so good.

But maybe none of that was true. The person behind that voice could be trying to trick her.

Addressing the woods and anyone in there, she announced, "I will not be intimidated by a spineless shadow. Be done with your bloody shenanigans. This is *my* dream. I do not want you here."

The faceless figure of the dark shadow appeared again and skittered quickly through the forest. Two more shadows joined that one, moving in a crisscross pattern. Then another. Dark, wispy shapes darted all around the tree trunks. Not one or two shadows, but twenty. Maybe thirty.

Or were they all the same one?

"Show yourself!" Brina ordered, raising her sword. How would she battle a shadow? *With my powers.*

That thought cheered her for a fleeting moment.

What powers did she possess, if any?

Howling erupted in the woods, then the shadows suddenly stopped wherever they were, scattered among the tree trunks.

What now?

Energy swirled between her and the woods. A prone body began to materialize on the ground twenty feet in front of her. Human in shape, it appeared to be a man.

He sat up and shook his head as if he'd had his bell rung. He was a handsome bastard, with beautiful dark brown skin covering powerful arms, and a bold chest that stretched his black T-shirt. She found his smooth head as sexy as the carved lips that twitched with unspoken thoughts.

This was not someone you called pretty.

A voice from the woods called out, *"We will have your blood and your castle!"*

Her head snapped up. One minute the voice was in her head and the next it was all around her.

The shadows started moving again, but toward her this time. Their faces took on shape and dimension.

The man on the ground pushed to his feet, smiling as if he'd heard nothing.

Didn't he at least see that horde closing in on her?

As the shadows emerged from the woods, physical details formed. Each one had rich brown skin and dark eyes. None had hair on their smooth scalps. They were all built like Spartan warriors and wore the same black T-shirt and jeans as the man now standing between her and the horde.

They looked just like him, except they were translucent and he was solid. Was this his army?

The sky changed swiftly back to a rich hue of blue. Had *he* done that?

She swallowed, preparing to face them all. No, she had a better idea. Leave this dream world now, but how? It wasn't as though she'd fall asleep standing in the middle of an attack.

The shadows now carried swords with strange triangular emblems. As one, they lifted their weapons and continued to approach.

Her palms dampened and her pulse skyrocketed.

A shiny sword identical to the ones carried by the shadows stabbed the ground at the man's feet.

He froze and looked up, shocked. "Brina?"

CHAPTER 5

Tzader watched Brina as he would a wild animal about to attack. She held the deadly sword her father had given her and looked ready to use it, in spite of wearing a deep aqua gown that hugged her pretty curves. "What's going on, Brina?"

Her eyes flicked past him, then back to his face.

He slowly looked over his shoulder. Nothing there.

When he turned back, Brina pointed her sword at him. "I will not die without drawing blood."

That wasn't a wild look in her eyes. It was terror and confusion. What gripped her mind now?

Tzader kept his voice soft. "You know me. I'm Tzader. I don't want to fight you. Please put the sword down."

Her eyes kept moving back and forth. "No."

"Why are you holding a sword?" Tzader asked.

"What game are you playin'? You think I don't see your army?" she asked with no give in her voice.

Oh shit. "Not my army, Brina. I love you. I would never harm you."

"Love me? Who are you to be sayin' such things? You think to trick me?" She swung her sword left then right, as if preparing for a battle.

With an army her mind had conjured.

This was worse than last time in the dream world with her.

She swung her sword in a liquid movement so like his warrior princess back when they used to spar. Before she became the warrior queen and carried a world of responsibility on her narrow shoulders.

Damn it. Her gaze still tracked something moving in the woods. The army she thought he'd brought here?

Or could there be a real threat he had yet to see? He doubted it. Not in the dream world where she had far more control over her power than even he had here. But the muscles in her arms tensed, ready to fight something.

He had to bring her back to him. There was no way to know how long Macha would hold off. He pushed power into his voice. "Look at me, Brina."

She jerked her head around, staring at him now.

He asked, "Tell me what you see and I'll help you fight it."

"You think I'm that easily swayed?"

He had to be careful how he replied. "No, but *they* may be tricking you, and I might be your only ally here."

She swung her gaze back to the woods and her mouth opened. "Where did ..."

Finally. Whatever she'd seen must have vanished. He said, "It wasn't real."

Turning to him once more, she gave him a measured look. "But you are."

He didn't like the suspicious sound of that. "You know me, Brina."

"You keep sayin' that." She studied him harder. "Your face and name are vaguely familiar, but ... I still don't know if you be friend or foe."

His heart dropped to his feet.

Until the past few days, he'd been able to talk his way past her dementia and disorientation, but the day before yesterday he'd spent a half hour just hunting her as she hid from him. They'd argued until he'd grabbed her arm when she tried to walk away. She'd turned back, swinging, but held up at the last second. With that touch, she began recalling bits and pieces until she'd finally walked into his arms.

Yesterday, he'd come upon her arguing with unseen opponents, but she had not called up a sword as she had today.

With a wave of her free hand, the gown she'd been wearing disappeared, replaced by jeans, a loose shirt, and lightweight boots.

Her normal attire for sparring.

Was this a positive change or not?

Her waist-length red hair snatched light like polished copper as it wove itself into a braid down her back.

She looked like the young woman who had stolen his heart in this glade. He smiled at the memory.

"You find this amusin'?" she asked, clearly not happy.

"I like your outfit," he replied, tiptoeing around each word.

"'Tis easier to battle without trippin' on a blasted hem."

He held his hands up in surrender. "Like I said, I'm not here to fight you."

"You think to have me lowerin' my guard until your army returns?"

"Think for a minute, Brina. I'm here alone. You know me. You chose this place to visit in the dream world because it's *ours*."

Confusion clouded her gaze. Her sword tip dipped an inch. She was at least considering his words.

He pressed his case. "We've spent a lot of time in this very spot."

"Doin' what?" she asked.

Now that was a tricky question. If he told her they'd made love here, would it trigger her memories, or cause her to doubt him if she *didn't* remember?

He'd won more battles by going on the offensive.

Tzader reached down and tapped the pommel of the sword stuck in the ground. "We sparred." They'd do that back on the real Treoir Island for long periods, then end up tumbling into each other's arms. He took a chance and added, "Sometimes we wore fewer clothes."

She smiled.

His heart tilted, wanting to be happy at that sign, but he waited.

Lifting a hand, she pointed at him and his T-shirt vanished. "Feel better now?" she asked.

He grinned. Yep, a very positive sign. Now they were getting somewhere. "Actually, it was even better when we both—"

Her gaze jerked back to the woods.

No, please no.

All humor fled her face, replaced by a fierce glare she turned on him. "You liar! You play with me then call back your army." She raised her sword and advanced, slashing at her invisible opponent.

Tzader's knives hissed and clicked in response to her swinging that wicked blade as she moved toward him. He spit out old Gaelic, ordering his knives to stand down. Both blades quieted, but Brina was coming closer. "Brina, stop. There's nothing there."

Twice as many shadow versions of this man, Tzader, had returned. They rushed Brina one at a time.

She fought furiously, striking each shadow's sword and blocking a hit, but never feeling a solid resistance even though she could hear metal clash with metal. Keeping track of their leader in her peripheral vision, she fought hard, slashing back and forth. Every time she made a clean strike, the shadow burst into tiny gray pieces that rained to the ground.

Another one attacked her. A third one wound its filmy hands around her neck and tightened its grip, strangling her. This would be a good time for those powers her memory had hinted at, if only she knew what she could do to these things. More waited in the forest.

Was Tzader calling them one at a time to wear her down?

She clawed at the hand clamped around her throat, wielding her sword with one hand. Anger rode her hard until power ripped from her. It blasted toward the woods, smashing shadows that stood in the way. But more stepped into the empty spots and waited.

For what?

She'd fought her way over to Tzader.

He stood there, staring at her as if he could see inside her mind. *Good luck finding anything there.* Still, his face and name stirred something deep in the recesses of her mind.

Who was he?

This was the dream world. Why couldn't she push her power out again and make him and the rest of his army hovering among the trees go away?

She wished for that with all her might. Nope. That one burst had happened all on its own.

Why was this happening? What did this man want?

Still, Tzader stood there without moving a muscle. He hadn't lifted the sword. He'd made no attempt to harm her, but all the shadow soldiers wore his face. At this rate, confusion would beat her to a pulp.

She let out a weary breath and asked Tzader, "What are you doin' here?"

"I always come for you here. I was here yesterday, the day before, and the day before. We've been doing this for many weeks. I'm here to remind you who I am and who you are. I'm here to help bring your memories back."

Her heart thumped at his words. Were they true or was this some hoax? Should she lay down her sword and trust him?

The shadow soldiers sucked in closer, murmuring. She listened, sorting out words until she heard, "Give up. All is lost. Treoir castle is mine."

Those shadows belonged to him, and they were moving in as one unit this time. She didn't bloody care who Tzader was anymore.

If she cut him down, would his army vanish?

Her mind might have doubts, but her body knew exactly what to do. She swung her sword to attack.

And look at that.

He dodged, and the shadows started receding. She'd made the right decision.

For a man of Tzader's muscular build, he surprised her with lightning-fast reflexes. He snatched up his sword with a curse, and blocked her next strike.

He met every swing of her blade, blocking with enough force that her teeth shook. Battling felt good, felt right. Her body had been dormant too long. Getting in better physical shape had to help her mind, but at the moment she was breathing hard.

Why? What did she do with her days if not train?

On the other hand, what training could she have been doing in that stupid gown?

How was she to know? She couldn't recall anything at will, but she'd had a fleeting vision of growing up in a castle when she'd heard the name Treoir.

She remembered this location, too, where a giant oak stood above a thick forest surrounding a lake, but not why this spot felt so important to her.

With a new surge of energy, she continued her attack, and it struck her that Tzader had yet to take an aggressive action. He could clearly handle a weapon. Out of nowhere, a memory flickered of fighting this same man ...

but with a younger face and a cut body, though not as beefed up.

Not fighting, but sparring.

She stumbled at the realization, and he pulled back.

Brina warned, "Lower your guard again and I'll not be apologizin' for drawin' blood."

"You never have." His eyes twinkled, taking attractive up to devastating. He was enjoying this?

She knew him and recalled practicing this way. Tzader had acted as if he hadn't seen the shadows. A sick thought churned her insides. Had she been hallucinating? That would be one step worse than having no memories.

Swinging right, then left, her blade clashed with his.

More images came to mind, of sparring in *this place* with him, but had that been in this dream world?

Was he a friend after all?

He challenged her for two steps, always careful not to make a deadly hit.

Her next strike surprised him. She expected anger.

He grinned and acknowledged her expertise with a nod.

The tension in her chest eased. Her lips twitched with a smile. She felt more alive than she had ... in a long time. Yes, she *had* done this before, and with him. Her attack changed to practiced moves, because she began to sense truth in his words.

She hoped she was not being a fool, but she wanted to believe he could help her.

Tzader met every swing, strike for strike, still never fully using the power in those massive biceps.

He hadn't even broken a sweat. He toyed with her, and though she didn't remember how she'd gained the skill, she was no pushover with a sword.

Tzader moved with the agility and confidence of one who had fought many battles, and won.

The more she sparred with him, the less she wanted to harm any of that smooth, ebony skin. She stumbled, more fatigued than she'd realized. She should have been paying attention instead of looking at the handsome man.

At her falter, his demeanor changed in a flash. His voice came barreling out with an edge of irritation. "Stop, Brina. I understand you're frustrated, but—"

She scoffed, cutting him off. He thought he knew what she was going through? *Try living with no mind to call up the simplest things.* Swinging again, she struck hard, and he blocked her. No mind, no energy, and no patience.

She snarled, "What do you know about frustration?"

Tzader blocked her next swing. "You of all people should know better than to ask me that. I—" He parried, spinning and moving faster, too fast for her to get a decent strike on him.

She had her own supply of irritation. "What, Tzader? You say you know me. What do you know that you think I should?"

He lost his smile. "Never mind."

"No!" she shouted, driving him back and striking harder with each word. "You will tell me what it is I should know."

With one mighty swing, he knocked her sword flying and chucked his to go with hers.

Glory to the gods, he was furious, deadly and magnificent. His deep voice shook when he told her, "That I waited four years to be with the woman I love, then I watched her disappear after being attacked with Noirre majik, with no idea when she'd come back." By the time he took a breath, he was grinding out his words. "Now you don't even know me."

Fire should be bursting from his mouth.

She had nothing to say, but she heard the sincerity in his voice. And the hurt. This man held his pain deep inside, but it was there. His last words hit her.

Now you don't even know me.

Waiting four years for the woman he loved ... who didn't know him. *Is that me?*

Couldn't be. She'd remember someone like Tzader.

Wouldn't she?

"Brina." One word, pleading from a man whom she knew without a doubt begged no one for anything. The emotion in his voice sliced across her heart. He whispered, "Please don't fight me, *muirnin,* when we have so little time left."

Taking a slow step toward her, he kept talking. "This is our place, where we hid from the world when you were a teen. I stole my first kiss from you beneath this tree."

Images floated free in her mind, exactly the way he described it. The more he talked, the faster the images came to her. He said, "You laughed at me when I missed the target with my knife."

"You told me later you had been throwin' left-handed." She touched her lips, surprised at how that popped into her mind.

When he stopped right in front of her, Brina's gaze flitted across his face and the gleaming perspiration on his chest.

She lifted her gaze to those brown eyes that looked at her as if she were the only woman alive. Those eyes had *always* looked at her that way. Her breath caught. "Tzader?"

That's all it took for a sigh filled with relief to escape him. He put his hands on her shoulders and slowly touched a kiss to her forehead.

Warm sensation rushed through her. Her body knew him. She wished her body would teach her mind a few lessons.

He tilted her chin up and kissed her gently.

That triggered a rush of memories. Images of this man kissing her in this very clearing assaulted her.

And of doing ... so much more here.

She wrapped her arms around his neck and leaned into the kiss. He growled, and his mouth claimed her now, demanding more the longer they touched. Or had she been the one to deepen the kiss? Who cared? She might not remember every detail of her life, but she knew this man. Knew his body. Knew that he had stood between her and danger.

He grabbed her by the waist and lifted her, swinging her around. He smiled and the world came to life. She laughed, enjoying the way her body sang with happiness.

When he finally lowered her, he murmured, "If I could only hear your laugh every day for the rest of my life, *muirnin,* I would die a happy man."

With him holding her and kissing her, the meaning behind that Irish term of endearment rattled another memory loose. He'd called her that many times before, in this very spot. And in the castle.

Still not sure of all that had happened in the past, she asked, "We *are* friends?"

"No."

She pulled up short. "What?"

His eyes filled with tenderness that tugged at her heartstrings. When he spoke, his voice came out rough with emotion. "You are far more than just my best friend in all the worlds. You are my love. You are life itself. You are everything I have ever wanted."

"The woman you've waited four years for," she repeated.

"The woman I would wait a lifetime for," he said, then studied her, making a decision of some kind. "Feel the bond of our power."

In the next moment, power surged around her and wrapped her body in a blissful cocoon of warmth. She felt him inside, where no one should be but her. "I feel—"

"I do, too. The day we swore our love to each other, we bonded, but this is the first time I've felt it since then."

Frustration boiled inside her. "Why? What's happened? Why do memories slip through my fingers?"

"Shh, *muirnin.*" He kissed her and wrapped her in his arms. "You are the Belador warrior queen. You were stuck in Treoir Castle for four years after the last of your family died in a battle. The castle was warded against immortals except for you and Macha."

Argh, that annoying goddess. Of course, Brina would recall Macha. "The castle should have been warded against her, truth be told. She's irritatin'."

He chuckled.

Brina sighed. "I'm so tired of thinkin' and thinkin' and thinkin', only to come up blank. I don't know what happened."

"I'll tell you."

He'd been so quick to offer that she asked, "Have you done this before? Filled me in?"

"Yes. A few times."

She sensed he wasn't telling her the truth about how many times. "For how long?"

He hesitated, then hugged her to him. "For almost two months, but I'll do it every day for the rest of my life if I have to, just to have you near me." He held her tight, but in a careful way.

Her body wanted him to do so much more. He could start with her breasts. They ached for his touch.

But what kind of woman would tell him that?

A woman who missed him and whatever they'd had. Hopefully, still had.

He continued explaining, "For four years, I couldn't get through the ward on the castle to reach you physically, until a battle between the Medb and Beladors broke out on Treoir."

She leaned back. "You said it prevented immortals from passing through."

"I'm immortal, just like you." He brushed a loose tendril of hair away from her face.

"Oh." She thought on that for a moment. "I'd best be gettin' my mind back soon if I'm goin' to live indefinitely." Tzader grinned. But the idea that he would also live and could be with her brightened her day. "What were you sayin' about our enemy?"

"I'll tell you about that another time, but when I finally managed to reach you, a traitor in our midst was casting Noirre majik on you. And Lanna. I killed the traitor." He asked, "Remember Lanna?"

A young woman's face came to Brina's mind. Curly blond hair. Full of energy. Busybody personality and scary level of power, but she had no idea exactly what the girl could do. Brina said, "Yes, I know Lanna. She was with me in a strange realm. I remember it looking like nothing ... no land or trees or sky, just gray."

"Right. You two disappeared in front of my eyes. It's a long story, but a Skinwalker named Storm, and Evalle Kincaid, one of your Belador warriors, helped bring you back. That was the good news. The bad news is that your memories have been corrupting ever since."

She leaned her head on his shoulder and let him hold her. "Could be that's why I'm so bloody tired all the time, and gettin' worse every day." Fatigue from mental stress made sense. The brief sword fight had also stolen her energy. She'd enjoyed the battle, even though it was clear now that Tzader had been careful not to harm her.

He loved her.

She opened her heart and her mind. She felt the flow of his love inside her.

Pieces of memory shifted around and fit together. She recalled a battle going on around the castle, then darkness, then Lanna's face and ... nothing. "Thank you."

"You're welcome, but I'm not done. I *will* find a way to return your memories. Do you recall this spot?"

She lifted her head and looked at the peaceful setting that gave her comfort now. "Yes. It took a bit, but I know it."

A hot gleam burned in his gaze. "Do you remember why we declared this our special place years ago?"

Images flashed in her mind of him wearing nothing but that intense gaze and driving into her. Damp heat swirled between her legs. Her damn breasts ached again.

More flashes of memory returned. A very graphic memory rose up and caused her nipples to tighten. "Tzader, did we ... make love here?"

Relief rolled over his face. He kissed her sweetly. "Yes. The day we committed ourselves to each other, we said the words we planned to repeat in front of a druid on our wedding day."

She might not recall every little detail, but the second his power had swept inside her body to greet hers, she'd known this was her man.

The one she loved.

A man she wanted to feel inside her again, physically, before her mind took another vacation.

She ran her hands over his carved chest, feeling warm skin flowing over the ridges of hard muscle. Hooking his neck, she pulled his mouth to hers, pausing long enough to say, "Touch me, Tzader. I need you."

He didn't have to be asked twice.

His hands gripped her at the waist and pulled her up as he kissed her with single-minded determination.

Rubbing her hips against him, she moaned at the feel of his erection, recalling how she'd been a bit daunted at the first glimpse of him naked.

But once he'd filled her with a powerful stroke, nothing had ever felt so perfect.

His hard member thumped against her, clearly just as ready to replay that memory in real time. She wanted him now. Heat and moisture pooled between her thighs.

"I've missed you, *muirnin*." He kissed her with the mouth of a raider determined to lay claim to everything he put his hands on.

Finally, she let go of her cares, content to live in the moment where she knew the man holding her. She knew her feelings, and cared nothing for the rest of the world.

His hand slipped under her loose shirt and caressed her breast. His thumb brushed across her sensitive nipple and she cried out, jerking at the shock that raced through her body.

Good goddess. That was ...

"It's been way too long," Tzader murmured, wanting to feel every inch of Brina's smooth skin. He missed ... them. Just the two of them together.

Why did life have to be so damned difficult?

Not life, but Macha.

Brina made a noise that sent heat rifling through him to his groin.

He couldn't think about the goddess right now. Not while he had Brina warm and soft in his arms.

He pulled back, wanting to see her, and let his gaze rake her from head to toe. He'd touched her only once in four years, and that had been two months ago while they were dream walking. He started to comment on how she'd changed in those years, but sometimes back in the castle the most innocent comment had brought on panic that more was changing than just her memory. Even her breasts seemed different now.

He kissed her, loving her with his mouth. "You're so perfect. Every inch of you."

When her nails dug into his back, he grunted, but with a sound of pleasure.

She whispered in a conspiratorial tone, "The girls miss you as much as I do."

Oh, man, she was killing him. He said, "It'd be so much easier if you had your gown on again."

"I don't want that stupid gown back on." Energy buzzed, and she'd removed her pants and boots, leaving her in only a shirt and panties.

Shock, then pleasure, spike through him. He looked down, then back up at her face, and knew she wanted him. "This place definitely likes you better than me. I could never get it to do anything like that."

She opened her mouth, probably intending to give him a sassy comeback, but he didn't want her thinking. He wanted her to feel everything, with no hallucinations or stress. Using one hand to pull her to him, he allowed his other one freedom to roam her lovely breasts.

"Oh, yes," she squeezed out. "Don't stop!"

As if.

Holding her bottom close to him, which was pure torture, he slid his hand inside her panties from the back and ran one long finger through her damp skin. She arched up, lifting into the air.

He pulled her back down. "Easy, love."

Then he contradicted that order by plunging the same finger inside her, moving it in and out. A second finger teased her sensitive folds at the same moment he pinched a nipple.

Tiny lightning bolts flashed around both of them. She called his name, and he loved it. Never letting up, he pushed her to give up all she had.

When she came back to reality, or as much as they had in the dream realm, he hugged her limp body to him. He whispered in Gaelic, telling her how much he loved her.

"Why can't we stay here forever?" she asked in a breathless voice. "Forget about castles and goddesses and enemies." She looked him squarely in the eyes. "All I need is you."

He kissed her cheek, trying not to admit how many times he'd thought the same thing. But she didn't realize she was getting worse and the dream world would not cure her. "I want you to be happy no matter where you are. You okay, love?"

"I won't be runnin' any races on these wobbly legs." Releasing the fierce hold she had on his neck, she eased down the front of him. He held her until she could stand on her own.

He loved being the one who rocked her world.

She quipped, "Your back may be a mess."

"It'd better be after that."

"I'm not finished," she said, matching his smug tone. She reached down to stroke his erection through the jeans.

He moaned, grasping her hand and stopping her. "You have no idea how much I want you, love, but—"

"But *what*?"

Tzader took a deep breath, pulling his honor around him to quench the inferno inside him. "Everything we do here has implications. Lanna tells me if we're killed while dream walking, we die." He wasn't sure how that would play out for two immortals, but wasn't taking any chances.

"If we make love..." His voice trailed off.

"Then we make love. What of it?" Brina punctuated that reply with a frown. Why would he be concerned? They had pledged their love long ago. "I'm not seein' a problem. I know you, right now, right here. I've no idea about an hour from now."

"And that's why we'll wait until you *do* know." Tzader had that unyielding look in his eyes. "I won't risk you ever looking at me and wondering if I took advantage of you when you had no idea who I was."

"What about the last time here? I remember us naked in a dream in this very spot."

"We were, but at that time I didn't know we were dream walking. Not until Lanna clued me in. I thought it was just *me* dreaming that I was making love to you." His eyes searched hers. "You'd tell me if you were pregnant, right?"

"Of course I would." Then she amended, "Well, I'd be tellin' someone."

Brina felt a sharp stab of hurt at the idea she could be pregnant with Tzader's child, but not remember whose it was. The good news was that she didn't feel pregnant and should know if she was, right?

He seemed relieved, though. "That's the reason we're waiting. I will not make love to you, then leave you confused about what's going on, *and* pregnant so that Macha can lock you away somewhere she deems safe."

He had a valid point, and he was making an honorable choice.

That didn't make it any better.

She'd tried to kill him because she hadn't recognized him, but now she wanted to kill him for leaving her without finishing what he'd started.

Of course, *she'd* started it, so it would be dishonorable on her part to blame him.

Tzader cursed, then pulled her back in for another long kiss. "I can't keep my damn hands off you. I want you too much."

That put him back on her good side. She smiled. "Nice to know I'm not the only one left wantin'."

"Not by a long shot. Once we have you a hundred percent, we're spending a month away from everyone."

That sounded wonderful until she took into consideration the part about her being fully recovered. "That may never happen, Tzader."

"It *will!*" he said with the ferocity of a leader ordering an army to attack. "Lanna gave me something to try that might help bring back some of your memories permanently."

"What is it? Let's do it."

He showed her his hand that had a weird drawing on it. "These are Cyrillic images she drew on my hand. She told me to hold your hand and repeat a chant right as we return to Treoir. If it works, you'll gain at least the memories I hold of both of us. Then you'd know enough to convince Macha that you remember me."

She felt his surge of pain at those words. "I don't know you when I'm in the castle, do I?"

His smile was sweet and sad. "No, love, but once you have enough memories intact to prove you're making progress, Macha will agree to let me continue to stay with you. If not, she'll send me away."

"I won't allow that."

He took her hand in his strong one. His words were gentle. "You may not remember ... *us* later on, love, but either way I don't want you battling her. And I don't want you worrying about remembering. I have a plan." Not really, but he'd come up with one soon. "In the meantime, I need to know you're safe no matter what."

"I won't fight her unless she thinks to harm you." Brina pulled her arms back and crossed them. Tzader muttered, "You're as stubborn as you are sexy." He took a long look at her and covered his eyes. "You have to put clothes on again or ... just please put the pants back on for my sanity."

She smiled, which was unkind since he was clearly suffering, but she loved the way he wanted her. "All done. I won't be distractin' you now."

Uncovering his eyes, he released another long sigh. "Yes, you will, but that gives me a fighting chance at keeping my hands to myself so we can return. Back to Macha. None of this will matter if she puts you out of my reach."

She nodded. "I understand. By the way, I'm sorry."

"For what?"

"Tryin' to kill you."

Arrogance flooded his grin. "I wouldn't have let you."

She cocked her head at him. "Don't be so sure about that."

He laughed. "There's my flame-haired hellion. Let's not argue until you have all your memories back, then have at it because I love making up with you."

Truly, he was a rogue. But he'd made her heart smile again and she felt his love as truth. "We should be goin' on to Treoir to see if Lanna's spell works."

"One more thing. When we get back to the castle, Macha is demanding to see us and for you to confirm that you do remember me as the man you intend to marry."

Thoughts she'd just held scattered from her mind. She looked at Tzader and still knew him, but ... *Macha*? Bits and pieces of an image floated through behind her eyes and out of reach. Brina argued, "Is what we do really any of that woman's business?"

Tzader's eyes bulged then his face took on a reserved expression when he calmly answered, "Sort of. That women does rule Treoir."

"Why? Is she family?"

He looked confused. "She's the Belador goddess, the most powerful being in our world."

All that came to mind was a loud woman in the castle. Brina didn't want to spend time talking about her. She waved off his comment. "Fine. We'll appease Macha, but I'm not sure I want her stayin' once we're married."

Tzader made a choking sound. "Can you keep that between us for now? We may need her help."

"If I must."

He kissed her one more long time then moved back slightly to take her hands in his. "Close your eyes, and prepare to leave this world."

She did as he said. When he felt Brina's hand lose definition, he quickly began the chant, "Take these words to heart and mind—"

He'd almost made it to the last sentence when a noise startled him from the trance-like state he'd fallen into.

Brina was already leaving the dream world. Her body had turned translucent.

But he could hear heavy footsteps getting close.

Tzader swung around with his arm outstretched, calling the Belador sword that flew to his hand.

A man approached, dressed for war and carrying his own sword. An old relic. The stranger yelled, "I've come for Brina!"

Tzader said, "She is mine. Any man who touches her will die."

Tzader, Brina's voice whispered through his mind. *Whose voice is that? Where are you?*

He answered her telepathically. *Go to the castle. I'll be there soon.*

But the spell?

Do not come back, love. He had to convince her, or she would return. *You are the warrior queen. You are vital to the Belador power. If you're harmed, it weakens me. A stranger is here. I'll be back as soon as I deal with this bastard. Please, do as I ask.*

Return soon, or I'll be comin' back for you.

He placed his wider body in front of her slender, vanishing form.

Brina finally gave in, even though it went against her nature. She preferred to stay and fight, but Tzader's words reminded her she had responsibilities. She continued forcing her body through the half-state of transitioning from one world to the other.

As she drifted off, leaving the dream behind, a vicious clash of steel on steel rang through the air.

Her thoughts fogged and she fought to clear them.

Images assaulted her, jumbling together. Faces jumped in and out of her mind.

"Open your eyes, Brina!"

When Brina managed to peel back her eyelids, a woman five or ten years older than her stood over her. Glowing blonde hair fell to her waist, then lifted an inch off her shoulders.

She was ranting about something. Her hair flew out around her head, moving frenetically.

Brina clamped her hands over her ears. If that bitch did not shut up, she was going to call up a sword and shut her up.

Wait. I can do that, right?

She chased that thought, but it vanished into the ether.

Brina shoved up to a sitting position, and thankfully, the maniac stopped shouting. Instead the woman asked, "Where is Tzader, and what has he been telling you?"

Brina said, "Who the bloody hell are you, and what's your problem?"

A whispered "Uh-oh," drew Brina's gaze to an adorable young woman with bouncy blonde curls. Who was she? Brina concentrated hard then snapped her fingers. "Lanna, right?"

Lanna gave her a weak smile and said, "Yes, but do not yell at Macha. She is goddess."

Brina's gaze went to the crazy woman. Goddess, huh?

Macha's hazel-green eyes flamed into bright orbs.

CHAPTER 6

With Brina gone from the dream world, Tzader faced the threat striding boldly across the private clearing. No one should be privy to this place in the dream world except him and Brina.

Who was this guy?

A warrior. There could be no doubt of that by the way he carried himself. Plus, he held a sword that required serious muscle to swing. He wore a billowy white shirt that had seen a few battles and a weathered leather vest, both of which covered obvious slabs of muscle. The sleeves of his shirt had been rolled to his elbows, and his pants, a faded black material, were stuffed into tall boots.

He looked like a warrior plucked from the past.

Those forearms were capable of cleaving a body in half diagonally with that sword and not slowing his swing as he did it.

He didn't appear to be in a hurry, but moved with an easy confidence as he closed the fifty-foot distance.

Just what I don't need in the middle of this mess with Brina. Worrying about her returning here and meeting some stranger. Her hallucinations were bad enough.

Had Lanna's spell taken hold before Brina left, even though Tzader hadn't finished the chant? Maybe Brina would at least retain the memories she'd grasped while here.

He shoved that aside. The sooner he dealt with this guy, the faster he'd return to Brina. Hopefully before Macha pushed her for answers.

Lanna's warning about actions having real consequences during dream walking kept harping in the back of Tzader's mind. Was this warrior also immortal? He'd like to have an instruction manual for the dream realm. Even without reading the fine print, he'd bet a fight to the death would mean just that based on what little he'd learned since visiting so often.

When the guy was twenty strides away, Tzader motioned with his sword to hold up. "Who are you?"

"You may call me Ceartas," he said, slowing, and yet still moving forward.

Ceartas was not a familiar name. In Irish, the word translated to *justice*. Maybe this guy's mind was out of whack in the dream world.

That brought up a new concern.

Could dream walking be causing Brina's issues to worsen?

Another thing Tzader would have to investigate later when he wasn't busy trying to get out of here alive.

Ceartas swung his sword back and forth in one hand, clearly warming up his muscles, and finally stopped. He had four inches on Tzader and maybe another thirty pounds of muscle, which was impressive since Tzader could bench press four hundred pounds.

This must be my day to get in sword practice. Tzader didn't need to warm up. He was still loose from his earlier skirmish with Brina. That'd been the first time he'd seen her wield a sword in a while.

She'd been happy. He wanted her happy every day for the rest of her life. That she'd conjured the sword her father had ordered custom-made for her warmed Tzader's heart.

She clearly remembered *that*.

"Pray, how are you with swingin' that sword?" Ceartas asked.

"Skilled enough to kill anyone who challenges me." It wasn't boasting. Tzader had never been beaten when he held a Belador sword, and hoped putting that statement on the table up front would make Ceartas think twice.

"I have no' battled one so worthy in many ... years," Ceartas said.

From the way he spoke, Tzader wondered if it had been years or decades ... or centuries. And more importantly, what the hell had he meant when he said he'd come for Brina?

He'd just as soon avoid bloodshed, but he had no idea where this was going and he couldn't just pop out of here with a sword at his neck. He asked, "How long have you wandered through this realm? Has it been so long that you've forgotten how to return to the world of the living?"

"I can return any time I wish."

"Then why don't you head back and—"

In one fucking quick move, the bastard attacked.

Tzader swung his sword up in time to keep his head still attached to his shoulders, and met each assault with the force he'd held back from Brina. In a blink he broke away, spun, and swung on the attack again.

Strike, strike, dodge, strike.

The clash of metal on metal zinged through the air.

Sweat poured across Tzader's shirtless body. He had to give it to Ceartas. If the guy had been dream walking for eons, he'd been swinging a sword the whole time.

His opponent smiled. He was enjoying the match way more than he should.

Ceartas lost his footing and Tzader attacked, calling up his Belador power to finish this off without having to harm the guy.

Energy flashed across the clearing, and Ceartas glowed all the way down his arms to the tip of his sword.

What. The. Fuck?

Ceartas twisted his neck back and forth, then nodded. "Ready."

Tzader sighed and moved forward, in no hurry.

Rushing into a fight gave up any advantage.

With the next swing of Ceartas's glowing sword, Tzader blocked, bringing him close to his opponent. They strained against each other, but Tzader could tell that this crazy guy's power was unlike anything he'd ever encountered.

Ceartas said, "Got any ale?"

Ale? Who asked for ale in the middle of a fight? "No."

"Damn. I would stop for a drink."

Lanna had told Tzader these were his dreams, and the elements in a dream world would respond to him. While he did not possess her majikal ability, he had envisioned a few things that appeared, much like the swords Brina had called up.

Easing his pinkie finger loose without giving up any ground, Tzader pointed at the ground and thought *beer.*

Nothing happened.

Never letting up on the pressure against Tzader's sword, Ceartas watched with a curious and guarded expression.

Maybe he needed more focus and detail. Tzader wished for two tall mugs of frosty beer ... that appeared. Damn. How about that?

Grinning, Ceartas shoved hard enough to send Tzader flying backwards and walked over to lift one of the mugs.

Tzader bounced up to his feet and shook off the jarring hit. He waited to see what came next. He'd been knocked off his feet with powerful kinetics before, but no *man* had ever sent him flying.

Besides, that hadn't been kinetics.

Ceartas carried power that he'd only allowed to peek out.

Realization struck Tzader between the eyes. This warrior had clearly been around for centuries or at least he was *from* another century—who the hell knew what was possible in this dream world?—which meant he was almost certainly immortal, and had the power to kill Tzader, even without a sword.

After downing a healthy slug of beer, Ceartas let out a loud belch and a happy sigh. He frowned at Tzader. "Are both o' these for me?"

Shaking his head to himself, Tzader materialized a scabbard and sheathed his blade. His sword would only delay the inevitable if this guy decided to kill him.

Waving a hand, Ceartas produced a log ten feet long and two feet in diameter, which meant he could have conjured the damn ale if he'd wanted. What was with this crazy bastard? Lifting the other mug, Tzader sat down, leaving plenty of room between them.

Ceartas stretched out his legs. "'Twas good to exercise. I've gone without for a while now."

"So you just wander around, looking for a fight?"

"No, but it would be better use of my time than what I do now."

"Which is?" Tzader asked.

"Not what I came here to discuss."

Great. Maybe Ceartas would finally make some sense and allow Tzader to get back to Brina. He played along, now that he wasn't battling for his life. "Fine. What do you want to talk about?"

"The dragon you're going to rescue."

So much for staying in the land of the sane. Tzader used the patient tone he saved for the demented. "I'd like to help you, but from what I've seen you can handle dragon rescues all by yourself."

"If that were the case, he'd already be free." Ceartas took another slug of beer and sighed, as if he hadn't tasted anything so good in a long time. "That's where you come in."

When in an impossible situation, play along and hope for an opening to escape. "Why should I get involved with this, Ceartas?"

"To save Brina."

The hairs on Tzader's neck stirred with warning, but they were finally down to the real question. How did this guy know Brina? Had he somehow learned her name by spying on her in this realm, and decided to use her to fuck with Tzader's head? "Save her from what?"

"Take your pick. Macha, who cares naught for Brina, only that she gets a Treoir heir. Or me, if you refuse to offer the aid I'm ... requesting."

Tension took on a life in the still air.

Tzader warned, "If I kill you, it eliminates one problem for Brina."

Of course, he'd have to return with an army of Beladors to back up that threat.

Ceartas turned up the mug, finishing off the beer and set it on the ground. "You won't kill me, even if you could."

"What makes you think that?"

"You need me to help you bring back Brina's memories."

Tzader stared at Ceartas, speechless. How could this guy know that about Brina? Had he listened to enough of Tzader's conversations with Brina to guess? "What do you think you know?"

Watching Tzader with great interest, Ceartas said, "I have little time to waste, so I will show you that I know far more than you do. A Belador traitor in league with Queen Flaevynn attacked Brina using Noirre majik. True?"

Tzader nodded.

That traitor was now dead, by Tzader's hand. Flaevynn had since been replaced by Queen Maeve, who had reincarnated ... from what he'd heard.

Ceartas continued, "It takes someone with knowledge of the actual Noirre spell used on Brina to reverse it."

Clearly this guy knew about the traitor's attack, which pushed Tzader to keep engaging. "But we had someone break that spell. That's how Brina returned from another realm."

"Oh? How did you bring her back?"

Should he answer? His gut said yes, because intel was intel, so he went with it.

"We brought in someone with demon blood, and with the help of his Belador mate, he broke the spell."

Ceartas grunted. "He managed to bring Brina back *physically*, but the Noirre majik is still working on her. That's why she continues to lose her memories. If that were not the case, she'd at least retain what she's experienced since she was brought home. But she hasn't, has she?"

Tzader didn't say a word. The logic was sound, and damn it, this Ceartas was correct about Brina failing to recall recent events. Tzader should be glad to have a smoking gun to point out as a reason for her memory loss, but this might be worse.

Not waiting on a reply from Tzader, Ceartas said, "Even if you could talk a Medb warlock or witch into trying to reverse the spell, they can't do it. In fact, Maeve can't either, because she wasn't around when Flaevynn developed that particular spell." He stared off for a moment, looking lost in thought and added, "Of course, if Queen Maeve ever figures out how to make Flaevynn's scrying wall work so that she can see everything that happened before she regenerated, I suppose Queen Maeve *could* reverse the spell after all."

Tzader still hadn't heard anything encouraging. "I hear a 'but' at the end of that."

Offering a grim smile, Ceartas nodded. "But we both know Queen Maeve will never lift a finger to save Brina."

This guy was still spot-on and every word from his mouth made sense. But what was his end game?

With few options already, and time slipping through his fingers, Tzader had to consider any opportunity. He asked, "How do you know all this?"

"You'll understand by the time we have a deal and the dragon is free."

"How do you communicate with the dragon?"

Ceartas stretched and crossed arms that bulged with roped muscles. "You're wastin' time on insignificant details. With Queen Maeve and the original Cathbad the Druid back in business, you're dealing with a nasty pair. They're plotting to undermine the Beladors in the human world, as a start. Queen Maeve is not the fool Flaevynn was. She has been around a long time, and is developing a strategy that will eventually win if left unchecked. By the time she pulls the last block out from under the Belador power base, it will be too late to stop her. Not even having Brina in Treoir will save the Beladors."

Tzader's heart beat harder than it had while he'd fought. Could all of this be true? While he reeled from those statements, Ceartas pointed out, "However, if you lose Brina, the war is lost before it's begun. The dragon will not lift a finger to help you *or* the Beladors if Brina is not protected from everyone who would do her harm, including Macha. And that will not happen if the spell is allowed to continue destroying Brina's mind."

No one had considered that the Noirre majik was still influencing Brina. What if Flaevynn was the only one who could reverse the damage? A lead ball of disappointment landed in the pit of Tzader's gut at that possibility.

This guy claimed the dragon could help.

Why would Tzader trust a stranger or some unknown dragon? He pressed his question again. "You still haven't answered me. Who are you to know all this?"

"I am the champion for a dragon who was cursed to remain in TÅµr Medb two thousand years ago. He remains there even now. Having no choice in the matter, he was present when Flaevynn created the Noirre spell your traitor cast upon Brina. The dragon heard Flaevynn talk about the traitor she used to deliver the Noirre attack. That dragon is the only one who can save Brina, and in so doing , also save the Beladors."

"Save the Beladors from what?"

Turning a cold, gray gaze to Tzader, Ceartas asked, "Who wields the most power over the Beladors?"

"Macha."

"That's what she'd have you believe. Has she not lied to you time and again? Told you she couldn't break the ward on the castle to allow you to be with Brina?"

"How do you know *that*?"

The warrior's face turned grave. "The Medb know many secrets the Beladors believe are safe. You underestimated Flaevynn, and Brina was attacked. Don't underestimate Queen Maeve and Cathbad. Let's just say, if it has been spoken of in the queen's chambers, the dragon knows it."

Fuck. Tzader rubbed a hand over his jaw. "What is the dragon's interest in Brina?"

"You keep asking the wrong questions."

"Not from where I'm sitting. How do I know this dragon will work in Brina's best interests?"

"If the dragon wished Brina harm, he merely has to remain silent and allow the mental damage to continue."

The guy had a point, but Tzader held his silence, waiting for more.

"Tell me, Tzader, are you willing to be Brina's champion?"

"That goes without saying. Of course I am."

"I believe you're willing to face a tangible enemy, but will you go up against Macha to save Brina? Will you risk all to free the only one who can reverse the Noirre spell?"

Tzader was torn between the hope that burst inside his chest and doubt over what it would take to fan that hope into an actual miracle.

Still, he had to know more, even as he began calculating possibilities. "What's stopping the dragon from leaving on his own?"

"He pretended to be Queen Maeve's sword arm many centuries ago so that he could get close enough to Maeve to save someone very important to him. When Maeve discovered what he was up to, she cursed him to spend the rest of his days as her throne. Then she killed the woman he was trying to protect."

"She turned a dragon into a *chair*?"

Ceartas looked insulted. "This log we sit upon is a chair. The dragon's shape is a throne."

Suspicion raced back and forth through Tzader's thoughts, but damn he was desperate to have that Noirre spell broken. "Why have you waited until now to free the dragon?"

"I'm a dream walker. That doesn't afford me a lot of opportunity for conversation with a dragon whom Queen Maeve has not allowed to close his eyes for two thousand years. She only recently permitted him to rest, and only for short periods. Speaking of sleep, Brina is sleeping more often, isn't she?"

Tzader swallowed, not wanting to admit to the truth in that statement.

He had no idea if it was the spell, or Brina preferring to stay in the dream world where she was happier and could hold on to her memories longer.

Nodding confidently, Ceartas said, "The TÅµr Medb dragon had me wait until the right moment to make contact. Now that she sleeps more often, it is clear that time is running out."

"This isn't the first time you've seen her here in the dream world, is it?"

"No. I've been keeping up with both of you."

Tzader considered what he and Brina had just been doing when they'd believed they were alone.

Ceartas must have picked up on Tzader's thought path. He said, "I have not invaded your privacy with Brina. I can tell when your power blends that you're having an intimate moment, and I do not intrude, but those intimate moments have not come often."

"That's none of your business." Tzader was not explaining why he'd avoided sex with Brina until she was whole again. He shouldn't have to explain it to anyone who had a conscience.

Placing his empty mug on the ground, Tzader crossed his arms and pressed for answers this guy hadn't supplied. "I'll ask again. Why did you wait until now?"

"To be honest, I've been waiting for you. She sleeps far more often than you do, which means she's here alone much of the time. The dragon demands I stand watch over her, so she's been safe."

"Why does the dragon care about Brina?"

"You may ask him when you free him," Ceartas said, as if that was any answer.

Tzader had been right to worry about the changes he'd recently noticed in her sleep patterns. "If I help you free this dragon throne, it will start a war between the Beladors and TÅµr Medb."

Amusement vanished from Ceartas's face, and anger took up residence. "That war was launched many thousands of years ago. A river of blood has been spilled, and is nothing compared to what Queen Maeve will unleash once she has all her game pieces in place. Many have died, but war continues for the living long after the dead no longer fight." His fists clenched and the ground shook. "If you fail to save the dragon, then you fail Brina. I will have no choice but to come for her. I will not kill her, but she'll never wake again to suffer life with Macha."

Tzader was on his feet. He stared down at Ceartas and put venom in his voice. "Do that, and I'll come for you with enough power to bring you down."

In the face of that threat, Ceartas actually seemed to relax. "You may return to the dream realm when you choose, but you'll not find me, or Brina, if she is with me. The only reason you see me now is because I made myself visible to you. I can tell that you are not versed in the skills of dream walking. Nor could you learn enough to ever find me again." He studied Tzader and added, "We both want the same thing. The dragon cares about Brina, and not in any way that would validate jealousy on your part so don't waste energy posturing."

When the silence stretched again, Ceartas added, "This is about more than Brina's memories, but that should be reason enough, considering what she means to the Beladors, and to you. If you make the wrong choice, the day will come when you'll realize you could have protected her and all the Beladors. By then, no one will be able to help you, and Brina will be long gone from your life."

Tzader didn't know if it was the months of strain from watching Brina struggle or the offer of hope, but he stopped fighting.

Unshakeable walls were closing in on his future and on Brina's salvation. "What is my guarantee that the dragon can break the spell on her and that he will?"

"You want a guarantee? The only things guaranteed are that Brina will not survive this spell and that Macha will do what she deems best for Macha." Ceartas paused, looking away in thought, then told Tzader, "What if, as a show of good faith, I tell you something no one except Queen Maeve, Cathbad, and the dragon currently know?"

"I'm listening."

"The dragon has been privy to all things in the lives of every queen ruling TÅµr Medb for the past two thousand years. When Queen Maeve first cursed him into the shape of a throne, she wanted no one to have the ability to pass the secrets from one queen to the next. That's when she made a rare miscalculation. Due to fear of one queen along the way gaining too much knowledge, Maeve added a caveat that the dragon could never be compelled to tell what he knew of the past. That means even

Queen Maeve can't compel him to share the history and secrets of past queens, which she's going to regret."

"Not as much as I'll regret starting a real-time war between the Medb and the Beladors *and* losing Brina if I make the wrong decision," Tzader muttered. He'd fight the world to save Brina, but wouldn't he put her at more risk with war?

"There are many things you don't know about the Beladors and the Medb."

Tzader gave him a blunt look of disbelief. "About the Medb, perhaps, but as to the Beladors, I beg to differ."

Ceartas raked a hand across his face, as if Tzader had said something that pinched a nerve. "Do you trust Macha?"

Tzader started to say hell no, but in spite of all the grievances he had against Macha, he'd given his word to stand loyal to her, and would not sound disloyal in front of a stranger.

He only said, "I'm a Belador, and we swear fealty to Macha."

Ceartas sat quietly for a moment. "Your loyalty is admirable, but you'll soon find that it's been misplaced and *misused*. I won't share more at this time, but I will tell you that Queen Maeve and Macha are two sides of the same coin. I know this for a fact. Flaevynn's attack on Treoir with the gryphons is nothing compared to what Maeve is capable of accomplishing. The only reason Flaevynn's attack failed was because she didn't know about Kizira and Quinn. Maeve suspects something, though, after viewing details of the attack using her scrying wall."

"Viewing what, specifically?" Tzader asked.

"As the battle raged, Kizira stepped between Quinn and an attacking gryphon that mauled her. Quinn held her as she died. Maeve does not know everything yet, but she will not stop until she does."

Quinn, Tzader, Lanna, and Evalle had shielded that secret. If Ceartas knew about Quinn and Kizira's child, he wasn't saying. Tzader battled to decide whether he was impressed or concerned that this one man knew so much.

Ceartas chuckled. "Don't be surprised. The dragon knows about so much more than the secret love Kizira worked to hide from everyone in the tower. That's why the dragon is the only one alive with knowledge of the Noirre attack on Brina. The traitor, who was Horace Keefer, by the way, held Brina and Macha responsible for the death of his family."

Horace had made that very accusation while he threw the Noirre spell on Brina and Lanna. Tzader ran back through his memory of the incident, picking out the people who could possibly know the traitor's name and that particular detail. Lanna had been the only one other than Brina to hear Horace make those accusations. Tzader doubted the young woman had told anyone beyond Quinn or maybe Evalle.

Neither of them would have said a word.

The only way the Medb would know was if Horace told them himself.

VIPER hadn't even been informed as of yet. Tzader wanted to keep the details quiet in case Horace had an accomplice who was also in league with the Medb, and Macha had agreed with Tzader's reasoning. Rats always deserted a sinking ship, so they'd put word out on the street that Horace, who'd been technically retired anyway, was taking an extended sabbatical out of the country.

The more Ceartas said, the more support he built for the dragon's case. He turned serious again. "Like I told you, Tzader, the war started long ago, and blood will be shed on both sides no matter what you decide. Queen Maeve is after Treoir. Always has been. You can't take responsibility for a war with roots as deep as this one, but you can prevent Maeve from winning. The sooner you free the dragon, the better chance all Beladors will have of surviving. Have you not noticed how, from what I've related, the dragon shows no loyalty to either Maeve or Macha?"

Tzader *had* noticed, but instead of admitting that, he asked, "And where does *your* loyalty lie?"

"I serve the dragon's family. I am the only one who can speak on his behalf at the moment, which is why he will honor any agreement I make for him. Keep in mind, I could have taken Brina many times over, and I could have killed you."

Ceartas might or might not know about Tzader's immortality, but Tzader had a hunch the man was speaking truth. Still, he lifted an eyebrow. "You could have tried."

Ceartas smiled, not the least bit challenged. "Give me your word that you will free the dragon, and I will give you mine that I will do all in my power to keep Brina from harm in the dream realm while you're gone. Also, I swear that once the dragon is free, he will reveal how to remove the Noirre spell on her. *That* is your guarantee."

If what Ceartas said was true, there was only one way to save Brina. Tzader had a hard time discounting this dream walker.

Strange things happened in his world all the time, but no one just showed up with this kind of information. Trusting this man could go either way—for good or for ill. But if Tzader were entirely honest with himself, he'd admit that Ceartas had struck a nerve when it came to trusting Macha.

The whole reason Tzader had hidden Brina's mental deterioration from Macha was because he feared what the goddess would do.

Now he just had to convince Macha to endorse his stealing the dragon throne, so she couldn't accuse him of breaking his Belador vows. While going after the throne without her authorization was honorable in Tzader's mind, defying her would be dishonorable to her and the Beladors, in her thinking.

That would be the same as signing his death warrant.

His silence must have sent a message of hesitation.

Ceartas reached inside his leather vest and withdrew something shaped like a rounded leaf the size of his hand. As he turned the thin disk, it changed from iridescent colors to brilliant red. Ceartas said, "I can appreciate that you have doubts. I will give you this to prove that I know what I'm talking about, and for Brina to show you the truth."

Tzader frowned. "What is it?"

"One of the dragon's scales. He shares this with Brina to help her while you're rescuing her savior. This scale can't stop the Noirre spell from continuing to infect Brina, but it will offer her a brief reprieve. She will remember you—"

Those four words gave new life to Tzader's hope.

Then Ceartas ruined it by saying, "But only for twenty-four hours once she touches it. However, she will remember you immediately and recall far more than she has in the last two months. Clamp it between your hand and hers when you see her again. Make sure she does not show this scale to anyone."

Tzader accepted the scale, surprised at the energy buzzing over the surface. He made his decision. "If this scale does what you claim, then I give you my word to try to free the dragon, but I'll need some time to figure out a few things."

Like how to get inside TÅµr Medb undetected.

How to break the curse placed on the dragon so that he would be mobile.

How to get *out* of the place with the dragon, before all hell broke loose and Queen Maeve turned them *both* into something far worse than chairs.

Rising slowly to his feet, Ceartas snapped, "You can't *try*, Tzader. This is an all or nothing deal, and time is running out. If you don't think so, go back and talk to Brina before sharing the scale, then have her touch it. And if you want to see proof of what I've said of Macha and Queen Maeve being no different, just ask Macha what she plans to do when Brina's memory does not return. I assure you, she'll turn Brina into nothing more than a mindless vessel for making babies."

Not while I still breathe, Tzader swore silently.

Much as he hated to admit it, Ceartas voiced the concerns about Brina's future that rode Tzader's heart every minute of every day.

He admitted something now that he never would have in the past. He did not trust Macha with Brina's well-being or her future.

Maybe not even with the future of the Beladors, if Macha gave Tzader reason to question her commitment to him and Brina.

Decision made, Tzader extended his hand. "By my word, we have a deal if this scale performs as you say."

"I would not give just anyone the dragon's scale." Ceartas shook hands.

Tzader winced at the amount of power flowing through this man. "What are you when you're not dream walking?"

"A very dangerous warrior to those who cross me," Ceartas said, without a bit of ego. "But you and I are allies. You have a day, if that much, which is another reason I'm delivering the scale now."

"What? Why?"

Sympathy softened the warrior's intense gaze. "'Tis not my timeline. That's the dragon's best guess at how long you have before the Noirre spell finishes the job it started. Queen Maeve is not aware of Brina's mental condition, but she's piecing together a picture of what Flaevynn did in the past. Once she has everything she needs, she'll know how to come after Treoir. She's already inserted an elite unit of warlocks known as Scáth Force into the human world."

That new information made Tzader's head spin. VIPER had no idea, or he'd have heard from someone about it by now.

Ceartas went on without slowing. "You will need the dragon very soon. Need his aid to protect Brina and the Beladors against Queen Maeve. You're a powerful warrior in your own right, Tzader, but remember. No one can win a war alone. You can save Brina and gain a powerful ally at the same time."

"So Flaevynn is definitely dead."

"Yes." He shrugged. "More like disintegrated. The power that brought Queen Maeve to this time took Flaevynn from it. The same thing happened to reincarnate the original Cathbad the Druid, who is Maeve's partner in all ways." Ceartas turned to leave but stopped, looking back at Tzader. "You must not tell Macha about any of this, and definitely don't allow *her* to see the scale."

Well, that fucked his only plan. Tzader snarled, "Why not?"

"She doesn't like the dragon any more than Queen Maeve does. Always remember one rule about Macha. Regardless of who she steps over to get what she wants, she will always put herself ahead of everyone and everything."

"How is it that you know so much about two goddesses?"

Ceartas looked away as if weighing his answer, then shook off whatever thought had come to him. "The dragon will answer all your questions. He is the one who knows most about Macha and Maeve. Free him, and you'll learn truths you have never been told. Truths about Macha that she has hidden for centuries. She will not be bothered if Brina loses her memories forever. Don't mistake Macha for a benevolent goddess. She has survived all this time by being just as ruthless as Queen Maeve. She won't allow anyone to get in her way. Not you and not Brina. And do not forget that if you fail to save Brina, the dragon will do nothing to help the Beladors."

Tzader didn't need that spelled out any simpler.

For whatever reason, Ceartas believed Macha was as much a threat to Brina as the Medb.

Or did this dream walker consider Macha the greater threat?

Ceartas's gaze narrowed until he peered out through slits. "Do you believe Macha cares whether you and Brina remain together?"

"Answering anything but yes would show a lack of loyalty to my goddess."

A sad smile appeared on Ceartas' face. "I know the answer. I asked you so that you might find the answer for yourself. If Macha felt any compassion for either of you, she would not have kept you apart for four years. She is a master of manipulation."

The truth of this stranger's words stabbed Tzader deeply. Hadn't he questioned that time and again? But Macha always found ways to turn Tzader's questions back on him.

Tzader suffered a shaft of self-disgust. What kind of warrior allowed a stranger to undermine his belief?

But in truth, Tzader would never allow that. Never *had*. Months of frustrated circling around the goddess and her twisted words had done that foul job long before this warrior ever appeared. Ceartas only echoed Tzader's own inner worries. Ones he'd shoved into the background in the name of duty and honor.

He'd done his duty for four long years while Macha had allowed a ward to separate him and Brina. Had Macha offered any help for them during that time? No. The goddess *had* manipulated Brina into pretending she intended to marry one of her guards.

Then when Tzader faced her with that truth, she'd turned the tables and made it seem as though *Tzader* had shirked his duty.

Macha *was* an expert at manipulation.

So maybe the better question Tzader should ask himself was what kind of warrior continued to follow blindly without questioning things he knew in his heart to be wrong?

He had never taken his Belador oath lightly. But now he had one goal first and foremost, and that goal would never change. Save the woman he loved, even if he died doing it.

He had to accept the truth of what Ceartas said, and reserve the rest for when he had more information.

The whole thing would be easier if someone else could vouch for this man's word.

"Our business is concluded," Ceartas announced. "I will find you, or Brina, again when necessary. And I'll know if you tell Macha anything about me, the dragon, or our conversation. You may not believe me, but I'm not telling you to hold a confidence on this to tie your hands. I'm saving you from Macha's wrath." He paused, looking away as if in thought again, then turned to Tzader. "I've debated telling you one more thing, but I feel it is something you deserve to know. If you don't return Brina's memories, Macha will expect Brina to marry immediately. Within days."

Would Macha really do that? How the hell could this man know in such detail what the goddess would do? "Macha might toss me out, but I don't see her acting that quickly. She'll have to at least offer the pretense of giving Brina a chance to ... become involved with someone else." Tzader almost choked on the words.

For the first time, Ceartas seemed to labor over his next words. When he spoke, his voice filled with compassion. "Macha will *have* to act soon. Brina carries the next Treoir heir."

Shock stole Tzader's breath.

He took a step toward the warrior. "The Medb cannot be privy to this information. How can *you* know this?"

Ceartas hesitated, then said, "I cannot yet reveal to you precisely how I know, but to ease your mind I will say only that when Brina comes to the dream realm, I sense the presence of the new life within her."

Tzader ran his hand over his face, processing the implications. That was vague as all hell, but Tzader would likely have more luck cutting this guy's head open and dipping the answers out than by asking for more.

Ceartas nodded. "The fact that you were not aware of the pregnancy means Brina has not told you. The only reason she would not have told you is that Macha is blocking Brina's awareness in some way to prevent her from recognizing the changes in her body, which means Brina doesn't know either. Beyond the drain of the Noirre, that's part of why she's sleeping so much. I have just shared what Macha hides from you. Is it so hard to accept the other truths I've told you?"

"I don't know what to think," Tzader said, clenching his clammy hands.

"Decide quickly, or all will be lost." Ceartas moved backwards. As he did, his face and hands became translucent until he vanished.

Tzader stared in disbelief.

Brina was pregnant?

He and Brina had made love in the dream realm two months ago, before he found out there were real consequences to actions taken here. Her breasts *had* felt fuller. She slept all the time.

Was she carrying his baby?

Is she carrying someone else's baby—someone she met dream walking but doesn't even remember?

What kind of asshole am I?

Brina might not be able to grasp her memories, but she knew Tzader every time they touched in the dream realm. No matter what state her mind was in, she'd never give herself to anyone for less than love, and deep inside she loved him. Fear for her safety and future was twisting him into an emotional pretzel. It was his baby.

Their baby.

Tzader looked at the red scale humming with power in his hand. He held the evidence he needed to end all debate, because the minute he went after the dragon without Macha's authorization, Tzader would be breaking his vows.

Especially if Macha hates this dragon.

Now he just had to return to the castle and figure out what the hell he would say to Brina. Sitting down, he closed his eyes and began the process Lanna had taught him for releasing his hold on the dream realm.

A pain clenched his chest and yanked with enough power to pull him apart. He grabbed at his chest where the ache ripped though him with sharp teeth.

"Tzader!" boomed in his mind.

His eyes rolled up in his head and he let go.

CHAPTER 7

Tzader curled in on himself, trying to ease the gut-wrenching agony of hurtling between different dimensions. His head should explode from the pressure building inside it from changing realms so quickly.

That couldn't have been his doing. He'd never had any trouble returning from the dream world. A woman had shouted his name in his mind.

Not Brina or Lanna, which meant it had to be ... Macha.

When everything stopped spinning, he opened his eyes. He was lying flat on the window-seat bed and staring at the ornately painted ceiling of Brina's sunroom in Treoir Castle. *Made it again.* He swallowed against his dry mouth and dragged in a deep breath. One day, his body would pay for the punishment he'd been putting it through for the past two months.

Tough shit. He had no time to waste. His body would just have to keep up.

Sitting up, he searched for Brina first. She stood ten feet away. When he leaned to his right, he found Lanna and Macha on the other side of the room.

He'd have only a moment before he had to deal with the goddess, so he jumped up and stepped over to Brina.

She backed away.

Macha called out, "How long did you think you would keep me in the dark, Tzader?"

No good answer for that. He spoke softly to Brina. "Please. I can help you remember." When she leaned forward, he grabbed her wrist.

· She tugged it back, but he tightened his hold so she couldn't pull free. The confusion in her face broke his heart. He opened her hand and clamped the dragon's scale between their palms.

Energy shot up his arm.

It must have done the same to Brina. Her eyes blinked quickly as if her mind raced through thoughts, then her gaze sharpened. "Tzader ... you and I, I remember ... "

He kissed her quickly and whispered, "Don't give up on me. I'll be back. While I'm gone, keep this and show it to no one." He hoped like hell that Lanna was doing something subtle to keep Macha from overhearing.

"I will not be ignored by you, Tzader Burke," Macha demanded. "Come here and face me."

To buy even a few seconds, he said, "I'm coming, Macha. I would never ignore you. I just need a moment to regain my bearings." When he spoke to Brina, he lowered his voice again. "Do you know why you sleep so much?"

Her eyes brightened. "Oh, Tzader, I ... uh." Her face clouded and she mumbled, "I forgot what I was about to say."

Damn. "It's okay, *muirnin*. Just do as I ask and don't cross Macha. I'll be back soon." He sure as hell hoped so. "But for right now, play along, please? Pretend you still don't know me and don't remember what we are to one another." That got a frown out of her. "Trust me, love?"

Finally Brina nodded, and he released her hand, which killed him. He had no idea if he'd ever have a chance to touch her again, but if he still breathed, he would move anything in his path until he did.

He strode over to Macha.

The best barometer of his reception would be Lanna, and she couldn't look any more worried if she tried.

Tzader went on the offensive. "I have something to tell you, Macha, and we don't have a—"

"You want to tell me the truth now that I've figured it out?"

Ah, hell. "I told you I was doing everything in my power to—"

"Lie and deceive me. Yes, I realize that."

Tzader would not blow his stack with Macha. Getting in the face of a goddess would be a short conversation. He'd wake up in either another realm *forever* or some godforsaken hole in the human world.

Taking a deep breath, he considered his options. Maintaining the false dialogue cover that he and Lanna had created to keep Macha off Brina's back was no longer on the table.

That left coming clean ... which made the most sense in the interest of time. "I admit I may not have been entirely honest in my dealing with this situation, but—"

"Your time is up," Macha announced with a chill that, knowing her power, might just freeze the castle.

If she'd let him finish one freakin' sentence he might be able to diffuse this situation. "Give me a chance to explain, Macha."

"There is no explanation for such dishonorable actions."

This was taking a deadly turn if she decided he'd already broken his code of honor. The Belador vows were about not taking a life without acceptable cause, treating others in a dishonorable way, placing the tribe at risk through betrayal, or failing to come to the aid of a Belador.

About acting with honor in all situations.

Not for misleading a goddess with unrealistic expectations in the face of all Brina was up against. What about Macha's actions? How was she behaving honorably? Any other man would have done the same in his shoes. No one had been harmed with his and Lanna's subterfuge.

He'd only pissed off Macha. He had not committed some heinous betrayal.

Not yet.

Macha said, "Brina, please wait for me in your private quarters."

He turned to Brina, who looked close to arguing. Tzader gave a tiny shake of his head and mouthed *I love you. Do this for me.*

Brina's face flattened into one of calm acceptance. She said, "Yes, Macha."

Macha's eyes glowed a bright hazel, a subtle sign she was close to pitching a catastrophic hissy fit. "Before you leave, Brina, tell Tzader who you are and if you have any plans to marry him."

Brina hesitated for only a split second before she gave Macha a small frown and asked, "Who?"

Macha's smile took on epic proportions. "This is Tzader Burke, one of our Belador warriors."

Tzader started to correct her and add that he was the Maistir over the

North American Beladors, but he no longer held that position. He'd handed it over to Quinn so he could come here to be with Brina.

"Oh," Brina said, then turned to Tzader. "As a Belador, you should know who I am, Brina of Treoir, warrior queen over the Beladors." Cocking her chin indignantly, she added, "I have no plans to marry anyone, and when I do, it will be someone I love. Not a stranger."

She walked out of the room.

He'd asked her to play along and keep Macha content, but hearing those words shredded his insides. The minute the power of that dragon scale ran out, Brina might mean everything she'd just said.

Tzader ran a hand over his head and shook with the need to kill something. *Not now.* He had to calm down and ask Macha's permission to hunt a cure for Brina. If he got that agreement out of her, he'd still be upholding his end of the deal with Ceartas.

The minute that dragon scale had worked, Tzader's mind was set. He was going after a dragon throne.

"Nothing to say for yourself, Tzader?" Macha chided.

His gaze bumped into Lanna's, and she barely moved her head in a careful side-to-side motion, warning him. He couldn't address her right now, not with the goddess on a tear. "Yes, I have something to say, Macha."

"This should be good."

"I've been busting my ass, with Lanna's help, to figure out how to return Brina's memories." Macha opened her mouth but he kept talking without a break, to avoid her interrupting again.

"But the truth is that Brina has made no headway. In fact, she's getting worse."

"I knew it," Macha said, biting out each word.

"Then you should also know that there is more at stake than the two of us marrying. Brina being whole is our first priority."

Waving a hand, Macha made a *pfft* sound. "You had your chance to commit Brina to marriage, and you failed."

"You're not listening to me. Brina is losing more of herself every day. You can toss me out of here—"

"I fully plan on it."

"—but you can't just pawn her off on another male."

"Don't think to tell me what I can and cannot do, Tzader."

"*Damn it, Macha!*" he roared.

Warning flared in her gaze. The building shook as if a volcano tried to erupt from beneath the foundation. "If not for the vow I gave your father that provided your immortality, I would remove your head from your shoulders. Challenge me again and I will do so regardless, and your father would support me if he still lived."

He wasn't through with Macha. "Kill me, and you'll still lose any hope of an heir."

"You may have been the man Brina loved once, but she's forgetting you. She'll move on. A man of honor would allow her to do so."

He locked his jaws so tightly his teeth should be crumbling. He should just gain Macha's consent to pursue a solution to Brina's problem and get going on it, but Ceartas had gotten through to Tzader and now Tzader had to know, "What'd you do? Compel Brina to be at peace with no memories and to not worry about anything?"

Lanna's eyes widened.

He shouted, "You did, didn't you, Macha?"

"I answer to no one, and I allow no one to raise his voice to me twice. Don't push me, Tzader."

"Oh, I see. You think that guard Brina pretended to be interested in before I breached the ward is going to just step in again? Even if you compel Brina to fall in love with Allyn—" Tzader had to catch his breath at the real possibility that Macha would do that. "Brina won't know even *him* in another three days. She'll turn into a body with no mind."

That got Macha's attention, but did nothing to remove the firm look on her face. "I'm tired of your games, Tzader, and of repeating myself. You wanted a chance. You got it and you're done. Move on."

Now what could he say? Tzader considered how far out on a limb he'd already crawled, and had nothing to go back to if this didn't work. "I think I may know how to help her."

"Give it up, Tzader. Allow her to live her life."

"Give up on Brina? On us? No. Never."

Macha's eyes narrowed. "This is the problem with you, especially in recent years. Being Brina's husband would require you to defer to me just as Brina does, but you constantly fight me at every turn. Treoir history has been dictated by necessity to retain the power, not by foolish emotions. Your actions prove you think only about your own emotional needs. I, on the other hand, have to consider everyone and especially continuing the Treoir dynasty."

What the hell? Tzader could hear Ceartas saying 'I told you so'. He went for the last gamble he had. "What if Brina is already pregnant with my child? We made love in the dream world."

"She's not," Macha said, dismissing the possibility with no consideration at all.

He believed in his heart that Brina did carry his baby. "Allow her nine months to be sure she's not pregnant."

Lanna's eyes couldn't get any wider. She looked close to exploding with the need to say something.

Macha waved away the request. "We can't keep waiting. I'd know if she was pregnant and she would, too. Has she told you she is?"

"No."

"Then she isn't."

"Why won't you allow her to wait even four months?" She'd be showing plenty by then.

"I'll leave Brina and Allyn to work out their future."

What? Tzader saw red. If Macha was blocking Brina from even realizing she was pregnant—and Tzader believed she was—then the goddess would absolutely compel Brina to believe she carried another man's child, and she'd also compel someone pliable like Allyn to raise it with Brina.

Tzader shouted, "What are you going to do? Compel Allyn to rape Brina when she turns into a vegetable?"

That was as close as anyone had ever come to verbally slapping Macha that Tzader knew of, and he'd known her a long time.

"Get out of my sight," she warned in a low voice that rocked the walls. "You are banished from Treoir. Never return."

"I'm not leaving until I talk to you about—"

Macha whipped her arms out wide and roared an unearthly sound.

Tzader's world turned into a mash of colors spinning so fast his head felt separated from his body. Had Macha made good on her threat and pulled his head off after all?

He landed hard on cold concrete, rolling twice before he stopped flat on his back. Why hadn't Macha just beaten him with a two-by-four? Couldn't hurt any worse.

"Tzader?"

Pushing up to his elbows, he found Lanna sitting on a bench. Dark had descended on Atlanta and it appeared they had been dumped in front of the Carter Presidential Center. At least Lanna was sitting, so maybe she hadn't been body slammed, but the young woman wore only jeans and a long-sleeved T-shirt. She wasn't dressed for the middle of a winter night in Atlanta.

If he had to guess based on the minimal traffic moving along Freedom Parkway, it had to be somewhere between ten and midnight.

And cold, which explained the snow flurries. Tzader asked, "Are you okay, Lanna?"

"Yes. Macha gave me smooth teleport."

Thankfully, the bitch goddess had not taken her ire out on Quinn's teenage cousin. "Sorry to have put you in the middle of that mess."

Unperturbed, Lanna said, "We must get back to Brina."

"That's not happening any time soon."

"You would abandon her?"

"Hell no!" He didn't mean to sound so surly when Lanna was just as worried about Brina as he was. "I don't mean to keep snapping at you. I appreciate all you've done to help Brina and me. I just need a minute to catch my breath after flying Air Macha."

Lanna smiled. "I must find out how to teleport that far."

Heaven help them all if Lanna ever figured out just what she could do. "That would be handy right now, since I'm going to need to teleport again soon."

"You have plan to save Brina?"

"Working on it."

"I will help. Cousin will help, too."

That sounded encouraging and comforting, but Tzader couldn't involve Lanna, Quinn, or anyone else he cared about. Still, he could try to confirm one thing.

He asked her, "Do you know why Brina has been sleeping so much?"

"Yes, but when I try to tell you the words disappear from my mind.

You know why. I heard you tell Macha."

"Brina is pregnant."

"Yes. Brina will be even more upset when her body changes and she does not know why. Macha keeps her from knowing."

Tzader hadn't really needed the confirmation. Brina's pregnancy didn't change his goal anyway, but now he had a child at risk, and that upped the ante.

He was going into TÅμr Medb to free a dragon. If he pulled that off and the dragon made good on curing Brina, Tzader hoped to live long enough to see life fill Brina's eyes again.

Who am I kidding?

He had no way to teleport, and no idea how to break a curse of any kind, much less one cast by an immortal.

CHAPTER 8

With a quick check on the doggy-critter perched on the passenger seat of Storm's truck, Evalle stayed at the speed limit while she worked her way to Rowan's home in Midtown.

All she needed was to be stopped by human law enforcement and have to explain a witch's familiar capable of taking off a hand.

Storm's truck was warmer than her GSXR motorcycle in the winter, but she missed riding her baby.

In spite of snow flurries, Atlanta never lacked for traffic even late at night.

The good news? No wrecks to turn the highways into parking lots. Evalle reached Rowan's Midtown neighborhood by midnight.

Please tell me Rowan is a night owl.

Evalle slowed to navigate the historic neighborhood full of homes with wide porches and double-hung windows. With all the remodeling going on at the building where she and Storm intended to live, Evalle had been getting an education on things such as how the two movable parts of those windows were called sashes.

Who knew?

Storm was having custom windows installed in their future home, which had once been a commercial building, just so she could open them on cool nights. After living underground for pretty much her entire life, the idea of owning just one window thrilled her.

She drove under a canopy of leafless limbs on big oak trees hovering over the road. The last time she'd driven Storm's truck to a house he'd owned in this area, he'd been trapped in another realm with an army of demons.

Let's not relive that memory.

She parked at the curb in front of Rowan's Victorian-style home. It fit in with so many others built a century ago, but this one had always *felt* different.

Rowan lived in the big old house with her younger sister, Sasha, and brother-in-law, Trey McCree, who was also a Belador warrior.

According to Trey, one of Rowan and Sasha's ancestors had built the house.

She checked her phone. Still no text reply from Rowan.

What to do now?

If Evalle called telepathically to Trey, he'd hear her and let Rowan know she was here. He was the most powerful Belador telepath she'd ever met, but she hated to disturb him. Between his and Sasha's new baby girl and Trey's Belador duties, the guy's hair had a perpetual bedhead look from exhaustion. Not from any sense of style.

Snuffling sounds came from the other seat, where her passenger had curled into a ball and closed its eyes.

Her dangerous sidekick needed a power nap, huh?

Might as well knock on Rowan's door and hope she didn't piss off anyone by waking the baby. She climbed out of the truck and had made it halfway down the dark path to the wide porch when a glow bloomed in a hanging oil lamp.

Must be nice to be a badass witch.

The leaded-glass front door opened and Rowan stepped out in a furry white house robe that stopped just above matching boot slippers. "Good evening, Evalle."

"Hi, Rowan. Did I wake you?"

"Not really. I was just napping so I could take a turn getting up with the baby, but I sensed someone here."

"I sent a text first."

"My phone is off to keep from waking the baby. She's been colicky."

"Sorry to hear that." But Evalle was glad to know Rowan hadn't been ignoring her message.

It wasn't enough that Rowan was the definition of drop-dead gorgeous, but the good-morning fairies had gifted her so she didn't even look sleep rumpled.

Evalle took in her outfit and asked, "Are you warm enough?"

"Oh, yes. I'm good. I'd invite you in, but the baby just got to sleep and she's showing early signs of her powers."

"Really? Is she, uh, more witch or Belador?"

"Hard to say yet." Rowan lifted a shoulder. "But she knows if a non-family member comes inside. Sasha will kill both of us if we wake that child."

"Ten-four."

"I'm surprised to see you here without Storm," Rowan said, taking a step down so that she could sit on the edge of her porch.

"Storm's home, getting our new place ready." And, for once, Evalle would be going home early due to the men opting to deal with Sen. She walked over and leaned against one of the waist-high stone walls bordering each side of the steps. "VIPER sent me and two others to hunt down a demon, but it turned out not to be one."

"Thought those were all caught."

"Reports of sightings still pop up, just not as often now. Evidently the Medb left a few extras just to give VIPER agents something to do." Evalle could accuse the Medb of being at fault only when talking to someone she trusted. She didn't need a new round of arguments between the Medb coven and the Beladors right now. Not with the Tribunal set to finally make a major decision affecting the Alterant-gryphons.

Currently, there were only seven others of her kind that were known, but this decision would also affect anyone else who woke up one day to find out they were of the same bloodline.

Evalle had been on her best behavior during every Medb encounter for weeks. She hadn't killed any. That counted for good manners, right? The other seven gryphons were hidden away on Treoir Island where they couldn't antagonize VIPER, the Medb, or a Tribunal member.

That put major responsibility on Evalle's shoulders to cause no trouble or give anyone a reason to derail the Tribunal vote on recognizing the gryphons as an independent race.

Her group had lived long enough with someone else pulling the strings on their lives.

Evalle might carry the blood of both Beladors and Medb, but her loyalty sat squarely with the Beladors.

Rowan shoved a handful of silky black hair over her shoulder. "The Tribunal and VIPER are fools for bringing the Medb into the coalition, and this world."

"Tell me about it, and I'm stuck as the liaison for the gryphons," Evalle groused. She hadn't originally planned to stay long, but since Rowan appeared to be wide awake and chatty, it was nice to talk to someone she could trust.

"Trey told me Tzader went to Macha about keeping you out of the middle of the Belador and Medb conflicts, but clearly that didn't happen."

"He did, but she didn't. I can't really blame Macha this time."

Rowan's eyebrows lifted. Her gypsy-shaped eyes questioned that comment.

Evalle chuckled. "Don't misunderstand me. I'm not defending her for any *other* actions, but the goddess wasn't present when Loki pulled his usual crap during a Tribunal meeting and twisted things around until I couldn't possibly say no."

"Ah. Got it," Rowan said.

"The Tribunal expects me to find a resolution for the tug of war between the Beladors and Medb over the gryphons."

"How'd *that* get dumped in your lap?"

Running her hands over her hair, Evalle grumbled, "Not by my choice. It started back when the Medb captured Alterants and made us fight each other. Those battles forced us to evolve into gryphons who could die and immediately regenerate back to life again."

Rowan sat up at that. "Really?"

"Yeah. None of us knew about that ability before then, and the regeneration only works three times." Evalle had suffered through all three. "Every time we die, we become stronger as gryphons when we return. Flaevynn compelled us to attack Treoir and sent their priestess, Kizira, to lead us. She died during the battle. Once that happened, she no longer had control of the gryphons, so the most powerful one in the pack became the leader. His name was Boomer. He was a huge SOB and went after Brina, so I had to fight him when he busted into Treoir Castle." She shrugged. "I won and became the gryphon leader by default."

Kill the biggest, baddest one on the team and, bam, you get to be in charge.

She hadn't wanted that position, but for now she had to deal with the responsibility.

Rowan leaned back. "Wow. Macha is so lucky to have you and the others. Why isn't she pushing her weight around in this mess with the Medb? She hasn't even shown her face in this world since the Medb started sending warlocks and witches into Atlanta, has she?"

"No. She won't leave Treoir, not with Brina still having problems with her memory. The closest I ever came to seeing Macha show real concern was when she thought Brina had vanished forever."

"But you and Storm brought Brina and Lanna back. Doesn't that matter to Macha?"

"You're asking the wrong person, Rowan. I'm lucky Macha didn't leave me locked up beneath VIPER headquarters last year. I didn't care for the deal she made, but she did get me out. All I know is that I have to perform my duties. If she wants to stay on Treoir, I'm the last person in a position to share my opinion. And I don't want anything to happen to Brina."

Rowan leaned forward and propped her chin on her hand in a thoughtful pose. "I can understand Macha's concerns, given that the entire Belador power base is dependent upon Brina being alive and on the island, but not stuck in that castle. Poor woman is a prisoner. Tzader is there. He's immortal, so why can't he watch after Brina?"

Evalle froze. How did Rowan know that?

Rowan chuckled. "Trey has told me nothing, but rumors did fly after Tzader died breaking through the ward on Treoir Castle ... and you brought him back to life. Now I understand how that happened."

"Yep. It was my last regeneration, and even then, the fact that it brought Z back was a miracle. One I can't repeat."

She smiled up at Evalle. "But you risked truly dying when you linked with him."

Evalle shrugged. "He'd have done it for me."

"I have no doubt. Isn't the warding around the castle still a problem for him?"

"Tzader said it's back up, but he can cross it." Evalle shrugged. "Don't ask me about majik. I just kill things."

Rowan nodded. "Back to my point, though, which is that Tzader can protect Brina as well as Macha, maybe better. His heart's in the right place at least." Rowan grimaced. "With Macha, who knows what beats in her chest? I doubt it's a functioning heart."

This was why Evalle had stuck around for a bit. Rowan called it straight, with no concern over politics. "I couldn't agree more, but I have no idea why Macha does or doesn't do anything."

Rowan shook her head. "I wouldn't leave my people to face off with their enemy. What's the point of being loyal to a goddess if she isn't just as dedicated to her people?"

Sitting back and supporting her weight with her elbows, Rowan struck another cover-model-worthy pose.

Men in this neighborhood who had turned in for the night were missing out, big-time.

Evalle marveled over how the chilly air didn't seem to bother Rowan, but *she* felt it all the way to her frozen toes. "I don't know how we're going to get rid of the Medb now that VIPER has allowed them to populate the city, but their coven members will eventually screw up. When they do, we'll nail them even if it means taking them down one at a time."

"Sooner would be better than later." Then Rowan added, "We think they may be attacking our witches. Some have gone missing."

"What? Did you report it to VIPER?"

"Yes, for what good it did. Trey delivered a message to VIPER for me, then returned with a curt reply. I was informed that I had no hard evidence to support my claim. Also, that if the white witch membership and council wanted access to VIPER's resources, they needed to join the coalition."

VIPER kept ordering the Beladors to smooth out relations with the Medb, but the coalition had no problem blowing off a powerful white witch who had kept tempers calm and prevented a massive witch war back in November.

Rowan sat up and seemed to shake off her irritation. "If you got your demon or whatever tonight, why're you here when I know you'd rather be home with Storm?"

Just hearing his name brought a sense of peace to Evalle, and deep longing to get back to him. She explained, "Like I said, we don't think it was demon, but this particular creature had been gathering food or something, because it captured a lot of dogs."

Surprise lifted Rowan's voice. "You got that *dog thief* everyone's complaining about? That's great ... wait a minute. I know this is going to sound bad, but why would anything preternatural grab an animal when it could have a human?"

"I don't know. We kicked around several theories, and Lucien suggested it might be a tikbalang, but we don't know for sure and we've got no idea who controlled it, so we're just making wild guesses."

Rowan's gaze narrowed at the mention of Lucien.

Much like Lucien's reaction to hearing Rowan's name.

What was going on between the witch and Lucien? Rowan didn't share her thoughts, so Evalle stayed on track. "I'm here because one of the animals was not exactly a dog. Lucien says it's a witch's familiar."

That brought Rowan to her feet. "What does it look like?"

"Cute in an odd way and not quite knee-high. Looks like a bichon frisé, but it has shaggy salt-and-pepper hair and—"

"—a horn jutting up from its forehead plus a mouth full of fangs," Rowan finished in a flat tone.

Score. Evalle would be headed home empty-handed soon. "Great. You know who the owner is."

"Yes, it's Mother Mattie. She leads a small, but powerful, coven of our oldest witches *and* she sits on the council, but ..." Rowan's voice drifted off. "I don't see how it could be Oskar."

Evalle was missing something.

Shouldn't Rowan be happy to get her friend's familiar back? Speaking of which ... Evalle cast a glance at Storm's SUV, where she found Oskar awake. He stood with his front paws on the window, watching them. His gaze went from Rowan to Evalle as if intent on keeping up with the conversation and waiting for a verdict.

That wasn't creepy. Not a bit.

Hooking her thumb in the truck's direction, Evalle asked, "So that's Oskar?"

Rowan took one look and said, "Yes." She didn't sound very happy to confirm the familiar's identity. "He's been with Mattie for over forty years."

"I didn't think dogs lived that long."

"It's *not* a dog, Evalle, and he's very dangerous. In fact, no one should have been able to put their hands on him. That couldn't happen unless ..." Rowan lifted her fingers to her lips, looking worried. "Unless Mother Mattie was out of the picture.

"You mean she's ... dead?"

"No, not dead... wait a minute." She pulled a cell phone out of her robe pocket and ordered the phone, "Call Mother Mattie."

She put the call on speaker. It rang and rang, but not loud enough to wake a baby inside the house. The longer Rowan waited, the more tension Evalle picked up.

Rowan stared with disappointment at the phone and terminated the call. "This is bad."

When Rowan said something was bad, Evalle took note. Pushing away from where she'd been propped against the short wall, Evalle asked, "You think something has happened to Mother Mattie, too?"

"I'm sure of it. She keeps her phone handy, and Oskar even closer. I told you we have missing witches. If the Medb are behind this, and that would be the first place I'd look, VIPER is playing with fire by ignoring us." Rowan glanced up. "Did you find *any* evidence of the Medb on that ... what was it?"

"A ten-foot-tall creature that held a dark, shadowy glamour until we fought it, and no, there was no sign of Noirre or scent of Medb. If they did create it, the Medb managed to hide their singed lime odor and—"

Energy flooded the air.

Evalle snapped to attention, turning toward the source in the center of the yard.

Rowan stepped down to stand beside her.

Power whipped around Evalle, then a massive chestnut-colored horse appeared ... with a man's upper body in place of the horse's head and neck.

A centaur.

Not just any centaur. Deek D'Alimonte.

This night would not end.

Or it *would* end, but not well

CHAPTER 9

Evalle tried to swallow against the dread clogging her throat. Call her a pessimist, but there could be nothing positive about the unexpected appearance of a bazillion-year-old centaur. She really had no idea of his exact age, but he was ancient. She said, "Hi, Deek."

Menace poured off him. He cut a scathing look her way, acknowledging her with one acidic word. "Alterant."

The horse part of Deek's body had to go at least eighteen hands at the withers. From there, the neck of the horse blended into the torso of a man built for fighting Spartan warriors.

Like really *capable* of battling those impossible-to-kill warriors.

In his centaur form, Deek towered over Evalle, and she was tall for a woman. He struck a mighty pose. The guy was oblivious to being in the middle of suburbia, and seemed unconcerned that one of Rowan's Midtown neighbors might notice him.

Evalle had also seen Deek in his human form, and she'd call him hot if not for the insane ego that came with the whole package. So, yes, he *could* shift.

He chose to be in this form.

Rowan demanded, "What do you mean by coming to my home and in that form, *centaur*?"

Did these two know each other?

Deek amped up the death threat in his glare. "This is not a social call, *witch*."

Yep, that sounded as if they were familiar.

If any more tension built between Deek and Rowan, the ground would split open and spit fire next. That'd be funny if it wasn't an exaggeration.

Two houses down from Rowan's, an engine revved to life and the car began backing out of the driveway.

Evalle interrupted the glare fest. "Humans are going to see, uh, you, Deek."

"Don't insult me by suggesting that I can't shield myself from a human, Alterant. They see me only if I choose so."

"Don't *you* insult a guest at my house, centaur," Rowan warned.

Clearly, names were not allowed at this impromptu meeting.

The driver of the car passed by and never noticed the strange half-man, half-horse, or Rowan dressed in fluffy lingerie.

Rowan went back on offense. "What are you doing here?"

Crossing his arms, Deek said, "Searching for Mattie's familiar." His gaze swiped over to Storm's truck, making it clear he'd found said familiar. "What's it doing here, and where is Mattie?"

Evalle decided to let Rowan take the lead, since these two knew each other. No one wanted to get caught between an angry witch and a scary centaur.

Rowan watched him as she would a grizzly about to attack, but her voice changed with a thread of suspicion. "Why are *you* asking about Mattie?"

Deek took a menacing step forward. "I answer to no one, witch."

"You do when it comes to my council members."

He leveled another laser look at her, wrinkling his nose. "You think I want to harm Mattie? If I wanted to harm *anyone*, you would not stop me." His horse hooves shuffled about, while neither he nor Rowan gave an inch.

Evalle had not known Deek to be a patient person. Who would give in first?

Deek surprised her when he finally conceded, "Mattie is someone who matters to my niece. Now, where is she?"

This could escalate quickly if someone didn't help diffuse it. *Guess that's my job.* Evalle offered, "Deek, Mattie is missing, and I was on a VIPER team that found her familiar, Oskar, after we killed a creature that had him cornered in a building. I brought him here to try to find the owner. Rowan just called Mattie, but she got no answer. Just before you showed up, Rowan was saying she's sure something has happened to Mattie. We don't have any lead on where Mattie is, or if someone *has* her, or why they took her if she was kidnapped. That's it in a nutshell."

His attention shifted wholly to Evalle. He studied her for a moment, then a sly smile lifted his lips as if he'd come up with a clever idea. "*You* will find Mattie, Alterant, and return her home immediately."

Evalle had planned to help Rowan in any way she could, but Deek was not making this *her* responsibility. "I don't have authority to do that because VIPER is not allowing agents to give aid to the white witches." She sensed Rowan tense at that, so Evalle quickly added, "But I absolutely intend to do everything I can to help find Mattie."

"Do not confuse my words, Alterant," Deek warned in a calm voice that would freeze water. "That was an order, not a request. You *will* find her, or have you forgotten our last conversation?"

"You have no say over Evalle," Rowan argued, hands going to her hips, which was probably the safest place for those dangerous fingers.

But Evalle had no argument. Deek had her. She owed him an open-ended debt.

During a Medb attack, Tristan had accidentally teleported Evalle into Deek's private office above the Iron Casket nightclub. Due to very old agreements, VIPER had no authority on Deek's property. Visions of Deek threatening to lock her in his dungeon assaulted Evalle's mind. She'd been at his mercy, and agreed to repay the debt in exchange for Deek allowing her to leave alive. The centaur could have held her forever, or until Tzader, Quinn, and Storm came after her, which would have ended with them dead.

Or he could have just as easily smoked her with a flick of his fingers.

Evalle put a hand on Rowan's arm. "Actually, I do owe him a favor."

"See, witch?" Deek said with a smug look. "'Tis as I said. The Alterant will find Mattie."

Evalle wouldn't go quietly into the night, though. "You're far more powerful than I am, Deek. Why can't you locate Mattie? You found Oskar."

"Because I have you to find her." He was pleased with his answer.

Rowan leveled a narrowed gaze on him. "What is Mattie to your niece?"

Fury stirred in Deek's dark gaze, but it settled after a moment and he shrugged. "Mattie's sister is my niece's godmother."

Rowan looked away, thinking, then snapped her fingers and turned to Deek. "Caron? The Fae princess? *She's* Mattie's sister?"

Sister? Fae princess? Evalle recalled rumors of Deek having once been involved with a Fae woman who broke off the relationship. Word was, Deek proceeded to create a nightclub so shiny and sparkly it would be irresistible to any Fae, and named it the Iron Casket.

Not exactly subtle about his hard feelings over the breakup, since iron was death to many Fae.

Deek's hooves pawed at the lawn. "Caron and Mattie are *half* sisters."

"What's up with Caron? Why can't a Fae find her own *half* sister?"

"Caron is none of your concern," he grumbled back.

"You don't want to tell Caron that Mattie is missing," Rowan said, sounding as if she'd figured out something. "Why?"

Evalle wished she could send Rowan a telepathic shout to stop aggravating Deek, but Rowan didn't share telepathy with Evalle.

Glaring clearly had no effect on the witch, either. She continued jabbing that sore spot of Deek's. "You listen to me, centaur. Don't come around here making demands when you're not willing to offer any substantial aid *or* explain why an all-powerful Fae can't help."

Deek released a fierce growl that could send a herd of lions running.

He snarled, "If you must know, they aren't speaking. Mattie sided with me when Caron and I separated."

"Oh?" Rowan appeared genuinely surprised.

"I last spoke with Mattie a month ago when she called to inform me that she'd invited Caron to visit this weekend. Mattie wanted to make peace with Caron before my niece's birthday. I went by Mattie's house to have her promise to contact me if Caron got out of hand. Caron and I are *not* communicating."

That sounded final. Evalle had been on the receiving end of Deek's anger, and could only imagine him and a Fae going at it.

Deek said, "When I found Mattie missing and came here, I expected to find Mattie's familiar dead and have someone's head to hand Caron when she arrived, but if that's Oskar, Mattie must still be alive."

Evalle thought on that. "Did you teleport into Mattie's house, Deek?"

"No. What kind of barbaric men are you around, Alterant? No man just barges uninvited into the home of a woman like Mattie."

Evalle rolled her eyes, noting he'd narrowed that to a 'woman like Mattie,' which probably meant all others might be fair game. "Then how do we know she's not there and unconscious?"

"Because I teleported in to check on her."

"Wait, what?" Evalle mumbled.

Deek's eyes narrowed to thin slits and light glowed from them. "I went in *after* Mattie failed to answer my phone calls and my knock," he said slowly, as if Evalle was a moron for not realizing the obvious reason he'd teleported in at that point.

Engaging in verbal battle with an ancient centaur would serve her as well as asking Sen to personally give her a mani-pedi. Evalle asked, "Did you notice anything out of place?"

"Other than Mattie and Oskar missing, no," Deek replied. His hooves danced around then he settled down, tail swishing. "Be forewarned. While Caron may be angry with Mattie for siding against her, she will allow no one to harm her family. If Caron arrives to find Mattie missing, she will level this city and every other one in her path until her sister or her sister's body is returned."

The way Deek kept moving around gave Evalle the idea that he was going to disappear soon. If she had to settle a debt with Deek, finding Mattie would be ideal, since she planned to help Rowan anyhow.

If she found Mattie.

But Evalle wanted a witness to the terms of her deal this time. "Deek, do you agree that if I find Mattie, my debt to you is paid in full?"

"Did you say *if*, Alterant?"

"I meant *when*," Evalle corrected, even though she had no idea how she was going to make good on that.

Rowan crossed her arms and cocked her head with challenge. "That seems reasonable to me."

Deek had been somewhat calm until Rowan spoke up. "Do not interfere."

Evalle sent Rowan a please-don't-help-me look and waited for Deek to agree or not.

It didn't take long. He said, "If you return Mattie safe and sound before nine on Saturday morning, the debt will be considered settled."

"Why by nine on Saturday?"

He smiled with victory. "'Tis the time that Caron is expected to arrive at Mattie's house."

Deek raised a hand and Evalle rushed to stop him before he vanished. She shouted, "Wait. What about Oskar?"

"Do not allow harm to come to him, or you will face me." Deek flipped his hand and blinked out of view.

The door on Rowan's house opened.

She and Rowan turned at the same time.

Trey walked out, running a hand back and forth through his disheveled hair. He had a thick, sleep-drenched voice. "What's all the shouting about? What's going on out here?"

Rowan waved him off. "Nothing that requires you to be up. I'll check on the baby. Get your sleep and I'll fill you in over breakfast."

Evalle said, "Sorry to wake you, Trey."

He nodded. "Call me if you need me."

She knew he meant telepathically and replied, "I will."

Once Trey closed the door, Rowan told Evalle, "I would be glad for this additional attention on finding Mattie, but not the timeline. I've heard stories about Caron. It was ugly when she ended her relationship with Deek."

"I can imagine."

"Maybe not, since it was before you came to Atlanta. The city thought a tornado had hit. Word was that Caron selectively struck every property Deek owned, and he owns a lot. She managed to do it without any loss of life, but she doesn't care one bit for VIPER, or shielding humans from the knowledge of nonhuman existence."

"Got it."

"I'm actually shocked to find out about Deek's connection to Mattie. He never gets involved with anything that isn't extremely important to him. Just coming to look for Oskar says a lot. Who knew that Deek had a soft spot for a little old white witch?"

"His niece is pretty important?"

Rowan said, "He's raised her since her mother, Deek's older sister, died."

"How could the sister of a centaur die?" Evalle wanted to know.

"Deek is the only one who knows the whole story. I've only heard rumors. I hate to give him any credit, but he raised his teenage sister and his niece." Shaking off a thought, Rowan said, "Mattie has never spoken about her family, Deek, or his niece that I know of, which was wise since that's a volatile situation. Caron is just as dangerous as Deek indicated."

That meant he hadn't been blowing smoke about Caron wiping out the city. Evalle tried to envision telling VIPER about this.

Yep. Not happening.

Rowan walked around, hands in pockets, sounding as if she was thinking out loud. "None of the homes of missing witches have been broken into, so that fits for Mattie's to also be undisturbed. The fact that Deek teleported in means that Mattie's wards were down, too. I've had council members trying to find the first three missing witches. Even I can't pull up anything by scrying." She sighed disgustedly.

"What do you have for me to start with?"

"Just a distinctive odor. We've found residue of Noirre majik at each kidnapping site, but it's too—"

"What?"

"Obvious. I know that sounds ridiculous, but tell me—how many demons were you hunting prior to the Medb coven being allowed to enter the city?"

"One or two a year.

"Exactly," Rowan agreed. "While not all demons can be verified as Medb creations, we both know they've created quite a few. They had to use Noirre majik to create the demons, yet any evidence, and the Noirre scent, has been hidden. Why go to that kind of trouble to cover their tracks so well with the demons, and yet leave clear evidence of Noirre in the homes of kidnapped witches?"

"Good point." One that Evalle had to run past Storm and Quinn for their feedback.

Rowan continued, "Even if I convince VIPER to send a team to investigate, and they confirm the Noirre residue present at the kidnapping locations, I have no doubt the Medb will accuse us of planting that evidence. I don't want to bring a Tribunal into this, but neither will I allow anyone to harm the witches under my protection and get away with it."

"Of course not," Evalle agreed. No one wanted the Medb run out of the human world more than she did, but in all honesty, this was the worst timing for Evalle to be caught in a conflict between the white witches and VIPER.

If someone was going to the trouble of planting leads at the crime scene, Rowan might not have a choice about this reaching a Tribunal decision.

Even worse? Everything Rowan said could end up clearing the Medb of any suspicion.

Any evidence would have to be presented to a Tribunal, which would involve Beladors investigating and Medb being put on trial. Fingers would point both ways. Accusations would fly. The Tribunal gods and goddesses would lose their tempers.

As bizarre as it seemed, the Tribunal would hold Evalle responsible for not keeping peace between the Beladors and the Medb.

I might as well be a tiny pebble trying to hold back a landslide.

Taking Rowan's side would also put Evalle in a hot spot, but back in November, Rowan had waded into war side by side with Evalle and Adrianna, against that crazy witch, Veronika, to help prevent her from grasping the Witchlock power.

If Veronika had pulled off her grand plan, the preternatural world as they knew it would have never survived. Well, all except the Medb. Rowan believed that coven would have probably joined with Veronika to turn any surviving witches into slaves.

The human world would have been wiped out first.

Plus, Rowan was Evalle's friend, and Evalle did not let her friends down.

You're responsible to the gryphons, too, and they're your friends as well.

Just what Evalle didn't need right now, a mouthy conscience.

If this caused a delay on the vote about gryphon rights for another couple months, Evalle would also have to face Tristan and the rest of her gryphon pack on Treoir. She had enough guilt to drown her over living free when the others weren't, without yet another delay happening.

All this drove home the point Rowan had made earlier. Where *was*

Macha during all of this? Why couldn't she leave Tzader to watch over Brina, and pop in long enough to give everyone a hand? When would she step in to back up her Beladors and speak up for the gryphons?

Okay, getting riled over that was still not helping.

Macha would never be a fairy godmother, so Evalle had to stop wishing for the impossible.

Rowan tapped her chin in a thoughtful look. "Once we find Mother Mattie, if the Medb are behind this, we'll have the hard evidence required to force Sen and VIPER to accept that the Medb are attempting to take down the white witches." She huffed out a long breath. "I shouldn't have to deal with Sen at all. I'd like to know who picked that jackass."

"You and me and about half of VIPER," Evalle concurred. Sen was a six-and-a-half-foot-tall thorn in Evalle's hide. The guy had changed his look recently, but his 'tude had stayed right where it had always been—on the putrid side of rotten.

In addition to his role as liaison between agents and the Tribunal, Sen doubled as the Tribunal enforcer when the deities ordered a decision carried out.

Everyone Evalle knew thought Sen functioned as liaison under duress—that someone had forced him into the position—but all they had was speculation.

He also claimed the top spot on the list of Evalle-haters. She'd never done anything to earn his disdain, but he'd showered her with it since the first day they'd met.

Rowan started typing quickly on her phone.

"Okay, what's the plan now?" Evalle asked, wondering who she was texting.

"Do you think Storm can track Mother Mattie, or the person who used the Noirre if the residue is in her house?"

"He can track anything he detects at Mattie's, and I know he'll try."

"Of course he will. He'd do anything for you." The warmth returned to Rowan's voice. She paused typing. "I'm glad you two found each other."

Evalle smiled at the truth in that statement. "I am, too."

"How's your new home coming?"

"I've been over there helping for more than a month, but Storm asked me to stay away for the past ten days. He wants our area furnished and decorated so I see the finished product." She didn't care what it looked like, but Storm did and that was fine by her. "We should be moving in any day now, according to Storm. He left early this morning and asked me to meet him at the building when I head home. I'll have a better idea then."

Life had calmed down into a nice rhythm. Feenix still hadn't warmed completely to Storm, but the arrangement they had was keeping the peace.

She took that as a positive.

Bullfrog croak-chirping erupted from the truck.

Oskar probably wanted out, and she had to get going. Did you walk a familiar? She asked Rowan, "What are you going to do with Oskar?"

Rowan took in the truck, then slid a weighted look at Evalle. "Oskar must stay hidden. No one can know that he's around. Whoever grabbed Mother Mattie missed her familiar, or more likely, Mattie might have shielded Oskar when she realized she was in danger. That makes sense, because he wouldn't have been out on his own without her. He was probably just hiding in the place you found him."

"That would explain why he hadn't attacked the dog thief, but there was a whole group of dogs corralled there. Finding Oskar there too strikes me as a little too coincidental. In fact, Lucien even suggested the tikbalang might have been using the dogs to try to bait Oskar. "

Rowan paced as she thought about that. "My hunch is you're right about the coincidence, but I don't have any answers. The bottom line is that Mattie's kidnapper might think Oskar could lead us to Mattie, and that means Oskar has to stay out of sight. We need him. I'm hoping that Mattie is still in the city and not somewhere like TÅµr Medb. In the meantime, Oskar is our best barometer that Mattie is still alive."

Evalle was still waiting for Rowan to suggest who could hide Oskar, but that last comment sidetracked her. "Why is Oskar a barometer?"

"If Mother Mattie dies, Oskar will lie down wherever he is and follow her."

"That's a serious bond."

"You have no idea."

Hmm. Evalle suggested, "If we could get Quinn's young cousin, Lanna, to touch Oskar, she might be able to locate Mattie."

"She has *that* gift?"

"Yes. Lanna has no idea what all is in her mixed bag of tricks, but I've seen her at least attempt to find someone that way."

"Where is she?"

"On Treoir Island, helping Tzader with Brina." Evalle thought on that and saw a snag. "Shoot. If I ask to be teleported there to talk to her, I'll have to explain to Quinn, then to Macha. Quinn won't be a problem—"

"Yes, that *would* be a problem for him," Rowan argued. "You'd put Quinn in conflict with VIPER now that he's the Maistir here. I'm concerned as it is about Trey sticking *his* neck out, but there's no talking him out of being in the middle of anything that affects Sasha, the baby, or me."

Trey was as honorable as they came, and would put family first no matter what.

Evalle couldn't argue with his thinking. He was rock-solid loyal, too. She, Tzader, and Quinn had come to his aid when he fought a Kujoo warrior determined to take Sasha. Trey made it clear that he would be there for the three of them anytime, anywhere.

She'd never had a family, not until Tzader and Quinn came into her life as surrogate big brothers.

Now Evalle had Feenix and Storm as well. She'd put the safety of those important to her before anyone and anything else, just as Quinn and Tzader would.

Rowan could be right about not involving Quinn. Evalle would make that decision if and when she decided it was necessary.

Pulling her back to their conversation, Rowan asked, "When do you think Storm can visit Mother Mattie's house to determine if there is anything to follow?"

"I'll know as soon as I go home and explain all this. In fact, let me get Oskar unloaded and I'm ready to go." Evalle turned to do just that.

"Uh... Evalle, he likes you and you're not a witch, so—"

Evalle spun around with her hands up. "Oh, no, no, no. I can't take him home."

"Why not?"

"I have Feenix. He barely tolerates Storm right now. I don't need anyone else new in his territory."

"Feenix can handle himself," Rowan said.

"True, but what if he decides to turn Oskar into a charred chew toy?"

"Your gargoyle has never harmed any living thing before, right?"

Rowan should have been an attorney with her quick arguments.

"Yes, but—"

"They'll be fine, Evalle. It'll be a play date for Feenix." The witch's eyes shimmered with humor.

Evalle's jaw dropped. "Are you mental?"

"No, and I really need to get dressed and get over to Mother Mattie's to see what I can pick up on before Storm goes in. I'll text you the address. Let me know if you need anything." Rowan had backed all the way up the steps.

"Rowan."

"What?"

"You are not leaving me with that, uh, Oskar."

"I don't have a choice, Evalle. *Nobody* touches Mother Mattie's familiar."

"What about me?" Evalle thumbed her chest. "*I'm* a nobody."

That did not come out right.

"No *witches*. You're not a witch."

Evalle narrowed her eyes. "I want the truth. No one wants to deal with Oskar, do they? Why?"

Rowan frowned and glanced away. Busted. "He's not that bad. I've really gotta go, Evalle. Let me know if Storm is coming over to Mattie's, okay?" She slipped inside and closed the door softly.

Crap. Evalle ground out a few choice words and headed back to the truck.

Three guys hunched against the cold as they walked past on the opposite side of the street.

Evalle waited a moment before opening the passenger door so Oskar could jump out. He walked around in the dark as if he could see just fine, marked a tree and a bush, then jumped back into the truck.

The little guy curled up on the seat again and stared at her as if he'd understood every word she and Rowan had exchanged.

Maybe he had.

Now she felt guilty for trying to unload him. She explained, "It's nothing personal, Oskar."

He didn't blink as his gaze piled on more guilt.

As if she had a choice at this point? "I really doubt this is going to suit you, but I'm out of ideas right now so I'll take you home."

A long forked tongue came out, swiped across his mouth, and went back in. He did that scary smiling thing again.

"Just kill me now," Evalle muttered.

"Okay, but you ain't gonna like it," a gravelly voice replied close behind her.

CHAPTER 10

Evalle slammed the passenger door on Storm's truck and whipped around, all in one motion, ending with her dagger in hand.

The wavering, semi-translucent form of Grady jumped back. Evergreen bushes in Rowan's front yard ruffled with the movement. Grady grumbled, "Whoa. Watch where you slingin' that thing."

Evalle glanced at the empty front porch. Rowan's white robe glowed in the window just left of the front door. She could probably see Grady.

Waving to let Rowan know she was fine, Evalle put her dagger away. She turned back to the old guy who was her best intelligence link for anything going on in Atlanta's underworld of nonhumans.

To VIPER agents, ghouls like Grady—known as Nightstalkers—were useful resources, but Evalle called this one friend in spite of his being cantankerous at times.

And in spite of his being dead. Details, details.

"What are you doing here, Grady?" The old coot usually hung close to Grady Hospital, his namesake.

"What I always do. Wander 'round 'til I find a VIPER agent wantin' to shake hands." He waggled his eyebrows. "You interested?"

Evalle glanced around, checking for humans. She doubted any of them could see an ethereal Grady, but his body was fading in and out of solid form at the moment. The three guys she'd seen a moment ago still walked away in the opposite direction.

Nothing to see here. Just a woman and a ghoul.

Even Rowan no longer stood at the window.

Evalle said, "I'm not looking for intel ..." She reconsidered. "Not unless you know anything about a creature stealing dogs."

"Naw. I ain't no dog catcher."

"I asked about an odd creature. Ten-feet tall. Has a horse head, but a human-shaped body. Wears a shadow glamour."

"Oh, nope. That's not what I have." He grinned.

Oh, great. He had something to share, but she'd have to shake or play twenty questions. She went in a new direction. "You know anything about missing witches?"

"Naw. You shakin'?" Grady prodded.

"Not if you haven't got something I need." As a VIPER agent, she had to adhere to the rule of only shaking hands with a Nightstalker who had information significant to a VIPER investigation. Once a ghoul shook with a powerful nonhuman for only a few seconds, the ghoul could take corporeal form for ten minutes. Since Nightstalkers were the homeless and forgotten who had died during natural disasters, some of them spent their ten minutes guzzling rotgut liquor.

Grady was no different in that, but in many other ways he was not like the rest of them.

For one, he sometimes allowed his keen intelligence to show through in spite of his street talk. Sometimes the street dialect disappeared entirely, and Grady sounded like an educated man.

She'd also broken the shaking rule one time and given him corporeal form for much longer than allowed, but it had been for a good reason. So sue her.

"I might have somethin' you need to know," Grady taunted her.

What was the easiest way to get him moving without hurting his feelings? Ghoul Psychology 101. "Nothing is going on that VIPER would approve for a handshake."

"Like you care what VIPER thinks these days?"

He did know her.

She'd consider shaking with him if she could find out enough to justify the decision. "Do you have information on anything pertinent to my duties?"

He lifted his shoulders. "Depends."

Talking to her knee-high gargoyle Feenix was easier some days, and

Feenix's vocabulary was only about twenty words. Half of those were numbers.

She didn't have to play this game with Grady.

She could finally go home, where Storm would be waiting to have dinner with her after she'd convinced him her assignment was nothing more than boring investigative work.

The bloodstains would be hard to explain, but she'd find a way.

Rubbing her hands together to warm them, she said, "I'll find you tomorrow, Grady, and we'll talk, okay?"

She'd surprise Storm by showing up early tonight. He'd been slowly getting better about his overprotectiveness and not stressing over her hunting nonhumans without him.

Evalle took a step back to leave.

Grady warned, "Not sure my information is going to be much help tomorrow."

Stopping, she pinched the bridge of her nose. "Okay, convince me I want this information, and I'll shake."

Grady grinned like a Cheshire cat. "You want it, but you may not be happy to get it. Just remember, I'm only the messenger."

She didn't like the confident slant of his grin. "What's it about?"

"Did Macha and Queen Maeve sort out their fuss over the gryphons?"

"Not yet." Hair danced along her neck at this specific topic being raised by Grady.

"So the gryphons are safe from Queen Maeve as long as they stay on Treoir, right? I mean, all but you since they let you stay here."

Thanks for reminding me, because I don't feel guilty enough as it is. "Basically, yes, and Queen Maeve isn't going to mess with me while she's trying to gain the other gryphons." Which Evalle would fight tooth and nail.

"But if those gryphons come here, they're fair game?"

"Yes," she said, turning further into an ice cube the longer she stood in one spot. "They all know that. I even had to deliver the message back in November that they could choose to come to the human world, but neither Macha nor VIPER would offer them protection. They chose to stay on Treoir, and she will not send them here, so what *is* your point?"

"What you think Macha or Queen Maeve would do if those gryphons just showed up in Atlanta?"

Macha would have apoplexy and that would probably result in an apocalypse. Queen Maeve would swoop in and scoop up as many as she could at one time.

"Why are we discussing this, Grady?"

He stuck out his stubborn chin. "You have to answer my question first."

She scrubbed a hand over her face and said, "If the gryphons somehow left Treoir on their own, and Macha found out before Maeve captured them, Macha would make an example of any gryphon teleported here without her knowledge. I don't think either of us can imagine just how hideous that backlash would be." Not to mention what Macha would do to Evalle, since everyone had made the gryphons Evalle's responsibility. "As for Queen Maeve, my guess is that she wants to imprison the gryphons and compel us to do her bidding, since that's what her predecessor, Flaevynn, tried to do. I'm done playing what-ifs. What. Have. You. Got?"

"In that case..." Grady stuck his hand out. "You might want to know where I saw Tristan in the city right before I got here."

Oh, shit! What the hell was Tristan doing here?

Forget Macha punishing that gryphon. Evalle would kill Tristan herself.

CHAPTER 11

"I gave Quinn our route. He'll be here any minute," Tzader told Lanna as they walked up a paved trail that paralleled Freedom Parkway just east of downtown. Knowing Quinn, he'd pull up as soon as Tzader and Lanna reached the intersection ahead—about fifty steps from now. Things were quiet here this time of night.

When Lanna said nothing, Tzader worried about the girl. She'd been through a lot in recent months and had just been kicked out of Treoir, where she'd said the old druid had been training her. "I can't make any promises, Lanna, but I'll tell Quinn that Garwyli was helping you and maybe Quinn can get you two back together."

"I am fine, Tzader." Lanna hadn't complained, but she'd said little, which was odd for the normally talkative young woman. She had to be cold without a coat. The chill didn't eat at him so much with his muscle bulk, but it had to be cutting through her. Would have been far kinder to teleport her to Quinn. Not that Macha gave two hoots about tossing them into an area within view of a major highway.

The plus side to the nippy midnight arrival? Fewer people around to see a grown man and teenage girl appearing out of thin air.

I should be glad Macha didn't drop me in the middle of the decorative pond instead of on the sidewalk next to it.

He had a hard time finding any appreciation for the way the goddess had thrown him out of Treoir and barred him from ever returning.

As if he'd just walk away from Brina.

Not in this lifetime.

Lanna gave him a curious look. "Brina said nothing when she returned to the castle, but I could tell she was upset. What happened when you dream walked?"

He wasn't about to tell the world's greatest busybody a thing about the dragon. "She's upset because her memory isn't coming back, and nothing we've tried is helping."

"That was all? Did you try the spell I gave you?" Lanna asked.

Ceartas interrupted that. Tzader wiped his hand over his face to prevent taking his frustration out on Lanna. She meant well, but pushing him about Brina right now was not helping. "We tried, Lanna. It didn't work out. I don't mean to sound rude, but I'm not up for talking about Brina right now."

"I understand," she said, her tone contradicting her words. She either didn't understand or didn't believe that was the whole story, but she changed the subject. "Cousin will help you, no matter what."

"I know," Tzader replied, hoping he wouldn't have to ask Quinn to get involved. His friend was still dealing with losing the woman he loved and managing the North American Beladors in Tzader's absence.

Why don't I ask him to work on my car while I'm at it? Until lately, Tzader had never asked anyone for much of anything, and didn't like having to put Quinn under additional strain.

One thing for sure, Tzader would deal with extracting the dragon from TÅµr Medb on his own, but he needed a few resources. For Brina's sake, he would tap his friends for any help they could offer with locating those resources. There were so many things to figure out, not the least of which was how to teleport into TÅµr Medb.

At the moment, he knew of only two teleportation options. He glanced at Lanna. Two *capable* options anyway—Macha or Sen.

Macha was not a possibility, and Sen couldn't be trusted even if he would help, which he wouldn't.

"We are almost there," Lanna said, stretching her neck to search the intersection. "Cousin is close to us."

Before Tzader could reply, Quinn's voice came into his mind. *I'm in the Lexus GX pulling up to the corner.*

"You're right. He's here." Tzader turned around as a pearl-white, luxury SUV angled out of the light traffic and parked along the curb.

Lanna jumped into the back and Tzader took the front passenger seat of the toasty car.

"Hello, Cousin."

Quinn twisted around. "It's good to see you, Lanna. Are you well?"

"Yes. All is fine for me, but Tzader needs our help."

As Quinn turned back forward, Tzader caught his questioning gaze and gave a little shake of his head. Quinn asked, "Where to?"

"I'm not sure yet. Let's grab something to eat," Tzader said out loud, then telepathically added for Quinn only, *I need to tell you what's going on, but not until we figure out what to do with Lanna.*

Pulling back into traffic, Quinn replied in the same silent way. *I've heard nothing about Grendal since the Beast Championship three months ago, but I'm still concerned about leaving her alone.*

I agree. Tzader thought on it a moment. *Want to leave her with Evalle?*

Now might not be a good time. I spoke to Storm earlier. She and Storm are moving into their new residence any day now.

"What?" Tzader said, regretting his outburst.

Lanna muttered, "Is rude to talk in your minds in front of me."

Quinn frowned up at his rearview mirror. "I've never heard of social protocol for telepathy."

Tzader caught Lanna's scolding look in his peripheral vision. "You should ask, Cousin. I would explain for you."

"I'm sure you would," Quinn muttered. He drew a long breath and asked, "Would you like to go to my hotel and have a spa day?"

"No, thank you."

"What? You really don't want that?"

Lanna huffed out a sigh loaded with exasperation. "I know something is going on and Tzader has problems. You will need my help even though you both have no idea of all that I can do."

"*You* have no idea of all that you can do," Quinn countered with a bit of sarcasm.

Tzader agreed. Lanna's powers had been off the charts and out of control, often at the same time.

Lanna conceded, "This is true, but I have not shown you what abilities I *do* possess."

"Let's make this simple, Lanna. Whatever Tzader and I do will not involve you. Understood?"

"Yes, Cousin." She stared out the window, clearly not happy with her cousin one bit.

But Tzader was glad Quinn had put his foot down. Lanna had survived several dangerous situations, including getting hit with the Noirre spell that still influenced Brina.

The two women had ended up in another realm, where Lanna convinced Brina to search for Tzader in her dreams. Brina had found him while dream walking, and that's when they'd made love. But Tzader hadn't realized at the time that it had been anything other than a normal dream.

Now Brina was pregnant.

But now that he thought on it, something bugged him about what had happened to Lanna and Brina. Tzader turned around. "Lanna?"

For him, the sweet Lanna returned. "Yes, Tzader?"

"Did the Noirre majik thrown on you and Brina ever affect you?"

"No."

Quinn asked, "Why do you think that was?"

"*Now* I am helpful, Cousin?" She bit out words borne of teenage frustration.

Quinn growled, and mumbled a Russian curse.

Lanna reminded him, "I am still fluent in Russian."

At that, Quinn raked a hand over his perpetually neat hair, turning it into a tousled mess.

Amusement twinkled in Lanna's gaze. She addressed Tzader. "I believe Noirre was meant only for Brina, not me. I was captured by the spell, but that was accident. Spell was not cast upon me specifically."

That fit what he'd learned during his dream walk. "Makes sense. The Medb wanted Brina gone to destroy the Belador power base."

Lanna shook her head. "You do not understand me."

"Nobody does," Quinn interjected.

She gave Quinn a quelling look that should make him think twice about annoying the little blonde terror behind him. Hadn't Quinn told Tzader about how Lanna could shake the foundation of a building when she got upset?

Tzader said, "Would you explain so that I understand, Lanna?"

Sitting up straighter, she gave him her full attention. "The traitor who threw Noirre majik on Brina chanted a spell. When I try to stop him, he shoved me over to Brina. That was how I got caught, but spell was not created *for* me. I heard very little chant before everything became blurry and we disappear, but I did hear him use Brina's name as part of chant."

That was something Ceartas hadn't mentioned, but he had said the dragon was the only one who could save Brina so maybe it hadn't been necessary to spell it out further. If it had been a blanket spell, the residual effect would have influenced Lanna as well.

Tzader asked Lanna, "So if someone knew how the spell had been created and the actual chant, could they undo whatever was done by the spell?"

"Storm and Evalle broke spell and brought us back."

"Let's say, hypothetically, a spell like that was thrown at someone else who didn't try to teleport away like you two did. Could someone *other than* the spell creator reverse the spell if Brina was present?"

Lanna pondered a moment, nipping at her fingernail. "Spell was created by Queen Flaevynn. To change or break spell, it would take someone with equal or more power." She paused and stared at Tzader. "I think it could be done, but exact spell originally used would be necessary. Why?"

He didn't want to share anything more with her. "I'm just replaying it all in my mind and thinking out loud about how it worked. That's all." He turned back around and stared at nothing. Ceartas had claimed the dragon was the only creature alive who'd been privy to the original Noirre spell Flaevynn had created.

Logic still dictated that the dragon was Brina's only hope.

It wasn't that Tzader still debated what had to be done. He'd made his decision back in the castle, but he couldn't overlook any opportunity to confirm that decision as the only one he could make.

Lanna sat forward and put her hand on the back of Quinn's seat. "Cousin, I have thought about Kizira and maybe if I touch her I will see something that will help us find Phoedra."

The young woman continually showed her backbone and how loyal she was to family. She'd tried holding a braided piece of hair that Kizira had given to Quinn. Several strands of the hair belonged to Phoedra, the daughter Kizira had birthed without Quinn's knowledge.

Hell of a thing to find out as the child's mother died in his arms.

Lanna's one attempt to use her gift for finding someone by holding something personal like hair, had ended with a protective spell burning her hands.

Quinn shook his head. "No. I appreciate your willingness to try once more, but I will not put you at risk again."

She sat quietly for a moment as Quinn wove the Lexus through the dark streets, probably heading for an all-night diner he'd eaten at with Tzader and Evalle.

Lanna's voice came out softly, no hint of her earlier aggravation with him. "I do not want to be the one to make you feel bad, Cousin, but you must not leave Kizira's body in the cemetery tomb."

"Trust me, Lanna, it's safe."

"You may think so, but many will want to draw her power out, and maybe her secrets, too."

He frowned with a look of concentration. "Are you talking about necromancy?"

"Yes. There is much evil in the city now that the Medb coven sends warlocks and witches in. It is not safe to leave her this way."

Quinn's throat bobbed with a deep swallow. "Like I said, no one can get to her."

Sighing, Lanna leaned back and glanced at Tzader, who had turned to watch her.

She shook her head and mouthed *He is wrong.*

CHAPTER 12

Gritting her teeth, Evalle pushed the speed limit on the way from Midtown back to Inman Park on the lower east side of the city.

What was Tristan thinking?

Did he want Macha to use him as an example to the other gryphons? Since the Medb attack on the castle, no one traveled into or out of Treoir's realm without Macha's permission.

And Evalle had no doubt that Tristan was AWOL, since Quinn had not been informed of any Alterant-gryphon coming to Atlanta. Quinn would have contacted Evalle immediately.

That handshake with Grady was the fastest she'd ever done, after shoving him into a bush so no human would see his body turn solid.

Tires on Storm's truck squealed as Evalle saw the turn she'd been hunting at the last minute. A streetlight there would have helped. Her headlights pierced the dark, catching on trees, garbage cans, and cars parked along the street.

She wanted her motorcycle back. Two wheels handled curves so much better.

Oskar sat up, calmly looking around. He seemed not the least bit bothered by the truck catching air when she took the fast corner.

When she neared the street in Inman Park that Grady had given her, she cut her headlights off, slowed to a crawl, and made her last turn.

She studied the mix of houses that included everything from Greek Revivals to Queen Anne architecture to bungalows built during the late 1800s. Storm had driven her through the older residential areas on the fringe of downtown, and that familiarity was coming in handy now as she hunted for her Treoir escapee.

Most of the neighborhood was dark, locked up for the night. All except for one quaint Victorian house where the outside security lights shone.

A guy who looked very much like Tristan from the side stood at the bottom of three steps leading to the front door.

At least he wore sunglasses to hide his glowing green eyes.

What was he doing here?

The elderly woman standing in the doorway handed Tristan something. Had to be a notepad, because he moved as if he scribbled a quick note, and handed it back before she closed the door.

Lights went out as he sauntered back to the street, heading in Evalle's direction.

She tapped her fingers on the steering wheel, waiting.

Tristan was an idiot for leaving Treoir when they were so close to a vote on the gryphons' right to be a recognized race.

He paused and lifted his head, searching. He looked in her direction.

Yep, gotcha.

As he stood there staring, Evalle started to worry. Tristan had the ability to teleport, which was not one of the usual gryphon abilities, because he'd been given a strange witch brew that had altered his powers.

When he continued striding toward her, she let out a breath and got out of the truck.

She shouldn't be so surprised that he was here.

Tristan had tried to teleport out of Treoir once before, but Brina had been missing from the castle, which diminished the Belador part of Tristan's powers. That attempt hadn't worked.

Had he figured it out since then, or had someone else teleported him?

He didn't have the decency to look guilty. He wore a dark hoodie, and shoved his hands in the pockets of his jeans. When he closed the distance between them, he asked, "How'd you find this address?"

She shut the truck door and leaned back against it, looking up at the black heavens, searching for patience. No such luck. She crossed her arms against the chill air and dropped her gaze to Tristan. "Don't even think I'm going to answer that. What the hell are you doing off Treoir? And, for that matter, *how* are you here? You told me you couldn't teleport between realms."

"I couldn't. Not until Brina came back and everyone with Belador blood got jacked up with a new load of power."

Evalle had seen Tristan on Treoir from mid-December to the end of the year while she'd stayed with the pack and in gryphon form to fly security alongside them.

He'd failed to mention any of this back then.

She watched his face and asked, "How many times have you teleported back here?"

"This year?" he popped off.

"You did this last year, too?"

"What? Should I have just sat tight and waited on yet another group to tell me what to do?" He unleashed anger that she knew had been simmering for a while. When she didn't reply, he kept going. "Don't give me any crap about this either. You'd do the same thing in my shoes."

She slapped her hands over her face and muttered, "You must be suicidal. What could make you..." She couldn't finish that sentence, because her mind had jumped to what would cause *her* to make the same gamble.

Storm and Feenix. She'd do anything to return to them. She lowered her hands, feeling the weight of seven other gryphons wanting at least what she had. Why couldn't the gryphons have lives without this crappy tug of war? Why couldn't they just live the way they wanted?

Tristan said nothing. She considered where she found him. He'd been leaving a note at that house.

Evalle took a guess. "Do you have a girlfriend here?"

Tristan leveled a hard gaze at her. "You know what? I was captured by Beladors and locked in a jungle prison for five years, *then* I'm captured by the Medb. They turn me into a gryphon and ship me off to fight a damn war on Treoir. Now I'm a captive *once again* on Treoir." His voice turned deep and furious. "No one, not one fucking person, has ever considered that I might have a life if I wasn't caught in the middle of all this shit that I did *not* ask for."

She had the same complaint, but that didn't change the fact that this was his life. It wasn't her fault. Wasn't his fault. They were both pawns in this stupid battle between Macha and Queen Maeve. "You didn't answer my question, Tristan, but nice sidestep."

"I don't have to answer your questions."

She'd dealt with him during many difficult situations. Allowing him to get under her skin never played out well.

Drawing a calming breath, Evalle said, "Listen, Tristan, I'm not arguing with you. Of all people, I get it. I want every Alterant-gryphon to choose how to live. I'm sick of being a second-class citizen, too."

"Second-class? Try not even a recognized race. Inmates in human prisons have more rights than we do."

"I know, but I've been sucking it up to do everything possible to keep all the parties happy. I've played nice with the damn Medb just to keep things calm here, because we're so close to getting a vote."

"On what? The equivalent of living on a reservation like the humans did to the Native Americans? Ask your tomcat what he thinks of that."

She could *not* get a break tonight. "What do you want me to do?"

"Nothing. I get your position here, and with the Beladors, but I don't have one. I'm just one more gryphon in the pack. You're the leader. We have to follow you at some point, but don't be surprised if you look around and I've decided to find out what happens if I don't follow you."

Crossing her arms, she leaned back against the hood. "I don't *want* to lead anyone. Besides, you've been the one in charge while I was gone."

"Don't remind me," he groused.

She frowned. "In fact, who's watching over the pack *now* while you're gone?"

He scowled and swung around to lean back next to her. "Believe it or not, they're adults and they've been doing just fine without someone standing over them. I don't stand over any of them when I'm there. All I do is keep them from killing each other out of frustration over being trapped, and I bring them—"

She jerked her head up, but Tristan had clamped his lips. "You've been bringing them back *here*? Are you crazy, Tristan?"

As if he wasn't already pissed enough, that did it. "No, I'm not. And the only reason they aren't completely off their rockers is *because* I teleported each of them here for a holiday break."

Shocked, she sat back, arms crossed, thinking. What was the point of arguing? He'd said it best. They were all adults, including Tristan.

Changing her tone to one of curiosity, Evalle asked, "Doesn't it strain your powers to teleport someone else?"

"Yes."

"How'd you hide that two gryphons were missing each time?"

"Until you came to the island during December, we were flying double shifts, which gave everyone extra time off." He shrugged. "I had to fly a few extras shifts each time to make up for my place in the rotation, but we all agreed to cover for the group."

Tristan could be the most infuriating man she'd ever met sometimes, but he had a streak of loyalty he hated to admit. He'd taken on extra duty and pushed his powers to bring members of the pack home for a visit.

Instead of yelling at him, Evalle felt bad about not having helped him. "When was your last trip?"

"The day you showed up to spend the rest of December with us. I'd just returned with Petrina and Bernie."

"Three? You teleported three at a time?"

He muttered a curse. "I sort of figured out under duress that I can teleport more than one if we link."

"What kind of duress?"

"Tell you about that another time, but that reminds me of something I did want to pass on."

"Like you would have found me while you were here?"

"No," he said with pure honesty. "But I'd have figured out how to send the information before I left."

"What is it?" she asked.

"There's a human group hunting for nonhumans. There. I've done my civic duty and told you."

She pondered on that for a moment. "Are you talking about that guy, Kossman? He's a medical researcher or something."

"Trust me on this, Evalle, he's hunting for nonhumans. He's not out to harm us, but he's putting big bounty money out. At fifty thousand a pop, it's bringing in plenty of calls. That's bad enough, but nonhuman traffickers are getting into the picture. They aren't taking their captures to Kossman. They're selling them on the black market to people like Queen Maeve. The only way I convinced the other gryphons to stay on Treoir right now is because it's too dangerous for them with VIPER, the Medb, and now greedy bounty hunters gunning for them."

Life just never got any easier. But that gave her an idea. "Have you heard of Kossman putting a bounty out on witches?"

"No. He's after something that no one would believe is real. A lot of humans know about witches."

"You mean he wants something like a gryphon?" Evalle joked.

"Alterants, to be specific."

She sighed. VIPER knew about Kossman, but didn't consider him a serious threat. She'd have to inform Quinn and Tzader that his hefty bounties presented real issues. "So what are you doing here, Tristan?"

"That's my business."

She silently bounced around her options, and only one made sense. "You can't stay out here. Come back to my place."

"With you, a fire-breathing gargoyle, and a Skinwalker who'd just as soon gut me as look at me? Pass."

"Feenix will not torch you, and Storm won't kill you. Not unless you do something to harm me." She grinned then a new thought hit her. "Can't you just teleport back to Treoir?"

"Not yet," he admitted. "Not without linking. I need time to rest and regain enough power to teleport alone, but don't worry. I've got a place to stay out of sight until then."

"Are you teleporting to this safe place?"

"No. I don't want to waste even that much energy. It was actually pretty easy when I linked with Petrina and Bernie."

When Tristan stepped away and turned to face her with goodbye in his eyes, she asked, "Really, are you involved with someone here? I'm not going to tell a soul, but she might be in danger when you're not around if someone finds out she's involved with you."

"I know that. I've taken precautions to protect her, but she's out of town right now. Out of the country, in fact. That's the only reason I'm not staying long."

That was all she would get out of Tristan. She angled her head toward Storm's truck. "I'll give you a ride."

That got his attention and softened the grim look on his face. "Deal."

Evalle opened the driver's door. "Hop in the back."

"What's the matter? You don't want to be seen with me in the front seat?" he chided.

She smiled. "Go ahead and sit in the passenger seat. I just thought you'd be more comfortable in the back."

He gave her a curious look, but walked around and opened the passenger door to get in.

Or, rather, he *tried* to get in.

Oskar stood up, showing his pretty teeth and giving Tristan a throaty bullfrog snarl. Impressive.

"*Shit!*" Tristan backed away from the door.

"Hey, be nice to Oskar," she warned.

"What the hell is an Oskar?"

"My new sidekick."

Tristan climbed into the back seat, sliding over directly behind Evalle. With everyone loaded, she watched the rearview mirror as he shoved his sunglasses to the top of his head. When he met her gaze, she asked, "Where to?"

He kept cutting his eyes toward the passenger seat, but Oskar had quieted. "You can drop me at the Ponce de Leon and Peachtree Street intersection."

What was there? Fox Theater came to mind. Tristan would not give her his actual address.

At this point, she didn't care.

She'd care later once she located Mattie, reunited Oskar with his witch, and returned them both safely home. As Evalle drove off, she warned, "Please stay out of sight, Tristan. If I get called into a Tribunal, there's no way I can cover and lie for you."

"So you *would* lie for me if it wasn't to the Tribunal?"

How did she get herself into these situations? "Just stay put, but let me know before you teleport back, okay?"

"Sure, Warden."

"Not funny, Tristan."

"Neither is living on that island." He was quiet a moment then he asked, "What would you do in my shoes, if you could teleport and had someone here you cared about?"

She did have someone in this world she loved, and just considering that question hurt her heart. All the gryphons on Treoir wanted some semblance of a life. She gave him the only answer she could. The truth.

"I'd come back every chance I got."

When she glanced up at the rearview mirror, Tristan stared back, surprised. Then he nodded and let it go.

She took Ponce de Leon back into town and pulled to the curb just before Peachtree Street.

Tristan opened his door, then paused and turned back to her. "I'll let you know before I leave, as long as no one comes for me in the meantime."

She twisted around. "Fair enough. Just don't get caught."

"Don't worry, Mom. I'll stay out of trouble." He stepped out, closed the door and sauntered off, blending into the night.

Just the fact that he was here contradicted his claim to stay out of trouble.

Whatever. She and Oskar were finally close to the downtown building Storm had remodeled. He planned for offices on the first floor, four rental units on the second floor, and their living quarters on the top two floors.

Plus the bonus rooftop he'd designed just for her, so that she could watch the sun rise and set without it turning her body into a fireball.

Storm had been running two crews back in November and early December. He'd backed off during the holidays so that everyone could be with their families, but he was determined to move her and Feenix in soon. Maybe even tomorrow.

She looked at her watch. Scratch that. Tomorrow was here.

Her phone played the ring tone for *No One* by Alicia Keys. That would be Storm.

Happy to talk to the one person in her life who didn't stress her, Evalle answered her phone. "I'm on the way to our new place."

"Good thing, sweetheart. The sooner the better."

She rubbed her eyes then put her glasses back on. "I'm sorry. I meant to get back earlier than this to help pack for the movers, but—" She glanced at Oskar. "Something unexpected came up."

"I have the movers handled, and I brought Feenix here myself."

"Really? How'd that go? Is he okay?"

"You aren't concerned that maybe he lit *me* up?" Storm chided, but she heard amusement in his voice.

"He wouldn't hurt you." She hoped. "He didn't ... right?"

Storm chuckled, "No, he was pretty calm. He's waiting on his beanbag for you."

Storm would have had to cloak Feenix to get him through downtown to the building, and he'd even thought to bring the beanbag for her baby. "I'll be there in less than ten minutes."

"Good thing. You have company."

"Who?"

"Tzader and Quinn. They—"

A crash sounded, and squawking came through the phone to Evalle.

"Ah, hell," Storm muttered. "Gotta go, babe."

Why me? Evalle gunned the motor, and Oskar started grunting again.

CHAPTER 13

Evalle pulled up to the first-floor garage of a building that had once housed light manufacturing, but had fallen into disrepair as the city grew and left this area behind.

From what little she'd seen in recent months, Storm had a keen insight when it came to investments, and particularly liked to reclaim abandoned properties.

She'd been so ready for an early evening at home with just him, but having a life full of people to love was still new for her. Besides, she shouldn't feel annoyed to have company when it was the two men who had been her only friends for a long time.

Why would Tzader and Quinn be here at midnight?

Quinn should have called her telepathically to let her know Tzader was back. Did that mean Brina was healed?

Evalle hit the remote button on the truck's visor to activate the overhead door on the street-level garage, then lowered it back into place as she parked.

Home. Had the movers finished and left? Had Storm already moved them in? She smiled as she opened the door and stepped out.

A grating bullfrog sound erupted.

She slapped her head and muttered, "Storm's going to kill me. Hell, I might help him."

Turning back to the interior of his classic Land Cruiser, she considered leaving Oskar in place for the moment. "I'll be right back and—"

With his eyes locked on her, he sank his front fangs into the seat.

"No. Don't do that."

The skin around his mouth lifted, showing the rest of his fangs not buried into the leather padding. One little push and he could probably bite all the way through.

She'd met humans who were less devious. "Okay, I'll take you with me."

Oskar released the seat and sat up with that disturbing, happy look on his face.

She ran around the truck and lifted him into her arms. "No biting, okay?"

He clicked his fangs together. Then his snake tongue made an appearance.

Oh, boy.

Hurrying over to the new door between the garage and the offices, she entered what would eventually be a reception area once it was walled off and had a corridor installed.

Right now it was one large room with occasional wall studs.

"We're in here, sweetheart," Storm called from the other side, where a hall connected to more of the unfinished ground-level area.

Only one part of this floor had been completed.

Soft light shone out of an open doorway. Storm had finished a conference room early on for meeting with contractors, decorators, permit officials, plumbers ... Everyone. It would eventually serve the people renting the office spaces. All the lights in the building had dimmer switches just for her.

She started toward the conference room. Just as she passed the stairwell to the second floor, she heard happy squawking.

Her little gargoyle came flying down the open chute.

Evalle jumped out of the way and spun with her back to the conference room.

Feenix zoomed into the reception area, flapping and chortling. "Evalle! Evalle! E—"

Oskar tensed and cranked up his grunting, sounding like a terrorized bullfrog with loud cricket chatter interspersed.

Feenix took one look at Oskar and reversed his flight, flapping as he backed away. He stared at Evalle with big orange eyes, shocked. Her gargoyle had a limited vocabulary, but he could say a lot of things with his eyes and face.

Right now, his expression cried betrayal.

She couldn't put Oskar down or hand him off in case he attacked someone. "Feenix ... baby ..."

Feenix demonstrated his ability to spin in midair, and flew back up the stairs.

Storm walked up behind her. "Wonder what upset Feenix? I had him all calmed down." He stepped around to the front of her and his eyes widened. "What's *that*?"

"Uh ..." Evalle stalled. "Oskar."

"You didn't answer my question."

"He's a witch's familiar."

At least Storm didn't back away like Lucien had.

Oskar opened his mouth, and let out a gruesome sound that he probably thought was a growl.

"What the devil is that sound supposed to mean?" Storm asked, studying Oskar with undisguised disgust.

"I think that might be his warning croak."

Only Storm would be amused that Oskar tried to intimidate him.

To avoid discussing it more than she wanted right now, Evalle hedged, "I didn't have a choice. Let me find some place to put him and I'll explain."

Looking down at the critter, Storm sighed and reached for Oskar. "I'll take him."

Oskar snarled and snapped his fangs.

Storm snatched his hand back and a deadly jaguar stared out of brown eyes that quickly glowed golden. "You don't want to do that to me," he warned Oskar.

Evalle had no doubt that Storm could make good on his warning, but harming Oskar would stir up more trouble than she already had. "He's okay. He seems to like me. I'll find somewhere to put him."

She turned to the conference room where Quinn and Tzader stood. Tzader had lost some weight, which honed his powerfully built body to sharper edges. He commanded a room just by walking through the door. That was a man born to lead. He took one look at Oskar and scowled.

An inch taller, and refined as usual in his mega-dollar suit, Quinn stared in horror. "What have you brought home this time?"

She snapped, "It wasn't my idea. I tried to get someone else to deal with this little guy and what can I say? I drew the short straw."

Oskar lifted his head and narrowed his eyes at her.

How much *did* he understand?

She asked Storm, "Do you have some towels I can put on the floor?"

"Is it housebroken?"

Now Oskar made a grinding sound deep in his throat.

If she had to guess, she'd say Storm had just insulted Oskar.

Trying to find some happy medium, she said, "That's not the issue. I just want something I can pile in the corner that he can lie down on."

Once Storm had the towels piled like a bed, the men all stood back to allow Evalle to enter the conference room and settle Oskar. She held up a hand. "I need a minute with Feenix."

"We're not in a hurry." Quinn waved her off.

Storm headed for the doorway. "He's upstairs."

Evalle dashed out behind him, hurrying up the steps. When she reached the second-floor landing, her eyes bugged out at the trim work and paint in the hallway. "Wow. When did all this get done?"

Storm turned around. "These apartments are finished, and the furniture was delivered yesterday. We already have a guest. I set up Lanna with a new set of sheets, and stocked enough food in the apartment from our supplies for her to be set for a day or two."

"Lanna's here?"

Storm led Evalle down to the first door on the left. "She was with Quinn, and he wanted to talk to you. I figured she'd be good company for Feenix. He must have heard your voice and made Lanna let him out."

One tap on the door and Lanna opened it, smiling. "Evalle! I am glad to see you."

Evalle was still working on allowing people to get close, but Lanna was basically family. She hugged the teenager, then asked, "Where's Feenix?"

Lanna had an 'oh-no' look on her face and tilted her head to her left.

Evalle stepped all the way into the room and found Feenix on his beanbag chair, hugging his stuffed alligator and ignoring her. She walked over and squatted down. "Hi, baby. Do I get a hug?"

He seemed torn between sulking and getting a hug from her. He finally dropped the alligator and climbed onto her lap, tucking his wings. She let out a sigh. She could fix his hurt feelings.

Then he whispered, "Mine?" and she flinched at the doubt in his voice.

Hugging him tighter, she said, "Of course I am, and you're mine. Okay?"

He patted her with his chubby paws. "'K."

Storm said, "I've been waiting to show you both something. Now seems like a great time."

Turning to him, Evalle hesitated. Feenix had just gotten over one shock, but the tenderness in Storm's gaze convinced her to trust him not to add to her little gargoyle's stress. "Sure. You good with that, Feenix?"

He lifted his soft bat wings in a shrug.

Lanna bubbled, "Am I invited?"

Smiling, Storm said, "Of course."

Once they were all in the hallway, Storm led them to the third floor. He'd kept the only door on that floor locked the entire time Evalle had been coming to the building. He said it hid a surprise, so she'd never pushed him to show it to her.

When he opened the room, she followed him in, unable to speak. All the floors had twelve-foot ceilings, but this space was huge and open and beautiful. Large video screens scrolled through different images. Pipes had been constructed into connected rectangular shapes in one corner, with an open platform eight feet up. Ten different whirly toys flew around the room. Half of the floor was covered in sod, and there were piles of toys and building block games scattered around.

This space was equal to ninety percent of the ground-level footprint. Two large beanbags had been tossed in as well.

Storm had made Feenix a playhouse.

Feenix was flapping his wings, trying to take flight.

Evalle gave his chubby little body a lift and let go.

He flew after something shaped like a four-winged bird that darted all over the place. And he was making the happiest noises she'd ever heard from him.

Lanna stood next to her, awestruck. "Beautiful. All this so good for Feenix."

Evalle finally found her voice, but it was thick with emotion when she stepped into Storm's waiting arms. He hugged her, and kissed the top of her head.

She said, "I have no words except thank you. I love you so much."

"Best words in my world," he murmured. "By the way, this doesn't mean I don't want Feenix in our living space, but in here he can't hurt anything. If he does, I'll replace it."

Lanna's sigh was all teenage girl. "I want a Storm."

Chuckling, Evalle said, "There's only one, and he's taken."

She turned in his arms in time to see Feenix catch a silver lug nut that shot off like a missile from the flying toy he chased. He snapped up the silver treat and chomped it.

"Wait one minute." Lanna ran out of the room, which reminded Evalle she had to get back downstairs. Evalle had to call Feenix's name several times before he fluttered back over to where they stood.

She squatted down to his eye level. "Are you happy, baby?"

"Yeth." He hadn't stopped smiling.

"Storm built all this for you."

Storm put his hand on her shoulder and squeezed. "That's not necessary."

"Yes, it is. I want him to know who did this for him. I want him to understand so he can appreciate this. He has to do his part here, too." She turned to Feenix. "When people do nice things we say thank you. Remember?"

"Uh-huh."

Argh. He was being stubborn. "Do you want to go back to our old place to live?"

Feenix's orange eyes strayed, taking in his playroom. He came back to Evalle and said, "Nuh-uh."

"Me neither. I like it here. I'm happy to be with you and Storm. It would make me *very* happy if you told Storm how much you appreciate this."

Feenix licked the tip of a claw, thinking. Then he waddled toward Storm and looked up. "Apprethiate thith."

Storm's face relaxed. "You're welcome."

"That's my baby." She opened her arms and Feenix lunged for her.

Lanna came back in, dragging Feenix's original beanbag that had his stuffed alligator on it.

Feenix jumped from Evalle's arms and landed on the beanbag. Pulling his stuffed toy into his arms, Feenix said. "Lanna thay."

Lanna called out, "Yes, I will stay, and look at that!" She walked over to a small barrel the size of a five-gallon bucket. Reaching in, she pulled out a handful of lug nuts and tossed one to Feenix. Feenix started clapping and chortling.

Seeing things calm again, Evalle told Feenix, "I have to take care of some business downstairs, but you can stay here or with Lanna, if she wants, for the night. I'll see you in the morning. That okay with you?"

"Yeth." He was ignoring her in a moment of lug nut nirvana.

Lanna laughed. "Is fine. He will keep me company. Much better here than in Treoir."

Evalle started to ask her what she meant, but Tzader would fill her in as soon as they got back downstairs.

With her pet gargoyle finally content, Evalle and Storm headed back down. She asked, "Where did all those shiny new lug nuts come from?"

He shrugged. "Here and there."

She snagged Storm's sleeve when he was a step below her on the stairs and pulled him around then kissed him, thanking him the best way she knew how. She loved this man to the point it scared her at times when she thought about anything happening to him.

He must have liked it. He started growling under his breath and made it clear with his next kiss he wanted full body contact soon. *Bring it.* She missed Storm the minute she left and never got enough of touching him.

Breaking away, he cursed in his Navajo language. She only knew that because she'd asked him to translate once. "What's wrong, Storm?"

His dark gaze churned with simmering heat. "Another second of that and I'd take you right here."

"Oh." She enjoyed the heady feeling of turning on a man as sexual as Storm. Leaning in again, she brushed a kiss over his lips. "I only wanted you to know I really appreciate all you're doing to make Feenix happy."

One of his dark eyebrows climbed up at that. "Let's get this meeting done, and I'll let you take more time showing me that appreciation. When you're done, I intend to make Feenix's mama a very happy woman."

Another word out of him, and she'd be the one crawling up his body right here on the stairs.

He smiled and kissed her forehead. When she stepped down, he slung an arm around her shoulders. "I feel better now that I'm not the only one ready to call it a night."

"I get it. Misery loves company."

"Think of it as motivation to make this a short meeting."

When they reached the conference room, Evalle took a chair at the table on the end near Oskar. He seemed to be sleeping. Good news on that front.

Storm sat next to her on the other side and whispered, "If he gets out of hand, I could calm him down with a little something special."

Oskar's head popped up and turned, much the way an owl's head rotated. He sent a withering look toward Storm, who watched him the way a predator studies something new in its territory.

She knew that look. Storm was assessing Oskar as a threat to her. Evalle said, "He'll be fine. Let's talk about it later."

Oskar's intense gaze slid over to Evalle. She smiled at him, and that must have been enough for him to relax. When she turned to the three men, she had a hard time deciding who had the more grim expression— Tzader or Quinn.

She understood Quinn's. He had to be juggling stressful situations related to being the new Maistir, but that was likely second to his grief. He normally kept his emotions shielded, but he would probably grieve in silence for a long time.

Evalle had no idea how you got over losing someone you loved that much, and didn't want to find out.

Tzader, on the other hand, shouldn't be back in Atlanta unless all was right with Brina.

Cutting a sharp look at Oskar, Tzader asked, "Now will you tell us what the hell is going on?"

Evalle arched an eyebrow right back at her friend. "I was about to ask the same thing. You first. Is Brina better?"

"No." Tzader seemed to force the words out. "I've been booted from Treoir, but I have a lead on how to help Brina."

"Booted? As in can't go back?"

"Exactly."

That was the last thing Evalle had expected to hear. "How bad is Brina?"

"Her memories continue to deteriorate every day, and I've discovered that the Noirre majik is still influencing her."

Storm sat forward. "But we—"

Tzader cut in, "—brought her back from wherever the spell sent Brina and Lanna. I know." He rubbed his eyes, and squared his shoulders, not giving an inch in any battle.

His emotions were clearly under siege from her illness.

Tzader explained, "We've been doing a lot of dream walking, because that's where Brina remembers more easily. But even there, she's been retaining less. I met someone in the last dream walk who said—" He shook his head. "This may be hard to believe."

Evalle's empathic ability wasn't as sharp as Storm's, but she picked up something she'd never felt from Tzader before. Fear. He was terrified for Brina.

Storm chuckled at Tzader's comment.

When Tzader tensed, Evalle suffered a moment of embarrassment. It was unlike Storm to make light of Tzader's situation. But then she realized the energy coming from Storm was compassion.

Storm must have caught her distress just as quickly, and placed his hand over hers. He told Tzader, "I'm a Skinwalker who shifts into a black jaguar *and* I have demon blood. Evalle turns into a gryphon and has a pet gargoyle. Quinn can mindlock with anyone, and you're immortal. All three of you have kinetics. What can be so hard to accept about our world at this point?"

Quinn cut loose a sound. Evalle couldn't believe what she heard. He was laughing. A real laugh. Not a big one, but more than she'd heard from him in a long time. Quinn said, "Good point, Storm. Just tell them, Tzader."

Evalle asked, "You already know, Quinn?"

"Some of it, which is why we didn't contact you telepathically."

Storm interjected, "Evalle trusts anything and everything you two say, so you have my trust, and I will hold your confidence."

That seemed to draw the tension from Tzader, who had fisted his hands together on the table in front of him. "A dream walker showed up today when I was in the dream space with Brina. I convinced her to leave the dream so I could deal with him without distraction. Once she was gone, we fought with swords."

"He attacked you?" Evalle recalled Lanna's warning about the potential of being injured or dying while dream walking.

"Yes, and no. He's powerful. So powerful that he could have killed me at any time. He swings one hell of sword, like he was born to it in the dark ages. In fact, I think he's pretty damn old."

"What did he want?" Storm asked.

"He wants me to help someone escape TÅμr Medb."

At that moment, Evalle realized this was not going to be a short meeting. "Why you?"

Tzader's grim face tried to smile. "Motivation. He knows what's going on with Brina. I was hiding Brina's deterioration from everyone except Lanna, who helped me conceal it even from Macha, but this guy knew about that. I could go on about all he knew, but it would be simpler to say that after a lot of debating, I believe him."

"How does he know so much?" Storm asked.

"That was one of my questions." Tzader took a moment, as if gathering his thoughts. "He said he gets his information from the person he's trying to free, and he claims that Noirre majik is still in Brina's system. Still affecting her. After hearing him out and questioning Lanna, everything he said makes sense. He also seems to know things about Macha and Queen Maeve, and the traitor who attacked Brina, things someone privy to the prior Medb queen's conversation and actions would know. Basically, the person trying to get out of TÅμr Medb is the only one who was present when the original spell was cast. That person can reverse the spell."

Evalle had spent a significant amount of time in TÅμr Medb when she and the other Alterants had been captured and were forced to finish their evolution into gryphons. She'd managed to pull out every person who mattered to the Beladors when the gryphons were sent to attack Treoir Island.

Had she missed someone? "Just who needs rescuing?"

Tzader took in all three of them when he said, "A dragon."

She thought on it. "They keep all kinds of creatures locked up near a fighting pit in their tower. How are we supposed to know which one?"

Storm swung around to stare at her, but didn't jump in. Yet.

Tzader drew in a long breath, and on the exhale said, "This one should be easy for me to locate. It's the queen's dragon throne."

"The *throne*? You've got to be kidding." Evalle shook her head. "Queen Maeve would go postal. That would be nothing compared to what Macha would do."

"I know. That's why I'm going in alone, but I need help finding resources."

Reeling from what he'd just disclosed, Evalle said, "No, you're not."

Quinn objected, "Absolutely not." He added, "I told you Evalle wouldn't go for it any more than I would."

Storm slapped a hand over his eyes. "This is suicide."

"Storm's right," Tzader said. "I won't put anyone else at risk. This is my battle."

Evalle agreed with Storm, but she also knew that look in Tzader's eyes. She'd seen it when he went into battle. He would not back down, and he would not accept defeat. "Tzader, are you saying that dragon-shaped throne is a ... *person*?"

"Evidently. Queen Maeve supposedly cursed a dragon shifter into the form of a throne two thousand years ago. He hates her *and* Macha. Doesn't trust either goddess, and to be honest, I can now see why when I couldn't before."

Storm lowered his hand. "What's the whole deal?"

Tzader laid out the entire conversation with this man called Ceartas, then said, "He gave me a red dragon scale that I gave Brina. It worked, just as Ceartas said it would. After my last argument with Macha, I'm convinced that she's as much a threat to Brina as any Medb at this point."

"In what way?" Evalle asked, still trying to wrap her head around what they were discussing. Tzader would never make it alone, but to do this ... that was no simple decision.

"I'll give you the details later, but Macha compelled Lanna not to tell me something about Brina, and Macha has shielded Brina from realizing what is happening to her own body."

"You mean her mind," Storm corrected.

"No. Brina knows she's losing ground mentally, but she doesn't know

... that she's pregnant. It happened during a dream walk, before I understood that actions taken there were real."

Stunned silence swept across the room until Quinn cleared his throat. "Did you really think I would let you go on your own with that at stake, too?"

Tzader sighed. "Sorry, Quinn. I know we haven't found your daughter yet, so I hated to even mention this."

"I will find Phoedra, and you'll be there to help me, but only if you don't try to steal a bloody dragon by yourself."

Evalle swallowed. "You know there's no love lost between me and Macha, but I'm at the bottom of the rung in her world. To treat you and Brina this way is ... well, I started to say unbelievable, but when I think of Macha it isn't that much of a stretch." Still, what kind of person would keep Tzader and Brina apart when Brina was pregnant?

The same goddess who failed to support me even when I was doing her bidding. The same one who lifted not a finger to help me find Storm, then teleported him back to Atlanta, knowing VIPER was hunting him, even after he saved Brina's life.

Evalle could spend hours listing all the things Macha had done to her, but she'd always assumed she was not worthy of Macha's respect.

Now that she saw how Macha treated Tzader, Evalle had to accept a simple truth. None of them mattered to Macha beyond the service they provided. That left her with an empty feeling she hadn't experienced since before she met Tzader and Quinn.

Looking physically drained and sounding emotionally bankrupt, Tzader said, "I just need a layout of TÅµr Medb and a way to teleport in."

Evalle shook off her mangled thoughts to jump back in. "No, you need a tactical team that includes someone who knows the tower layout, plus someone who can teleport *and* someone who can break the curse on that throne."

Storm leaned in on his elbows. "And since I know that means Evalle intends to be on that team, you'll need me to cover everyone's six."

"Even better?" Evalle announced. "I have someone who can teleport us, plus Adrianna is the best chance we have at breaking a two-thousand-year-old curse."

A new tension radiated from Storm. "*Who* can teleport a team between two realms?"

Quinn lifted his chin. "Yes, who is this person?"

Oh, crap. She'd stuck her foot ankle-deep in her mouth. "This is clearly a top-secret project, right?"

Tzader lifted both hands. "Everyone just hold it. You and Quinn haven't realized something, Evalle. One of the conditions Ceartas laid out for me to gain the dragon's help is that I can't tell Macha about any of this. Entering TÅµr Medb and stealing the queen's throne will come with repercussions. Going after that dragon without Macha's consent will translate into me breaking my Belador vows in Macha's eyes, because there's every reason to believe the Medb will declare war. There is no way she'll see my actions as anything except betraying the Beladors, and her." He paused then added, "But she wouldn't authorize my plan anyhow."

He swept a tense gaze around the room before continuing. "I'm thinking that as long as I go alone, to avoid war, Macha will claim I was rogue, then point out that the Medb recently had a rogue warlock who wrongly accused Evalle of murder. She'll call the incident a wash even if she can't return the dragon. She might get away with diffusing a conflict if I'm the only one involved ... and penalized."

At one time, Evalle would have rushed into battle with no thought, because she'd support either Tzader or Quinn. No question.

Was she ready to break her vows?

Tzader was acting honorably, in Evalle's opinion, but every Belador swore fealty to Macha and gave a vow of honor. The goddess had final say on guilt or innocence.

If Macha decided anyone had behaved dishonorably, she had the right to sanction that person with lethal force on the spot.

Judge, jury, and executioner.

CHAPTER 14

Evalle's heart pumped so fast and loud it pounded in her ears. She couldn't look at Tzader, Quinn, or Storm, who all sat quietly around the conference table, each probably lost in his own thoughts.

If she broke her vow to Macha, what would happen to Storm and Feenix? Macha could sanction family members as well, but Evalle and Storm were not married, and Feenix was not a blood relation.

Would Macha still go after them in a fit of vengeance? Would she blame Storm for Evalle's rebellious attitude?

To be honest, that would be a fair accusation.

Until meeting Storm, Evalle had gone along with whatever was asked of her in order to keep peace and not rock the boat. But he'd shown Evalle her own worth, and that her needs were important. Now she wasn't nearly as compliant as she had been.

And she was damned tired of being jerked around by one goddess or another. She felt Tristan's words from earlier even more acutely now.

She'd told him she hated being treated like a second-class citizen, too. He'd scoffed at her, and thrown it back in her face that they weren't even a recognized race.

Macha hadn't lifted a finger to do a thing after a Tribunal, once again, manipulated Evalle into falling on the sword and accepting the position as gryphon liaison. If a Tribunal sent Evalle into TÅµr Medb to negotiate on behalf of the gryphons, Evalle would end up captured, and Macha would not lift a finger to save her. She knew this from experience.

Storm wrapped his fingers around her hand and leaned close,

whispering, "Follow your heart, and I'll follow you."

Was he giving her his blessing for breaking her vows? Was she really going to do this?

Did she have a choice?

Not if she wanted to face herself in the mirror.

Hadn't she said time and again that any or all of these three men would put their lives on the line for her? She would do no less for them. Storm knew she could never live with herself if she didn't help Tzader now.

She told Storm, "I'm trying to figure out how to help Tzader and keep you and Feenix out of the backlash."

"I can take care of myself, and I won't allow anything to happen to you or Feenix. I know you have to do this. We'll do it together."

That was the man she loved.

Quinn stepped in. "I have information that may also influence your decision, Evalle."

She shot Quinn an incredulous look. "That's not necessary. I'm not allowing Tzader to go alone any more than I would allow you to do something like this alone. The three of us have always watched each other's backs. We've held each other's secrets since we met that night we were captured by the Medb. Of the three of us, I'm the only one who's been inside TÅμr Medb. My hesitation has been from concern about Macha lashing out at everyone close to all of us. But I have full trust in Storm."

Storm gave her hand another squeeze, letting her feel his pride over her belief in him.

Tzader wiped a hand over his face. "I don't want any of you in this mess."

"I understand," Quinn replied. "But you and Evalle still don't know—"

"It doesn't matter, Quinn," she said, getting ready to start planning. "I've made my decision. After hearing what Macha is doing to Tzader, I can only wonder where the rest of us stand with her. I'm certainly at the bottom of that list."

"That's what I'm trying to tell you," Quinn said sharply, and with a hint of censure after being interrupted twice.

Cranky much? Evalle's empathic senses picked up worry from Quinn, mixed in with his irritation. "Sorry. What did you have to say?"

Quinn clarified, "There is something else you have to know about, but I had intended to discuss it after this meeting. I found out just before I picked up Tzader and Lanna."

"What the hell?" Tzader groused.

Quinn lifted a shoulder in his friend's direction. "When I drove up, you looked as if you'd been run over a few times by a Mack truck. Telling you then wasn't going to change anything. We needed the time while driving and eating for you and Lanna to catch me up to speed. I figured you could wait to hear yet another bit of disturbing news."

Evalle drummed her fingers in a silent pattern on the table. "What news?"

Not happy spread across Quinn's handsome face. "Trey contacted me. Macha sent word for him to have me arrange for Sen to teleport Evalle to Treoir immediately."

Tzader and Evalle shouted, *"What?"*

Anger joined tension barreling off of Storm. "Why?"

Evalle leaned forward, hands curled into fists. "For how long?"

Quinn's jaw quirked with an angry muscle twitch. "Macha has decided that since Evalle is a gryphon and their leader, she should reside *permanently* with the pack, not here in Atlanta dealing with human issues."

Storm snapped, "Hell, no."

Tzader looked stunned. "Was that all?"

Quinn's throat bobbed with a hard swallow. "Actually, no. Trey is no happier about this than I am. I told him I would come by to see Evalle myself, since this was not news to receive over the phone or via telepathy. He said Macha made the comment that she'd never approved for one of her gryphons to mate with any being, especially not a Skinwalker. Trey did his best to convince the goddess you were needed here, Evalle, and Macha took his head off. She told him you have until Sunday to present yourself to her at Treoir or suffer her wrath."

Evalle's world shifted. Macha thought she could snap her fingers and demand that Evalle walk away from Storm, Feenix, and everything that mattered to her?

Maybe at one time, when Evalle had been all alone.

Not anymore.

Storm was on his feet. He seared the air with curses in two languages and snarled, "She can't have Evalle."

Tzader stood and slammed his hand on the table. "This is my fault. Damn her goddess hide. It would be just like Macha to screw with Evalle and claim she'll allow her occasional visits home if I give up all claim to Brina."

Anger swept off of Storm in massive waves. "I'm done with Evalle dancing on Macha's strings and for every other person's demands."

"We can't allow Macha to do this to Evalle," Quinn scowled, rising gracefully to stand.

This wasn't the first time Evalle had been expected to sacrifice what mattered to her just to appease Macha.

She cared for every man in this room raving about the injustice to her, but she was no longer an abused teen trying to find her way in life.

Pushing up, Evalle shoved the chair back. She crossed her arms. "Anyone interested in *my* opinion?"

They quieted at once and turned to her, sitting again.

Taking a breath, she said, "I've been persecuted the entire time I've upheld my vows to Macha. That wasn't good enough for her. When I was imprisoned beneath VIPER headquarters, she didn't come to me to offer her support, as Tzader did. No, Macha came with an offer for my release *if* I did her bidding, which I did and, as usual, put my head on a chopping block with VIPER by doing so."

Not pausing for commentary, she continued, "The only reason Macha put in the original petition for Alterants to be recognized as a race earlier last year was because she wanted control of them. Of *us*. She made it clear her offer was good *only* for those who swore fealty to her. The gryphons currently patrol Treoir Island, and yet she's done nothing to push for the vote to recognize us as a race, because that means we could make our own decisions. She leaves all of our Beladors to fight her battles as the Medb infiltrate our world. We're expected to put our lives on the line, even with our hands constantly tied by VIPER."

Her gaze swept to Tzader. "And now Macha is willing to compel Brina to marry another man and not even allow Brina to realize she's having your child. That's abominable." Evalle would never stand down if she were in Tzader's shoes, and she would not step back while he went into battle alone. That's what it meant to care deeply for another person. "I appreciate that you're all willing to stand up for me, but I'm taking my own stand. I gave a vow of honor. I expect the same in return from the goddess and, in my way of thinking, Tzader's proposal is based on honor."

Evalle didn't have to look at Storm.

All at once, she felt his burst of pride and love roll over her.

This was a scary step, but she'd been down similar paths with Macha, and had barely escaped with her skin more than once. If they could return Brina's memories, Evalle believed Brina would stand firm about her relationship with Tzader, and would support her Beladors. Brina had asked for Evalle's trust in the past and, unlike Macha, Brina had earned that trust more than once.

Now it was time for the Beladors to support their warrior queen, because Evalle saw no hope for any of them to have a life without Brina in power.

Returning to the topic, she settled in her chair again and nodded at Tzader. "You said Ceartas made the point that this war has gone on for thousands of years. From all I've heard since joining the Beladors, he's right. The way I see it, we're just the current pawns in a game between those two goddesses. I will not be sent back to Treoir as a prisoner, and no other gryphon should be forced to stay against his or her will. Once this is done, I'll find a way to free them, too."

Storm reached over and took her hand.

Evalle left no question about what she was saying. "Storm and I will go with Tzader to rescue that dragon to cure Brina, and to find out what he knows that we don't about Queen Maeve's plans ... and about Macha."

Tzader said, "I believe this Ceartas. I think this dragon may be our only hope once Macha finds out what's going on. He's keen on Brina being protected at all costs. I don't know why, but I'm banking on whatever he has up his sleeve to protect her ... and any of you who go with me. But that doesn't change the fact that if Macha doesn't see it the way we do, she has the right to take our lives and that of everyone in our families. I don't have any more family, except Brina, but the rest of you do."

Evalle said, "Understood." She put a fist against her chest. "But *we* are the Beladors. Based on what you've said, the dragon is agreeing to support *us* for helping him and Brina. Who will support us once Macha takes full control of Brina? We have a choice and we have duties, but we have never agreed to blindly follow anyone. I'm willing to put my faith in Tzader and the dragon."

Storm spoke up. "If this goes badly, I have a backup plan, and anyone involved in this will be welcome. I agree with Evalle, and am willing to join you for the chance that Brina can be restored to power so we can stay here. I don't care where we live, but given a choice I know Evalle would rather stay here. That won't happen if Macha is left unchecked."

She squeezed his fingers.

Quinn had listened quietly. "I second everything Evalle and Storm have said. I, also, have had concerns about Macha for a long time, but I never wanted to create problems for the Beladors. I will not stand by while she hands Brina and your baby to another man, Tzader. I know you wouldn't if our places were reversed. If Macha finds out that I have Kizira's body in a mausoleum here in Oakland Cemetery, she'll very likely consider that a broken vow as well, so I'm taking no new risk by joining you. My only concern would be leaving our Belador warriors without a Maistir while I'm gone. I can't deal with Lanna right now, but neither do I want to send her home with her at risk from Grendal."

Storm said, "Lanna will be safe here. The building is warded. Anyone can leave if there's an emergency, but no one can scry inside or enter with malicious intent. But you still need to be the Maistir while we're gone, Quinn. We'll need the ground support back here at home. Someone who can cover for us."

Quinn started to argue.

Tzader stood up, and everyone fell quiet. "As I said, I don't want any of you going with me—"

"Can't stop us," Evalle pointed out.

Tzader gave her a stern look and added, "I know. I'm saying if you're determined to be a part of this, then we need a plan. I will not do this half-assed and put you at risk any more than you obviously have to be." He sent his next words in Quinn's direction. "Storm's right. We'll need Queen Maeve and Cathbad drawn away from TÅμr Medb when we're ready to teleport in. You're the only person who has a chance of getting them out of that tower when it's time."

Pondering that a moment, Quinn said, "Yes, that would be key to a successful insertion. Dragging them into a Tribunal meeting should do it."

Before they got strategizing further, Evalle said, "We have one more issue. That little critter in the corner is called Oskar. He's a witch's familiar. Lucien, Casper, and I found him with a bunch of kidnapped dogs tonight."

They all took in the black-and-gray pile of shaggy hair for a moment before she continued. "I went to see Rowan. Oskar belongs to Mother Mattie, one of the white witch council members. Rowan thinks the Medb may be behind three missing white witches, and that they now have Mother Mattie. Rowan went to VIPER when the first one disappeared, and Sen said the Tribunal would not listen to her accusations unless the new witch council wanted to join the coalition."

"That bugger Sen," Quinn grumbled, echoing Evalle's thoughts. "The whole point of creating the witch council was to keep them from having to join the coalition. VIPER makes exceptions for trolls, for crying out loud, but not witches who will support us?"

"Exactly," Evalle said. "I need Storm to go with me to track a Noirre residue at Mattie's house before we leave to free the dragon. Hopefully, we'll find something that might give us a lead on where they're holding Mattie, *if* the kidnapped witches are still in the human world."

Tzader said, "Noirre residue is enough evidence to authorize a VIPER investigation."

"Rowan doesn't want to call them at this point," Evalle explained. "She thinks it's odd for the Noirre residue to be so obvious when the Medb clearly shielded their scent when they created demons. Even the creature we killed tonight had no Medb scent or any evidence of Noirre. She thinks the blatant Noirre clue is a trap, and the minute she shows that to VIPER the white witches will be accused of trying to frame the Medb."

Storm murmured, "Could be. Keep in mind there could be another player. There's always been a black market for that kind of majik, plus a lot of Noirre was traded during the beast championship on Cumberland Island."

Now for the punch line. Evalle said, "We have a time issue. Mattie's sister is a powerful Fae who is coming to see Mattie Saturday morning. At this point, the sister doesn't know Mattie is missing. If we don't find Mattie before this Caron visits, Caron will flatten the city."

"*Caron* as in Caron of Sídhe Orlaith? That Fae is her sister?" Quinn asked, appalled.

"Half sister, but yes, that sounds right. We have it on good authority that Caron will take the city apart to find Mattie, and with no regard for human witnesses." No point in mentioning that Deek was the good authority. Storm hadn't forgotten that Evalle owed Deek a favor. She'd have to break it to him later about agreeing to find Mattie to pay her debt.

Quinn shared, "Caron destroyed seventeen different commercial property locations belonging to Deek D'Alimonte." He described how Caron had cherry-picked the targets for destruction, not killing a person.

"I heard," Evalle confirmed. "If we don't find Mattie before we leave for TÅµr Medb, we'll need Quinn to work covertly with Trey to find the witch."

"Understood." Quinn speculated, "I might be able to use that in some way to draw Queen Maeve and Cathbad into a Tribunal meeting."

"And one more thing," Evalle said. "We can't tell anyone that Oskar is alive and here, because Rowan says the kidnappers will realize we might be able to track Mattie through Oskar. If tonight's hunt doesn't pan out, I'll ask Lanna to touch Oskar's hair to see what that shows her. I'd ask her now, but she looked whipped, plus we have to go to Mattie's and I don't want to rattle Feenix again tonight."

Tzader stood up and shoved in his chair before addressing Quinn. "Queen Maeve and Cathbad are cagey. Just don't give the Tribunal any reason to retaliate against you." He took a look at his watch and asked, "How about a ride to my place?"

"Certainly. With Lanna here, I can drop you, check in with VIPER to see if anything critical is happening, plus talk to Trey and stop by my hotel before returning." Quinn suggested, "It's after two now. I say we convene back here at eight. Sound good?"

Evalle said, "Yes."

Storm nodded.

Tzader looked as if he wanted to overrule that.

Evalle walked around and put her hand on Tzader's arm. "We'll get the dragon and, with a little luck, no one will know it was us, but if they do we'll face the consequences together. Once the dragon returns Brina's memories, she'll be a game changer with Macha, who wouldn't dare push

Brina at that point. We do this together. Just like we always have. If Macha's willing to betray you and Brina, plus treat me and the other gryphons as if we're only beasts to be ordered around like trained dogs, then she's not a person who deserves my loyalty."

"You have a lot to risk these days, Evalle," Tzader warned.

"That's exactly why I'm willing to take a stand with you and Quinn, and why Storm will, too." She leaned in and kissed Tzader's cheek, then told him, "You look exhausted. Meeting at eight will allow me the time I need for a few things, too. Get some sleep before you come back."

"I'll be ready," he said.

She doubted he intended to rest, but hoped exhaustion would win out.

Storm stepped over. "If you're not sharp, you'll put your entire team at risk."

"Point taken," Tzader said, clearly accepting that everyone was in agreement. He walked out with Quinn.

She turned to Storm. "I don't want to go back out, but—"

"We need to check Mattie's house right away before something happens to disrupt the scents."

"Right." She waited as he locked up behind Tzader and Quinn.

On the way to the Land Cruiser, Storm said, "Don't think for a minute that I didn't notice how you failed to inform the other two about who would be teleporting the team. It's not Deek, right?"

"No." She hurried over to the passenger door, hoping to jump in and come up with a way to avoid this conversation by the time he got in.

Storm's hand came down on the top of the door before she could open it. Crap.

She flipped around. "What?"

He dropped his head until their noses almost touched. "I only know of one other person you could ask to teleport us, but he's still flying his gryphon gig on Treoir, right?"

Storm had been born a human lie detector, so she didn't waste effort sidestepping the question. "Tristan is in Atlanta. Grady told me about it tonight as I was leaving Rowan's house. When I found Tristan, he said he's been experimenting. He's teleported three at one time between Treoir and here. I know you don't like him—"

"Understatement. To be more accurate, I don't trust him," Storm corrected.

"Right. But he's our best hope for making this work."

Storm put his other hand down, caging her between his arms. Any other time, this could lead somewhere interesting, but at the moment Storm wouldn't let this Tristan bone go.

He said, "This is the same person who put you in a jam with Macha and a Tribunal."

"Well, yes—"

"Tristan also grabbed his group and ran, while you stood between him and a black ops team sighting in on all of you."

"Technically, I asked him to—"

Storm interrupted, "He walked you into a Medb trap and—"

"Teleported me away so I could escape," Evalle managed to say.

Storm's face became even fiercer. "Yes, Tristan did teleport you ... right into Deek D'Alimonte's private office, and almost got you killed by that centaur."

She gave up defending Tristan.

Storm sizzled with renewed anger at the Alterant whose actions Evalle had tried to defend. He said, "If Tristan agrees to teleport the team both ways, then so much as hiccups at the wrong time and puts you in danger again, he'll be unable to ever teleport, fly, walk, or eat without a straw when I'm finished with him."

Storm kissed her forehead and opened the door for her.

Yep, this was shaping up to be so much fun.

Not.

CHAPTER 15

TÅµr Medb, home of the Medb coven

Queen Maeve passed through the tall double doors carved with disgusting erotic scenes, and entered her private chamber in TÅµr Medb. If she planned to stay here very long, she'd reconstruct most of the tower, but there was no point in wasting majik on this place when she'd be moving to Treoir Castle soon.

Cathbad the Druid waited with his hands tucked behind him and a smug smile on his face. He enjoyed dressing in the modern styles, wearing a dark gray suit today with a black turtleneck pullover. Pale brown hair had just enough curl to add to his devilish attraction. Striking eyes the color of a dark beer followed her as she crossed the room.

He was the druid who'd first come to her aid two thousand years ago, and he was still her partner today.

The doors swung shut upon her silent command.

She spared a glance for Daegan, the dragon she'd cursed to serve as her throne. His silver eyes were trained on her and shooting death wishes her way. "Don't make the mistake of allowing your eyes to close, Daegan."

A deep rumbling shook the throne, but she had not freed his tongue since the last time he mouthed off at her.

Cathbad threw Daegan a derisive glance, muttering, "Keepin' that beast alive so long concerns me."

She found that amusing. "Seeing him shackled in that shape is entertaining. He's not a threat."

Cathbad waited until he was closer to say, "I've been told the dragon's eyes were green while you were not queen, but they be silver now. What if that beast is gainin' strength?"

An interesting observation, but nothing she considered significant. "He's locked in that spell. His body could change color and I wouldn't care, so you shouldn't."

Still not convinced, Cathbad pointed out, "He's been privy to everythin' said in this room for two thousand years. 'Tis a mistake to allow him to continue listenin' to our plans now."

She made a scoffing sound in Cathbad's direction, dismissing his argument. "The only mistake I made with Daegan upon cursing him was to prevent anyone from compelling him to talk."

"'Twas a good plan so he did not share anythin' with successive queens who ruled until we returned." Cathbad angled his head, thinking. "However, it would save us considerable time if that beast could be compelled to tell us how to access the history in the scryin' wall."

"Agreed." Queen Maeve dismissed Cathbad's concerns. There was only one place Daegan could be a danger to her. He'd never see that place again.

Not unless he could figure out how to open his wings and fly as a throne.

No, Daegan was just fine where she had him.

This way she could enjoy his misery every single minute possible. If not for him, she wouldn't have—

"Are you ready for an update on Ossian's integration into VIPER?" Cathbad asked.

Ignoring the dragon's evil gaze following her every move, she turned to Cathbad. "Tell me about my gryphons. I've waited long enough. I want them. Now!"

"I have no' heard from the Tribunal yet."

"Send a message. The Tribunal's deadline for this decision has passed. What is the delay?"

Cathbad strolled several steps. "Could be nothin' more than arrogant gods and goddesses makin' a point, or it could be they don't have three willin' to work together yet to form a Tribunal. Not all the pantheons joined the VIPER coalition and, of the ones that did, not all get along. I canna be seen in Atlanta at the moment, not until VIPER sends word. It's part of the sanction for what trouble our rogue warlock caused with the Witchlock mess."

"The Tribunal deities are fools to think that sanction means anything to me."

He sighed heavily, the way he always had when he'd try to appease her in the past. "I hear ya, but if we are to keep up this ruse of pretendin' ta be a part of the coalition ... " He stretched his arms out and shrugged. "We need to play the part."

She wished for something to kill. Nothing eased her anger like a bloody death. Letting the topic go for the moment, she said, "Very well. Do you bring me good news?"

"I believe so. Our man Ossian has inserted himself into VIPER, and has been receivin' agent assignments."

"How is that news?"

"I should be more specific." Cathbad held up a finger then cocked his head, which meant he was speaking telepathically with Ossian. Nodding once, he waved his hand and Ossian appeared.

Or a *version* of Ossian.

Cathbad had created a unit of elite warlock warriors and endowed them with a few extra perks, such as being able to mask their Medb scent.

He'd hand selected Ossian to be even more special. After weeks of majikal influence, Ossian was capable of polymorphic changes to his outer appearance.

Today he was slight in size with narrow shoulders. Maintaining his footing in a strong wind would be a challenge. His inch-long, mud-brown hair had a disturbing shape, but she'd seen his hair much darker and longer, with a striking face to match. Not this time. Dark-rimmed glasses he didn't need for his vision perched on his too-long nose, and his thin lips parted to show crooked front teeth. He wore an unflattering dove-gray suit and white shirt, standard clothing that turned human men invisible once they joined a herd of similarly dressed males at jobs in their world.

Cathbad beamed. The druid did enjoy showing off his handiwork. "Ossian has encouragin' news. He has recently been assigned to an intelligence team that answers directly to Vladimir Quinn of the

Beladors."

"Oh?" The queen moved her attention to Ossian. "Are we closer to gaining access to the mausoleum where Quinn hides Kizira's body?"

"I hope so, my queen. I'm making headway in developing a closer association with Quinn, though that Belador is one surly bastard at the moment. It is difficult to gain a meeting with him, and he's distant on the rare occasions I can draw his attention. But he's becoming accustomed to seeing me around VIPER. The agents believe I'm a warrior mage from the Julian Alps in Italy. I actually lent a hand to save a Belador from a demon attack last week." Ossian hurried to add, "Of course, I performed that action only as part of my duty to you."

She overlooked his aiding the enemy since Ossian was doing exactly as he'd been told. His instructions had been to infiltrate the Beladors and gain the confidence of Quinn. She qualified, "No one suspects who you really are, correct?"

Ossian shook his head. "Not even the other members of our Scáth Force team have been allowed to see me in this specific disguise. I change to my natural form to meet with them in secret, then I change back when I return to VIPER as a contractor."

"Do you have anything new to report?"

"Yes. With my access to VIPER, I hear about anything related to our coven. We're being blamed for every infraction in the human world right now. Even those we haven't committed."

Cathbad inquired, "Such as?"

"White witches have disappeared. I heard that Rowan Armand, the head of their council, sent word to VIPER, but Sen dismissed it because they're not part of the coalition."

"Best move ever when our queen joined that coalition," Cathbad said, looking over at the queen when he gave that compliment. "No one expected it, especially Macha, and we now have a layer of insulation from the Beladors and the new council."

Queen Maeve would normally enjoy being credited with any harm to white witches, but she killed anyone who dared to take an action on her behalf without her explicit consent. There were rules in the supernatural world when it came to that sort of thing. Actions had power. Members of the Medb coven were soldiers in her war to take back Treoir.

They were not generals to map out strategy on their own.

Anyone acting without her authorization would regret assuming that autonomy.

Returning to the conversation, she told Cathbad, "Our Scáth Force is excelling in covert operations, but we could use a team of Ossians."

He smoothed his fingers over his trim beard. "True, but it required a considerable amount of power and resources just to give Ossian the ability to change his physical appearance at will, plus gift him with a semblance of mage abilities. Took me several days to recoup my stamina after that, but it's been worth the effort. He's the reason we know what is happenin' with the Tribunal and VIPER, but creatin' another one would be unwise."

"Understood." She caught his meaning. They could control one such as Ossian. After having dealt with a rogue warlock recently, it might not be wise to hand a second one such gifts. She changed topics. "When will we be able to send *all* of our warlocks and witches to the human world?"

The sooner she could undermine VIPER everywhere, the sooner she'd begin to weaken Belador resistance and implement a large-scale plan.

Ossian replied, "Based on comments Sen has made, the Tribunal is not in favor of changing the rate of our coven's entry into the human world. I believe Sen would allow it, but not because he favors us. His motivation appears to be more about irritating the Beladors than accommodating our coven."

"Odd that he would be allowed free rein," Cathbad commented.

"True," Ossian agreed. "I've been able to find out little about him, save that he's been liaison between VIPER and the Tribunals for years. He has been in place for as long as any current VIPER associates recall, and he has not aged the entire time, which leads me to believe he is immortal. Everyone speculates that he's been forced into his position, which is peculiar, considering how he, at times, displays godlike powers."

Cathbad's eyebrows danced with interest. "Keep surveillance on him as well."

"Yes, my lord."

Maeve floated across the room and turned to the men. "I'm not interested in Sen. I have no gryphons, and I'm sick of being held accountable to those far beneath me. Beladors flood their world, but VIPER limits the number of my followers allowed to enter. I want my island back!"

"Patience, my darlin'," Cathbad cooed. "After waitin' two millennia to destroy Macha, what is the harm of playin' along for a wee bit longer?"

"Waiting is not in my blood." Maeve wheeled around so fast, sparks flashed all around her and across her new deep-blue gown. "You and I created the Alterants." If not for the two of them, the Alterant-gryphons would not exist. They'd magically taken sperm from the male children of the ancient berserker warrior Cú Chulainn and a Medb witch.

Together, she and Cathbad had devised a plan that brought the sperm to the present day world and bonded it with Belador descendants.

The result had been greater than even she or Cathbad had anticipated. Cathbad had created a prophecy, and she'd powered it with her own blood. In the end, Alterants were born of human women with Belador bloodlines, fathered by the powerful Medb—Cú Chulainn bloodline. What spawned were beasts that eventually evolved into gryphons.

My gryphons, by the gods. That bitch Macha was not stealing anything else from her.

"Ya know, my darlin'," Cathbad said, looking intently at her. "Macha does no' have all the gryphons. 'Tis not possible. There had to be many more than ten."

"She has only *eight*, to be precise. We'd have ten available if Flaevynn had not been a moron." Hundreds of red candles at different levels around the room flared with the angry energy Maeve released. "How could she have risked *any* of the gryphons, but particularly the ones with golden heads? It's a good thing her death powered my reincarnation, or she would not have survived my displeasure." Waving off that irritation, Queen Maeve said, "We need a plan in case Macha comes up with a way to convince the Tribunal to deny my claim on the gryphons."

"True," Cathbad agreed. "We have two potential outcomes. We end up with half of the eight gryphons, or none at all. I don't see us gainin' the entire group, at least not yet. With Evalle as leader, she'll have to deliver our gryphons."

"Unless we request Evalle as part of the first group."

Cathbad blew out a breath. "That will take some doin' with her loyalty to the Beladors, which I find strange considerin' that Macha has not treated her well."

"How do you know that?"

"From Ossian." Cathbad nodded at his special warrior. "And from what the rest of our Scáth Force has learned. The more knowledge we gain about all the parties involved, the more powerful you will be when it is time to capture Treoir. I promise we will gain that island again."

She *would* rule Treoir. Flaevynn had almost destroyed her gryphons in that insane attack on the island. Unlike any queen who'd ruled in her absence, Maeve knew *all* of Treoir's secrets.

Flaevynn, the stupid slut, had wanted to wipe out the Beladors, which would have ruined Maeve's plans. *Those* warriors belonged to her as well. She and Cathbad had allowed others to think the Beladors and Medb coven were merely enemies. Macha knew the truth, and she had to be quaking in her boots right now over the return of the real Queen Maeve and Cathbad the Druid.

Macha had to know what was coming, and that she would not survive.

Kill all the Beladors? Never.

Queen Maeve would kill only those who failed to submit to her power.

For now, her druid had a valid argument for not upsetting the status quo in the human world.

Moving back to her original point, she said, "The Tribunal asked us to wait until now to deal with the right of possession of Alterant-gryphons. The first of the human year has come and gone. It's time to force Macha to hand over the beasts. I want all of them, but I'll start with half, and those will provide valuable intel on Treoir's security operations."

Ossian remained silent and still as a statue.

Cathbad shoved his hands in his pockets. "What's the word on that, Ossian?"

"As far as I know, the Tribunal has not sent word to Macha about this issue. I believe the delay is because the Tribunal intends to vote on the Alterant petition this week. If they declare the Alterants an independent race, they can finally wash their hands of the whole possession battle."

What? The queen warned Cathbad, "That would be a disaster. If the Tribunal turns those beasts loose they'll scatter. We might lose one. We have to take possession while they're still together." She floated back across the room and spied Daegan watching her with chilling intensity.

Do you finally regret crossing me so long ago, Daegan? He couldn't hear her thoughts. She smiled at him, which was as good as taunting him.

He lowered his lids partway in defiance, but he couldn't sleep while she was here.

Opening his arms, Cathbad said, "I agree, my darlin', but I have no answer yet. This delay could be nothin' more than ... "

"—the Tribunal unable to find three deities willing to work together at the moment," she finished for him before he could repeat it.

Ossian spoke up. "That is possible, my queen. I did overhear a VIPER agent joking that the witch, Veronika, might still be waiting to appeal her case to the Tribunal ten years from now. Of course, she did threaten everyone with powers."

Maeve sniffed at that. "She's of no consequence."

Cathbad argued, "Veronika might have been a dangerous force, had she succeeded in takin' control of the Witchlock power."

"I heard about all that. It had to be blown out of proportion. That power died out generations ago," Maeve argued. "Witchlock hasn't been around since—"

"—before you first challenged Macha over Treoir Island," Cathbad interjected.

"Must you use that for a time marker?" She glowered at him, then turned her attention to the dragon throne. "I had traitors all around me back then."

Smoke curled from the dragon's large nostrils.

"If I may, my queen?" Ossian asked cautiously.

She swung around and scowled. "What?"

"I would never contradict you, but I feel it is my duty to share everything I've learned about Witchlock and Veronika."

She gave the soldier credit for taking care in how he broached a subject. "Very well. What have you found out?"

"If the VIPER agents are to be believed, Veronika was indeed the chosen one meant to take control of Witchlock. It's been said that she had a long-range plan for wiping out the majority of the supernatural power in the human world and turning the witches she allowed to survive into her slaves."

Queen Maeve laughed at that. "She's lucky they caught her before she had to face me."

Cathbad turned his head to her. "I think we could have struck a deal once we showed her it would be wiser to be allies."

Ossian's gaze bounced back and forth between his superiors until Cathbad nodded for his soldier to continue. "According to what I could research, chosen ones of the ancient KievRus covens could take possession of Witchlock only during a full solar eclipse directly after a blue moon month."

She waved her hand in dismissal. "Yes, yes. We heard about that."

Speaking cautiously and keeping his attention on the queen, Ossian said, "I heard that when a powerful black tornado spun down from the eclipse, Veronika called it to her. But she was in the midst of a battle with the white witch council members and the Sterling witch, Adrianna, at the time."

"What happened?" Maeve asked.

"I'm not entirely sure, but I believe Adrianna took possession of Witchlock and now wields that power."

"Why haven't you told me before now?"

Ossian dipped his head. "My apologies, my queen, but I learned the majority of this information only in the last two days when I was put on guard duty watching Veronika."

Cathbad asked, "You have access to her?"

"Not on any set schedule. VIPER pulls agents at random and sends us to guard her. She's locked in a high-security cell beneath VIPER headquarters."

Circling the room as she thought, Maeve considered this and kept moving until she reached Ossian again. "Does Veronika possess any power now?"

Lifting his head, Ossian's eyes sparked with excitement. "Oh, yes, my queen. She likes to show off, and crippled one guard before Sen came down and threatened her with something strong enough to bring her under control. The Tribunal may not ever listen to her pleas. Not after she stated her intention to go after even the gods and goddesses."

"Ambitious," Maeve murmured. "I want to know when anything changes in her status."

"Yes, my queen. I may not be sent back to her for a while, but I'll try to finagle another turn at guard duty."

Witchlock actually existed, and a Sterling witch had taken possession of it.

Would wonders never cease?

Addressing Cathbad, she asked, "I wonder if Veronika, or another powerful being, could take Witchlock away from the Sterling witch."

"I don't know," Cathbad admitted, sounding thoughtful. "But I intend to spend time tracin' the origins of that power and findin' out as much as I can."

"Good. Once you do, we'll put our Scáth Force on finding out just what that Sterling witch intends to do with Witchlock."

"Can she be bribed?"

Ossian made a sound, and Maeve said, "Speak."

"Doubtful. She's a friend of Evalle Kincaid, who is loyal to the Beladors. By that association, I believe it would be hard to sway the witch. As for Evalle, VIPER agents say she would die before breaking her vows."

Maeve rolled her eyes at that. "No one is *that* loyal when she has no say over her future. The Macha I've known for so long would hold her people through fear, not mere sworn fealty."

Agreeing with a tilt of his head, Ossian said, "True. Evalle is also close friends of this Quinn we've been tracking, who has taken over as Maistir of the Beladors."

Queen Maeve ignored Ossian for the moment to use Cathbad as a sounding board. "We may be going about this all wrong. Evalle has shown us her weak spot. She cares what happens to her friends and that Skinwalker you told me is always with her. She should be willing to do whatever we demand if it means saving the lives of Quinn, Tzader, and her mate."

Cathbad said, "If the Tribunal does not come through, then Evalle may be our next option." Sending a pointed look in Ossian's direction, Cathbad said, "I believe that is all we need at the moment. You may have an hour to rest in your private quarters here before you return."

Ossian dropped in a low bow to each of them. "Thank you, my lord, and my queen."

Cathbad lifted a hand in Ossian's direction and the soldier vanished. He scratched the back of his neck. "I just wish we knew what had been goin' on between Quinn and Kizira. They were clearly involved, based on what we saw in reviewin' the scryin' wall history. But what could she have said to him with her dyin' breath that she wanted shielded from anyone observing the battle through the wall?"

"The minute I lay my hands on her cold body, I will know everything she knows," Maeve pointed out.

"I know, my darlin', and I will find a way to bring you that body, but Ossian is our best hope for learnin' enough about Quinn to find out how to access the mausoleum holdin' Kizira's body. You heard Ossian. He's gettin' closer with Quinn, and he knows to alert me the moment he has anythin' that will help us."

"Waiting two thousand years was easier than waiting the past two months," Maeve groused.

Cathbad suggested, "We might be able to prove Quinn was in league with Kizira to attack Treoir. Show that the Beladors are blamin' us when they're actually creatin' problems and makin' us the scapegoats. Maybe drive a wider wedge between them and VIPER."

"Who would believe that?" Maeve asked, with a sour attitude.

"A Tribunal tired of all this hagglin' between you and Macha. They want an end to the infighting, and might just jump at a reason to hand you the gryphons if we managed to convince them that would put an end to all this."

"Which it wouldn't," Maeve clarified. "I like it. Have our people create evidence, then you can present it to the Tribunal."

A sly smile captured his face, reminding her of the druid who'd seduced her when they were younger. He said, "I will do exactly that, if the Tribunal ever sends a messenger."

Cathbad paused with his head cocked then turned toward the door and pointed at it.

Both doors swung open, revealing one of their Scáth Force soldiers standing at attention. Her soldiers dressed battle-ready in dark cargo pants and a long-sleeved thermal top that allowed ease of movement. The most deadly Medb warlocks were priests, such as this one with the mark of snake tattooed around his smooth scalp. The snake's head rested on the warlock's forehead above the bridge of his nose. These Medb priests had exchanged their robes for the new modern look to fit into the human world.

Cathbad addressed the soldier. "Yes, Zerko."

"Someone has requested a meeting with the queen."

Maeve asked, "Is it a message from the Tribunal?"

Zerko answered, "No, my queen. A stranger overpowered one of our warlocks and held him captive. That soldier contacted me."

"What?" Cathbad interrupted. "Overpowered one of our Scáth Force?"

"Yes, my lord."

"Why is he still breathin'?"

The soldier dipped his head in respect. "Our soldiers could not kill him." The soldier rushed ahead to say, "But the stranger did not harm our warlock or use his majik in any other way to attack us. He claims to have an offer that the queen will want to hear."

Cathbad looked over at her and said, "This visitor may have overpowered our warlock, but he canna survive fightin' the two of us. Not here."

She took that under consideration and asked the soldier, "What *is* he?"

"He says he is a wizard, which would explain his power."

"Did he say anything else?

The soldier quickly replied, "He told our warlock to pass this message to you. 'I know what you want from Vladimir Quinn, and how you can obtain it without conflict involving the Beladors or VIPER.'"

It was a rare thing when someone surprised Maeve. This wizard had to be referencing Kizira's body. How did he know so much?

Cathbad crooked his head in her direction. "This might prove interestin'. I prefer to have a look at this wizard first, and can teleport to the human world briefly without being detected. If all seems acceptable, I'll teleport him here."

Maeve said, "Very well. Tell him his meeting is granted, but warn him that if he disappoints me, he will live only long enough to regret this visit."

Grinning, Cathbad rubbed his hands together and disappeared along with the guard.

CHAPTER 16

"Why do you live out in the boondocks?"

Tzader had almost dropped off into sleep. Quinn's question woke him. He sat up and rubbed his gritty eyes, looking around. "I'm not much for city life."

Quinn had driven him a half hour east of Atlanta, to a rural part of Covington where Tzader kept a house hidden in the middle of seventy acres. He had no animals to maintain, and no yard to tend since he'd carved out just enough space to build a one-level log home in the woods.

At least it appeared to be only one level. He'd planned the basement to be a recreational space that doubled as a bunker.

The main floor had four bedrooms, all with individual baths, a great room, and large eat-in kitchen.

Too big a place for one man.

He'd hoped to make this house a home that he, Brina, and their brood could use when they visited the human world. That had been the idea five years ago. He'd built it as a surprise he'd planned to show her after they'd made their commitment to each other.

Then *he'd* suffered the worst surprise of his life.

Her father and Macha had warded Treoir castle against all immortals except Macha and Brina.

When Brina's father and brothers went off to battle, Tzader's father had joined the team. Before leaving, his father asked Macha to pass his immortality to Tzader if he died in battle.

He died. Brina's father and brothers died.

No one realized Tzader had been barred from entering the castle, and Brina could no longer leave for fear of being killed. The Belador power required a living Treoir descendant residing on that island. That would be tough enough on any young woman, but Macha believed Brina was safe only in the castle.

Or was that simply the easiest way for Macha to maintain control of Brina?

Tzader pointed out the turn for the dirt road to his house. When Quinn pulled off and started through the woods, the vehicle dipped into a deep gully. Anything but a tall SUV would have bottomed out.

Quinn groaned.

"Sorry to ding up your new ride, Quinn."

"That's not a big deal. I was actually thinking about this mess with Macha. I want to ask you something."

"What's on your mind?"

"I would've asked sooner, but I was too lost in my grief over Kizira right after the battle. I tried to ask Evalle, and she brushed it off. What actually happened when you broke into the castle when the traitor was attacking Brina?"

That moment raced back to Tzader as if it had been yesterday. He swallowed hard. "That sucked."

"Never mind, Z. I shouldn't have asked."

"No, it's okay. Really." Tzader blew out a breath. "During the battle, I stood outside the castle with the last line of our defenses against the Medb coven and the gryphons. At that point, I believed the gryphons were all still compelled by the Medb to kill any and all Beladors."

"I would have thought the same, because of the one that attacked me and—" Quinn paused, then said, "We both know what happened then. Please continue."

Tzader would never forget the look on Quinn's face when he came walking up holding Kizira's body.

"Anyhow," Tzader continued. "A gryphon blew us aside like we were bowling pins. I didn't know it at the time, but that was Evalle, and she was trying to keep us out of harm's way."

"Of course."

"When I came to, I heard two gryphons crashing around inside the castle, and all I could think was that they were going to kill Brina. I ran inside."

"But the ward ..."

"Yep. It got me. Enough power exploded across my body to light up Atlanta. I hit the floor and felt my life force draining out. I went to a dark place, and I couldn't feel anything. Then all of a sudden, I sensed a flicker of life inside. I couldn't feel my heart at first, but then I heard blood pounding in my ears. When I opened my eyes, Evalle was telling me telepathically that she was the gryphon. I called off the guards, she shifted back to human form, and we found the traitor throwing the spell on Brina and Lanna."

"So Macha *does* know you literally died getting to Brina during the Medb attack, and she was still going to withhold knowledge of your child from you *and* Brina. I keep having a hard time with that."

"Me too. I argued with Macha one time about her not offering any help for breaking the ward so that Brina and I could be together. She convinced me I was being dishonorable to ask her to basically break her word to my father. I apologized and let it go."

"Something tells me you've changed your mind."

"I have nothing to base it on—yet—but I can't get past thinking it was just one more time she's manipulated me and Brina."

"Didn't Macha give you her blessing for marriage?"

"Sort of. I thought she had, but—"

"What?"

"It may just be me being paranoid about everything now that I know Macha's been keeping the baby from me, but maybe she never wanted Brina with a Belador. It's the only thing that makes sense to me right now."

"What about Allyn? You told me Macha was ready to marry Brina to him at one point and he's a Belador."

"You're right." Tzader considered that.

Quinn navigated the twisting, bumpy road silently for a bit. When he spoke, he sounded thoughtful. "Maybe it's not about you being a Belador. Maybe Macha specifically wants someone she can always manipulate. You would never stand for it once you and Brina married and had a family."

"Damn right."

"I'm very interested in hearing what the dragon has to share with us."

Tzader tried not to think about it. What if the dragon's champion lied and the dragon either couldn't or wouldn't help Brina? Tzader would have put everyone he considered family in jeopardy and lost Brina forever ... as well as his child.

After more directions, Quinn pulled up to Tzader's house and commented, "I've always wanted to see this place, Burke. Very nice."

"It might be if there was more than a foldout sofa."

"How long have you been here?"

"Close to five years."

At the look Quinn gave him, Tzader explained, "I expected Brina to decorate our home the way she wanted." He pushed those words out past a lump in his throat. "Thanks for the ride. I'll meet you at Evalle's at eight."

Quinn parked, sitting still in the dark. "How are we going to get Brina to the dragon if we manage to free it?"

"Honestly? I don't know, but I'll sell my soul to Deek D'Alimonte if that's what it takes to save Brina. He's probably the most powerful being I can get to at the moment."

Quinn's silence shouted louder than if he'd voiced his concern. Finally he spoke. "No one comes back from Deek if he makes that type of deal."

Tzader swallowed a lump of emotion that kept threatening to climb up his throat and strangle him. "I know. But no matter what it takes, I won't leave her in limbo with no memory, subject to Macha's whims forever."

"You're immortal, Tzader. Forever will be a long time at Deek's mercy."

"I've thought of that."

"Very well. Get some sleep."

CHAPTER 17

TÅµr Medb, home of the Medb coven

While Cathbad teleported away from TÅµr Medb to check out the wizard requesting to meet her, Queen Maeve had time to poke at her surly dragon to gain new information.

When she turned to her throne, the dragon's head faced her, but his eyelids were at half-mast.

She threw a slap of power at Daegan's head, lighting up the entire throne.

His eyes blinked open, blazing with hatred. As the energy settled down, black diamond centers appeared in his silver eyes.

"We have an agreement that you would not sleep when I am present, or would you prefer I take away *that* privilege for another millennium?" she taunted. She'd recently allowed Daegan to rest, but only as a means to an end.

He remained silent, that deadly glare always in place.

She snapped her fingers. "That's right. You can't *speak* either. I granted you that privilege as well, and you abused it." She flipped her index finger at him, releasing his vocal chords.

Smoke swirled when Daegan puffed out a breath. He cleared his voice. "What do you want?"

Hmm. Her patience with him might just pay off after all. "You *know* what I want. To pull all the history from that gaudy scrying wall. There is more than we've found. I know there is."

That scrying wall held secrets it was going to give up.

Daegan's voice had been smooth as warm ale at one time, but he'd spoken only a few words in two thousand years. Now his words rumbled out rough and gravelly. "As you know, I'm limited in what I'm allowed to see when I'm barred from moving my head."

"Yes, yes, the other queens didn't fawn over you so often by allowing such freedoms the way I do." She rolled her hand. "You were saying."

He growled something under his breath. "When Flaevynn first came into power as queen, she destroyed a large scrying bowl originally placed here for each queen's use, and built the stone waterfall. That wall holds only what has happened during *Flaevynn's* reign. A mere six hundred and sixty-six years," he added with sarcasm. "She sent members of the coven covertly into the human world to find the largest of rare stones. When it was finished, she believed her wall a masterpiece."

More interested in recent events of the past decade, Queen Maeve could live with seeing only Flaevynn's time here. "Our tastes clearly differed. Basically, she had none." Maeve cast a look at the towering design composed of many different gemstones. A waterfall cascaded over scarlet emeralds, diamonds, black opals, jadeites, and more. Most were fist-size and dazzling, but some were far larger. A spectacular assortment, but the assembly looked ridiculous. Something a novice would design.

On the other hand, Cathbad had yet to break the chant Flaevynn had used to create it.

For as much a fool as Flaevynn had been, she'd built in exceptional security to prevent others from accessing her wall.

Maeve tired of this game they played. "What was the chant that powered the wall, Daegan?"

"The words were cloaked from me."

"You are worthless. You know that? What do you offer me in trade?"

"I know of Kizira."

Maeve let out a hefty sigh. She answered in a droll tone. "I saw the battle scene, and even know the name of the man. Vladimir Quinn. If you want to be of use to me, then tell me what Kizira said to Quinn as she died."

"No one knows. You are correct in thinking Kizira shielded her last words from Flaevynn... from everyone except the Belador warrior, Quinn. What you do not know is that Kizira was the one who placed the security on the scrying wall. Flaevynn would not risk draining her power, and so compelled Kizira."

Well, well. That was new. Just as Queen Maeve had suspected, Kizira could answer many questions.

Daegan's eyes blinked slowly with the focus of a predator. He asked, "Why have you not brought the Belador Quinn here to torture for answers?"

"Why would you care?"

"I don't. As you said, I have nothing more to do for the rest of eternity so I have decided to discuss these things with you. Note that I just shared significant information about Kizira. If I share more, I will expect something in return."

She concealed her pleasure at this first chink in his stubborn emotional armor. Evidently Daegan enjoyed the tastes of talking and sleeping she had given him. He believed himself superior to everyone, including her, and capable of resisting all temptation, but he was no different from any other captive who had suffered for years upon years.

They all broke eventually.

She took her time, breathing deeply and acting as if she thought hard on his comment before replying. "Quinn is too powerful for simple torture. He would require more time than I'm willing to invest to gain answers. I accept your offer to trade for information."

"Ask me what you will. I will share what I can."

She didn't believe he would be quite so accommodating as he sounded, but this was a start. She tested him. "Which Alterants have you seen here?"

"All ten that Flaevynn brought to TÅμr Medb, before they were forced to evolve into gryphons."

"Once that happened, were the gryphons united behind Evalle?"

"Not when they left to join the battle at Treoir. The most powerful gryphon at the time was called Boomer. He hated Evalle." He added, "Boomer was one of the five with golden heads."

Queen Maeve thought back over the Treoir battle scenes she'd reviewed when Cathbad had managed to replay them on the scrying wall.

"I didn't see this Boomer on Treoir."

"You're saying Evalle leads the gryphons now?"

"Yes."

Daegan was silent a moment before saying, "Once Kizira died, Boomer would have become the leader, as he was the most powerful gryphon. If Evalle now leads the pack, that means she killed Boomer at some point."

Correct, since Queen Maeve knew there were now eight gryphons. She'd seen one that did not have a golden head die during the battle. What Daegan said made sense.

She couldn't believe how careless everyone had been with her gryphons. Kizira's name came up in relation to practically every topic. The dead priestess had been privy to everything in TÅµr Medb. She could shed light on so many things.

Queen Maeve said, "We believe Quinn has entombed Kizira's body within a cemetery in Atlanta. I wonder why he did not burn her body and salt the ashes. Why is he saving her, when others could make use of Kizira's body? What do you think he has in mind to do with her?"

Silver eyes smoldered with menace. Daegan remained silent so long, she began to think he needed another energy slap.

He said, "Perhaps Quinn wanted her body close so that he could commune with her spirit or grieve in private. His actions would be a mystery only to those who lack compassion. What would it matter what he's done with her body, since Kizira is out of reach for others? Unless you think to act as Flaevynn would and destroy the mausoleum just to punish Quinn."

Maeve did not rise to the bait of Daegan's dig over her lack of compassion. In truth, she took it as a compliment, but he hadn't intended it as such.

But why be so foolish as to goad her?

"Unlike Flaevynn, I do not resort to chaotic tantrums. I can withdraw the answers I want from Kizira, dead or not. Only fools such as you underestimate me." She smiled, and floated away as if she dismissed the conversation.

She watched Daegan from the corner of her eye as she moved past the throne toward the scrying wall, pretending to leave his field of view.

He slumped his head, eyes softening with relief.

Did he really think she would allow his impudence to go unpunished?

As his eyelids closed, Maeve pointed her finger at Daegan and said, "No, no. Bad boy."

His eyelids jerked open and would stay that way, unable to blink until she left this room again.

The throne shook and rumbled. Smoke boiled from his nostrils.

"Careful, Daegan, or I'll put plugs in your nose." Laughing with delight, she circled the room and returned to the center just in time to see Cathbad appear with a freakish-looking man.

The wizard.

Cathbad began introductions. "This is Grendal, who requested a meeting with you. Grendal, this is Queen Maeve, who leads the most powerful dark witch coven in all the worlds."

Grendal had yellow skin. Not jaundice-like, but a dingy color that came from pushing dark majik to extreme limits at personal cost. He had half-inch-long hair, much brighter yellow than his skin. Why would anyone with that hideous coloring wear a robe the color of spring leaves? Runic symbols had been embroidered on the robe with gold and red thread.

Whoever had given him that hooked nose did him no favors.

Just looking at him hurt her eyes.

"Queen Maeve." He dipped his head in deference to her and began, "I have captured four white witches from the Atlanta covens."

She tilted her head back to look down her nose, as she would to observe a rodent. "Why would this matter to me?"

"I used a Noirre spell to trap them."

Cathbad stepped over to stand next to Maeve. "You failed to mention that when I came for you, Grendal."

"I thought you might delay my meeting."

Power sizzled around Queen Maeve. The effort to keep from slamming this Grendal into her scrying wall took all her control. "Where did you gain Noirre majik?"

"It was a gift."

"I find that hard to believe, when it is our proprietary majik and we do not *gift* it to anyone," she countered.

Grendal lifted the palms of his hands in a show of peace. "I stand corrected. *You* did not give it to the witches whom I *persuaded* to part with it," he clarified, smiling. "Your predecessor, Flaevynn, was not as discerning when it came to sharing Noirre. She offered it in exchange for Alterants at the Achilles Beast Championship."

Cathbad turned to her. "Our warlocks spoke of this when I interrogated everyone. I dismissed it as inconsequential, based on the amounts they believed to be used in the trades. As I understand it, Kizira was sent to oversee a sponsorship our coven provided for the battles between Alterants and other beings. The games were blocked from view on the scryin' wall, which means the venue was a heavily warded location."

What Cathbad was not saying is that they had no way to know exactly how much Noirre had been exchanged.

Giving her a meaningful look, Cathbad said, "What Grendal claims may be true."

"It *is* true," Grendal reinforced. "I have no reason to lie about that, since many knew that Noirre was traded. VIPER chose to overlook those rumors. Or I should say that Sen allowed those who made illegal trades to slip away while he waited to capture Evalle, but she had already been teleported here."

Maeve seethed at yet another careless use of Medb resources. Noirre should be treated like their blood, and protected at all costs.

Grendal added, "Your coven is being accused of the white witch kidnappings, and of being behind a missing witch council member."

Waving that off, Maeve said, "I'm not concerned about petty issues in the human world. The white witches and Beladors accuse us of every discomfort they suffer, but VIPER requires proof. It will be difficult to prove we have committed any crime when we have not touched a white witch." Then she amended, "At least, not in the last two months."

"You are correct ... as long as there is no proof," Grendal said with a sly undercurrent. "However, if VIPER did receive evidence of the Medb kidnapping these witches, that would shift VIPER support in favor of Macha and the Beladors again. Such a pity after you went to so much trouble to get the coalition in the palm of your hand."

Cathbad said, "The solution is simple. We hand you to VIPER, and their missin' witch case is solved. This smacks of blackmail. We do not pay for such things. We make the problem go away. Permanently."

"I'm not here to waste my time or yours. Trying to overpower me will waste majik we can both put to better use."

Trying to overpower him? Maeve told the wizard, "You have one minute to convince me not to send you to our dungeon, which would require a smidgeon of *my* majik."

Grendal opened his arms in a gesture of understanding. "I am here to offer you a way to gain the upper hand with the coalition once and for all, plus offer what you want from Vladimir Quinn at the same time."

This odd man intrigued her as much as he invited death by annoying her. "Why should I care what VIPER thinks?"

"As I understand it, your coven is allowed to enter the human world only in small numbers. It will take a long time to build your numbers there at this rate."

Cathbad sent Maeve his don't-rock-the-boat-until-we-know-everything look.

She shrugged and asked Grendal, "What is it you *think* I want from this Quinn?"

"The body of your priestess who died in the attack on Treoir."

Schooling her face to remain barely patient, Queen Maeve intentionally took her time answering. Any sign of interest would work in this wizard's favor. "What do you know of Kizira's body?"

"More than you would expect. I traveled from Ukraine to Atlanta to find someone who ran from me. The Beladors hide her. In searching for her, I've discovered things of value, such as the fact that Vladimir Quinn returned to Atlanta after an attack on Treoir. He carried Kizira's body home with him." Grendal paused then added, "And he has concealed it in Atlanta."

Why does everyone think they know more than I do? She made a production of sighing. "Tell me something I don't know."

"Her body is hidden in Oakland Cemetery."

"Still waiting."

Grendal seemed genuinely surprised at her lack of reaction. "If that body belonged to me, I would want it back. Perhaps I made this trip in error. Do you not want Kizira's body back?"

Maeve glanced away, thinking. Her gaze landed on Daegan, who gawked at her with his eyelids stuck wide open. Everyone tested her patience today.

She turned back to Grendal. Who was this wizard? "Let's say that I would like to have it returned."

Grendal's thin lips tilted up. "I know how you can gain the body, and avoid conflict with VIPER or the Beladors."

Maeve thought on all the ways she could torture what she wanted out of Grendal. He held himself in high regard, but he had no idea of the danger he toyed with at the moment.

Cathbad murmured, "Hmm ... tell us more, Grendal."

"I have said all I intend to share until we strike a deal."

It was time to stop dancing around. Queen Maeve asked, "What do you want?"

"The one thing that has brought me this far from home. I want Quinn's cousin by the name of Lanna Brasko delivered to me, alive. She is mine."

"Where is she right now?" Cathbad asked.

"That is what I have not been able to discern. As I mentioned, the Beladors hide her. I've gotten close twice when she's drawn on her majik, but she's managed to vanish just as quickly. I tire of this hunt, and am here proposing we help each other."

His offer of gaining Kizira's body with no fallout piqued her interest, but Maeve would not agree to produce someone out of thin air. "You want me to do what? Look into my scrying wall to find this Lanna?"

"No, I could do that myself, and have tried to locate her in similar ways. I want you to use your Scáth Force to track her down. Once I realized you had an elite detail of warlocks secretly inserted into Atlanta, I found the answer to my quandary. I don't believe VIPER or the Beladors realize the extent of the covert force that moves among them."

The normally exuberant Cathbad had quieted considerably as Grendal continued to present his offer.

Maeve doubted the wizard realized that Cathbad would see Grendal as a loose end that had to be snipped. Cathbad would make it a clean cut across the neck, but not until they managed to squeeze all they needed from this unexpected source of information.

Grendal explained, "Once you deliver Lanna, I'll share with you how to gain Kizira's body without incident. You're fortunate in that Quinn chose to keep her body intact. If Macha finds out what he did, neither Quinn nor that body will last very long."

He'd put some effort into learning much about the Medb operations.

If they struck no deal, this wizard would find a way to inform Macha of Kizira's body without implicating himself. And he would not have come here without leaving a way to bring the coalition down on the heads of the Medb if he ended up in a dungeon.

Queen Maeve replayed his first words in her mind. "Why did you tell us about capturing white witches?"

Grendal snapped his fingers. "Ah! I have more to share. Once I have Lanna and you have Kizira, I'll leave the kidnapped council members—"

Cathbad broke in. "*Members*, as in more than one?"

"Not yet, but there will be soon. One must always have plenty of backup. As I was saying, once we both have what we want, I will leave those white witches to be found alive in a way that implicates a dark coven possessing Noirre, but unrelated to you. When that coven is discovered as the culprit for kidnapping the white witches, it will reflect badly on the white witch council for pointing a finger at you *and* on the Beladors for supporting them."

Cathbad asked, "How does this benefit our queen, since the presence of Noirre is not enough to prove we've taken anyone?"

Grendal gave them a sympathetic expression one normally reserved for the simpleminded. "That would be true, if not for the fact that evidence of Medb involvement *does* exist."

And now the truth struggled to the surface. She ordered, "Spit your words out clearly, wizard."

Showing no reaction to her acidic tongue, he calmly said, "If you fail to deliver Lanna to me, then I will leave the *dead* white witches in a way that clearly points to the two of you. You may not be concerned about going up against VIPER, but the Tribunals have become hostile toward this whole Belador and Medb conflict. If VIPER is turned against you, functioning in the human world will become nearly impossible, especially now that a witch in league with the Beladors controls Witchlock. She may lead them here, in fact."

Cathbad's icy tone could raise fear in the dead. "You dare to come here and threaten our queen?"

Grendal's frown-wrinkled skin sagged around his eyes. "Please, let's not turn this into a conflict, when that was not my reason for coming here.

I have the white witches and currently one council member as insurance. Once the queen and I complete our deal, all will be fine."

"What is Queen Maeve's insurance?"

Spreading his arms once again, Grendal said, "What would you ask of me?"

Maeve allowed the hint of a smile to tilt the corner of her mouth. She swirled her finger about and a shallow dish three feet in diameter and ten inches deep hovered waist-high between her and the wizard. She wiggled her fingers over the empty vessel and water filled the bowl, then herbs rained down onto the water, causing ripples.

Grendal stared at the liquid with more curiosity than concern. His black eyes lifted to meet hers. "I'm listening."

"This will be a binding spell. Not for one to bind the other, but to be performed by both of us."

After considering that a moment, Grendal said, "I accept."

She explained, "You will give your oath first, then sprinkle your blood in the water. I will give mine next and do the same. Once the blood is blended, we will both be bound by our words."

Grendal slid his deep sleeve back to expose an arm scarred in vicious ways. He produced a T-handled boline and drew the sharp knife across his skin.

Cathbad said nothing, merely sending her a questioning arch of his eyebrow before returning his attention to Grendal.

The wizard's blood drizzled into the water.

"I, Grendal, from the House of Miron in Transylvania, give my word that, upon mutual execution of this agreement, I will not implicate Queen Maeve, Cathbad the Druid, or the Medb coven in the white witch kidnappings I have performed and will continue to perform, plus I will share how to gain Kizira's body without conflict with VIPER or the Beladors if Queen Maeve delivers Lanna Brasko to me alive and without implicating me in Lanna's capture ... within three revolutions of Earth around the sun from this moment. If these terms are not met to the letter as sworn, this agreement is unbound, and I am free to take action as I choose."

"Three Earth days?" Cathbad questioned.

"All agreements need a time limit. That is mine. Do you accept?"

Maeve lifted her arm, which was as smooth and perfect as the rest of her skin. She used a long black fingernail to slice across her skin. Blood bubbled, then dripped straight down, pausing before it touched the water.

"I, Queen Maeve, ruler of the entire Medb coven, give my word to deliver Lanna Brasko to Grendal in three days, and in exchange, I will receive information at that time as to how I may gain Kizira's body per conditions of the agreement. Also, Grendal agrees to leave all who belong to the Medb coven, including Cathbad the Druid and me, blameless for any actions associated with white witch kidnappings currently underway in Atlanta. Additionally, for receipt of Lanna Brasko, Grendal will expose the kidnappings in such a way that VIPER is convinced the Beladors and white witches orchestrated the kidnappings to wrongly blame the Medb. If these terms are not met to the letter as sworn, this agreement is unbound, and I am free to take any action I choose." She held Grendal's gaze the entire time she spoke, and enjoyed a smug moment when he blinked at the way her blood waited for her command.

She released her blood. The water boiled and churned with her majik.

Grendal cocked his head, with concern this time, but he said nothing.

Once the bubbling water settled down, black smoke rose from the center and swirled in the air.

Maeve brushed a finger over her cut, and it closed immediately, leaving her skin as good as new.

Not to be outdone, Grendal blew softly on his arm and the cut sealed, but left a thin scar.

That should have shown Grendal who was the more powerful. She'd never had a doubt.

Daegan angled his head to stare at the wizard, and she stifled a chuckle at the way his eyes were practically bulging with the need to blink.

Cathbad cleared his throat. "Now that you two have reached an agreement, how will we locate you once we have Lanna?

Grendal slid one of many rings from his fingers. The one he chose was of a dark metal and carved with symbols the queen did not recognize. Grendal said, "This will work only if we are in the same realm. I will be in Atlanta for the time being. When you're ready, place this wherever you want to meet with me and call my name, then allow me one hour to reach that location."

Accepting the ring, Cathbad told Queen Maeve, "I'll be back in just a moment once I've returned Grendal to Atlanta."

Good to his word, Cathbad vanished with the wizard, then returned ten seconds later. He said, "That was an unexpected gift."

"Only time will tell if it's a gift or a curse."

Cathbad snorted with a smothered laugh until he took in Daegan's wide-eyed state. "What has this one done to provoke ya now?"

"Just being himself."

She thought back on the meeting and revisited something that still needled her. "We've been to the cemetery. Kizira's body is there. What has Grendal discovered about removing the body that we don't know?"

He sighed. "I've no idea, but I intend to find out. Remember, we've been reincarnated only two months. Grendal has been around the human world longer than we have. He knows more than we do about VIPER and the Beladors. He discovered we have our Scáth Force there, and no one should know that. I want to find out what he knows, and how he got the information. If he tells it straight, we could turn the tables on Macha in a big way."

Queen Maeve tapped her thumb against her cheek. "Before we make any trade, I want to know what's so special about this woman. She must have a power that Grendal wants."

"Aye, that would be my guess. The man's skin is disgusting. He's misused dark majik more than a time or two. If I were to guess, I'd say he needs her to continue living. Death is his shadow right now."

She agreed with that assessment. "Have Ossian and our Scáth Force find this Lanna *and* the missing white witches. Have them bring Lanna to me."

Cathbad's eyebrows lifted high. He grinned. "I do love how your mind works. You intend to remove his bargaining chip and turn the tables on him. Well done, my queen."

"Now, about Witchlock. It intrigues me."

CHAPTER 18

Tzader was spent, but the idea of sleep offered no sanctuary for him. He took a shower and meandered around, trying not to notice the empty echo that reminded him this house had been built for a family.

His eyes were gritty from being up so long. Maybe he'd grab a battle nap, where he wouldn't sink deeply enough into sleep to enter the dream realm.

Much as he would love to spend the time with Brina, he didn't want Ceartas coming around to ask what progress he was making.

An hour later, he had sucked down a nuked frozen meal and stretched out on the sofa. He set the alarm on his watch. Yes, he needed more sleep, and definitely deep sleep, but if he went under that far, the alarm on his watch might not wake him.

Tzader closed his eyes and started drifting off into a half-alert sleep state.

Energy tingled across his face and neck.

Someone was inside the house with him.

He cracked his eyelids just enough to see shadows, but didn't move another muscle. His heartbeat picked up even though his mind refused to believe anyone had been able to cross the ward he'd had an old druid put around this house.

Allowing his eyes to adjust, he slowly searched the immediate area.

"Tzader?" whispered very close to him.

No point in pretending to be asleep now.

Rolling his head to the left, he found Brina in glowing hologram form.

"*Brina!*" He was on his feet and reaching for her when his brain reminded him he couldn't put his hands on her. "What are you doing here?"

"Are you not glad to be seein' me?"

His hands shook with the need to touch Brina. "I'm thrilled to see you, love. Being apart is killing me."

"Me, too. We need to talk without Macha around."

It dawned on Tzader that Brina had never been in his house. Their house. "How did you find me?"

"It was strange. I kept thinking that I had to leave and find you, but Macha pitches a fit if I dare to leave the castle now, even in hologram. I was rubbing this thing you gave me—"

That's when he noticed that she had her hands cupped against her chest. She wore a peach-colored gown with a billowy skirt. He'd seen her in gowns most of the time these past years, but they weren't the clothes she preferred. She wore them only to appease Macha.

"—and the next thing I knew, I was standin' here watchin' you sleep."

What kind of majik was in that dragon scale?

Or was she able to locate him through the bond of their majik?

He didn't want Brina stressed out, especially with her pregnant. "I told you I'd be back, *muirnin*. I don't want you to worry while I'm gone."

Her fists flew to her hips. She had the scale clutched in one hand. "I'm no fragile flower to be kept locked in that castle."

"No, you're a warrior queen, but we need you to be safe. I need you to be safe."

She waved her free hand around. "I know. I'm constantly reminded of the Belador power and my responsibilities. I've had more memories in the last few hours than in two months. I feel like myself again."

His heart jumped with joy at that.

"Then I put this thing down." She held the scale up. "All those memories started swimmin' away from my mind."

"Don't put it down," Tzader said, with more force than he'd intended.

The temper attached to all that beautiful red hair surfaced. "Do not be givin' me orders! I'm sick of people tellin' me what to do. I picked this up again right away and my memories returned."

Shoving both hands over his face, he gripped his head. "I'm sorry. I didn't mean to shout at you."

"There ya go, actin' like I'm gonna break again."

He was damned no matter what he did. His Brina had always had attitude, but she'd never been quite so ... irritable. What had her snapping at him?

The baby.

He brightened. What he wouldn't give to have her in his life every day, snapping at him because her hormones were all out of whack. What drove most men crazy would be a blessing for him.

"You find this funny?"

Dropping his hands, he sighed. "No, this isn't funny. I just had a happy thought for a moment and it made me smile."

She got quiet, studying his face. "Was it about me?"

Her voice had gone from battle ready to vulnerable.

He shook with the need to hold her and reassure Brina that he would keep her and the baby safe. "Of course it was about you, *muirnin*. Just thinking about you lifts my spirits, and knowing we will be together keeps me fighting to have you at my side. I will not let you go, no matter who tries to stop me."

She cupped her hands in front of her, still clinging to the scale like the lifeline it was. "Macha is gettin' on my nerves."

"That's not new."

"I hadn't realized it so much until my memories returned with this thing." She waved the scale. "But I'm recallin' everythin' in sharp detail, like when she convinced me to pretend that I was ready to move on from us and to show an interest in Allyn."

Tzader growled at being reminded that Allyn was still around. "Once I learned the truth about what Macha has been trying to do, I warned that guard to keep his distance from you."

"He is, but I think Macha is tryin' to convince me to take a serious look at him again."

"How serious?"

"She wants me to invite him into my sunroom."

"Did you?"

"Not yet."

Tzader would prefer not to harm the guard, but he'd already made it clear to Allyn that Brina was off-limits. He said, "If he comes around uninvited, give him a message from me. Tell Allyn I thought he had a better sense of self-preservation."

Brina said, "Don't be gettin' huffy around my guard. He's done nothin' wrong. I'm the one who dragged him into this mess when Macha coerced me into her shenanigans."

"He isn't quite so innocent," Tzader argued. "I saw the way he looked at you. He had far more on his mind than just guarding your person. Keep your distance from him or he'll face my sword." What about if—*when*—the dragon scale's power ran out and Tzader had not returned to her?

Macha would push Brina and Allyn together the minute Brina lost her grasp on her mind.

He longed to tell her about the baby, but Brina had a tenuous control over her mind. If she slipped and let Macha know that she knew, Macha might snatch Tzader back into Treoir before he had a chance to reach the dragon.

And it wouldn't be to congratulate him on his impending fatherhood.

Brina took a breath and went on. "I've been pretendin' I still don't have memories and testin' Macha to see what she'll do. She's pressurin' me, and warned that I should bond with someone now to begin buildin' new memories."

"That bitch."

In a rare moment, Brina allowed the curse to pass unchecked. "When I told her I was too tired to be considerin' another man at this moment, she told me it was imperative to my health that I not delay. I know I'm more tired than usual, but ... what could she possibly mean by that? Tell me the truth, Tzader," Brina demanded. "Don't keep me in the dark. Am I dyin'?"

"What? No. You're just tired from ... trying to regain your memories. I won't allow anything to happen to you." He'd said the first words that his heart shouted out, but guilt swamped him over hiding the fact that she *did* face dying. If Ceartas had told the truth, Brina would become incapacitated, maybe even comatose, which would put her and the baby at risk once she could no longer maintain her health.

He also hated the fact that he couldn't tell her she was pregnant. Brina would deal with Macha to buy Tzader time to deliver an answer for her situation, but if Brina knew of her pregnancy and Macha pushed too hard, his stubborn warrior queen might try to teleport away from Treoir to protect the baby.

Macha would never allow that, and Tzader did not want to give the goddess any reason to escalate things before he had a chance to free the dragon.

If successful, he'd suffer the consequences of crossing Macha.

And he'd lay waste to an entire world that dared to separate him from his family.

Brina looked around the room, which was too dark for much to show. "Where are you, Tzader?"

Should he tell her? What if she never saw this again? He said, "In the house I built for us. It was to be my engagement surprise for you, but ..." *Life and commitment to duty conspired against us,* he finished silently.

"We will have our chance," she said with fierce determination. "In fact, I don't want to see it now. I want you to show the house to me when this is all behind us. That brings me back to why I was wantin' to see you. What is it you're doin' before you come back to see me, and what's this red thing I'm holdin'?"

His heart hurt at the idea of not including her in his confidence. He wanted to tell her about going after the dragon to remove the Noirre spell still influencing her, but the less she knew about his plans, the better for her and their child.

Macha couldn't be trusted. She might even compel Brina to tell what she knew.

He didn't want to outright lie to Brina either. "You're holding a scale from a dragon. Don't allow Macha to find out about it." If he hadn't rescued the dragon by the time the scale's power ran out, it would be because Tzader was either captured ... or dead.

"Stop treatin' me like a wee bairn, Tzader. You told me about not showin' it to anyone and I won't be showin' it," Brina snapped, her short temper surfacing again. "That's why I'm wearin' this ridiculous gown, so I can hide the scale in my pocket. I feel normal as long as I touch it, so at least we have this."

"Right," he said, rather than admit the scale had a limited shelf life. "I've got a lead on a way to fix your memories so you won't need that scale."

"Macha didn't mention that."

"It's because she doesn't know. I tried to tell her after you left the room, but she wouldn't listen to me and, to be honest, I think she may not want me for your husband."

Shock and fury warred in Brina's face. Fury won. "Macha's goin' to suffer serious disappointment if that's the case. I'll have no one but you. Not even a goddess will change that."

There was the woman he'd fallen in love with when she'd first challenged him to a knife-throwing match.

"What's this plan you have?"

He couldn't tell her that, but neither did he want to keep handing her one lie after another. "I don't want to say until I have all my answers and that isn't being evasive. I just want to be sure before I say more." *I also don't want to give you anything Macha can find out about.* But he'd keep that to himself.

With a flick of irritation, Brina brushed a handful of hair from her face and said, "Fine. But tell me you won't be goin' off on your own with no help."

He could do that. "Evalle, Storm, and Quinn are going to help me find what we need to fix your memories." That sounded far better than saying they were joining forces to go rogue and steal a Medb throne. "We're meeting in a couple of hours to get started. I just came home to shower and catch some shut-eye."

"Where is this meetin'? I should join all of you. I can clearly still travel in hologram."

"No!" He regretted shouting the minute that word shot of out his mouth.

"No? As in you think to be tellin' me what I can or cannot do?"

"Of course not, Brina." Even in hologram form, Brina could unleash her power. Calming his voice, Tzader said, "You said you were tired. The more you rest, the easier it will be for that red scale to help you regain your memories." That *might* be the case. "Also, you'll want to be rested and at your best when I return. I'll need you then more than ever."

Suspicion swept across her narrowed gaze. Brina was not easily fooled, and he wouldn't have a chance at it if not for her trust, which left him with a bad taste since he was taking advantage of it.

She shoved her hands in the deep pockets of her gown. "I suppose you're right."

"I wish I could kiss you, *muirnin*." He'd feel better about convincing her to stay away if he could apologize without the words, but he couldn't have her showing up while they were discussing the dragon.

Her eyes shone, but she forced a smile to her lips, refusing to allow a tear to slip out. "We'll catch up on our kissin' and lovin' soon. Until then ... " Her voice drifted off. She normally left quickly in this form but her hologram faded slowly, as if she couldn't bear to let go of watching him. At the last second before she blinked out, Brina said, "Meet me in the dream world."

Hell. He wanted her so much, he was tempted.

She yawned and came back into focus.

Some days, Tzader just wanted to be a man and for Brina to be a woman. No Beladors, no Medb, nothing but the two of them. "You're tired, love. If I go to the dream world, you won't get any rest."

"Ah, but you're wrong. Every time I return after seein' you there, I'm recharged."

"Really?"

"I would not lie to ya."

Guilt pummeled his chest. He'd lie to her, but only to save her. Sleep dragged at him, pulling him down. He could reset his alarm and spend some time with her. "Go sleep, love, and I'll join you as soon as I can."

Her eyes brightened. "I don't feel so tired there. Maybe this time I can convince you to do more than before." She waggled her eyebrows, flirting with him.

He wanted to hold her so much it physically hurt. It was the one place Macha had not interfered. Could she find them in the dream world if she knew about their meetings? If so, why hadn't she yet? Macha was not one to respect anyone's privacy.

But every minute that went by might be the last he'd have with Brina.

If he thought too long on that, it would cripple him.

He would not give up hope until his last breath.

CHAPTER 19

Storm followed Evalle's directions to Mattie's house and parked along the street.

He caught the confused look on Evalle's face as she took in the empty driveway.

Storm explained, "Faster to leave from out here than a driveway, if necessary, and nobody can block me in."

"That makes sense. I like the way you think."

If they were alone, she'd really like what he had in mind, but they had to deal with this first before he could get her where he wanted her... in the middle of their new bed.

She stepped out and surveyed the neighborhood, with its eclectic mix of houses from recent remodels updated for wealthy urbanites, to original structures created of stone and brick that were built close to a century ago. Some of the structures had shingle siding and most of them were tucked in close to one another.

Most, but not Mattie's. Her quaint, 1930s-era brick home sat on a half acre of land, with a driveway that stretched from the road to a detached garage in the back. A half acre in this area translated into a piece of real estate worth seven figures.

The prestigious Emory University Hospital had been good for property values.

Evalle said, "Mattie's house looks like it belongs in a fairy tale."

"Like Hansel and Gretel?" he quipped.

She rolled her eyes.

Storm's empathic sense picked up nothing unusual, but his survival instinct was telling him to look at the house, and then get Evalle away from here. Or maybe it was just his need to have her alone without carpenters, decorators, or VIPER agents around.

Still, he wouldn't discount anything he sensed. Someone other than the Medb might be after white witches, but he was suspicious by nature and he could see this being a way to draw Evalle even deeper into the Belador-Medb conflict.

Starting for the house, Evalle said, "I bet the neighbors have no idea who lives among them."

"I won't take that bet." Storm caught up to her and angled past the front porch. "Where'd you say Rowan left the key to the back door?" He disturbed layers of dead leaves as he headed across the front yard, but his empathic senses went haywire when they picked up a decidedly female interest focused on him.

He spun around to face Evalle.

She jerked her gaze up from where she'd been watching his butt. She mumbled, "What? Oh, the key. It's in a metal box stuck inside the air conditioner."

Lifting his palms to her face, he leaned in and kissed her, then said, "I'll let you take the lead next time so *I* get the hot view."

"Not if I have any say about it," she teased.

He loved the easy way she had with him. That hadn't always been the case, and he cherished every smile and touch.

She brushed a lock of hair off his face that had fallen loose from where he had it tied back. She sounded wistful when she said, "I really don't want to be here now."

He gave her his wolf smile and slowly moved his hands to her shoulders. "Glad I'm not the only one ready to get naked. I'm so hard just thinking about you, I'm in pain."

She didn't blush often, but neither would she be outdone. Her voice dropped to a sexy tone. "In case you need any more incentive, I can't wait to feel you inside me."

Mother of mercy. "You can't do that to me unless you want to see how quickly I can get you out of those clothes."

She laughed. The vixen.

"Think that's funny?" He dropped his hands to her chest and brushed his thumbs over her nipples.

Her humor fled and she moaned.

He backed away, chuckling.

"No fair," she accused, quick to catch up.

"Oh, really?" He kept heading toward the back of the house. "You can say that after you said you can't wait to feel me inside you?" He sighed. "You'll be the death of me."

She jogged past him when they reached the corner. He waited as she retrieved the key.

Rowan had confirmed that Mattie's wards were not in place when she'd come by earlier to check out the house. Storm walked up onto the ten-foot-square back porch and, sure as hell, he didn't feel any ward. He entered through a mudroom that connected to a kitchen shrouded in shadows. Evalle stayed right with him.

A nightlight had been plugged into a wall socket at the end of the room. With Storm's jaguar vision and Evalle's equally sharp night vision, there was no need to turn on lights.

He lifted a photo off a mahogany drop-leaf table shoved against the wall with both leaves down. The photo was of a sweet-faced, elderly woman sitting on the chair positioned at the end of that same table. She was smiling, as though she knew he was here looking for her.

Evalle stepped up. "Rowan left that picture for us."

She stood still as he moved around, scenting the kitchen. When he finished, he said, "Not picking up any Noirre in here or any Medb scent. Just Rowan and Mattie's, and a few people I don't know, but I smell those unknowns on different areas of the kitchen as if they were here for coffee."

"How did you get Mattie's?"

"It's on Oskar."

"Oh."

Giving Mattie's photo a thorough look, he suggested, "Let me go through the rest of the house first to see if I pick up anything else. Why don't you see what you can find here?"

"Sounds good."

Evalle poked around through white cabinets filled with well-used baking pans, which sent her mind back to the witch in Hansel and Gretel. But Mother Mattie wouldn't lure kids here for anything nefarious. Not a white witch, especially one associated with—and protected by—Rowan.

Porcelain figurines of fairies cluttered the counters and any open cranny. The windowsill above the sink held a unicorn, an unfinished clay figure that looked similar to Oskar, and a hobbit trinket.

Mattie collected knickknacks.

Evalle paused to look closely at another photo, but this one was inside a small gold frame. It appeared to be Mattie, around ten years younger, standing with another woman who had her head tilted down, shielding her face from the camera. Mattie had a hand on her friend's shoulder. The other woman wore a wide-brimmed, red hat that hid everything above her shoulders.

"Who is that, Mattie?" Evalle murmured.

The hat shifted as the woman in the photo lifted her head, revealing a beautiful face with burnished skin and exotic, diamond-blue eyes that sparkled as though struck by sunlight. In a flash, the sparkle changed to a predatory look of threat.

Evalle pulled back, holding that gaze in spite of her mind yelling to disengage.

The hat tilted down and the picture returned to the original static state. Evalle remembered to breathe.

Had the movement in the photo been Fae shenanigans? Was the woman in the red hat Caron?

With nothing else of interest in here, Evalle rubbed her arms and stepped out onto the back porch. A tall privacy fence protected the yard on three sides. Winter had shriveled the garden areas, but Evalle could imagine this place in full bloom.

A greenhouse stood in the back left corner. No witch's garden would be complete without herbs, and Mattie must keep hers going year-round. Condensation was evident on the inside of the glass from the heat being used.

A bright yellow object the size of a water bottle had been abandoned halfway between the porch and an oak tree that dominated the center of the open space. The more Evalle studied the yellow thing, the more it looked like a plastic toy.

Was that Oskar's?

Feenix dragged his stuffed alligator everywhere.

Oskar might be more at ease with something of his while he stayed with Evalle and Storm. She took her time surveying the area. That came from years of walking streets brimming with dangerous nonhumans mixed in with the human population.

Leaves had scattered across every surface, but just as many remained on the massive old tree.

After a thorough visual sweep of the area, she stepped down and started across the yard. As she neared the toy, she recognized the shape as a yellow duck with a witch's hat.

When she bent to pick it up, the toy tumbled in a roll toward the tree.

Oh boy. Had Auntie Caron given that to Oskar so that he'd have something to chase around the yard?

Sighing, Evalle walked under a canopy of branches and reached down.

Energy rippled over her skin.

She whipped upright and kinetically called up her dagger as she did. The handle slapped her palm. Nothing moved in the yard as she turned slowly to look toward the house. She waited to release the blades in her boots, which required stomping. No sudden movements until necessary.

She slowly looked up. Nothing in the tree.

Three feet above her, a branch as thick as her head moved slightly. There was a light wind, but not that much.

What was up there?

Leaves ruffled twelve feet up.

She waited for another move, preparing for whatever jumped out.

Something that felt like a massive hand wrapped her neck and lifted her two feet off the ground. Kicking her feet to unbalance her attacker, she swung her dagger, stabbing blindly. When she finally hit a surface, it was as solid as the tree.

It shook her like a ragdoll. Stars shot across her gaze.

Don't pass out.

She stabbed again and put kinetic power behind it, driving through some sort of shield.

A gray arm came into view, jutting away from her neck.

Warm liquid dripped down on her. Smelled like sewage.

She might not kill it, but if she made it bleed, this thing would lose its glamour.

Another invisible hand slapped at where she held her dagger embedded in the thing's flesh. If it had flesh. She couldn't get a breath to order the dagger to stay put.

Her lungs screamed for air.

She was losing consciousness.

She shoved the dagger back and forth, still kicking her legs to make it as difficult as possible to hold her.

How big *was* this thing?

It made a muffled, mournful sound, and the arm trembled. She had to be cutting muscle, but it still held her tight. Using her other hand, she slapped it with a kinetic fist, banging repeatedly. Black spots flashed in her vision.

To pass out is to die.

It jerked her up to the first row of limbs, practically pulling her head off.

Her heart rate leaped. She needed air. Couldn't think beyond trying to stay conscious. Adrenaline plowed through her body.

The emerald Storm had attached to her chest with majik warmed.

"Evalle, where are you?" Storm roared.

The point of wearing black clothes was to meld with the darkness, but she'd trade for something white right now.

In her peripheral vision, Storm leaped from the back porch, exploding into a huge black jaguar with fangs the size of her fingers by the time he hit the ground.

She took back all the grief she'd given him over sticking this emerald on her.

Storm launched into the tree, snarling, and slammed into the invisible form as it gashed his side. The smell of fresh blood hit her just as the creature jerked her around.

She grabbed the dagger handle with both hands and reached up, trying to cut through whatever muscle held her. Tears ran from her eyes at the strain. She was making gurgling noises, and everything was getting dim.

It yanked her up again, banging her arm backwards against a limb. Ow.

Her mate attacked, ripping chunks away from an invisible shape that turned gray as Storm tossed the pieces aside.

Wild snarling and growling erupted. The creature struggled to break free of Storm, but still it held her as if ordered to do so even in death.

What kind of beast could do that?

Beast. Damn. She had another weapon.

Evalle called up her Belador warrior form. Her neck expanded, forcing the creature's fingers to open further. Her biceps and forearms thickened. Then her power jacked up.

The thing howled and hit Storm, knocking him sideways off the higher branch. He flipped in midair like the cat he was, landing surefooted one branch down.

Evalle gripped the arm holding her and wrenched in two directions, snapping bones and ripping muscle. She snatched her dagger out of the thing and shoved it sideways into the heel of the creature's hand, but its fingers had already let go. She managed to use her kinetics to break the twelve-foot fall so she could land on her feet

It howled a painful sound of agony.

Storm attacked again, leaping higher this time and clawing viciously.

The creature dropped its cloaking, or couldn't hold it, as it tried to shield the head that Storm had finally found. An oversized horse head, with a ten-foot-tall, human-like body, but this one was covered in short gray fur with blotchy patches of rhino hide.

Had to be related to the dog-thief creature.

It dove from the tree, dragging Storm with it.

Breathing hard, Evalle called her dagger back from the creature's hand. Were the horse-head things demons after all? Her vision cleared gradually and she moved forward to back up Storm.

But she knew better than to jump in at the wrong moment and put him at more risk.

Energy powered up, slapping her skin. The creature had called up majik. It shoved Storm twenty feet to the side. Storm hit the ground and spun, ready for the kill.

That's when the creature bent its legs and leaped over the house into the front yard.

Storm landed in the empty spot, snarling and looking up. He hunched down and jumped onto the roof, raced up to the crest, and paused. He stared out toward the street for a long moment, then padded back down and landed silently in the yard.

In two steps, he shifted into his human form, walking the rest of the way. He pulled her into his arms without a word, and held her as if this moment was all he lived for.

Even after she'd joined the Beladors, she fought her own battles, never expecting anyone to take care of her.

To protect her.

Storm had come along and changed all that.

But she loved the feeling of being safe within Storm's arms. When it came to her, he'd jump in with no thought for his own safety. She'd do the same for him.

That's why Macha was not taking him from her. Ever.

When he finally eased his fierce grip, she said, "That was like the thing that captured the dogs and Oskar. Did you pick up the Noirre scent inside?"

"Yes. In the house, but Rowan's right. I think the Noirre is planted. The residue was in one spot, as if someone had literally placed it in a circle around Mattie's bed."

"Do you think they teleported her out of here?"

"No, I smelled some of her clothes, and that combined with what I got off of Oskar is plenty to determine what belongs to Mattie. A scent trail of Mattie plus a really unusual one, which is nowhere else in the house, led from the bed, then out the front door to a space two car-lengths down from where we parked. That's where I was when your emerald alerted me. I'm thinking somebody was able to breach Mattie's wards, force her out of the house, and then drive her away. Once they got in the car, though, the trail disappears." He shook his head, staring off. "Whoever did this is powerful as hell. I've never encountered a trail I can't track as long as the target didn't teleport, but this trail vanishes at the street."

"We have nothing then."

"Yes, we do. That creature we fought had a scent I've smelled before. And it was the same odor that was with Mattie's scent from the house to the curb. But the scent trail of that thing we fought disappeared at the top of the house right after the creature went over."

"Where'd you smell it before?"

"At the beast matches in the mountains, and at the beast games on Cumberland Island."

"Can you pinpoint it?"

"No. I have to think on it some. I may have to go back to that valley in the mountains and scout it to find the spot where I smell it again. Once I find it, I'll know what I saw in that spot."

"What do you think that creature was tonight?"

"I don't know."

"It made weird noises, and you know what?" Evalle turned in a circle and looked around, considering. "I haven't heard even one dog bark around here."

"I think the weird noises were because its tongue had been ripped out, and whoever came for Mattie must have put a protective sound and scent spell on the yard to prevent dogs or humans from detecting that monster. Might be a demon, but *being* one, I would normally recognize the blood of another. That wasn't demon blood. Not even sure it was blood at all."

"You are *not* a demon," she corrected him. "You only have demon blood."

"Semantics, sweetheart." He let his red demon eyes flash at her, then kissed her quickly. "I've had enough of investigating. Let's get you healed up, then go home."

She hugged him to her. "I'm ready. I can heal on the way there. How's your side?"

He twisted. His Skinwalker gifts were already healing the gash. "Be good as new as soon as I get a shower."

While Evalle brought him a spare set of jeans and T-shirt that he kept in the truck, Storm locked the house and grabbed what was left of his original clothes.

"Good thing for the privacy fence," Evalle noted as he pulled away. She called Rowan and filled her in using the speaker on her phone.

Rowan mused, "If it's not Medb, then I wonder who has our witches. Do either of you have an idea why they would leave a sentry at Mattie's house?"

Evalle had been thinking about that. "Maybe it was there to capture more witches that came by."

Storm shook his head. "We have to assume it might have been there when Rowan stopped by. She'd be a high-value capture, but it didn't show itself to her."

The discussion paused. Evalle said, "Storm said he's smelled the creature's scent before, back during the beast games, and it matched a scent that was in the house."

"That's more than we've had," Rowan offered.

Nothing fit in any of this for Evalle. "That creature would not have been there on its own, so it belongs to someone." She kept piecing her thoughts together. "I don't think it would have attacked me if I hadn't discovered where it was hidden. If that's the case, it could have been left there to keep track of who came by and report to the master."

"That makes sense," Rowan replied. "But we're back to the question of why. Why steal the witches? What do they want?"

"I don't know," Evalle admitted. "Quinn will get in touch with Trey today to discuss how to search for the witches without alerting VIPER to what they're doing."

"I've already told Trey to let me know if any of you have ideas that would require my abilities."

"Thanks, Rowan. We will." Evalle wished Rowan could help with breaking the curse on the dragon, but Rowan did not deal in dark majik. "I'll be in touch once we know more about the strange scent."

"Thanks."

Storm pulled into the garage at a quarter to five, and hustled Evalle into the unfinished office area. He released a heavy sigh. "I had hoped for a calmer evening, or morning, to do this, but let's go see our new living quarters."

So much had happened she'd forgotten about moving in today. "We're really all moved in?"

"Yes." He walked her up the three flights of stairs and told her, "Close your eyes."

When she did, he led her twenty steps and said, "Open your eyes."

She blinked, and started smiling. All the things she'd labored over choosing with Storm had been placed right where she'd envisioned each piece. For the past few weeks, she'd stressed over the furnishings, and he'd given only minimal input. He'd pointed out that he furnished his house in Midtown, but he wanted this to belong to him *and* Evalle.

For that to happen, she'd had to go shopping.

He'd even arranged for some places to stay open later in the evening to allow her extra time on the nights she had free from her duties.

They still had plenty of open areas for adding new pieces, but the overstuffed leather furniture already gave the space a comfortable feel. Mixing glass and teak for the tables and burnished copper for accents looked even better than she'd imagined in the showrooms.

Her heart thumped a crazy beat at seeing their home for the first time. She'd loved her underground place with Feenix, because before that she'd been living in a storage unit.

But this ... was a home.

Her home with Storm.

He pulled her back against his chest and wrapped his arms around her. "I love everything you picked out."

She hadn't realized until that moment just how worried she'd been about screwing up the decorating. "Really?"

"Yes, sweetheart. We have enough to make this livable, and we can take our time to add more as we find things that interest us. That's what will make this *our* home."

Our home. Two words she'd never thought to hear together. "I love it, too."

"I'm sorry this is a quick tour, and there's more to see, but we'll have to be back downstairs in less than three hours."

"I know you're tired."

His fingers slid down her front then back up under her shirt, and higher. She held her breath, waiting for him to touch her. When he did, her knees almost folded. Her bottom bumped into the front of his jeans.

He murmured, "Does that feel like I'm tired?"

She tried to sound nonchalant, which was beyond her acting skills with a man like Storm making it clear he wanted her. "I need a shower and—"

He spun her around and started pulling clothes off, walking her backwards. "I can help with that."

She was down to panties and a bra in three steps. How did he do that?

She put a hand on his chest. "I'm not taking off another piece until you catch up."

The grin he shot her was pure devil. He shrugged out of the jacket. Crossing his arms, he grabbed the tail of his shirt. He peeled it off his body, revealing each ridge of an eight-pack and chest muscles that begged to be licked.

When he flicked the shirt away, he unzipped his pants and stepped out. That's right. He'd gone commando when he'd dressed at Mattie's.

Storm had always been comfortable in his skin. Literally. He'd have no trouble walking around naked all the time.

She wouldn't care either, as long as no one saw him but her.

He reached for her waist and nipped at each side of her bra, giving her shivers. His carved biceps flexed when he lifted her, and she felt heat wick down between her legs. The man held her without a bit of strain.

They were moving. Him walking. Her floating in a frenzied sea of passion.

His mouth was doing incredible things to her stomach, lifting her higher and kissing lower.

When he let up on the sweet torture and brought her back to the floor, he turned her slowly so she could take in the bathroom.

She opened her mouth, but nothing came out.

This bathroom—theirs—was the size of her whole bedroom in her old apartment. A whirlpool bath that would accommodate a small group had been installed so that half of it was below floor level. A glass shower stood next to the bath, large enough for two and then some. Multiple showerheads pointed from every direction.

The entire place had slate floors, sleek dark granite counters, and teak cabinetry. Not a decorator showcase, but deeply personal.

He'd kept this hidden from her, wanting to finish the bathroom himself. To surprise her, he'd said.

When had the word surprise become inadequate?

In that moment, she took in all the love he'd poured into this. He'd listened to her apologize constantly because she was embarrassed every time she saw him in her tiny apartment bathroom after being in the spacious one at his Midtown house. Even that one paled next to this one.

He tugged her around. "Do you like it?"

"I love it." She smiled, reflecting the pleasure lurking in his gaze, begging to break out. "Love you. Love us."

His eyes turned thoughtful and he kissed her softly, with a sort of reverence. When he lifted his head, he reached around and released her hair from the ponytail. His smile caught fire and the gleam lit his eyes. "Good. I have plans for ways to have you on every surface."

Her nipples perked up. This man could twist up her insides with just a look, but he'd turned on the jets in the shower and had unclasped her bra just as quickly.

"You going to shower in those panties?" he asked.

Just to see what he'd do, she said, "Maybe."

He grinned, then grabbed her and hauled her into the shower that blasted her from all directions.

She shouted, "Wait. I'll take them off."

"Lost your chance." He put her down and spun her around.

Water pinged over her too-sensitive skin. His hands cupped her breasts and she forgot about the panties. Shower or not, they'd be wet by now anyhow. His hands swept down the front of her, taking his time as he went. He slowly pushed the underwear down and kissed the backs of her legs, then at the last moment, ripped the material. It hit the corner with a splat.

"Those were ..." She gasped when his lips caressed the backs of her knees. "New."

Moving around in front of her on his knees, he said, "You have a new Victoria's Secret charge card. Buy plenty."

His eyes glittered up at her, full of challenge and promise. Reaching around to cup her lower back, he said, "Lean back. I've got you."

As if she'd deny him anything?

She arched back and the water tortured her breasts, raining down with a thousand tiny pricks on her skin. At the same moment, Storm's mouth closed on her and she had no idea if her feet touched the floor any more.

Sensation overload. Water cascaded like a thousand electric fingers, sizzling over her aching breasts and skin.

Storm's tongue lashed across the fragile folds between her legs, stroking and not stopping in spite of her crying out. She shook with her release that went on and on.

Then he was there, pulling her to him and holding her in his arms—the only place she'd ever felt truly safe. And loved.

Water continued to rush over them. She took a shuddering breath and murmured, "That all you got?"

Storm's chest shook. He was laughing. "Don't ever change from the hellion I fell in love with."

"Still waiting." Strong words from a woman with boneless legs. She'd get her second wind any minute now and torture him the same way.

His erection pulsed against her and she wanted him.

All of him.

She had to find the kinetic energy to call a condom to them, but she didn't even know where they were. Storm must have, because she heard the crisp sound of a package opening.

He swore he couldn't read her thoughts, but his empathic ability gave her away just as easily. He hoisted her to eye level. She hooked her legs around him, never taking her eyes off of him as he lowered her down, down, down until she sucked in a breath at the feel of him sliding inside her.

And Macha thought she'd walk away from Storm?

Foolish goddess.

CHAPTER 20

Evalle, are you and Storm home from tracking Mattie?

She sat up, disoriented. Shoving hair out of her eyes, she took in the dark room, then the incredible male body lying next to her. She was at their new home. Got it.

She called back to Quinn telepathically. *Yes. How close are you?*

After a brief hesitation, he asked, *Should I give you more time?*

She leaned over Storm to see the time on the nightstand clock. Sixteen minutes. She'd dressed in less time. *We'll be ready, Quinn. See you in a few.*

Storm's hand hooked around her waist and pulled her against his chest. "Where do you think you're going?"

"Quinn just called me telepathically. He's on the way. He and Tzader will be here in sixteen minutes."

"Oh, hell. Is it eight already?" His lips twitched. "Easy to forget about time when I'm sleeping with a woman who keeps me up half the night, having her way with me."

Evalle smiled at his gruff morning voice. "How long will it take you to be ready?"

"Depends on what I'm doing." He flipped her over onto her back and loomed above her, all dark and sleepy eyed. He lowered his mouth to play havoc with her neck.

If her body had a vote, it would go with Storm's plan. But she didn't want to have Quinn and Tzader show up with her and Storm tangled up. "Don't start that, or I won't have time for a shower."

Growling like the jaguar he kept hidden inside, he pushed up from the bed, still gloriously naked and definitely in the mood for sex.

She teased him, "Such a shame to waste *that*."

"Then let's not." He scooped her up.

"Storm. We don't have time to—"

He sucked on her breast, and she forgot about the clock.

Storm mastered in multitasking. He'd managed to get them both showered while fitting in a quickie, and now brewed coffee as she raced downstairs with her wet hair pulled back.

Just as her foot hit the office area at street level, Quinn and Tzader walked in from the garage access door.

She pulled up short. "How'd you get inside without me opening the garage door?"

Tzader looked at Quinn, who sent a chiding look at Evalle. "I called Storm and he activated it from where he is. I *am* as adept at using a telephone as I am telepathy."

Had Quinn made a joke? "Ah." When in doubt, make a noise that could be construed as a reply.

"What the hell happened to your neck?" Tzader said, eyeing it as if blood gushed from a wound. She had four vivid bruises.

"We ran into something at Mattie's place. Tell you about it as soon as Storm comes down." She moved ahead of them to open up the conference room, which still smelled new to her even though it had been in use for two months.

Oskar sat up on his towel pallet. The yellow duck-with-a-black-witch-hat squeaky toy she'd remembered to bring home from Mattie's was tucked between his front legs, and he'd drunk half the water in his bowl.

"Have you determined how to maintain that beast?" Quinn asked.

Baring fangs in Quinn's direction, Oskar erupted in grunting frog-and-cricket sounds.

Evalle was coming to realize that Oskar understood some, or all, of what was said about him. "Don't insult him, Quinn."

"You're jesting, right?"

"No. I'm serious."

Quinn opened his mouth and closed it.

"I fed him raw hamburger last night. He seemed to like that, but he also opens his mouth and laps at the air, sort of like he's sucking in energy. Weird, but it works for him. And he *does* take exception to some of the things said around him." Evalle went over and squatted down to pet Oskar's head, calming him. "Want to go out, Osk?"

Mattie's familiar didn't jump up, wagging his bushy tail.

He stood on all four paws, walked at a dignified pace, took the long way around the table, obviously to avoid Tzader and Quinn, and paused at the door, waiting for her.

Tzader and Quinn stared at Oskar with the same expression they'd wear if Evalle started speaking in tongues.

No, actually, that probably wouldn't shock those two as much as realizing Oskar had understood her perfectly.

By the time she returned to the conference room, Storm was there with an urn of coffee, and all three men held mugs.

Lanna sat at the conference table, looking refreshed with her blonde curls contained behind a headband and wearing a purple long-sleeved knit top and jeans. Quinn must have brought her things this morning. She dipped a tea bag into a steamy cup of water and looked up at Evalle, then down at Oskar. "Who is that?"

Unlike everyone else, Lanna had addressed Oskar as a 'who,' which meant she recognized something about him. He wagged his bushy tail. Once.

Still, for Oskar, that was the equivalent of dancing around on two feet to show how pleased he was with her.

This was as good a time as any to find out if Lanna could pick up anything to help them find Mattie. Lanna set down her teacup and stood. Evalle said, "His name is Oskar. He's a familiar who belongs to a witch known as Mother Mattie. She's missing."

Lanna's eyes lit up as Evalle and Oskar came forward. "What a pretty boy."

Oskar preened. It would be hard to describe it to someone who hadn't witnessed his effort, but he literally sat up at her words.

Someone chuckled, clearly enjoying the Oskar show.

Quinn asked, "Any leads yet on the white witches?"

Evalle had stopped an arm's length away from Lanna. She hoped for any clue on finding Mattie. "No, but Lanna may be our best hope at finding her quickly. You haven't heard what happened to us this morning."

"The neck bruises?" Quinn asked.

"Yep."

That sobered Quinn and Tzader.

Evalle eased a little closer as Lanna smiled and ducked her head to meet Oskar's gaze. "Hello, Oskar. You are very special."

"Why do you say that, Lanna?" Quinn called over.

Evalle gave him a don't-screw-with-this look, but he ignored it.

Lanna said, "I feel power coming from him."

Really? Evalle hadn't picked up on that, but Lanna was special in her own way. "I thought if you petted him, you might be able to help us figure out what happened to Mattie. But turn your hand for him to sniff it first." She hoped that worked with familiars the way it did with dogs.

Lanna straightened. "I will try."

Evalle picked up Oskar and held him in her arms, facing forward. Lanna smiled again at the familiar. "Oskar, I would like to be your friend."

This girl was good.

Oskar grunted. To Evalle, it sounded happy. She could feel his excitement.

Lanna reached out slowly, showing the back of her hand.

His shaggy body wiggled with anticipation.

When Lanna's hand was an inch away, Oskar inhaled deeply and scrambled backwards. He swung around and tried to climb up Evalle's shoulder. The little guy had sharp claws.

"Ouch." She tried to pull him back down and away, but he was wailing and grunting as if something had hurt him.

Was Oskar having a panic attack?

Storm cursed, and heavy footsteps came rushing around the table. "Let me—"

"Don't!" Evalle shouted, even if it was Storm. She had to calm Oskar down, and that wouldn't happen if anyone else grabbed him.

The familiar finished crawling over her like a giant sandspur on steroids. Once he reached her neck, his front legs wrapped around each side of her like a monkey, claws still digging in.

Every spot he'd grabbed burned.

Now that a mop of gray dog hair didn't block her vision, she had a great view of a pissed-off trio—Storm, Tzader, and Quinn—all shaking with the need to do something.

"You're bleeding," Storm said, his jaw clenched tight. Tzader and Quinn were making similar noises.

Oskar clutched her neck tighter, and stuck his mouth around to snarl.

Storm growled right back at him, a noise so chilling he could have cleared an entire jungle of animals. In two seconds, he'd established himself as the alpha in the room.

Oskar quieted and pulled back behind her, whimpering. His claws curled tighter, digging deeper into her skin. Warm liquid ran on her exposed neck and upper chest.

Storm's eyes glowed bright yellow.

Red would be next.

"Not helping," Evalle told the lot of them. She slid her fingers under Oskar's paws and pried them loose, exhaling at the relief. "I'm not going to die from a couple of little claw marks so everyone just chill out."

"I am sorry, Evalle," Lanna said in a heartbreaking tone.

"It's not your fault," Evalle told her softly. "He hasn't taken to anyone but me for some reason. Everyone please back up and give me some space for a minute."

Tzader, Quinn, and Lanna moved all the way around the big conference table.

Storm took one step back. That was as much as she could expect from him.

Squatting down, Evalle lifted the stiff legs and said, "Oskar, you can get down now. I'm going to let go of you."

She released his front legs.

Using his hind legs for a little push, he dropped to the floor on all fours.

The second she stood, she called up her inner beast, the Alterant side of her that lay dormant until needed. Just a few months ago, shifting had meant turning into a powerful but hideous monster form. Now that she'd evolved all the way, she could shift into a gryphon.

Of course, she and the others like her did not have authorization to do so in this world. Just another way of handcuffing Alterants around the rest of the preternaturals in the world.

For the moment, she drew just enough power from her Alterant side to close the wounds, but not enough to call her beast all the way to the surface. Storm left the room and returned with a wet washcloth to wipe off the blood.

Oskar slinked over to his pallet, pulled his yellow witch ducky to him, and curled up. So pitiful.

Evalle frowned, trying to make sense of it. "I don't think he meant to react that way to Lanna, and I know he didn't mean to hurt me."

Storm sliced an angry look at her neck then sighed. "I know. Oskar was terrified."

"Exactly, but what would make him react that way? He clearly doesn't tolerate men, but at first it looked like he might allow Lanna to touch him."

Quinn suggested, "It appeared that he scented something about Lanna that panicked him."

Tzader grumbled under his breath and scrubbed at his bloodshot eyes. "That's a dead end for finding Mattie. What else have we got for locating the witches, Quinn?"

"Trey, Lucien, Casper, and a new guy called Emilio are searching."

"Can Emilio be trusted?"

"I think so," Quinn said with an easy confidence. "He and Sen have gotten into it a couple of times because Emilio questioned Sen's orders. I stepped in on the new guy's behalf."

Evalle snorted. "That couldn't have gone over well."

"No, but the guy had just helped us save a Belador from a troll attack. He's new and no one wants to partner with him. It's been up to me to put Emilio on cases, and he's worked alongside Beladors with no issues. He seems to be an adept chap and he's quiet, always willing to do his part. If he doesn't find a place in this region, VIPER may send him somewhere else. Emilio has a son in Canada he wants to bring here, but not until he feels his child will be safe. Sen made it clear that he can't choose agents based on rug rats. In retaliation for Emilio's questioning him in front of other agents, Sen has taken him off field assignments that pay more and has him doing errands for VIPER. That basically means Emilio has time on his hands and is knocked back to half pay. That's not what he wants when he's trying to get settled to bring his kid here."

That bastard, Sen. Evalle would like to backhand whoever moved the rock that let him crawl out and escape.

Tzader suggested, "Let's get busy with all we have to get done. Evalle and Storm can tell us what they found at Mattie's, then we'll need to work out..." His gaze jumped to Lanna. "The rest of the issues at hand."

Quinn caught the hint. "Lanna, please excuse us."

"You need me," Lanna argued.

All three overprotective men said, *"No!"*

Evalle glared at the trio. She didn't want Lanna harmed either, but they could have just said so. Storm had the good sense to look apologetic.

Lanna gave the men a classic teenage eye roll. "I know you are doing something to save Brina. If you have to go somewhere secretly, you will need to move around without being seen, yes?"

Evalle had to admit that the young woman had a valid point, and Lanna didn't even know what they were planning.

Lanna took advantage of her opening and pointed out, "I can cloak you, but I will need to be with you. Does not work from a distance."

Evalle sent a telepathic message to Quinn. *Lanna is right, but Adrianna can cloak us and has far more power—or at least she has far more control of her power. Besides, we need Adrianna's input on this mission. She should be up and about by now.*

Quinn didn't reply to Evalle, but told Lanna, "If we find ourselves in need of your skills, I will discuss it with you. For now, I would appreciate it if you'd allow us to have our meeting."

To do anything but comply would make Lanna look like a ranting teen when she wanted to be treated as an adult, which she *was* at the age of eighteen. Good luck convincing Quinn of that.

Lanna expelled a long sigh intended to let everyone know they were wasting her exceptional skills.

There was a certain truth to that, but Quinn had lost her and Kizira at the same time. Thankfully, Lanna had returned with Brina. Quinn would not bend when it came to avoiding putting her at risk again.

They all waited for Lanna to make it up to the next floor and shut her apartment door, then for Storm to confirm that she was no longer in the hall.

Evalle checked on Oskar. Poor little guy seemed to be hiding his face, so she took a place at that end of the table again. She told Storm, "I sent a message to Quinn that we do need cloaking, but Adrianna can do it. We'll have to ask her, but the way I see it, we're going to need her help for sure with breaking the curse to free the dragon."

Tzader, the only one still standing, put his mug down and kept moving around, looking too antsy to be still. "She's never been to TÅµr Medb, has she?"

"No, but do you know about Veronika and Witchlock?"

"Quinn filled me in." Tzader pinched his lips, frowning in thought. "Powerful witch from the KievRus coven in Ukraine came here to take possession of Witchlock, but when the time came Adrianna took it?"

"That pretty much sums it up. But Adrianna didn't want Witchlock. She had a twin, very powerful Sterling witch, although Adrianna was no slouch at the time. Veronika cooked her twin's majik as part of the process of taking over the power. When everything in the universe lined up just right, Witchlock descended as a tornado, and Adrianna's sister begged Adrianna to take the power. That was the only way to free her sister's spirit, because the body was gone. Adrianna did, and it's a good thing or we'd all be hunting for somewhere to hide. Veronika intended to wipe out anyone with power who wouldn't be her slave."

"Damn."

"Right." Evalle's phone rang. She pulled it out and muttered, "Speak of the devil," before answering the phone. "Funny you should call now, Adrianna. I was about to call you."

"My reason for calling is not a bit funny. I left you two messages."

Evalle thumbed her phone. Huh. Yep, two messages. "What's up?"

"I'm making a delivery. Where are you?" Adrianna snapped.

"At our new building." Evalle gave her the location. "Just press the buzzer by the garage. What are you delivering?"

"I'll be there in six minutes. I want tea. Good tea." Adrianna hung up.

"She's on the way," Evalle said. "She has something to drop off and doesn't sound happy about it."

"Finish telling us why you think Adrianna can break the curse on the dragon," Tzader said, but he had a distant look in his eyes.

Something about the Sterling witch bothered him?

Evalle replied, "I'm still not clear on everything that happened to

Adrianna when she accepted Witchlock. There's probably no way to know for sure if she can break the curse until she sees the dragon throne, but she might have some insights."

Storm interjected, "I could feel the difference in her energy when she walked up to us after it all went down." He looked over at Evalle. "She cloaked you with little more than a thought."

"Right. She'd gone to far more effort to cloak the two of us only a half hour before, and that cloaking was very limited." Evalle thought back on that day. "Here's the thing. Veronika inadvertently opened a channel to Adrianna's twin that, when everything was over, allowed Adrianna access to some of Veronika's thoughts. Adrianna found out that Veronika had more ambitious plans than anyone suspected, and that Veronika specifically wanted the dragon from TÅµr Medb."

The room went silent. Tzader's head snapped up and he stared at Evalle. "The dragon throne?"

Evalle said, "We need to ask her if she can tell whether that dragon *was* the throne dragon, and see if she's gained anything from Veronika since then."

Quinn quietly stirred his coffee. "I doubt Adrianna has picked up any telepathic noise or impressions since we locked Veronika away beneath VIPER headquarters."

"I don't know."

A buzzer sounded at the garage entrance.

Evalle jumped up. "That's got to be Adrianna."

Storm crossed the room in two strides. "It's daylight outside. Let me get it."

Evalle followed as far as the open space that would eventually be the lobby, and waited while she heard Storm speak to someone.

Boots tapped a brisk staccato from the garage, across the concrete floor through the door to the lobby.

For a short woman, Adrianna made the most of her size through meticulous choice of clothes. She'd wrapped her voluptuous body in a black denim jacket, black turtleneck, and black jeans. Blonde hair that normally fell loose around her shoulders had been pulled back, revealing a smooth oval face, smoky blue eyes, and ruby lips.

One smile from her and most men would drop to their knees to give her what she wanted.

Not Storm, though.

Evalle smiled over the thought, but she no longer had concerns around this Sterling witch.

Irritation snapped in Adrianna's gaze the minute hers met Evalle's. She stopped, arms crossed. "They're all yours now."

Evalle shook herself mentally. "Who?"

A pair of twin teenage males entered next, with Storm right behind them. Kardos and Kellman had changed in the short time they'd been away. They were close to six feet tall, their bright blond hair had darkened to a rich gold, and someone had trimmed the wavy locks. They were dangerously attractive for seventeen-year-olds.

Storm swept around the trio and, as he continued past Evalle, he slowed to whisper, "Good luck."

What was that all about? "Hi guys," she called to the boys, who both showed off their infectious grins.

Kellman had always been the quiet one she could depend on to use common sense.

Kardos, however, tested the limits of Evalle's patience at every turn.

She had the strange urge to give them a hug, but she'd only recently started accepting hugs from a very few people and was still feeling her way. These two were homeless street kids. Out of respect for their space, she squashed the idea of a public embrace.

Adrianna looked like *she* might need a hug, but Evalle would defer to someone else for that. Best to keep a reasonable distance from a witch that powerful who looked close to exploding.

"Thank you," Evalle told Adrianna. "I planned on picking them up this week." But she'd rather shove a stick in her eye than take Storm anywhere near Isak Nyght, even though Isak had recently shown an interest in Adrianna. Two months back, when the twins were at risk from Svart Trolls invading the city, Evalle had asked Isak's mom, Kit, if she'd keep them away from the trouble for a few days.

A few days had turned into weeks, then into months.

Evalle had to find a way to thank Kit for her generosity. The boys had filled out some, which meant they'd been active and had eaten on a regular basis. Before Kit, Evalle and her Nightstalker, Grady, had done their best to watch over the twins, but that wasn't the same as a stable home. Kit had been good for these two.

"You're welcome. You owe me," Adrianna said through clamped jaws.

Oh boy, now what? "I'll reimburse your gas."

"I don't want money. We'll talk about your *debt* later."

How much trouble could it have been to drive them from the Nyght facility forty-five minutes away, to downtown Atlanta? There was more to this. Adrianna enjoyed driving, and wouldn't make a big deal out of a simple favor.

Kardos leaned forward, getting close to Adrianna's ear, and spoke in a conspiratorial tone. "You never gave me your number for that date."

Adrianna ignored him, but lifted a sharp, perfectly shaped eyebrow in a see-what-I-have-to-deal-with motion.

Evalle warned Kardos, "Trust me, she's so far out of your league you'd need the Hubble telescope to figure it out."

"No woman is out of my league."

Spare me from teenage hormones.

Adrianna added, "I was at the Nyght facility when Isak asked me to drop them off before Kit decided to bring them."

Yep, she owed Adrianna.

Storm smothered a chuckle from the conference room, but it reached Evalle's ears. After seeing Adrianna roll in with fire practically spitting out of her eyes, he must be standing just inside the door to monitor everything.

Evalle glared in Storm's direction, then turned back to Kardos, going straight for the simplest fix. "Just a word of advice. I wouldn't be making passes at Adrianna and piss off Isak Nyght, if I were you."

All color leached from his face. Kardos quickly stepped back. "Had no idea."

Adrianna gave Evalle a withering look. "Really? You had to go there?"

Isak and Adrianna had hit it off like gas thrown on a hot coal, especially when he'd stepped between Adrianna and danger.

Evalle found this new development highly amusing, mainly because Adrianna did not. Evalle suggested, "Why don't you go into the conference room and I'll be there in a few minutes?"

Adrianna said, "Fine. You better have tea."

Storm stepped into the hallway. "We do. It's over here." He led Adrianna in to meet the others.

"How was life with Kit?" she asked the twins.

As if a switch had been thrown, both boys started talking at once.

Kellman jumped in first. "Kit was very nice to us, but I'm glad to be back. We missed Atlanta ... and you. How's Grady?"

"He's good. He asks about you two all the time. I told him you'd return soon."

Kardos tried to sound imposed upon. "Tell her the truth. We were in the country. Like with cows and things. It was crazy. I can't do that again."

Giving his brother a weary sigh, Kellman said, "You were all happy when you found out how hot the girls are in the country."

"Until Kit told me she'd ..." Kardos shut his mouth.

Storm came back to the hall just then and asked, "She told you what?"

The calm, down-to-earth brother answered, "That if Kardos laid a hand on that young woman, Kit would peel his skin from his body and make him watch as she fed it to the wild animals on her property."

Kardos turned a deep shade of humiliated red. "She's scary."

Evalle had to agree about Kit, who would fit right in with Navy SEALs, all five foot two of her. Given a choice between crossing Adrianna or Kit, who was only human, Evalle would choose Adrianna. But she wasn't about to admit that to Kardos, who would eventually bring it up at the worst time.

She told the twins, "You can't go back on the streets, guys."

Both boys froze, and Evalle knew it was from the implication that local authorities were getting involved.

Kardos gave her a wary look. "You're not going to try to send us somewhere, are you?"

"Of course not."

"Because we're both eighteen now," Kardos added.

"Really? When was it?"

"It's two different days." Poking his thumb at himself, Kardos said, "Mine is December 21st and his is December 22nd."

A Sagittarius and a Capricorn. Evalle was not up on zodiac signs, but that helped explain the huge difference in their personalities. Of course, that was based on the astrology she gleaned from the newspaper each week, which everyone knew was *soooo* accurate. Just as dependable as what she found on the Internet.

"Kit had a birthday party for us," Kellman mentioned. "It was ... nice."

Evalle bet it was amazing since they'd avoided discussing their birth dates in the past, and for all the time she'd known them they'd never had any semblance of family.

Storm tilted his head toward the conference room, reminding her of the waiting group.

They had to get to the meeting.

She pushed the topic back to discussing a place for them to live. "Here's what I had in mind. I'm going to be living here, so I was thinking maybe Quinn could work something out with you two for my old place."

"Underground?" Kardos asked, sounding appalled.

"Yes. It's a nice place." Her old apartment was nothing like where she lived now, but way better than the streets where these two had spent years.

Kellman's face registered concern when he glanced at his brother. "We know you're making us a great offer, but Kardos has—"

Kardos cut in. "Shut up."

His brother turned to him. "Evalle is not going to tell anyone." They both looked at Storm, who said, "I won't share your secret either, and everyone in the conference room is on their phones."

Kardos looked ready to slink away.

His brother said, "I think Kardos has taphephobia."

Taph-huh? Evalle asked, "What's that?"

"Fear of being buried alive, which doesn't exactly fit fear of living underground, but it's the closest I could figure out."

Crap. Now what was she going to do with them?

Storm cleared his throat, catching her attention. He said, "We have a two-bedroom apartment available here."

Looking embarrassed, Kardos put a hand on his brother's chest. He clearly didn't want anyone speaking for him. When he did reply to Storm, Kardos sounded more mature than when he'd left. "Thanks, but we don't have any money, and we're not going to mooch off of you and Evalle."

Evalle held her thoughts, allowing Storm to say what was on his mind.

Storm hooked his hands on his hips. "No mooching involved. Everyone here pulls his or her weight. We'll need someone on hand to do odd jobs and to help when we start showing the offices down here, then managing them. You two could share that position in trade for the apartment, plus we'll pay a stipend for food and such."

The twins looked at Storm as if they'd just learned they had a fairy godfather. "Really?" they chorused.

Evalle's heart squeezed at the longing in their voices. It was times like this that she couldn't believe how fortunate she was to have found Storm. Or more like he'd found her.

Storm nodded at the twins. "Yes, but it means respecting the agreement. As you pointed out, you're both adults. You're old enough to make your own decisions. I'll treat you like the men I believe you can be, and you'll give us the same respect in return."

With that one short speech, Storm had put them on notice that they were in charge of their destinies and screwing up came with a price.

Dual nods followed.

"The apartment has basic furnishings. When the decorator returns to finish other work, you can give her a list of anything additional you need. Everything we buy for the apartment belongs to the apartment. Your apartment is 2B. All floors above that are off limits unless one of us invites you up. No one unauthorized is allowed in this building at any time."

Evalle smiled. These two boys had to love knowing they wouldn't be attacked by someone trying to steal their bedding in the middle of the night.

"Holy sh—"

Kellman elbowed Kardos in the ribs. "You'd better not let Kit hear you."

"She's not here." Kardos rubbed his ribs.

"We just made a deal based on acting like adults. So act like one."

Kardos said, "Okay, okay. I agree, but ... race you to the apartment!" He shot up the stairs.

Kellman hesitated, looking at the stairs then at Evalle.

She said, "Go and keep him under control."

"Yes, ma'am." He dashed away.

"Ma'am?" Evalle looked at Storm, who found that funny.

When they returned to the conference room, Quinn furiously thumbed keys on his phone. Adrianna swished her finger over hers, scrolling something, and Tzader paced across the end of the room opposite Oskar's bed.

Quinn shoved his phone in his inside jacket pocket. "Were those the twins I heard?"

"Yes." Evalle refilled her coffee mug. "Storm has hired them."

Tzader stopped walking. Quinn said, "Considerate of you, Storm."

"It was that, or watch Evalle race around trying to keep them out of trouble. This way they'll have something to do in exchange for room and board."

"A fine arrangement." Quinn sat down, paused, then shot right back up. "Are they staying on the same floor as Lanna?"

"Yes."

"No."

Evalle could not deal with one more drama. "Quinn, she's an adult and—"

"Doesn't matter. She's not safe."

Adrianna stopped scrolling and spoke with impatience that hadn't abated. "Is this the Lanna who saved the boys and others when she used her majik to fight Svart Trolls? Wait, no. Let me just go ahead and answer that. Yes, it is, which means she's got a load of power, far more than those two hellions put together. You should be more worried about the boys. If either of them steps out of line, she's liable to roast them."

Oh boy. Adrianna was in some kind of mood.

Evalle knew that look on Quinn's face. She'd seen it often on Storm's when he had to stay out of her way and let her handle her own battles. Evalle added, "On top of that, Quinn, they're good boys. You can't stop Lanna from growing up."

Tzader said, "Are we ready to get moving or not?"

Quinn sat, then Evalle took her place at the end of the table near Oskar again, but she doubted anyone would try to invade his space. Storm sat between her and the witch.

Adrianna put her phone down and lifted her tea, looking past Evalle to the corner. "Is that the familiar?"

"Yes." Evalle told her what had happened with Lanna and asked, "Think you can touch it and find Mattie?"

"No. I heard what happened earlier. Sounds like he is not fond of men, and he's already given me the evil eye, which leaves you as sole caretaker."

Tzader still hadn't stopped moving. He stood at the end. "We need to clue Adrianna in. I'll let Evalle do it."

Good thing. He needed to sit before he crashed.

Evalle stood, pointed at a seat, and told Tzader, "Sit. I have the floor."

He didn't want to, but he pulled the chair out and plopped down.

"We have a couple situations," Evalle began. She outlined the missing witches, then went on to explain Ceartas and what was happening in Treoir. "To sum it up, Tzader has been banished from the realm. Macha expects me to walk away from my life, regardless of my being mated. In fact, she's made it clear I don't have her approval, and gaining it no longer matters to me. We've made our decision to go after the dragon throne, but we need help."

Adrianna put her mug down softly. "I'm listening."

"The dream walker representing the dragon claims that the Medb are currently sending in a highly skilled force disguised as nothing more than resident witches and warlocks. It's called Scáth Force. He says the former queen, Flaevynn, was nothing compared to Queen Maeve, which is a scary thought since Flaevynn came close to gaining Treoir Island. If she had, there would be no Belador force to protect this world."

With his elbows propped on the table, Tzader had been using one hand to support his head. He lifted his head and began filling in more details. "I'm starting to think there's a lot we haven't been told by Macha. Either way, that's a different issue. I don't want anyone involved besides me, but these hardheads refuse to stay out of it. I don't want to ask you to get involved and put you in danger if we end up surrounded by an army of warlocks and witches."

Adrianna's half smile finally showed up. She evidently found that amusing.

Tzader paused at her reaction then continued, "However, based on what Evalle told me, Queen Maeve might be the only real threat to you, and we won't leave until Quinn has Queen Maeve and Cathbad in a Tribunal meeting. The truth is that we need your help for several things, but you need to know the stakes up front, and now is the time to say no if you don't want to be involved."

Adrianna considered her tea for a long, silent moment. Lifting her head, she took in everyone with one studied glance. "I was going to contact Rowan next after dropping off the boys, but clearly she's busy. I've been attending council meetings."

That was news to Evalle. "I know Rowan's glad, but why are you getting involved with white witch politics?"

"I'm having dreams about battles with nonhumans."

Evalle snorted. "That's business as usual in our world."

Adrianna didn't crack even her half smile. Placing her hands on the table, she said. "I'm talking intense battles. War. One that we won't keep from the humans if it breaks out."

"Who, precisely, is in this war?" Quinn asked.

"I don't know exactly," Adrianna admitted. "I'm not sure of all the players on the field yet. That's the main reason I'm going to these damn council meetings. I wanted to get to know Rowan and some of the elders better. If things had worked out today, I was going to mention my dreams and see if anyone knows something they haven't been sharing with those outside of the white covens."

Storm asked the witch, "Do these dreams have any sort of time marker?"

"No. My sister had visions while awake, but my visions always come through dreams. Or they did in the past, and I'm not sure if that's going to change at any point. I'm sure you will understand when I say the clearest of visions is often vague at best when it comes to pinpointing a timeline and specifics."

"You're right." Storm sat back, waiting with the rest of them to find out where Adrianna was going with this.

She asked Tzader, "Do you have any idea what color this dragon is?"

"I'm guessing he's red, since the scale the dream walker gave me turns red when the light hits it a certain way."

"I see," Adrianna said, with the precision of taking each word and shaping it before she gave it life. "The dreams were disturbing before, but learning what I have just now about Tzader's experience, I'm wondering if my dreams and his quest are connected." She paused, as if gathering her thoughts. "In my dreams, a giant red dragon threatens to kill everyone in his path. He flies like a jet fighter, blowing fire across everything. Are you *sure* you want to free this one?"

CHAPTER 21

Tzader had been fighting exhaustion until Adrianna shared that she'd dreamed of a dragon threatening to kill everyone.

A red freaking dragon.

He sat up sharply, taking in Quinn, Evalle, and Storm's shocked expressions, then asked Adrianna, "Are you sure it's the same dragon I'm talking about? The one I'm after was cursed to be Queen Maeve's throne."

Adrianna gave a small shake of her head. "No. I have no idea if it is or isn't the same one. I'm just saying the timing of my dreams and your dream walking experience leads me to believe they could be connected."

Evalle tapped her finger. "Could the dreams be somehow connected to Veronika?"

"I don't know." Adrianna's forehead crinkled at a silent thought. "The only way I could say for sure is by being in the same room with her. That might help me determine who the dragon is or belongs to, because after I took possession of Witchlock, I lifted a thought from Veronika about her wanting a dragon from TÅµr Medb."

"I told them," Evalle said. "But you never figured out exactly what Veronika thought to do with the dragon."

"No." Cocking her head at Tzader, Adrianna asked, "You'll need cloaking, correct?"

Tzader answered, "Yes."

"What else?"

"We either have to break the curse on the dragon to free his form there, or bring him back and do it here. Evalle believes you're our best chance at breaking it."

She stared at the table for a moment, then said, "Depending on where he was cursed and how he was cursed, you may kill him if you try to teleport him across realms as a throne." She had more to say, but was not in a rush. "I may or may not be able to break his curse. I would say absolutely not if I didn't have Witchlock, but since I do, and it's very old, there's a chance. It depends on what the dragon recalls about the curse placed upon him."

Tzader pushed up to pace again. The longer he sat, the more his body felt like it was turning to lead and wanted to lie down. "I think he'll know the curse word for word, based on what the dream walker said about the dragon being the only one who knew the exact Noirre spell used on Brina."

Evalle interjected, "I know this screws us, but knowing what we do about our enemy, Queen Maeve would love to get her hands on Witchlock, which we can't allow to happen."

"True," Tzader agreed, then eyed the witch. "You really shouldn't go with us. I can't stop Storm, because Evalle's determined to do this. Maybe you can tell Storm how to break it."

Adrianna shifted her attention to Storm, her silence questioning his thoughts on Tzader's suggestion.

Storm snorted. "I've got witch blood in me, but compared to Adrianna it's a drop in the ocean. I'm a more powerful demon than I am a witch."

Evalle made a noise of irritation.

Storm covered her hand. "They all know it's true, sweetheart."

Drawing herself up, Adrianna said, "Thank you, Storm, for not making me toot my own horn, but you're right." She shifted her attention to the others. "I'm not sure I can break the curse, but we have no other witches with my power now, and in particular, none with a dark witch pedigree."

Tzader admired the way Adrianna stated facts without stroking her own ego. She was simply putting all the information on the table.

The witch glanced around the room, taking in all four faces. "Here's my proposal. I will help you. You say you have a plan to pull Queen Maeve and Cathbad from their tower while we go in, correct?"

"Yes, we do," Quinn confirmed. "But why make yourself a target for the Medb?"

"Are you questioning if she's sincere, Quinn?" Evalle said with a slap of censure.

"No. I understand the motivation for everyone else in this room. I want to know hers."

That's fine, Evalle." Adrianna smothered a chuckle that held no mirth. "It's not a matter of if, but *when* Maeve comes hunting for me. I'm a threat to her power. I have no desire to hide in a hole for the rest of my life. I'll look for your support in return when I have to go up against her. I've been the target of every dark coven in existence from the moment I was born. That's why my sister was sacrificed. If they'd realized that we had nearly the same level of power, they'd have traded me just as quickly. If freeing that dragon will aid the Beladors, then it's in my best interest to join with you. You may not agree, but I believe VIPER is showing signs of imploding. Sen has never been dedicated to the coalition. He doesn't care if any of us survive." She asked Evalle, "Has the Tribunal voted on the Alterant-gryphon right to be a free race?"

"No."

"If they haven't yet, I doubt that they will." Adrianna had started this thread of conversation, and continued, "I've heard rumblings about the Tribunals becoming more difficult to organize. If there's a power play, I don't see those deities sticking together. If they do, it won't be in our best interests. They can barely manage to pass judgment lately without attacking each other."

Quinn washed a hand over his face. "I will admit I've begun to wonder if the Tribunal is fracturing as well." He let his hand slip down. He'd pulled himself together for the sake of his responsibilities, and yeah, he'd cracked a joke or two. But his eyes had a hollow look that hadn't left him since Kizira died. He asked Adrianna, "Your dreams showed the humans exposed to our world? To us?"

Nodding, she said, "I second what Tzader's dream walker said, but I'd put it more bluntly. A war is coming. I'm not sure what exactly is going to happen, but I'll have to choose a side. I'll never be allowed to live in peace. There's strength in numbers. If I stay here when you go for the dragon, and you fail to free him, then he may escape later to kill all the Beladors for letting him down. If I help you free him, I can only hope he'll make good on the vow the dream walker gave Tzader, claiming to protect those who come to his aid.

Adrianna paused, taking in the room. "Until Evalle and Storm stepped in to help me with my sister, I'd fought alone for a long time. I honestly think we're all facing the end of life as we know it if we stand back and do nothing. After I took possession of Witchlock, I believed we were safe, but that's not the case."

Storm quipped, "We're only as safe as we are strong."

"True," Adrianna said, then looked to Quinn. "I'll need access to Veronika to see if being near her firms up any of my visions, and to trick her into telling me what she knows about the dragon."

Quinn leaned back, arms crossed. "Tzader can't get you in without being reinstated as Maistir—"

"Which Macha is not going to do at this point," Tzader said. "In fact, I have concerns about how long she'll allow Quinn to continue, because of his association with me."

"Especially when I don't deliver Evalle so that Sen can ship her to Macha," Quinn added.

"That's not happening," Storm muttered.

"Understood." Quinn's grim turned a shade darker. "I can escort Adrianna to Veronika's cell. I'll tell VIPER that she is consulting with us about contracts we believe Veronika left in place to attack the Medb. Sen's on their side these days." He cut his eyes at Storm. "That won't be a problem as long as you're not there to call out the lie."

"I'll be here with Evalle making preparations. If I'm called in, I'll find a way to be delayed without raising suspicion."

When Quinn nodded in agreement, Tzader pushed on. "Okay. We have cloaking, and hopefully a way to break the curse. We'll need teleportation." He caught an exchange of looks between Evalle and Storm.

"Let's come up with a list," Quinn suggested.

Tzader counted the fingers on one hand. "Sen—"

A chorus of "No!" followed.

Tzader shot a censuring look across the room. "I know that. I'm just naming everyone I know who teleports." Then he said, "Deek."

Evalle said, "No. I owe him a favor as it is, and he can't be trusted with sensitive information."

Storm sat forward and Tzader saw Evalle give him a let's-discuss-this-later glance as she continued talking.

"If we get lucky, we'll get in and out without Queen Maeve knowing who stole her dragon."

Tzader nodded, "Now for teleporting. Didn't you say you had someone, Evalle?"

Evalle fidgeted. "Yes."

"Who?"

When she hesitated, Tzader pressed, "Is it someone hostile?"

"No, but this person's identity needs to be protected."

Tzader was not splitting hairs at this point. "Done. What have you got?"

"Tristan might be able to teleport a group."

Disbelief pinched Quinn's face. "He can teleport from this realm to another one?"

"Yes. He linked with others, and it boosted his power."

"What makes you think he can teleport an entire group, even if we can get him out of Treoir?" Tzader asked.

"Because Tristan already has and he's ... here now. I saw him earlier this morning."

Macha would go ballistic the minute she found out, but that was nothing compared to how she'd react to Beladors breaking into TÅµr Medb to commit theft.

This was not the time to nitpick or vacillate. Tzader said, "Let's do this."

Adrianna stood. "I'm ready to go to Veronika when you are, Quinn."

Quinn carried his mug to the side bar and asked, "Do we have a tentative time for this mission to go wheels up?"

Tzader considered that and what everyone had to do. "The power of the scale to hold Brina's memories lasts only twenty-four hours. After that ... she may have no way to recall anything, if the dream walker is right about the timeline and the Noirre finishes what it started. The scale will be of no use by ten tonight. I'd like to go there, get the dragon, and return by nine at the latest. The insertion team will meet back here at six."

Quinn said, "If you want to leave by then, I'll need to start now to put things in motion for a Tribunal meeting with Queen Maeve and Cathbad. We'll coordinate the timing. I'll have Adrianna returned here in time, even if I have to call in a driver to transport her."

"That works," Tzader acknowledged.

Storm called out, "Quinn, give me a minute to check on something upstairs, and I'll clear the alarm for the garage door."

"Will do."

Evalle flashed Storm a quick smile. "Want to be my driver?"

"Where to?"

"Pick up Tristan. I had to give him a ride this morning."

"I assume that's why I smelled him in the truck."

She kissed his cheek. "Thanks for not yelling about that."

Storm said nothing, just taking in a deep breath and letting it out. "Let's pick him up. It'll give me a chance to make sure he understands the ground rules going in."

"We need him, Storm."

"And he needs both of his legs. There should be no problem reaching an agreement."

Evalle rolled her eyes. Clearly ignoring her mate's overprotectiveness, she told Tzader, "Storm has this building warded so everyone staying here is safe, but since you really can't do anything right now, would you hang around and keep an eye on the place?"

"Sure, but what are you going to do with that critter?" Tzader nodded toward Oskar.

Storm said, "We have a place for him."

Evalle didn't look as confident, but she pretended to know what Storm meant and told Tzader, "You really need some rest, Z."

"I'll use this down time to rest." He needed more than the brief nap he'd gotten at home, but he'd worry about sleep once Brina was safe.

Tzader brought up one last thing. "We can link with Tristan, but he'll have to teleport two non-Beladors one way, and three coming back."

"Oh. I hadn't thought about that. Let me talk to Tristan." She picked up Oskar and left.

He hated to hear the doubt in Evalle's voice, and if Tristan couldn't teleport them, Tzader needed a plan B.

Let me think. There is no Plan B.

Once Evalle wrote Deek off as a security risk, even that avenue was off the table.

Tzader jerked awake when Evalle and Storm walked right back into the room. He glanced at the giant clock on the far wall. Actually they *hadn't* come right back. He'd lost ten minutes to nodding off.

"You want to stretch out in one of the apartments upstairs, Z?" She walked over to stand next to him. "You have to sleep. We can't do this without you at a hundred percent."

"I'm good down here." If he let his body fall into something soft, he might not be able to force it back into motion again. "What'd you do with the beast?"

"His *name* is Oskar," Evalle chided. "Storm had the idea to put him in with Feenix, which I thought was nuts, but it seems to work. Storm made a shielding spell that allows Oskar to stay in one corner of Feenix's playroom. My little gargoyle flew over, took a look, and went back to what he was doing."

Adrianna shouted from the garage, "While I'm still young, Evalle!"

"Crabby witch." Evalle and Storm hurried out.

Tzader dropped his head back against the chair, feeling every minute of stress he'd been enduring for months. He considered their plan, and Evalle was right. There was nothing he could do but wait, and damn he hated to sit still.

He shoved his feet up on the next chair, then swiped his finger in the general direction of the light switch. The room fell dark.

He dropped off into sleep and slid deeper with each slow breath. Darkness seeped into his mind, shutting out the flash of thoughts that had battered him constantly. His body gave up the fight to keep moving and every muscle eased until it was limp.

For just a moment, he had nothing to do. Nothing worry would fix.

"Tzader!"

The harsh whisper brought him awake. Brina's hologram leaned forward. She huddled, as if hiding somewhere. "I have to talk to you. Now. We have a problem. Meet me in the clearing."

She blinked out of sight.

Slamming his eyes closed, he breathed in and out slowly, pushing himself into deep sleep. It was taking too long. He had to calm down, but how could he do that after seeing Brina in a panic? He stopped thinking about going after the dragon, about Macha, about anything else except seeing Brina. His muscles loosened and he was falling deeper when someone touched him.

Could Brina be pulling him to her? She'd never done that. He focused on reaching the dream world.

Invisible hands gripped him hard, dragging him from deep subconscious to ...

He opened his eyes. No sword flew at his head. Nobody reached for him.

Soft clouds floated overhead through bright blue skies. He sat up and looked around. This was the clearing, the location where he and Brina had always rendezvoused.

He pushed up and looked around at the landscape that went on forever. Where was she?

"She's not here."

Tzader jumped up, and swung around to find Ceartas standing where he'd heard no one a moment ago. "Where is she? She just told me she was coming to meet me here. She had something to tell me."

Ceartas shook his head. "That's unfortunate."

"What the hell do you mean?"

"I've been watching for Brina since you left. She would normally have slept twice since then, but she hasn't returned. Macha must have decided to put a stop to Brina meeting with you in the dream world. Once you free the dragon, he can call Brina to him, even from a different realm as long as Brina holds his scale. Get to the dragon before Macha finds that scale and hides Brina from all of us."

Tzader felt sick at the dream walker's grim tone. Whether it was fair or not, he lashed out at Ceartas. "It would have been good to know that about the damn scale."

"Now you know," Ceartas said.

Tzader was too tired to banter with this dickhead. "Since you're Mr. Information, any chance of Queen Maeve and Cathbad leaving TÅµr Medb soon, or does that dragon have any idea on how to get them out of the tower?"

"The queen is curious about a witch who possesses a power called Witchlock. She and Cathbad ... " Ceartas was yanked back a step, then his body literally looked as if it were being pulled like taffy. He squeezed out,

"I have to go."

He vanished as the last word reached Tzader's ears.

CHAPTER 22

Grendal dismissed his tikbalang. It could once again turn invisible, now that Grendal had repaired its injuries. The hairy gray beast plodded out the side door of the empty building Grendal had warded to use as his temporary headquarters.

Making those two creatures had drained too much of his powers.

That blasted Skinwalker and his Alterant mate almost destroyed this tikbalang, but the stupid beast should not have allowed himself to be detected. Grendal walked through the musty corridor and down the stairs to the basement level.

Queen Maeve and Cathbad underestimated him.

The arrogant queen had sent her people to search for Lanna, but she'd also sent a team out to hunt for him. Did she think he hadn't considered that possibility? Didn't she realize he'd developed a network of snitches during the months he'd spent in this miserable country?

He missed the tranquility of Transylvania.

Yes, he had to keep an eye on that pair in Tảµr Medb. The Scáth Force would capture Lanna, and then Queen Maeve would try to keep the girl. She'd also try to capture *him*, but she would fail at both.

He stepped off the stairs into the musty basement where five witches were tied to elevated tables he'd had built just for them.

Not all witches. One civilian.

Those four white witches had been *so* secure in their power.

Until someone unexpected showed up.

Much like how Queen Maeve and Cathbad would soon lose their

arrogance when they realized they could not outmaneuver Grendal.

His servant stood against the wall on his right, where she had a clear view to guard all five tables.

He called out, "Leeshen."

She turned to him. "Yes, Master?"

No emotion tainted the eyes outlined in thick kohl, so stark in her simple face. Russet-colored skin shone along her bare arms, showing off the carved definition these American bodybuilders wished to achieve. Grendal considered Leeshen's musculature one of his finest masterpieces. He took full credit. After all, she'd been only a witch before he'd recreated her.

Lambskin crisscrossed her breasts. She wore shorts of the same soft skin. Silky lavender hair cut even with her chin swished on one side of her otherwise bald head.

Her dark-purple lips parted when she addressed him. "Master."

Someone on the far end of the room groaned.

Leeshen's head swiveled toward the sound. She walked over and lifted a two-inch purple fingernail that was tipped in pure gold and filed to a point. She pierced the captive in the side of her neck.

The witch arched up, keening and shaking, then fell to the table.

Once the prisoner was silent again, Leeshen turned back to Grendal. She never annoyed him with endless questions, always waiting for instruction. She didn't complain about cold or discomfort. He'd stripped away the desire for anything but pleasing him.

"Very good," Grendal said. "You may rest."

She dipped her head in acceptance of his glowing praise. Then she went to the corner and crouched.

He didn't understand why others with his power criticized his creations. Of course, they did so only once, then he'd send Leeshen after them.

Stepping over to the second table, he smiled down at Mattie. "Wake up. It's time for your next treatment."

She blinked, her wrinkled eyelids slow to open. When they did, she struggled to focus. "What is ...?"

Grendal slapped her papery cheek.

Her head snapped sideways hard from the hit. She licked her lips where blood trickled.

Once she appeared cognizant, he reverted to speaking in the calm voice he used to manage the mentally challenged. "Pay attention, Mattie."

The witch's rheumy eyes sharpened. "What do you want, you son of a whore?"

"Let's not pull my dear mother into this. She died in that whorehouse, after all."

Mattie blinked, and her eyes flared slightly either at his lack of reaction or his admission. She licked her cracked lips again. "Who are you? What do you want?"

"That is more like it. My name is of no consequence for someone in your position. I wish to have a conversation. It will save time if you know what is expected of you."

"I won't help your kind."

"You only think you won't. I require a constant source of energy to keep my power level high and to maintain a healthy body."

Her eyebrows climbed toward her frizzy gray hair at that.

"You've met Leeshen."

"The one that looks like a demon left out too long in the sun? Yes, I met her, it, whatever."

Leeshen could hear everything from her position in the corner, but showed no reaction to the insult.

Grendal smiled again at her metamorphosis. Leeshen had been a powerful witch. She'd proven a solid energy source as he'd transformed her, but now he required a more powerful subject to work on. He'd had a perfect power source until that miserable child had destroyed a section of his castle and escaped. Lanna would not get a second chance.

Returning to Mattie, Grendal stroked her gray hair. She pulled away as far as her arm restraints would allow. "Power must be given willingly, Mattie. I want a willing participant, someone worthy of the metamorphosis that takes place. I can take the power, but that often drains me and influences the transfer."

"You're out of your mind. I won't give you anything, even if it means I never leave here alive. I've lived my life in the light, and will not support the dark side in any way."

He continued petting her, speaking as if he hadn't heard a word she'd said. "There is, of course, a ritual involved, and it takes hours for the spell to mature to the point of transfer. Once the host is compliant, I must be physically connected to the host when I draw on the majik, and feed on her blood as she receives my power through her. It's a complete cycle. It generally takes five sessions for the host, a witch, to completely morph into a version similar to Leeshen."

Mattie's mouth fell open. She trembled in horror. When she could speak, she said, "What kind of animal are you to rape me for my power?"

"What?" He straightened away from her. "No, no, no. I have no intention of drawing the power from you. You're too far past your prime and too combative. I need young flesh for this. I had an alternate plan for locating the one I prefer, but someone is interfering. I'll need your help calling the other young woman to me."

"I won't do it."

"I believe you will."

"Call in some innocent girl to be raped and turned into something like that monster you call Leeshen? Go ahead and kill me. Won't happen."

"I've already given a succulent young thing of twenty-six, who hides her witch blood, a workout. While she put up a rigorous fight that entertained me to no end, she isn't as powerful as my first choice, or as you. You'll understand why I found that odd when you look to your left."

Finally, Mattie's vulnerability rose to the surface. She turned her head slowly.

He mentally counted down. Three, two, one...

"*Nooooo*," she screamed. "*No, no, no* ..." Her wails turned into sobs as she stared at the bloody fingers of the naked woman stretched out on the next table. That half-alive woman stared back at Mattie with empty eyes, her face a mottle of bruises. But not so many splotches of blue-green that Mattie wouldn't recognize the only grandchild to inherit her gift.

"I'll take your reaction to mean you will wholeheartedly help me locate Lanna Brasko."

He'd probably have to repeat himself later once Mattie became coherent again. This had turned out far better than he'd originally planned when he'd captured her to trade with the Medb.

Her granddaughter did possess an exceptional amount of energy, but Lanna was superb. Comparing this young woman to Lanna was like holding up a candle to outshine the sun.

CHAPTER 23

Evalle headed to the garage of their building while Storm ran upstairs to check in one last time on Oskar and Feenix, and to inform all three teens to stay in their apartments until someone came for them.

They had food, Internet, and television.

Where she would've simply asked them to stay in, Storm politely made it clear that leaving the building was not an option.

Quinn had excused himself and stepped away to make a call, leaving Evalle with Adrianna, who asked, "What are you going to do if no one ever holds a vote on the gryphon race petition?"

"Your guess is as good as mine," Evalle quipped. "Macha isn't helping. I can't keep telling the other gryphons that it's going to be soon, when soon has come and gone. In fact, once we get the dragon out of TÅµr Medb, I'm thinking about helping Tristan teleport the gryphons out. They were offered the chance to leave, but it was a double-edged blade. Leaving back then meant it would be reported to VIPER, which is a hotline to Queen Maeve these days."

"Doesn't sound good."

"No. The situation has to be bad for me, Tzader, and Quinn to break into Queen Maeve's domain to steal her throne without Macha's consent and support. Just because we see it as honorable doesn't mean she will, especially if a war breaks out from this. Once I do that, I might as well go free the other gryphons. No point in going halfway. The penalty for crossing Macha is the same."

"What will Macha do?"

"I'm past the point of speculating, and making this up as I go, but Storm has made it clear that we have options. I may have to consider those options."

Adrianna whispered, "What do you really think Macha is going to do when she finds out you've crossed her? If you bring back Brina's memories, do you think she'll let you just walk away?"

"No. But she needs Treoir and she needs the Beladors to follow her. The way I understand it, gods and goddesses grow in power the more followers they have who believe in them. In her right mind, Brina will stand behind Tzader, and Macha cannot harm Brina because Brina is the power behind the Beladors. If she destroys the Beladors, she says goodbye to her support group. We have the largest force of warriors in the world, which means she currently has the largest base of support. Tzader would risk all for Brina, but he'd never put the entire Belador clan at risk for personal gain. The thing is that Tzader's goal will also end up supporting Macha's power base because, apparently, the dragon demands that Brina be saved. That dragon seems to know a lot about Macha and Queen Maeve. I can't fence-sit. I'm going to believe in Tzader."

Adrianna ran a hand over her hair and down her ponytail. "With the dreams I've been having, either this dragon is going to lead all of you to victory, which keeps my world safe, too, or we're all going to be fighting one hell of a threat. I could feel his power in my dreams. It shook me. Even with my possessing Witchlock, the idea of his turning that on me was terrifying."

"If war did break out in the supernatural world, where do you think Sen would stand?"

Adrianna lifted a shoulder. "No clue. VIPER isn't going to be able to control the situation, and you know as well as I do that the deities are going to cover their own asses. At that point, all humans would be at risk."

That sent Evalle's next thought to Isak. He'd be in the middle of it all. The Nyght armory designed weapons specifically to take down preternaturals.

Quinn finished his call and headed for his car, parked in the last position in a garage fit for ten vehicles.

Plus one GSXR motorcycle.

Evalle had a hint of tease in her voice when she asked Adrianna,

"Speaking of favorite humans, how's Isak?"

"I know that tone of voice. Don't play matchmaker. You're out of *your* league with that. Let's just say I haven't unleashed a spell on him, but he's stepping dangerously close to finding out what I can do."

"What happened?"

"I ignored him for a week and he sent a black ops team to put me in a van and bring me to him."

Evalle started chuckling.

Adrianna didn't look impressed by Isak's dating techniques. Yep, Evalle had been there, done that, gotten an Italian dinner out of the deal. "How'd it go?"

Adrianna managed a sly smile. "I turned the wheels on his van into stone. He's probably still chiseling those off."

Why couldn't I have done something like that? "I would have liked to see that."

"It was funny, but I wish *he* had to do the chiseling instead of his men."

Quinn called to Adrianna, who nodded and started his way.

Evalle fell into step with her. "Wait until you meet Kit."

"Not happening. Isak and I do not mesh."

From where Evalle stood, those two seemed perfect. Adrianna had the kind of experience—and the witch juice—a woman needed for dealing with a hardheaded alpha. While Isak did respect the word no, he was stubborn once he set his sights on a target.

Right now, he had his romantic crosshairs set on one deadly little witch.

Evalle waved them off and headed for the office to activate the garage door from a remote control panel Storm had put there so she wouldn't catch an accidental shaft of sunlight through the big overhead door while using the controls in the garage.

Storm met her at the base of the stairs. "Everyone is set. I have the boys' computer linked to the flat screen with controllers, and signed them into an account for downloading games. I gave Lanna a laptop and showed her how to work her flat screen. In a little while, she's going to bring Feenix to her room to keep him entertained. There's food in both apartments. Oskar is snoozing, and I told Feenix you had a surprise for him when we get back."

"Hold it." Evalle held up her hands. "Unless you've been holding back on what you can poof into existence with that witch juice you say is a drop in the ocean, exactly how is it that the boys are all set up out of thin air?"

He took his time answering. The other side of Storm's being a walking lie detector was that he suffered pain if *he* outright lied. He had double-talk down to an art when he needed it, but that wouldn't fly right now and he knew it.

She crossed her arms, waiting.

He grumbled something. "I knew you weren't going to be happy with the boys on the street and figured you'd try to set them up in your old place. Quinn told me in passing that as soon as you were finished with your old apartment and we got moved in here, he's remodeling your entire building, including your downstairs place."

Huh. Evalle hadn't known that, but she wasn't surprised that Quinn wanted to update the old building.

Storm continued. "It was only a matter of time before the twins ended up here. Planning for it saved all of us headaches and simplified it for the boys. I didn't know Lanna would be here, but she's welcome for as long as she wants to stay."

"Quinn will take care of her rent."

"He's already offered, and the answer is no. Where else can we get an occasional babysitter for Feenix who'd love him as much as Lanna does? That's priceless. I have all the apartments stocked with basics in the cabinets and refrigerators. Those three will be happy with pizzas and cold drinks."

Storm hadn't discussed any of that with her in advance, but she was honest enough with herself to admit that she would have argued about his going to the trouble and expense. Instead, she gave him what he deserved.

"Thank you, but I don't want you to take on everyone else's burdens."

"I'm not. Having your friends be okay makes you okay, and that makes me okay. Anything that matters to you is not a burden."

Every day she got a little better about accepting the life she hoped to live with him. "Should we do something else with Oskar if Lanna is going in there?"

"No. She won't go near him, and he can't escape where I have him."

Placing her hand against his cheek, she said, "Thank you for doing all that. I'm going to have to make it up to you later." She winked at him.

He grinned. "I am so holding you to a private thank-you session."

"We have to go get Tristan." She headed for the garage and Storm's truck, which was warded against the sun for daytime use.

She could feel how the mention of Tristan had instantly soured Storm's good mood.

He asked, "Why don't you just call Tristan telepathically?"

"He doesn't have to listen to me, and I don't want to risk him taking off. It's always better to deal with him in person and—"

Evalle! Tristan's voice shouted in her head.

She held up a finger, and pointed at her head to let Storm know she was engaged in telepathy. *Tristan, what's up?*

You said to let you know when I was teleporting back. I'm ready to go.

Shoot! *Don't do that, Tristan.*

Why not? Suspicion came through his telepathic voice.

I've got an offer you can't refuse. She hadn't expected the silence that followed to stretch so long. *Tristan?*

Does this have anything to do with the Beladors?

She hedged. *Sort of.*

Be specific.

Tzader, Quinn, Storm and I need your help.

The only thing that comes to mind is teleporting, and I'm not blowing my ride back to Treoir on you four. If I'm not back this evening, Macha will come looking, and her next target will be my sister.

It won't take that long. Silence again. *Tristan? Tristan!* She looked at Storm. "He may have teleported away."

CHAPTER 24

VIPER Headquarters, North Georgia Mountains

Quinn forced himself to stride through the bowels of VIPER headquarters with a confident carriage, stifling the turmoil inside him at facing Veronika once again. He still shuddered at how the vicious witch had exploited his grief over Kizira.

No one had ever controlled him, not with his powerful mindlock ability.

But she had.

In one fleeting, vulnerable moment, Veronika had almost gained control of thousands of Belador warriors under Quinn's command. The disastrous possibilities sent chills up his spine. Drawing a deep breath, he shoved away his concern.

This was not the place to ever show weakness.

Adrianna's heels clicked against the stone floor close behind him, reminding him this meeting had nothing to do with him.

Veronika and Adrianna had faced off over Witchlock.

Veronika had lost that battle.

She waited on a Tribunal sentencing and stood to spend the rest of her life in lockup beneath the North Georgia mountain that housed VIPER headquarters.

On occasion, the justice system put in place by their coalition actually functioned properly.

It would be nice if he could go to a Tribunal and ask for help locating his daughter, but that would be expecting too much of the self-centered gods and goddesses.

He no longer trusted Macha enough to ask for her help with anything, especially this. When she'd found out about his past liaison with Kizira, Macha had taken it personally. He would no more trust the goddess with his daughter's welfare than he would with Brina and Tzader's.

He slowed for Adrianna to catch up with him. When she did, he said, "I want to ask you about something, and no is a perfectly acceptable answer. I do not wish to impose on you, but I'm looking for someone to help me with an issue."

A foot shorter than he was, she looked up without slowing down. "Evalle mentioned your *issue* to me recently in private, and said she'd gotten your okay for the conversation."

Thank goodness for that, since Quinn didn't want to mention Phoedra's name in here.

"Good. That simplifies things. If you could touch something or ... someone ... connected to a missing person, would you be able to locate the person in question? I'm concerned about your being harmed by residual majik."

"I don't think that would happen, in particular with the object in question, but as to the more extreme measure, let's just say ..." She paused and lowered her voice. "I'm not a necromancer, and I'm too unfamiliar with Witchlock to know how that power will react to someone with ... extreme levels of residual majik."

She meant because Kizira had been a Medb priestess.

"You must understand *all* the risks if I try this," Adrianna added. "If anything I deem deadly rises up, I would be forced to destroy the host to prevent that power from lashing out at everyone around."

"I understand what you're telling me." Quinn got that Adrianna would have to blast away the corpse, and the dark energy with it, if something arose from Kizira's body when Adrianna touched it. He'd have to think on that.

When he heard her steps tapping faster than his, he slowed his long-legged stride even further.

She commented, "I've never been in this part of VIPER headquarters."

"That's because this is reserved for the deadliest criminals. VIPER prefers few visitors in this area even though it's heavily protected against escape."

Her gaze swept from side to side. "The energy running through here is ... unusual. Do you feel it?"

"Yes, but I doubt that I sense it as strongly as you do. I'm guessing the visual evidence is for those who may not pick up the power flowing across these walls." Quinn had been down here only once before. He glanced at the luminescent color that rippled across the rock surfaces forming the corridor, twelve feet tall by ten feet wide. No, now that he thought about it, *across* wasn't the right description.

The color didn't appear reflected but rather a part of the wall, a living energy similar to bioluminescence emitted by organisms such as fireflies.

This undulating glow, however, was not of the natural world.

Adrianna commented, "I assume this is some kind of security put in place by Sen, correct?"

"Yes." Quinn explained, "As I understand it, only one guard is required in this area. He or she has but to touch the wall for a second and shout of a prison break, which Sen will then hear. At that point, Sen activates the energy along these walls to prevent an escape."

"Prevent? Or disintegrate the escapee?"

"Good question. I'd put my money on disintegrate."

Sen allowed no majik or power except his to be used inside headquarters.

It took a full minute to traverse the tunnel. At the end, a floor-to-ceiling gate formed of silver crossbars prevented access past this point without authorization.

The minute the Belador guard realized Quinn approached, he straightened his stance and drew his shoulders back. That pulled his collared shirt tight over the bulky upper body. Warm brown eyes peeked respectfully from the guard's pale face, and freckles dotted his nose, softening his lethal look. But that appearance would deceive only those unfamiliar with him.

"I didn't know you were down here, Lionel," Quinn said, greeting the twenty-eight-year-old warrior. Turning to include Adrianna, Quinn said, "Adrianna, this is Lionel Macaffey, one of our Belador warriors who normally runs surveillance along the Chattahoochee River." In explanation, Quinn added, "VIPER sets up a rotation so that most of the field operatives spend one, perhaps two days at most, down here each year."

Adrianna asked, "Why not assign one group to guard this area? Wouldn't that be more efficient and allow them to become familiar with protocol?"

Lionel answered, "That's actually the reason we each take a turn. If no one is here more than once or twice a year, there's less chance a guard will become vulnerable to an inmate's influence."

"Ah. That makes sense."

It had been a while since Quinn had spoken with Lionel. The Belador's voice was a little deeper than Quinn remembered, and the fuzzy carrottop he'd last seen on this man was now buzz cut to a manageable quarter-inch length. Ready to get this dog and pony show moving, Quinn said, "We're on a tight timeline. I'm taking Adrianna to speak with Veronika. Did Sen inform you?"

"Yes, Maistir. He alerted me just ten minutes ago."

That would have been right after Quinn had convinced Sen that his people had picked up a tip that Medb were going to be targeted. As the Belador Maistir, it was imperative that Quinn be allowed to take whatever action necessary to prevent that from happening, or the Beladors being blamed.

When Sen had balked, Quinn added that he would be willing to discuss this with the Tribunal if Sen lacked the authority to grant them audience with Veronika.

Sen had given him a cold stare and said, "I don't want to hear a word from anyone if that witch spins your heads around. Literally."

Lionel faced the gate and spoke three strange words with long vowel phonemes, which sounded almost Asian. Another mysterious component of Sen's background.

The gate opened into the cellblock.

Quinn asked, "Do you know what those three words mean in English, Lionel?"

"No. Sen made me repeat them until I had the enunciation perfect. I've never heard it before. The code changes daily, and I'm betting none of us knows that language. Just another of Sen's secrets."

"True."

Lionel told Quinn how to find his way to Veronika's cell, adding, "Both sides of all the walkways will appear solid until you reach her. The corridor wall to her cell will vanish as you approach and reappear as soon as you walk away. A ward prevents her from exiting, but allows conversation. I'll remain here unless you need me for anything."

"We'll be fine on our own." Stepping aside, Quinn waved a hand. "After you, Adrianna."

Once they were inside, the gate closed behind Quinn. He prepared himself to meet the witch who had shifted herself into Kizira's image the last time they'd met. But she would not get to him this time.

If not for Adrianna being on the VIPER team, and now a friend of Evalle's, plus Tzader needing his help, Quinn wouldn't consider spending a minute in any witch's company ever again.

He took the lead again as they navigated the endless corridors lit by a stingy strip of light glowing along the ceiling above them.

At one point, Adrianna flinched and stopped, looking to her left.

What had she sensed? "Adrianna?"

She shook it off and said, "Sorry. It's just that I'm constantly experiencing different things since taking on Witchlock."

"Did you feel something even through that stone barrier?"

"Yes. Whatever is on the other side is ... disturbing."

Quinn didn't know if he should be impressed or terrified at her ability to breach Sen's security shields. Sen would definitely not be impressed. Once they were out of here, Quinn would warn Adrianna to be careful allowing anyone else to realize she could do that. He continued to the third turn and, as he rounded the corner, a wall twenty feet ahead on his left began to disintegrate.

That bastard Sen had better have the mother of all wards on Veronika's enclosure.

A wicked laugh started, building in volume as they approached.

Quinn slowed, then picked a spot in the center of the viewing area. He didn't know what he'd expected, but not this.

Veronika's long, dark hair had not taken well to prison life. Limp black locks fell past her shoulders, knotted with matted clumps. Her hands and feet were encased in stone gloves and shoes, all four limbs shackled to the wall behind her with fifteen feet of chain. A sink and commode had been tucked into the corner.

Her red robe hung on her, tattered and dirty, much like the skin clinging to her emaciated body.

The only part that had changed not one bit was the cruel gaze.

She sat on the ground, hunched and broken.

Adrianna's lips quirked.

Quinn had no sympathy for this woman, but neither did he find the situation humorous.

Evidently, Adrianna did. "How sad, Veronika," she said, sounding anything but sympathetic.

The wretched prisoner grunted. "What do you want?"

"I had hoped to offer you a chance to gain some relief while here, but clearly all you need is a bath. If Sen is alerted to your poor hygiene, he'll bathe you himself. I doubt you'll enjoy that, but maybe he's more fun than he appears."

Quinn wanted to caution Adrianna to curtail the taunting, but she'd asked to do the talking once they faced Veronika.

Veronika scowled and rose to her feet without even struggling. The chains fell away. A red cloud whirled around her, then the pristine robe returned. Her skin no longer sagged. A vicious beauty stood proudly before them, just as she'd been when she'd plotted to rule the world.

Except for the stone gloves.

The witch had been manipulating her audience even before Quinn and Adrianna laid eyes on her. She'd been setting the scene to gain sympathy. Such a fool to believe Quinn would drag up that emotion for this malicious bitch. Adrianna had not only seen through it, but had known how to handle it.

She impressed Quinn more by the minute.

Adrianna arched an eyebrow in amusement. She was the picture of calm, standing with her hands behind her back and her usual stoic composure. She watched with nothing more than mild interest showing on her face as Veronika finished her machinations.

So at ease. He envied her that poise in the face of his nemesis.

Or so it seemed, until Quinn's gaze slid down to where he caught sight of Adrianna's white-knuckled grip hidden behind her.

Maintaining his own blank mask, he focused his attention on the drama queen now standing in the center of her stage.

Veronika floated around. Now that she had an audience, she appeared ready to show off. "I know why you're here. You need my help to figure out Witchlock."

The comment had been directed at Adrianna, who said, "It must be crowded in there, living with an ego the size of an elephant."

Swirling to face them, Veronika twisted her face into a snarl. "You should take care how you speak to me. I will not be in here long."

"Oh?" Adrianna chuckled lightly.

Veronika said, "There is *always* someone who craves access to a power such as mine."

Releasing a soft sigh, Adrianna acknowledged, "Maybe, but Witchlock trumps anything you have."

Quinn held his breath, wondering if Adrianna's plan was to infuriate Veronika to the point that she tried to break the ward.

But Veronika surprised him by smiling. "You can't fool me. I spent years studying Witchlock. I know what it demands of you. I was ready to accept it and willing to bind myself to it, but you? You never wanted it. I heard your sister's thoughts while I milked her majik. She wanted to save you, and you wanted to save her. But she was gone, already turned into a power vapor. You both lost. And now ... you need me."

The silence stretched, thin and taut.

Veronika had found a sore spot, and kept digging at it.

With the two women focused on each other, Quinn spared Adrianna a quick look and found her hands had unclasped. She used one hand to hold the palm of her other one open behind her back.

A white sphere of power, the size of a marble, spun above it.

Adrianna had been inside VIPER enough times to know the rules. Specifically, no use of majik under any circumstances.

Still, Quinn whispered, "You're not going to use majik in here, are you?"

She never took her eyes off of Veronika, but spoke so softly he could barely hear. "Technically, what I intend to use is not majik. Witchlock is a power just like your kinetics, but when joined with a witch like me, who wields majik, it becomes something greater. I know Sen doesn't allow use of power in here either, but I allowed a small amount of the Witchlock power to escape as we walked down the halls. It didn't seem to affect the energy skating over the rock surface. That makes me think Witchlock might be older than Sen, which wouldn't surprise me. If this goes as I plan, Sen will either not be alerted, or I'll simply blame Veronika if he shows up and claims his rules were broken."

Quinn took in the walls, where energy still rode calmly along the surface. Nothing *had* changed there yet.

What Adrianna said made sense, but only when dealing with a reasonable person, a description Quinn would never assign to Sen. If Sen caught her using Witchlock here—power or majik—he still had autonomy to execute both Adrianna and Quinn and claim it was within his authority to do so.

Adrianna addressed Veronika again, sounding bored with the whole conversation. "We'll be out of time soon, so if you'd rather spend every minute pretending the world is your oyster, we have no reason to continue this conversation."

For the first time, Veronika's chilling, blue-eyed gaze switched to Quinn. "What is it *you* want?"

"He's only here as my guide. I'm the one with the questions."

Veronika held his gaze another ten seconds before crossing her arms and switching back to Adrianna. "Very well. What?"

"What do you know about white witches being captured? Did you contract with anyone to kidnap members of the council?"

"What if I did?"

Quinn wondered where Adrianna was going with this line of questioning. He thought she was here to gain knowledge of the dragon.

Adrianna lifted a shoulder. "If you had any part in the crime, you can plan on sharing more than a bath with Sen."

Veronika's smile slipped. "I find your humor crude."

"Be that as it may, I'll inform the Tribunal of anything you tell me that aids in our investigation ... or anything that hinders us."

Dark vapors smoked away from a hissing Veronika. "Do you really think you can come in here and threaten me?" she shouted.

Chuckling, Adrianna said, "Remember? I have Witchlock. You have nothing."

What had happened to the reserved Adrianna who maintained calm control at all times? Who was this braggart who had taken her place? Quinn could do nothing but support her at this point and hope she really did have a plan.

Veronika's hair shot out wide like a dark sunburst, then whipped around her as it fell again. She shook, but not from fear. That was raw fury bubbling, and Quinn had concerns about what would happen when she boiled over.

Taking a step toward the ward-protected opening, Adrianna said, "*I* am the more powerful. *I* can make you kneel to me."

Veronika screamed and lunged at the opening, stopping short of being fried alive.

Quinn moved toward Adrianna, but she whipped her open palm in front of her and held it up, shoulder high.

The sphere blossomed to the size of a baseball. Tendrils of white vapors flipped away as it spun. The energy that raced over Quinn's skin was only a tiny amount of what he'd felt the day of the battle between these two, but even at that it was extraordinary. As powerful as he was, this was far denser and stronger. Hers was a fifty-foot tidal wave she held back from crashing down on everyone, where his now felt like a gentle surf rolling up on the beach in comparison.

Frightening, because his was no gentle wave of power.

Veronika froze, staring at the sphere.

Adrianna kept her eyes on her adversary until Veronika jerked her head up, eyes wild, and started backing away, rising higher off the floor. She grabbed her head, shaking it from side to side. "No. Get out. Get out of my head!"

Energy along the walls hissed and sizzled like grease splattering on a hot skillet.

Adrianna's face never changed from intense concentration for a long thirty seconds, then she snapped her hand shut, and the orb disappeared.

Veronika hit the floor as if she'd turned to lead.

She moaned, and tears of blood dripped from her eyes. When she looked up, an insane beast stared at Adrianna. "You will regret that. I will do far worse than kill you."

Stoic once again, Adrianna said, "I hope you have the opportunity. That would mean you've escaped, and nothing would stand between us. Come for me. I will not spare you a second time."

Bloody hell. Quinn took one deep breath in, then out, and murmured, "Are you done?"

Adrianna said, "Yes." She turned to leave.

Quinn felt his gaze dragged back to Veronika, who now saw only him. She swept forward, close to the invisible barrier. "I know your secret. You told Kizira you had not found her. You told me about Phoedra, and that secret will buy my way out of here. When it does, I'll find her first."

His body stopped moving or breathing, paralyzed by her words. He tried to move just a finger and couldn't.

Adrianna stepped between them and lifted her palm, fingers folding in to close. "Would you like a second taste of Witchlock, Veronika?"

In a flash, Veronika turned away and Quinn was free to breathe again. He backed away and stepped past the cell. Adrianna followed and the stone reformed across the open space.

When she reached his side, Adrianna asked, "Are you okay?"

He ran a shaky hand through his hair. "Bloody witch. I'll be fine, but she can never leave that cell. At least not until I find my daughter." He glanced over at Adrianna.

"I'm not going to help her escape, if that's what you're thinking."

"I wasn't thinking that, but I'm glad to know it."

Lanna had warned him that Kizira's dead body could give up secrets, that he was making a huge mistake to leave her in that tomb. But how could he destroy Kizira's body before their daughter had a chance to mourn her mother?

Knowing the way Kizira thought, and how much she'd hated the life she'd been born into, Quinn was certain she would have hidden their child somewhere safe and away from the supernatural world.

He shook off the cold chills. With a potential war now on the horizon, he was glad that no one knew where Phoedra was.

The next guard showed up right on time. A Belador who looked at

Lionel and said, "How are the inmates?"

"Quiet. Nothing to report."

"Okay, you're free to leave. Have a cold brew for me."

Lionel laughed and shook his head, walking away. He met two more VIPER agents on the way out of the mountain who stopped him to chat, but he broke away by explaining he was in a rush to pick up a birthday gift.

Once he located the pickup truck he'd been using, he drove fifteen miles down the road back toward Atlanta. When he hit the right exit, he pulled off and parked behind an empty strip center where he'd arranged to have his beige sedan delivered.

Stepping out of the truck, he stood still and allowed the change to come over him, switching the Belador's clothes, face, and body for his usual attire as Emilio, the warrior mage from Italy.

He would now give his aid in locating the dead Belador who had donated his truck, clothes, and guard shift.

CHAPTER 25

Evalle followed Storm through the unfinished lobby to the conference room of their building.

A disgruntled Tristan trudged along behind her. He popped off, "You do realize that dragging me here against my will constitutes kidnapping."

Storm paused at the doorway to the conference room, shoulders tensing. He would turn around, and Evalle would have to separate the two men again.

Evalle said, "We'll be there in a minute, Storm."

His head moved, acknowledging her words, before he continued into the room.

She turned on Tristan. "What *is* your problem?"

"Do we have time to list them all, Dr. Phil?"

"Could you dial back the wiseass enough for us to have a serious conversation?"

He circled the space, muttering to himself, and came back to stand in front of her with his arms crossed. The frigid weather falling across Atlanta hadn't seemed to affect Tristan at all. They'd found him walking along Peachtree Street two blocks from the Fox Theater.

Actually, after a lot of time spent searching the old-fashioned way, since Evalle had to stay within the warded truck to avoid exposure to the sun, Storm had finally gotten out and tracked Tristan by scent.

Bad enough that Tristan had been on the move all day, but Storm was even less happy that Tristan had put Evalle through hell by pretending to be gone when he failed to reply to her telepathic calls.

She put her hands on her hips and leaned in, keeping her voice down. "What's it going to take to get your head out of your ass long enough to hear what's going on?"

"I don't care what's going on. Whatever mess you've gotten yourself into isn't my problem. I tried to tell you that before your tomcat got his back up and dumped demon majik on me."

A chair in the conference room scraped.

She got the message. Storm was letting her know he'd heard Tristan, and that the Alterant was dangerously close to getting his mouth permanently shut.

"Storm did that to get you into our truck," she shoved back at him. "A reasonable person wouldn't have made that so difficult."

Tristan dropped his chin low and chewed each word as it came out. "There is nothing reasonable about any of this."

"Dammit, Tristan. Don't you want to get your sister and friends out of Treoir? Don't you want *all* the gryphons out of Treoir?"

"Is that a trick question?" He sounded wary.

Don't strangle our only option for teleporting. Evalle said, "No, it's me trying to get you to listen. I need your help. If you help us, once we're done I'll link with you to teleport gryphons back here until they're all out."

For the first time since she'd forced him into the truck to come here, Tristan quieted, and his face shifted as he considered her words. "Why would you do that? The minute Macha realizes what happened, she'll come after both of us."

"Yep. If I finally have your attention, I'll tell you what's going on." Evalle gave him the bullet point version, which included sharing concerns over Macha. She concluded, "I've come to realize a lot of things. One is that the minute Macha gets me inside Treoir, she'll never let me leave. This isn't about my not coming home, or I'd just take my chances since Storm feels confident he can hide both of us from VIPER and Macha. This is about me taking a stand for all of us. If she's willing to lock me away, then she cares nothing about any relationship with VIPER or my being a liaison for the gryphons. We'll become her captives. I would never have left any of you there if I'd thought this would happen."

He chewed on the edge of his thumb, pondering away.

She gave him one more thing to think about, but had to say it in a way that preserved his secret. "The dragon I told you about believes war is coming no matter what we do. He'll support our side if we help him escape. Adrianna has seen this war in her dreams, and said if it does come to pass, humans will be involved. We'll watch over those humans tied to our Belador clan first."

He dropped his arms and swallowed, finally getting her message. The woman he cared for would be at risk.

Evalle didn't want to talk to him telepathically. If he was going to be on this team, he had to speak so that all could hear, including Storm. She needed this conversation to show Storm that Tristan was committed.

She asked, "Do you understand what I'm saying, Tristan?"

"Yes." Taking his time, he said, "We may not get all the gryphons out. I want a guarantee that if you and I get stuck there, my sister will be safe here."

Tzader stepped out of the conference room. "I'll guarantee that."

Evalle turned, hoping he looked better. Not much, but she prayed he'd at least rested. She asked, "Is Adrianna back yet?"

"Should be here any minute. She called to say she was on the way. Quinn is staying at VIPER to demand an emergency Tribunal hearing with Queen Maeve and Cathbad."

The door to the garage opened behind Tristan, and Adrianna waltzed through wearing jeans, short boots, and a knit top covered by a brown leather jacket. Evidently, Storm had given her an access code. She must have made a side trip to change clothes.

Adrianna stopped abruptly when she saw Tristan. "Color me shocked."

"No more surprised than I am."

Tzader called over, "Can we move this along a little quicker? We have to be ready to go the minute Quinn calls."

That got everyone into the conference room.

Evalle took a seat next to Storm, and he handed her a mug of coffee. The elixir of life.

Adrianna fixed another cup of tea and sat across from Tristan, who had pulled out a chair close to the door and plopped down. That was also the farthest point from Storm.

Tristan said, "What now?"

Finished dipping her tea bag, Adrianna said, "First I need to let you all know that Veronika *was* after the dragon throne, and it is a red dragon. She knew more, but I had to pull out anything I could quickly before she managed to block me. I discovered that she believed she could take the dragon from TÅµr Medb."

"That's good, right?" Tzader asked, hope so strong in his voice Evalle wondered if that was what kept him upright.

"Perhaps, but she also thought as I do ... that it might kill the dragon to teleport him out of that realm as a throne."

Evalle cleared her throat and offered, "It doesn't change the basics of what we have to do. What else?"

Tzader had remained standing and her words shook him back into motion. He started detailing the trip, addressing Tristan first. "Since you and Evalle know the TÅµr Medb landscape, we'll need you to teleport us into a space close to the throne room, but not in the actual room in case someone besides the dragon is in there."

Tristan scrunched his forehead. "The throne room is part of the queen's private quarters. Once we're in the tower, I can teleport someone into her space. But what's your plan at that point?"

Adrianna said, "I cloak the two of us, then you take me into the room. Once we confirm it's empty and no guards are in the immediate area, you leave me and bring the other three in while I start working on the curse."

Tristan cocked an eyebrow at her. "I never said I was going *inside* the throne room."

Evalle placed a hand over Storm's, silently asking him not to take Tristan's head off. She looked to Tzader, who had no sense of humor whatsoever when it came to a mission.

Tzader told Tristan, "Fine. If you're afraid, just get us to that first room and we'll do the rest until it's time to leave. If we get captured, you're free to teleport away and save your ass."

"I never said I was going to abandon anyone, either," Tristan snapped.

Evalle caught a dose of surprise coming from Storm and snippets of the same from Tzader and Adrianna. It had taken Evalle a while to figure out Tristan, but she'd come to realize he had backbone and pride, and a healthy dose of honor. Few others knew that because he buried his good traits beneath layers of jerk personality. He hated to give any impression of being a hero or loyal or dependable, but he was all of those things.

He was finally showing more of his true colors.

She gave him a little help accepting his role. "Tristan, do you remember the TÅµr Medb room where Lanna and I were held before I evolved into a gryphon?"

He nodded.

"That would be where I'd teleport in. What do you think?"

Sitting forward to lean on his forearms, he ran a hand mindlessly through his hair. "That would work. I don't know if the soundproofing spell on that room is still in place, or whether it will hold against the new queen, but it's our best shot for entering undetected." His eyes flicked around, the way they did when he worked out an answer for himself. "I have teleported individuals I couldn't link with, but those times happened with plenty of recovery in between. I'm talking days. I can link with Tzader and Evalle for additional power, but just in case, we need to find a way to bind Adrianna ..." He glanced at Storm. "And *him* to the group."

Evalle wanted to thump Tristan on the head. He'd been doing so well acting like a normal person. But that evidently just got too freakin' taxing. She turned to Storm. "Think we can make this work?"

"Should be able to." Storm asked Adrianna, "Can you weave an invisible chain around all of us?"

"Hmm, I see what you're saying. I think I can do that. Sort of like creating a spell that affects a group instead of just one."

"Right. Make it so that everyone is affected the same way."

"Not too tough, actually."

Tzader interjected, "Good thing, because you're going to need all you've got to break that dragon's curse, and I just heard from Quinn. We're leaving in five minutes."

CHAPTER 26

Lanna peeked through the crack in the door to Feenix's playroom. She watched Feenix fly around the room and dive-bomb Oskar, who danced around on his hind legs with no effort.

Evalle had told her Feenix was fine with Oskar, maybe even liked having company. Oskar was locked in an invisible cage, but Feenix could fly in to visit.

She didn't understand the strange noise that Oskar made, but she could tell he was not at all intimidated or frightened by the gargoyle.

Feenix flapped slowly, landing inside Oskar's invisible cage.

Oskar dropped to four feet, then sat as a dog would.

Feenix said, "Play?"

He got an empty stare for that.

Using one of his chubby hands to pat Oskar's head, Feenix appeared confused. "Name?"

Lanna couldn't watch any longer.

It was in her blood to offer help anywhere it was needed, and lately she saw many opportunities, but had few takers. Like Cousin Quinn and his friends. They accused her of interfering, but she had used her majik to help them many times. She'd checked the conference room and they were all gone. Before leaving, Evalle stressed to please not be caught in the room with boys or Cousin's head might explode.

Poor Cousin had been left to find white witches.

She'd tried his cell phone and left a message to call her, but she'd heard nothing. Cousin had too many things worrying him. He needed her help, but he did not know how to ask for it.

Family took care of family, and she was the only one here for him.

When she stepped into Feenix's playroom, Oskar jerked around and started making that awful frog squawking, if a frog could squawk.

Feenix looked upset with Oskar. "Lanna friend."

Lanna eased closer. "Thank you, Feenix. Oskar is just scared of me."

"Othkar?" Feenix echoed.

Oskar quieted and looked back at Feenix, who grinned a little two-fanged smile.

"I need something, Feenix," Lanna told her favorite gargoyle. Not that she knew any others, but Feenix would always be special to her even if she met a thousand more.

Feenix said, "Lug nuth?"

She grinned at his favorite food and walked over to grab three from his small barrel. When she turned back, she tossed one to him.

Feenix flapped his bat wings, lifting in the air to snag it. He chortled as he swooped around the room like his NASCAR idol, Danica Patrick.

Lanna clapped for him. "You are so smart. Here, grab this one." She threw the other lug nut toward the pen where Oskar waited as Feenix flew back, excited.

The lug nut flew within six inches of Oskar, whose forked tongue shot out and snatched it into his mouth.

Feenix landed and stared at Oskar, horrified. "No. Mine."

He had just offered Oskar one a moment ago. Lanna said, "I have more, Feenix."

Oskar kept turning the steel chunk around in his mouth until he spit it out.

Feenix backed up and made a sound that was the gargoyle equivalent of *eww.*

Guess he didn't want a lug nut with Oskar saliva and hair on it.

Lanna stared, realizing she had what she needed. Gross, but that would work. "Feenix. Can I have the lug nut Oskar spit out?"

His big orange eyes widened as if he had no idea who she was. Feenix said, "Yuck," as if warning her she didn't want to touch that.

"I know, but I want to use it to find Oskar's mama. I would touch his hair, but he got very upset when I tried." She wasn't sure just how much Feenix understood, so used the simplest explanation she could.

"Hair?" Feenix got a gleam in his eyes when he looked at Oskar. The gargoyle reached out his hand, palm facing down, to pet the familiar.

Oskar closed his eyes and dipped his head for Feenix. On the last pat, Feenix swiped a sharp claw over the hair sticking up and sliced off several strands.

Oskar didn't seem to even notice.

Feenix picked up the loose hairs and waddled over to Lanna. "Hair. No yuck."

She took them and felt a vibration. "Very good, Feenix. Be nice to Oskar while I'm gone. I'll be back soon to play."

Clapping his fat little hands, Feenix laughed. "Lanna play!"

Oskar danced around on his hind legs, no worse for the loss of hair.

Lanna tossed Feenix two more lug nuts. He scarfed them up and kept flying, clearly not willing to touch any with Oskar spit on them.

Racing back to her room, she grabbed a jacket and thought about telling the boys she was leaving. But that would be a bad idea.

They would want to join her. Too many people would draw attention. All she had to do was find the witch Mattie and call her cousin. Simple. No trouble that way.

Cousin could not yell at her for getting into trouble, and would surely want to reward her with much shopping. She needed new clothes. Brasko women must always dress well.

After thinking through potential problems, she left a note for the boys that she would be back by midnight so that they didn't call anyone because they were worried about her. She also suggested they stay away from the third floor so Oskar did not bite them ... just in case Feenix could get across to anyone that she looked for Oskar's mama.

When she made it down to the lobby, she found the electronic security had not been activated. Storm had left it off, thinking the ward would keep bad people out.

He would not leave Lanna and others trapped in an emergency.

He'd tried to keep Lanna contained with a spell once before. She had defeated that, and she had gained even more skills since then. If Cousin Quinn had taken the time to ask her, she would have informed him of all she had learned about herself and her abilities.

Lanna smiled. She turned the handle and pushed the door into the garage. Her hand stopped at first, blocked by the ward, but she extended tendrils of energy out around the door and created an opening in the majik. She pushed again and the door swung easily. On Treoir, Garwyli said she had power unlike anything he had seen born to a human in a long time. He trained her during the times that Tzader and Brina needed privacy.

He specifically told her to be patient, and that logic was one of her greatest weapons.

Willing her power to rise, Lanna stepped over close to the exterior door and teleported out to the street. She felt the sizzle as she passed through the outer ward and landed on the sidewalk, up against the building.

Just as she'd thought. Storm had to have set up the ward so that his group could teleport out.

Using the snippets of Oskar's hair, she followed the pull taking her toward the heart of downtown.

In her mind, she started seeing a building with columns. It had been built a very long time ago. She paused at the first corner and clutched the hair tightly while closing her eyes.

Two cross streets came to her.

The building was very close to that intersection.

She kept to herself, but stayed close to any group of pedestrians she found until she saw a policeman. Once he gave her directions to the cross streets, Lanna looked for a place to duck out of view between two buildings, then cloaked herself.

Grendal had not been seen for a while or Cousin would have told her if the monster had been spotted. Still, she would not risk his seeing her. Garwyli had shown her how to use her powers more efficiently, reducing the chance she would alert Grendal by drawing on too much energy at one time. Cloaking took only small amount now.

Walking through the city felt refreshing, even in the cold. She'd been cooped up too long between being caught with Brina in another realm, locked away in hiding, or stuck in Treoir. She wished Grendal would be captured.

She wanted her freedom back.

Excitement rushed through her when she approached the intersection she'd been hunting. She took in the park on her left as she walked up to the corner so she could peer in all directions.

There was the building just down on the right, as she'd seen it in her mind.

She looked at her hand, which was still translucent. Cousin did not realize how much stronger she had gotten in Treoir. Cloaking held much longer than before.

The hair in her hand warmed and vibrated.

Confident she was hidden from view, she walked slowly toward the building.

The doors and windows had been boarded up long enough to have dirt piled along the ledges. No one had disturbed that in a long time.

She climbed through bushes at the side and searched for a way in. Flashes of images came to her, of women strapped to tables. One cried, and Lanna sucked in quick breaths at the pain another woman suffered.

Using the cell phone Quinn had given her, she tried her cousin and got his voice mail. She couldn't breathe. Whatever was happening here had to be bad majik. She pressed the button for Trey McCree. Cousin had said to call him any time, day or night, if Evalle or Tzader was not around.

She said, "Trey, this is Lanna. I am—"

Trey asked, "Quinn's cousin?"

"Yes. I found Mother Mattie, but ..."

Lanna dropped the phone and doubled over, trying to hold onto what she'd eaten for lunch. The phone fell into a crack in the foundation. This was awful. She had to hold on and tell Trey more.

A hand slapped over her mouth and an arm hooked around her waist, yanking her up. Lanna reached up, trying to pull the hand away.

That's when she saw that her arm had turned solid.

Her cloaking had failed.

CHAPTER 27

Tribunal meeting—Nether Realm

Quinn held himself rigid, feeling like one of the Queen's Guard in London as he waited for the three Tribunal deities to appear on the raised dais he faced.

But the Queen's Guard was part of the human realm where rules and laws applied. There were no absolutes here in the Nether Realm, unless you considered being subject to a god or goddess's mood or whim to be a rule.

Calling in three gods and goddesses for yet another conflict between the Beladors and Medb could just about guarantee a cranky trio, which would require deflecting their annoyance onto the Medb as quickly as possible.

Sweat drizzled down Quinn's neck, but no one would see him sweat beneath the suit he wore. Still, when five minutes had come and gone without anyone manifesting on the dais, he started to sweat in earnest.

Tzader would be leaving for TÅμr Medb based on what Quinn had told him.

Quinn knew of no prior Tribunal meeting where the gods and goddesses had failed to appear. What now? He fought the urge to pull at his collar so he could breathe. He'd decided on the way here that he had to go strong or go home.

Shoving power into his voice, he called, "Sen!"

Energy swirled next to him and the liaison, who stood another four inches taller than Quinn, said, "What?"

"Where is the Tribunal? As Maistir, I have too many agents depending on me to stand here doing nothing."

"Would you rather come back later?"

What the...? "Why would I do that? No. I have something that requires Tribunal attention now." Quinn narrowed his eyes at the boil on the butt of creation. "You did inform them, didn't you?"

"Oh, yes." Sen looked up, putting his bent index finger to his chin. "I might not have mentioned the time. My bad. I'll tell them now."

I'll kill this prick. Give Quinn one shot at Sen's mind and he'd squeeze all the snide comments out along with the gray matter. Sen's attitude came from Quinn's refusal to drag Evalle in to be teleported to Treoir until she finished the assignment he had her on.

Sen disappeared without a word. In the next ten seconds, three beings gradually took shape on the dais.

Quinn groaned inside. Could he not get a break? Why was Loki here? That god had screwed with Evalle more than once, and his only point in living was for others to keep him entertained, which sometimes included their dying in interesting ways.

Loki stepped up. "You should be forewarned that to curb constant bickering between the Medb and Beladors, we've instituted a penalty for frivolous use of our time.

Quinn's heart stomped around in his chest, but he kept his breathing calm. "Understood. I agree that your time is far too valuable to be squandered."

Loki grinned, as if he knew just how much of a lie Quinn had just told. But Quinn hadn't glowed bright red, the sign of lying to a direct question.

Quinn had stated an opinion, merely agreeing with Loki.

Indicating the Egyptian woman on his left, in an ankle-length robe with hieroglyphic embellishments, Loki said, "Ma'at, known far and wide as the goddess of truth and justice, joins us."

What had prompted Loki to acknowledge anyone other than himself?

Quinn got his answer when the Egyptian goddess sent Loki an admiring glance.

Her jet-black hair stopped at her shoulders, cut straight as the blunt bangs chopped across her forehead. A carved gold band as thick as Quinn's little finger circled her head, both ends twisting together in the front to form a small cobra-head ornament. Thick kohl surrounded eyes as dark as night. Wide bands of gold circled her upper arms and outlined the half-moon collar that swept from shoulder to shoulder. Her sandals had been tied past her ankles, half way to her knees, and she wore a simple shift, belted with a red sash.

Loki made no move to introduce the deity on his right, but Quinn had heard of prior visits from Varpulis, a Slavic god who should have withered into nothing by now after running in place for eternity. He had pale skin and wiry muscles, and the only color on his all-but-emaciated body was a pair of yellow shorts so bright Quinn needed sunglasses to look at them.

Varpulis showed no reaction to being snubbed by Loki, who smiled at holding all the power in this room.

Loki said, "State your grievance."

Quinn hoped like hell that he'd made the right gamble. "In the interest of keeping this as brief as possible for all of you, I would ask that Queen Maeve and Cathbad the Druid be present." Had that appealed to Loki's ego? Would he call up the queen and her henchman?

Sen appeared and spoke to Loki. "How may I be of service?"

"Send word to Queen Maeve and Cathbad the Druid. Tell them we request their presence, and if I am displeased by this grievance I will award them all of the gryphons."

Quinn sucked in a harsh breath.

He hadn't seen that one coming.

CHAPTER 28

TÅμr Medb, home of the Medb coven

Tzader took in his team to make sure all five of them had survived the teleportation into TÅμr Medb. No welcoming committee had waited for them in this bedroom suite, thank the gods, but the distinctive smell of burned limes clung to the air in Medb Central.

Evalle asked, "How're you doing, Tristan?"

Running his hands over his head, Tristan said, "That was hairy, but we're here. Let's get this done and get out."

Tzader had hoped to hear cockiness instead of uncertainty in Tristan's voice, but they were here now and there was nothing to do but move forward with the plan.

Adrianna stepped over to Tristan. "Can you jump to the throne room, or do you need a moment to recharge?"

"I'm good. Do your little cloaking trick."

"Little cloaking trick?" Adrianna gave it a beat then said, "I'm not entirely sure how Witchlock will function here. Maybe I should test it on you and seal your mouth shut. It would be so much nicer if all you could do was nod yes or shake your head no."

"Who peed in your crispy doodles this morning?"

Evalle stepped over. "Tristan, would you just do your part without acting like a jerk?"

He lifted his hands in surrender. "Fine. Wouldn't want to upset your witch buddy."

Evalle shook her head and gave him a wry smile. "I'm trying to preserve your family jewels. I have no doubt she can remove them with a flick of her hand, but reattaching them ... now *that* might actually be some trick."

Color washed out of his face. "Not funny."

Tzader said, "We're not here for fun. Get moving if you want to stay alive. The sooner we're out of here, the better chance of that happening."

Tristan said nothing after that unless someone asked him a direct question. Once Adrianna had them cloaked, Tristan teleported them away.

Storm had been checking out the room. "How did you keep Lanna hidden once you figured out she'd traveled here with you?"

Evalle said, "She could cloak herself, but she also kept practicing teleporting."

"How far could she go?"

"From the bathroom on the other side of that door." Evalle pointed. "To this room, and she kept hitting her head on the wall when she missed."

"No wonder she gives Quinn fits," Tzader commented.

Tristan appeared right in front of Storm. They both jumped back. Tristan said, "Stay out of my landing spots."

Storm countered, "Put an X on the floor next time."

The next time Tzader needed a black-ops team, he was leaving at least one of these two behind. Right now, he needed both. He asked Tristan, "Is Adrianna working on the dragon, or do we need to take out some guards?"

"She's on it, and the hall outside the queen's quarters is empty. They must know when the queen is on-site or gone. Bunch up and I'll take you there."

The jump to the throne room was quick enough that Tzader didn't feel his stomach do backflips. So this was the heart of TÅµr Medb, huh? Adrianna stood in front of a throne that was, by the gods, shaped from a dragon. She said, "I can't break a curse unless you can tell me what it was."

The dragon grumbled and the throne shuddered. Smoke curled from his nostrils.

Evalle walked over to stand next to the dragon, who stopped making noises. His big silver eyes looked Evalle up and down, then shifted over to take in the men before returning to Adrianna. He tried to make noises but his mouth was not opening for him to talk, growl, or whatever he could do.

Storm joined Adrianna and Evalle, saying, "Can you free his jaws or tongue to somehow release his voice?"

Adrianna thought on it several seconds. She addressed the dragon. "I can try something, but it might require breaking your jaw. I won't do it unless you give me permission. Puff out one time for no and two for yes."

Silver eyes thinned at that suggestion, but he puffed out twice.

"I was afraid you'd say that," Adrianna muttered. "Everyone stand back. I'm using Witchlock, and I'm not sure what the radius of influence will be."

Tzader and the other three backpedaled quickly. All he could see was her raising her right arm and holding her palm out where ... a damn ball of white energy appeared and spun, throwing off wisps of power.

She was saying something, but he couldn't hear the specific words. That might be a good thing.

A loud pop sounded and a deep groan followed. The dragon's jaw fell down, loose. He made gargling and choking sounds, but in the next twenty seconds his lower jaw moved upward. He cocked his head right and left then cleared his throat. "I hope your plan to break my curse does not require breaking all my bones."

The dragon could talk?

Tzader should have expected that after what Ceartas had said, but still it was strange hearing the head on top of that throne actually speak.

Before anyone else had a chance to reply, the dragon called out, *"Tzader!"*

"That's me." He took a step toward the throne. "Who are you?"

"I am Daegan. If you're done socializing, we need to be out of here soon. I have no idea how long the queen will be gone, and you must destroy her scrying wall behind me before we leave."

Tzader said, "A man I trust is keeping her and Cathbad busy in a Tribunal meeting." Did the dragon know what that was?

"Not yet he isn't. Queen Maeve and Cathbad have gone to meet with someone who offered the queen a trade."

Quinn didn't have those two tied up with a Tribunal?

Tzader ordered, "Adrianna, you get busy on reversing his curse.

Tristan, you keep watch on the hallway and conserve your energy. Storm and Evalle, come with me."

When Evalle strode forward, she asked, "What's so important about the scrying wall? She'll just build another one."

Daegan's voice had a rough, unused rasp to it. "That wall holds history of almost seven hundred years that Queen Maeve will use against anyone outside her coven, starting with Beladors."

Tzader fell into stride with Storm. "Can you cover the noise?"

Storm frowned. "I can shield some noise, but breaking that wall may cause a sonic boom if the power in it explodes. I can't keep that from rocking this place."

The dragon called over, "You don't have to blow it up. Just pull out at least three stones and destroy those. That's enough to corrupt any images they try to pull out of the archives."

The wall sparkled with a king's ransom in gems ten times over, and had water rushing down the surface. Tzader told Evalle, "While Storm covers our noise, I'll take the left side and you take the right. With our kinetics, we should be able to break some chunks out."

Evalle stepped over and waited for a sign from Storm. He began chanting, and nodded at them to get busy.

Tzader kept up with Adrianna's progress by how much snarling the damn dragon was doing.

Daegan said, "Listen *closely* and I'll give you the entire spell so you can reverse it *if* you can recite the counter version exactly. Doesn't work if you mangle it."

Evalle paused to glance at Tzader with a he's-an-idiot look she normally saved for Tristan.

Adrianna said in a sweet voice, "Speak to me again as though *I'm* the idiot who got cursed into a throne, and you won't like how your head fits on your body when I reverse it."

Tzader hoped Adrianna didn't blow up the damn throne. He ignored those two and planted his feet on each side of a spectacular deep-red stone the size of his head. Grabbing the rock, he growled and put his back into it, pulling for all he was worth.

He strained, grunting and yanking. Nothing moved.

Evalle had no better luck with the sapphire she was going after.

Pausing in his chant, Storm walked over to look at the wall. The tower of oversized precious gems ran twenty feet up, then faded into nothing.

Storm reached down to pull out one the size of a basketball and, after a moment of grinding effort, he stopped. "We don't have time for this. We need more power."

Tzader turned to see how Adrianna was coming along. Not very well. They couldn't waste another second.

Storm's comment about more power gave Tzader an idea. He told Evalle, "Link with me."

Her power hit Tzader so hard he took a step back. "You've gotten stronger."

She smiled. "Must be my gryphon evolution. What now?"

"You and I both put our hands on one stone and see if we can channel our kinetics into crushing it."

"Good thinking," Storm said, then his chanting kicked up again.

Evalle asked, "Which stone?"

"This big sucker in the middle." Tzader positioned himself on one side of a giant ruby, palming the stone with his hands a foot part.

Evalle moved until she faced him, and placed her hands on her side in a mirror image.

Tzader said, "Now!" He drew all the energy flowing through his body and forced the kinetic power to flow through his fingers. Sweat poured down his face and stung his eyes.

Rainbow-colored sparks shot from his fingers, then from Evalle's. A squealing noise started thin and tinny then built until it sounded like a giant drill.

Brina's sad face came into Tzader's mind, and the rage he'd kept tucked out of the way swept through him.

The stone made a popping sound as if chipped by Thor's hammer.

Adrianna paused in her incantation, "I feel an energy moving this way."

From over by the door, Tristan said, "We have to go. No one can get us out of the dungeon in this place."

Straining, Tzader felt his muscles reaching the point of failure any moment now. Evalle would be right behind him.

Adrianna argued, "Reversing the curse isn't working. If we try to move this dragon between realms in this form, it may affect the curse."

Tzader was out of options, time, and patience. "Maybe it'll bust him free."

"Or kill me," Daegan snarled.

Tristan said, "Hey, no one said there wasn't a downside."

The dragon growled something then ordered, "Break that cursed scrying wall now!"

I may kill that bastard myself. Drawing so much energy at one time was squeezing Tzader's body from the inside out. One look at Evalle's pale face said she was putting all she had into it. If Storm looked over, he'd drag her away from this.

All of a sudden, a loud cracking filled the air. Jagged lines wicked out from the center of the ruby. It broke into seven chunks.

Evalle stood up, gasping for breath.

Storm's head whipped around. "Are you okay?"

"Yep," she answered. "But I don't think we'll crack another one."

Tzader wiped pools of sweat from his eyes and forehead. "Let's get out of here." He strode over to the throne. "Time to teleport."

Tristan was up and moving, but he still looked ragged around the edges. "What are we doing with the chair?"

Smoke rushed from the dragon's nostrils, engulfing Tristan's face. Daegan growled, "I'm not a bloody chair."

"Semantics." Tristan swatted away the thick cloud. "That smells like a box of burned matches."

Adrianna said, "The energy coming our way is getting closer. What are we doing?"

Storm asked Daegan, "Would you rather stay here alive, or risk dying during teleporting?"

"That's not much of a choice," Evalle commented.

Storm looked at her. "It's better than none."

Tzader ordered, "Everyone shut up."

That quieted the room, but another stream of smoke poofed out. The dragon said, "Just do it. I will not stay here another two thousand years."

Tzader pointed at Tristan. "Link now. Evalle is still linked with me." He told Adrianna. "Sit on the throne."

She looked appalled, but climbed up in the dragon's seat.

"Evalle stands between me and Tristan," Tzader went on giving directions. "Tristan, you grab one arm of the throne. I'll grab the other, and Evalle holds both of our wrists."

Storm moved behind Evalle, putting his arms around her waist, just as he had last time.

A blast of energy rocked the room with the power of a hand grenade being set off.

Five warlocks appeared in urban combat clothes. One had a tattoo of a snake circling his smooth skull, with the snake's head stopping just above the bridge of his nose.

A Medb priest, but the last one he'd seen had worn a robe.

Tzader had fought them before and respected that warlock's ability to take them all out.

The priest-warlock pointed at Daegan. "Cathbad warned her to kill you, traitor. Now, *I'll* do it, and hand her five prisoners to boot."

Tzader shouted at Tristan. "Now!"

Nothing happened. Tristan's neck muscles stretched taut with the effort.

Lifting his hands as high as his head, the warlock flung his hands at them.

In an explosion of color and a deafening roar, the world spun out of control. Whips of power lashed across Tzader's face and arms.

Everyone shouted.

Blood rushed through his ears.

The dragon roared and howled. The sound could only be described as a Kodiak bear being torn to shreds.

The spinning Tzader had always associated with teleporting slowed as it whipped around him. Power drained away as they traveled, leaving his body tired but no longer in pain from the fast exit.

He hated watching when he teleported, but had to see if all of his team had made it out.

Faces and parts of bodies flashed by looking like a macabre version of the tornado scene from the *Wizard of Oz*.

But he could still feel the chair arm or at least the part he'd been holding. Closing his eyes, he waited for the disorientation to end.

When it did, wind blew him backwards, head over heels, slamming him onto his back.

Rolling sideways over a bumpy surface, he opened his eyes in time to take in the thousand-foot-plus drop off the side of a mountain.

What the hell? His body jiggled back and forth with movement. He was on top of a railway hopper car full of coal.

"Get over here!" Daegan roared.

Tzader was on his feet and balancing his weight against the movement and wind. The bottom fell out of his stomach when he found the dragon throne rocking back and forth, dangerously close to falling off the cliff he'd just stared down.

Tzader lunged to grab the throne. His boots sank into the coal.

Storm jumped to the other side and they pushed the throne to the center of the car. Tzader yelled, "Don't you have a tail for counterbalance?"

Daegan growled an unearthly sound. "It's part of the throne."

Tzader did a quick search for the rest of the group, although he had no doubt Storm had made sure Evalle was safe before turning his attention to anyone else.

He said a silent thank you that they'd taken off after dark for Evalle's sake, but now there was a strange, dim glow hanging over their railcars. That had to be Adrianna's doing.

The train moved at a fast clip, rocking back and forth, which was hard enough to deal with before adding the wind whipping around.

Adrianna had landed on her hands and knees, perilously close to the edge where the two cars were connected. If she fell, she'd be crushed. Evalle had Adrianna's arm, lifting and turning her back toward the center. They stumbled sideways, swaying with the rocking car.

Tzader looked around. "Where's Tristan?"

"Little help!"

Adrianna was on her feet, and latched onto Daegan's chair arm. She pointed her free hand. "There he is."

Tristan dangled upside down from the side of the next car, close to the corner. He was digging his heels into the coal, but his bent legs didn't have enough room for a good grip to hold his weight. One good bump, and he'd be an Alterant splat. His body flopped around, banging the metal wall.

Evalle started for him, but Storm pulled her back and showed his jungle cat agility when he leaped to Tristan's rail car, landing surefootedly.

Tristan shouted.

Storm lunged and clamped down on Tristan's calves just as the back of his ankles hit the edge.

Tzader left Evalle and Adrianna to hold the throne, and hurried to the edge of his coal car. Looking over at Storm, who nodded as if he got what Tzader intended to do, Tzader shouted, "Do it."

Storm slid his grip to Tristan's ankles.

Tristan looked up at Storm as if he thought the Skinwalker was going to let him go. Then Storm stood up, lifting Tristan by the ankles, and swung him away then back toward Tzader, releasing Tristan at the last minute.

Tzader used kinetics to catch Tristan and flip him overhead and in the direction of the throne.

Tristan did a midair flip and landed with bent knees that hit the coal. He stood up and grinned, but it was an effort and his hands shook. Tristan said, "We made it back! Not too shabby a job of teleporting, eh? Sometimes I take myself for granted."

Daegan yelled at him, "You could have killed all of us! We have to get off this infernal thing. Now."

"Hey, I don't have endless energy, dragon boy."

"Dragon boy? You should enjoy your next minute. It will likely be your last."

"You gonna kick my ass from over there, *chair*?"

Evalle, ever the mediator, stepped between them. "Not now, guys. We do have to get out of here."

Rumbling noise from the dragon grew. "I won't have to crush you, Alterant," he said to Tristan. "You've left a trail a blind enemy could follow. If you were at all adept at teleporting, you would have landed us somewhere we could defend ourselves."

Storm had jumped back to their car, rejoining the group along with Tristan.

Tzader asked, "The Medb can follow us?"

In answer, two warlocks appeared on the flatcar ahead of theirs, which was loaded with steel plates, and three more warlocks showed up on top of the hopper car following behind where Tristan had just been hanging.

Got my answer.

That's when Tzader realized he was still linked with both Evalle and Tristan, but now was a bad time to stay that way. If one of them was killed, they'd all die. He ordered, "Unlink!"

Sidestepping at the immediate loss of power, Tzader shook it off, took two steps and planted his feet, waiting on the two warlocks that had jumped down between the cars and were climbing up the front of Tzader's.

The Medb-priest warlock had dark-purple nails an inch long and sharp as needles.

When the first head popped up, Tzader pushed kinetic power into his legs and booted that warlock across the chin.

His howl followed his body into the open space that dropped off forever.

He clawed the air on his way down.

Warlock number two stayed out of sight, and Tzader started to go look for him when a blast of something flew out of the trees they passed. Hawks emerged from the branches as if something magnetic pulled the solitary predators in to converge on Tzader's group. Screeching built as they flew into a swirling circle and came in like miniature fighter pilots.

That was not normal.

Those beaks and sharp claws could shred skin and blind them. Tzader swatted and lashed out with short kinetic bursts, shoving them back and off to the side. If these were real hawks, he didn't want to kill any normal creature unnecessarily, but neither could he let his people get ripped to pieces. Feathers clouded his view as beaks and talons dug into his skin.

His sentient blades snapped and hissed, but he hesitated to use those when he had no way to keep them from slicing one of his team who might jump in to help. He slapped more kinetic blasts at the birds.

Tzader smelled the sharp, metallic scent of his own blood.

Adrianna's voice cut through all the noise. That little woman had some serious lungs. She kept shouting something, but he was too busy protecting his eyes to pay attention. He swung a wide kinetic sweep, knocking thirty birds away. Just as many filled in behind them. Damn it.

All at once, the birds exploded away from him as if they were his polar opposite. Go, Adrianna.

The warlock who had sent that barrage finally appeared, lunging up at

Tzader.

Birds screeched, flying erratically as the warlock still tried to force them in. Adrianna's voice picked up volume, and the birds were finally swept away in one big, flapping cloud of feathers and screeching noise.

Tzader concentrated his kinetics into his arm, and drew back to slam the warlock in his face.

But the bastard blinked out of sight a second before an arm snaked around Tzader's neck in a chokehold. The warlock whispered, "I should take you to my queen, but she'll understand that there are always unexpected casualties."

When the sharp point of the warlock's fingernail pricked Tzader's skin, he dove forward, dragging the warlock with him as Tzader shoved his head into the coal. Damn, that hurt. He flipped all the way over, grabbing the edge of the train car as he rolled off the edge.

Momentum tossed the warlock off his back and down to the tracks, where he screamed until the wheel severed his head and slung the rest of his body into the void.

Tzader had both arms hooked around the wall of the rail car, hanging on. He swung his feet up and used kinetics to make it all the way over. Once he landed, he turned to see Tristan laid out on the coal close to the throne, Storm battling one warlock and Evalle the other one.

They must have dealt with the fifth threat already.

Adrianna was struggling alone to keep the throne from falling over.

Daegan spied Tzader and ordered, "Spin me around and point me at the warlocks! Then get out of my way."

Tristan struggled to reach his feet, and made it to one side of the chair.

Tzader called to Evalle telepathically. *Both of you let those two warlocks drive you back, then jump to our car and get out of the way. Daegan's got a plan.*

Got it, she replied then must have said something to Storm. They both retreated as if beaten back.

Tzader grabbed one side of the throne with his hands and his kinetics and told Tristan, "Now!"

They turned the throne to face the fight.

Daegan roared, "Let me at them!"

Evalle shoved a quick blast of kinetics at her warlock.

Storm spun like a top and kicked his opponent as they both jumped down to the home team's coal car.

Both warlocks started forward, their faces gleaming with confidence, but then paused and started backing up until they dropped out of sight.

Had they fallen between the cars?

No. If Tzader got that lucky, he'd buy a lottery ticket when they got home.

Adrianna lifted her voice. "That's not good. They're probably partnering up to drop something nasty on us that will trap us." She positioned her hands in front of her and started to unfold the fingers of her hand that hid Witchlock.

Daegan said, "Stand back, all of you. As you people like to say, I've got this."

The Sterling witch lifted an eyebrow at that and stepped aside, muttering, "You do realize you're the only one not fully mobile, right?"

A snort puffed from the dragon.

Tzader weighed the risk of pulling Adrianna back into place, because Daegan had no idea the power she controlled. Hell, Tzader didn't know the entire extent of her abilities, but he recalled Evalle saying she'd rather go up against a Medb army than Adrianna and her Witchlock power.

Storm shouted, *"Heads up!"*

When the attack came, it was fast and hairy-looking.

Just as Adrianna had predicted, the two warlocks were now blended together as one wide blanket of purplish-black wraiths. Both wraith heads joined as one that led the front edge of the deadly screen. It flew across the top of the boxcar, heading straight for Tzader's group.

Evalle, Tristan and Tzader shoved their hands up to hit the deadly mass with kinetics, but at the very last possible second, Daegan opened his jaws and flames shot fifteen feet out, lighting up the flying wraith pack.

The Medb conglomeration screamed and twisted in midair, still moving forward at high speed.

The fiery mass shot over the top of Tzader's head, close enough it would have singed his hair if he'd had any. As he watched, the flames engulfing the warlocks burned for ten seconds then vanished, leaving a blanket of ashes that disintegrated in the next sharp whip of wind.

The damn chair was of some use. Tzader called up his healing and his cuts began sealing. He asked the dragon, "Can any others follow their trail?"

Daegan's deep voice boomed, "Only to this point. The warlocks followed us here because that Medb priest tagged us when he threw majik. That allowed him to follow the link. Without a second majik trail from here they won't find us, but we have to leave immediately or we'll have to fight the next wave."

Tristan asked, "Again? You want me teleport again? Now?"

Evalle cut in. "Hold on, everyone. I just got telepathic word from Trey that they found Mother Mattie."

Tzader said, "We can't deal with that right now, Evalle. We have to turn Daegan into a dragon before the energy is gone from that scale. If we teleport anywhere, it's going to be to Treoir."

"Treoir?" Tristan shouted. "No one is listening to me. There's no way I could teleport to another realm right now. Maybe not for another day."

Daegan glowered at Tristan. "Then your ability to teleport is as much use as a gelded stud."

"It was good enough to get your ass out of TÅµr Medb," Tristan argued back.

"Would you two can it a minute?" Evalle shouted. Once Tristan and the dragon quieted, she told Tzader, "Trey found Mattie, but it's not all good news. Storm asked the twins staying with us to keep an eye on Lanna while we were gone and to call Trey in case of an emergency, or if anything unusual happened. They just called Trey to say Lanna was missing, but he hung up as Lanna called him and said she'd found the witches. Something happened during the call. He heard the phone fall and scuffling noises. He traced her phone to a building downtown and went hunting her. When he got there, five Medb warlocks slipped into the building from a side entrance. He needs reinforcements, but Tzader told him to check before bringing other Beladors in on this—"

"No." Tzader had four too many lives standing around him already at risk. "If the white witch situation blows up in our faces, I don't want more Beladors involved, but we can't leave Lanna there."

Evalle said, "We need to go help Trey. The only person he can call is Quinn, who's still in the Tribunal trying to keep everyone out of our way." She leaned toward Tzader and added, "I gave Trey enough to know what we were doing so he'd be up to speed."

"Good."

"We *have* to go to Treoir," Daegan said, with the kind of authority that didn't invite argument.

Tzader agreed one hundred percent.

Time was running out, and if he didn't get Daegan and Brina together soon, he'd miss the tiny window of time he had left. Once Queen Maeve found out her throne had been stolen, she'd question her security. Tzader had no doubt that the warlock priest had left a detailed description of Tzader and his team before chasing them down. The queen would be able to turn all of VIPER on him and the four who had already risked so much.

But he still couldn't put any of them ahead of Lanna's life.

"We're going to get Lanna back first," Tzader announced.

Daegan roared in fury.

Tzader stepped over to face Daegan and roared right back, "I know what's at stake. At the moment, Brina is safe, you're safe, and we're not locked up yet. Lanna has helped all of us, but more than that she's family. We don't turn our back on our own. Prepare to teleport."

Tristan opened his mouth.

Tzader pointed at him. "Not a word. I know you're exhausted, but you can do it one more time with us linking. I know you can."

Tristan blinked at the show of confidence from Tzader, but the moment passed. He said, "Fine, damn it, but hold on to your asses."

Daegan blasted a harsh exhale through his nose. "You'll wish you'd listened to me."

"That may be, but right now we do what I say," Tzader slapped back at him. Worry balled in his gut over expending their last teleport and the lost time, but he couldn't live with himself if anything happened to Lanna. Quinn had lost too much already.

"Oh, crap," Evalle groaned. "We're coming up to a bridge over water. There will be nothing to block that wind we've danced around."

Storm noted, "Looks like we're somewhere in North Georgia."

"Get in position to teleport," Tzader snapped.

Adrianna rolled her eyes and stepped on the base of the throne to push up, then landed hard on the seat.

Daegan grunted. "The minute I get out of this—"

"Yes, yes." Adrianna waved a hand at him. "We know. You'll rain terror down on all of us. Let's skip ahead to the part where the curse is broken and you're out of my sight."

"*Tristan!*" Evalle called, her gaze turned to the bridge.

Wind whipped across the top of the car.

"Ready?" Tristan called out.

"Do it," Storm growled.

Ten warlocks landed all around them on the piled-up coal.

CHAPTER 29

Grendal led his party from the hangar in a regional airport near Charleston, South Carolina, to a van large enough to carry his crated shipment. From here, it was on to the ship waiting at the docks. Casting a compulsion spell on an Atlanta-based shipping agent a month ago had ensured a way for Grendal to leave quickly and quietly with his precious cargo.

Just in time.

Pulling back his sleeve, he studied his arm. His skin had turned a splotchy, dark shade of mustard since yesterday. Lanna's decision to run had caused him unnecessary discomfort.

She'd have a chance to make that up to him, especially since his time with Mattie's granddaughter had been cut short.

It would be more painful than necessary for Lanna.

Still, he could appreciate small favors.

He'd have to wait until the ship was out to sea to draw on her. No interruptions at that point. Even with Leeshen to protect him, he would be at his most vulnerable once he started the transfer.

If not for all the useful information Nightstalkers had provided, locating the shipping agent would have taken much longer. Such a shame he didn't have the same intelligence sources in his country. He should work on developing a ghoul network, which would make him that much more powerful.

Snow floated down, sprinkling the pavement and making him homesick for his castle deep in the Carpathian Mountains of Romania.

He'd be returning victorious. His plan couldn't have worked any better.

The crate jostled when one of one of the three men he'd hired stepped in a hole.

Leeshen barked an order at the man, who straightened up and grumbled something about taking orders from a bitch.

Grendal touched her shoulder, letting her know he was pleased with the discipline she demanded. He whispered, "Once the crate is loaded, take the driver's place."

"Yes, Master." At the van, she held her corner of the crate with one hand and used her free hand to open the tall, rear cargo doors. She issued orders on how to position his precious shipment, forcing his motley crew to shape up and handle it with care.

Using Medb warlocks would have been so much easier, but first he'd have had to capture them, then control them. Controlling warlocks not bound to him required too much majik. Using any more than he needed between now and getting settled on the ship would put him at too much of a disadvantage.

It was a shame to miss seeing Queen Maeve's face when she read the note he'd left for her. She was so sure she'd be able to call him to her by using the ring. He'd found four of her warlocks running around Atlanta, given them identical messages, then cast a spell on each so that the ring's pull was transferred to those four. When the ring was used to call Grendal, it would draw those warlocks, who were now at the farthest east, north, west, and south points of the Atlanta area. By the time the queen or her druid received his message and figured out how to follow Grendal, he'd be home in his own territory.

Queen Medb had no valid complaint. She hadn't captured Lanna, after all, and she could still figure out how to clear her name with regard to the white witches.

It would take some work.

Besides, Grendal had learned while handing off those notes to the warlocks, that Queen Maeve and Cathbad were on their way to a Tribunal meeting. The four designated warlocks might not even reach them with his message until after that meeting.

To be honest, Queen Maeve owed Grendal her appreciation. His two-word note more than fulfilled his part of the agreement. The note explained how to gain Kizira's body per the terms of the blood oath, *if* the queen and druid could figure out the significance of those two words.

Grendal watched the three men lumber around with less intelligence between all of them than one of Grendal's tikbalangs. Such a shame to kill that last creature. It had been a decent informant. If there had been any way to bring the beast back with him, Grendal would have. The first one had been a complete disappointment. Grendal had told him to search for the witch's familiar.

What had he done?

Rounded up dogs. He'd *deserved* to be killed by those VIPER agents.

All things considered, this entire operation had actually worked out quite nicely.

After the queen's Scáth Force soldiers had been informed of where to find the white witches, Grendal was told they'd send a group to take possession. Of course, Grendal had vacated the premises within minutes of capturing Lanna in order to avoid that confrontation.

Let the Medb and VIPER figure out who was at fault for the kidnappings.

"Everything is ready, Master," Leeshen informed him, her usual emotionless mask in place.

As one of the men closed the rear door, Grendal stood a few feet away while he waited as Leeshen walked up to the driver's door.

Grendal addressed the three men. "That concludes my need for your services."

"You gotta pay us," one of them reminded him.

"Of course I do." He glanced to the side where Leeshen wrenched open the van door and yanked the driver out, as if he were some skinny little guy and not a six-foot-tall man with a huge gut.

The driver started complaining. "What are you doing? I—"

Using her free hand, she stabbed a long fingernail into his eye. It made a popping sound, then the driver squeaked out a noise just before her nail penetrated his brain and he slumped to the ground.

The three men facing Grendal shifted their attention and tried to lean forward, trying to see around the van.

Grendal took a step, blocking their view, and said, "Your payment?"

At the mention of money, they lost all interest in any strange noises.

Nightstalkers had told him where to find men with no families, no conscience, and unfortunately, even less concern for hygiene.

He stepped over to them and held out his hand, where a small, charcoal-grey stone with runic carvings glowed in the middle of his palm. "I'd like you to see something very rare."

"What the fuck?" the middle guy griped. "I just want my money."

Keeping his voice calm, Grendal began whispering, "By all the power 'tis mine to wield, I bid thee wander on until ... "

All three men were mesmerized within seconds as Grendal cast his spell. He watched them turn as one and walk away.

Tomorrow, two of them would be found a mile from here with their throats slit. The last one would plunge the knife over and over into his own chest.

He tucked the Slavic runestone into his coat pocket and walked around to climb up to the passenger seat.

"She is stirring, Master," Leeshen informed him.

Grendal listened, and heard Lanna muttering something.

The girl carried power unlike anything he'd ever experienced, and one wrong word said while semi-comatose could send this van cartwheeling.

Dragging up another surge of energy, he snarled at the box.

The wood vibrated.

A high-pitched screech followed, muffled by the wooden crate.

Then silence.

Turning back around, Grendal said, "Hurry, Leeshen, but do not break the speed limit and draw attention. She's fighting her way back to consciousness. That may not hold her long. I hope we make good time, because if she wakes again and puts us at risk, you'll have to sedate her."

Which would mean having to wait another twelve hours until Lanna could be drained, but they were safe as long as she did not call up her powers.

Lifting her index finger with the sharp nail, Leeshen nodded understanding, and placed her finger back on the steering wheel. "We have an eight-minute drive according to the electronics."

His faithful servant pulled out of the lot, and Grendal leaned back to rest. Finally, no one would stand between him and Lanna. This time tomorrow, no one could make a difference.

CHAPTER 30

Evalle's stomach wanted to shove everything she'd eaten earlier back up her throat as the spinning subsided. "I hate teleporting."

Storm had his arms around her, but even that could do only so much after three trips in such a short span, two through different realms, and with a severely drained Tristan piloting.

He had to be the all-time worst teleporter in history.

She opened her eyes to find that they'd landed in one of downtown Atlanta's small parks. If her cheap watch wasn't fried yet, it was nine already. She searched for the street signs.

Look at that. Tristan actually hit close to the mark she'd given him. They were at the corner of Auburn Avenue and Piedmont Avenue in the Sweet Auburn district of Atlanta. The few evergreens in this little downtown corner park offered almost no cover.

At least Tristan hadn't dropped them *in* a tree.

Or in the middle of the intersection. Traffic didn't rush by, but no driver could miss something that just appeared in his or her path.

Tzader stood to one side, shaking off the residual effects, and Adrianna had already stood up from the throne and begun cloaking them.

Evalle said, "Thanks."

Adrianna dipped her head in acknowledgement, but kept feeding her power into shielding five people and a dragon throne.

Good thing, since small groups of young people, probably Georgia State University students, walked past wearing a mix of sweaters, hoodies, and coats.

"Where are we?" Daegan demanded.

Tzader replied, "Downtown Atlanta, very close to the location where the witches and Lanna are supposed to be. I'm calling Trey now." His weary voice sounded as if he'd been dragged the hundreds of miles they'd teleported from North Georgia to downtown Atlanta.

Evalle sniffed at the smell of Caribbean food and forgot about her queasy stomach. She could eat, but that wouldn't happen any time soon.

Daegan got cranked up again. "This is a waste of time."

Adrianna swung around to the dragon. "I'm beginning to think rescuing you is a waste of time."

"You should take care with your tone," he warned.

"And you should keep in mind that I'm trying to break that curse. Don't give me a reason to reconsider."

"Enough," Tzader said in a soft tone that Evalle recognized as his I'm-at-the-end-of-my-patience voice, which meant someone might die soon if they pushed him too far. "Where's Tristan?"

Evalle swung around and searched. "He should be here with us."

"He wasn't last time," Daegan pointed out.

"Over here," Tristan said, sounding pained.

Evalle searched behind the throne, which had landed near a brick wall.

Tristan sat ten feet away with his back against the bricks. She dropped onto her knees beside him. "Tristan?"

His head drooped. Blood seeped from his eyes and ran from his nose and ears.

Tzader was there next. "Heal yourself, Tristan."

"Can't. Too much effort."

Evalle put her fingers on his wrist and felt energy flowing through him, but very slowly. "I'll link with you then you can use my power."

"No. I can't ... fight. Don't use your power."

She looked at Tzader. "What are we going to do?"

Adrianna's soft voice called over, "Trey's here. I'm opening the cloaking for him."

Trey made eye contact with everyone, gave the dragon throne a slow look, and asked Daegan, "What'd you do to piss off someone badly enough to be turned into a chair?"

"Are you all dimwitted?"

Trey looked at Evalle, who said, "He's touchy about being ... that."

Everybody stared at Daegan, who poofed out smoke and ignored them. Trey glanced around then squatted next to Tzader. "What happened to Tristan?"

Tzader explained the multiple teleportation trips, which included two fights with the Medb. "Where are the witches?"

Pointing across the street, Trey said, "Just past that empty lot is a building that's boarded up. I've found a way in at the back, but there are still five warlocks in there and I'm betting they're the Scáth Force you told me about."

"What is it with them sending out groups of five?" Evalle muttered.

Storm shrugged. "That allows enough for three to fight, one to circle around and attack from the back, and one to escape so he can report. Any more than that is too many to move covertly, and any less might be overpowered. That last group of ten was the second wave planned only if five couldn't do a job."

"He's right." Tzader wiped a hand over his mouth, thinking, and spoke softly to Trey, "You may need to leave at this point. Evalle and Tristan chose to come with me, but we're all rogue. Macha isn't going to cut anyone who helps us any slack."

"After Evalle told me where you were and about having the dragon with you, I talked to Sasha and Rowan. They know you three wouldn't be doing this unless you thought it was in all of our best interests. The Beladors' best interests. None of us trust VIPER since they accepted the Medb into the coalition. You, Evalle, and Quinn had my back when the Kujoo tried to take Sasha, and nobody else came to help me. I'm not walking away now."

Evalle worried about all of her friends, but she respected Trey's position. She hoped this dragon was worth the lives being risked.

Tzader nodded and looked around at their group. "Adrianna will have to stay here and keep Tristan and the dragon cloaked."

"No," Daegan ground out. "Do not leave me here with a witch and a half-alive gryphon."

Evalle murmured, "He's really getting on my nerves."

"I heard that."

Tzader stepped around in front of the dragon. "How are we supposed to fight the Medb coven's elite warriors while carrying you around, trying to keep you hidden, *and* keep the Medb from taking you back?"

"Break the curse, and you'll have a warrior like no other on your team."

Evalle came around so there was no confusion over her intent for him to hear her. "Have you always had trouble with self-esteem?"

"I believe the saying in this world is, 'It ain't braggin' if you can do it'." His big jaws curved into a smile.

Adrianna stepped up to the conversation. "I've got the cloaking stable if I'm staying in one place. I'll give breaking the curse another try, but we weren't making any headway back in TÅμr Medb."

Daegan sighed, which was a strange sound coming from a dragon. "That's because the most *difficult* place to break this curse was TÅμr Medb."

"Is there somewhere that makes it easier?" Adrianna asked, sounding just a bit exasperated at that information.

"Yes, but we have no chance of going there right now with the gryphon down."

"I see. Everyone step away from the dragon." She waved her arms to spread everyone away from the throne. "If teleporting in that shape didn't kill you, I guess you'll survive whatever I do."

"You can't kill me."

She arched a challenging eyebrow at him. "Lucky for you I agreed to do my best to keep you alive."

He did that dragon grin again until she added, "For now."

His silver eyes swirled, and the black diamond centers sharpened. "Get on with it, witch."

Adrianna cut her eyes to Evalle who said, "I know. We'll owe you big time. Please don't kill him or turn him into a coffee table."

Opening her palm, Adrianna called to the Witchlock power that rolled up in a swirling white ball. Energy steamed away as it spun on her palm.

Daegan got serious, asking, "Do you remember the spell and how we decided to break it?"

"Yes. Everyone please be very still, and stay out of my line of sight or you might be affected."

Evalle, Storm, Tzader, and Trey backed up several steps. Tristan was safe on the ground where he'd slumped. They had to get him to Treoir so he could recharge faster, but he was the only one who could teleport.

If she linked to him and drained her power, she risked Storm, Tzader, and Trey's lives when they fought the warlocks. Trey was the most rested and they needed his strength.

Still, she couldn't leave here without knowing Tristan would be okay until she returned.

Adrianna held the bright orb out toward Daegan and began speaking in Gaelic. Evalle knew that only because Adrianna had spoken similar words once before to trick a warlock's body into turning on itself.

Power poured from Adrianna's hand in a white vapor, wrapping around the throne again and again, growing brighter as she called out word after word of her chant.

The throne started shaking and the dragon stretched its head from one side to the other, as if trying to force his body out of that shape.

Adrianna's skin turned translucent and her lips went from ruby red to deep purple. Her blue eyes glowed and the words took actual form as they left her mouth, circling the dragon.

Daegan clenched his big jaws. Evalle flinched at the sound of tendons stretching and bones popping. His body was being torn apart. Muscles flexed and bulged along his neck, back, and arms.

The clawed fingers on one hand formed slowly, each digit breaking away from the fixed shape.

Then nothing.

Gasping for air, Adrianna slowed her chanting, then finally dropped her hand with the orb, which vanished as she closed her fingers. "That's all ... I can do. I can't break it. I'm sorry."

Even the dragon was fighting for air.

Worse than all that was the heartbreaking misery in Daegan's eyes. That misery spelled defeat.

How could anyone suffer being locked into that form and left alive for two thousand years?

Evalle offered, "Let's rescue Mattie and the other witches, then we'll see if Rowan can help."

Adrianna shot her a look of doubt, but said nothing.

Hope danced once more in Daegan's eyes, breaking her heart again, because Evalle couldn't see how Rowan, a white witch, would succeed after Adrianna had used Witchlock on him. But Evalle had learned over the years that it ain't over 'til it's over.

One of Grady's strange sayings, but it somehow made sense at times like this.

Tzader cleared his throat. "Sounds like a plan." But his eyes contradicted the conviction in his voice. "We'll be back as soon as we can."

Evalle checked on Tristan again. "Let me give you some power before I leave, something to just get you started healing."

"Don't. I haven't died three times. I still have one regeneration left if this goes sideways."

She wasn't sure the regeneration would work with him so wiped out that he couldn't call up his beast or shift into a gryphon. "Okay, but tell Adrianna if you need help before I return. She's still got some juice even after that attempt at breaking the curse."

"I'm good. Go kick their asses so we can find a place for me to rest, or we'll never get back to Treoir."

She didn't have it in her to tell him that he couldn't teleport them soon enough to make it work for Brina anyway. Instead, she said, "Rest. I'll be back soon."

Adrianna opened a slit in the cloaking that Trey walked through with Evalle, Storm, and Tzader following.

When she crossed the street and looked back, the park appeared empty and would stay that way. Adrianna's cloaking also deterred any visitors.

Now if they could just make good on their vow to save the white witches.

CHAPTER 31

Tzader kept an eye on his team as they walked nonchalantly past the original Atlanta Life Insurance Building, which had been vacant for quite a while. Four stately columns stood along the front wall, reaching up to the third floor.

The captured white witches had been hidden right under their noses in the heart of the Sweet Auburn district in downtown Atlanta.

Shielding this from scrying or tracking must have taken a massive amount of power.

Queen Maeve and Cathbad would have that level of power, but no reason to stash the witches here instead of taking them back to TÅμr Medb.

With a quick look around, Trey slipped into the shadows at the far side of the building. When he pointed up at the half-covered window where some of the boarding had rotted away, Tzader stepped up and cupped his hands.

To conserve their energy, Tzader signaled that he'd give Trey and Evalle a boost up to the ledge. Trey stepped into Tzader's cupped hands, and Tzader used kinetics as he tossed Trey up to the third floor.

Evalle went next, then Storm, who bent his knees and leaped silently to the ledge like a jaguar on steroids.

Tzader backed off and took a running start, then pushed off in a flip, shoving the palms of his hands down to use kinetics for a last push the rest of the way. He landed hard.

They all paused to listen for any disturbance below.

When no one came charging up, they huddled.

Trey said, "They're in the basement. I saw them through an opening where a vent came out, and heard the warlocks talking about guarding the witches until their queen showed up."

Tzader asked, "Did you see Lanna?"

"No."

Hopefully the young woman had been stuck somewhere out of view from that point. Tzader owed Quinn more than he could ever pay for keeping Queen Maeve and Cathbad occupied. He could not lose Lanna while Quinn stood in the gap for all of them.

Turning to his new team, Tzader explained, "I'll take point. Let's find the stairs and try to get down there without alerting them."

Easier said than done in an old building, but they were in luck. The steps to the basement were metal, which didn't creak as wood might.

He slowed as he neared the basement, which had no door blocking their way. No one spoke, but with his Belador hearing powered up, every shoe scuff came through loud and clear.

He eased forward to peek into the room.

Five beds that looked like sacrificial pedestals each held a woman, strapped down. The three on the far end of the room were middle-aged, average-looking women. The fourth one coming back this way was a younger woman who had been stripped, and her head sagged to one side. If the eyes staring at him were alive, that one was locked in her own personal horror.

The closest table held a woman with the wrinkled skin and white hair fitting Mother Mattie's description.

Where was Lanna?

If Queen Medb had taken her, why leave the rest of them here?

Tzader hoped Mattie could give him answers. Using hand signals for Storm's benefit, he told his team there were two guards at the far end, two at this end, and one on the far side who had a clear view of the entire room.

Trey gave a signal that the first warlock on the left appeared to be the leader, from what he'd seen earlier. That made sense. The other four stood still while their leader kept checking his watch.

Evalle's voice filled Tzader's head. *Storm just whispered an idea to me.*

He'll go down there as a jaguar.

Tzader said, *They might kill him on sight.*

She looked at Storm, who held her gaze until she told Tzader, *His majik will protect him and give us the element of surprise while they focus on him.*

Tzader gave Storm a thumbs-up. Storm turned and left, hurrying back up the steps.

Where'd he go? Tzader asked Evalle after she'd shared the information with Trey.

I don't know. He told me he had a plan, so I trust him.

A huge black beast raced down the stairs, yellow eyes glowing and lips pulled back to expose sharp fangs.

Storm burst into the room and roared so loudly the windows should be exploding.

Tzader dove down the stairs and around the corner right behind him.

Warlocks were yelling and throwing hits of power at the jaguar's coat, striking him glancing blows.

Storm flew around the room, slapping sharp claws at anything standing that could bleed.

Tzader engaged the warlock Trey had fingered as the leader, who kicked and spun his hands like a ninja set on fast-forward. He hammered a kinetic blow at the warlock's head before the Medb could release whatever he was spinning.

The guy flew backwards, slammed the wall, and came down on both feet, ready to fight.

Damn, that sucker was going to be tough to kill.

Evalle and Trey each engaged a warlock. Storm leaped onto the back of one and chomped down on a big shoulder. The warlock screamed.

If he had any idea of what Scáth Force could do, Tzader would link with Evalle and Trey, but they did not link unless they were certain they could defeat an enemy. Scáth Force were unknowns at this point.

Tzader kept tossing kinetic slugs, right, left, right, left.

Blood sprayed from the guy's nose on the last one.

Lifting the warlock by the throat with kinetic force, Tzader had intended to slam him down.

The bastard's black lips opened, and a torrent of purple smoke boiled in

Tzader's face, blinding him momentarily. He couldn't let go unless he was ready to die.

Boot heels ran across the floor behind Tzader.

That had to be the one who'd planned to escape and bring back reinforcements. Just as Storm had said.

Listening to the footsteps, Tzader spun twice and threw the smoke-bomb warlock in the direction of the noise with every bit of kinetic power he possessed.

Bones cracked as bodies smacked together and hit a solid wall with a crunch that should mean dead.

Eyes burning from the acidic smoke, Tzader could barely make out the two warlocks as they scrambled to their feet. Both launched their bodies at him. Not *nearly* dead enough. This was taking too damn long.

Everyone and every*thing* kept delaying his getting to Brina.

Screw it. He was done. *I will not lose the woman I love.*

Running toward them, Tzader lifted his hands and shoved his energy into a kinetic wall powered by all the frustration of the past week. The force slammed into the duo, driving them back into the concrete wall.

They hit so hard this time that both heads shattered like crushed eggs.

Tzader kept ramming them anyway. If not for the Medb, Brina would not have had to be locked away for years. Now he had to yank a dragon out of a throne shape, and he couldn't even do that. He'd avoided accepting it, but that damn scale would run out of energy in less than an hour.

There was no way to reach her before that. Maybe not ever.

Someone grabbed an arm on each side of him.

Evalle said, "Tzader, they're dead. We're done."

He shook with the adrenaline flooding him, but he dropped the connection and the bodies fell in two mangled heaps. Turning, he sucked in a deep breath, aware of Trey and Evalle watching him. "I'm fine. How are the witches?"

Trey said, "Those three at the end of the room are dead."

Evalle ran up the stairs and came back just as quickly with an arm full of clothes. "Over here, Storm," she called to the big cat still stalking the room, like a predator pissed off because his hunt had been cut short.

She dropped what he needed in a clean spot and used his coat to cover the young woman with the blank eyes. "This one's got a pulse, but she's cold and in bad shock."

Tzader moved over to Mattie and started freeing her legs from the leather straps. Mattie made a noise. Tzader stepped up to face her. "Are you okay? Is anything broken or ... hurt?"

"I'm fine." She sounded drunk, but he doubted she'd had a drop of alcohol. "My granddaughter." She turned to the side and whimpered. "What did he do to her?"

"Are you Mattie?" Tzader asked, trying to engage her again.

Sniffling, the witch looked around. "Yes. Where is he?"

"They're all dead."

She tried to sit up and Tzader put his arm behind her fragile body. She said, "Those are Medb warlocks. They didn't kidnap us."

"What?"

Her words were still a little slurred, but new strength wound through her voice with each word. "That bastard. A disgusting, yellow-skinned wizard."

Grendal? Please tell me I'm wrong. Tzader didn't want to ask the next question, because he knew the answer would make him sick. "Did you see a young woman here by the name of Lanna?"

"Yes. His creepy assistant captured her sneaking around outside. She's a sweet girl. When that slimeball questioned her, she said she'd used a bit of animal hair to find me. She said it loud so I would hear. She was letting me know my Oskar was safe. Look around you. This whole, horrible thing was about finding that girl. The wizard had offered to trade Queen Maeve *five* of us for Lanna, but then he found her first."

Shit. Shit. Shit. Tzader turned to Storm, who had just pulled his shirt over his head, finished dressing. "Can you scent Lanna in here, Storm?"

"No, and I didn't scent her outside either. The wizard must have cleaned her scent or replaced it. I *could* smell the strongest scent in here, and it's the same odor I encountered twice a few months back. I didn't recognize it last night at Mattie's house," he said, walking over to Tzader. "The trail was somehow concealed from that point, too, which was not normal."

Tzader admitted, "I think Grendal's the wizard behind all this."

Evalle walked up. "It's got to be him, Storm. He was involved in the beast games. You picked this scent at Mattie's house that you recognized as being from the illegal beast fight in the mountains where we met Imogenia." She cringed in Tzader's direction. "That you don't want to know about since you were Maistir at the time, so forget I mentioned that."

"The least of my worries right now." Tzader swallowed. "Grendal has Lanna. This was all set up just to capture her."

Evalle said, "We heard. What are we going to do now?"

Tzader looked at his watch.

All he could think about was that the dragon scale Brina had was losing power by the second.

She'd be alone, and vulnerable to whatever Macha had in mind, none of which was in Brina's best interest.

If Macha hadn't done something already.

Brina's last time in hologram form had him worried. The fact that she'd been failing to dream walk concerned him even more. He'd been refusing to focus on any of that because, if he did, he'd lose his ability to think clearly or to lead his team.

Mattie stared at her granddaughter and snuffled softly.

Tzader patted Mattie's shoulder. "Our people will be here soon. We have druids who can help her."

"We have Adrianna outside shielding some of our group, too." Evalle said as she walked around Mattie's table to stand next to Tzader.

Mattie turned her nose up. "I don't need any Sterling witch to take care of my family."

Ah, hell. Tzader didn't want to put those two anywhere near each other. Adrianna's patience had already been tested severely by Daegan.

When Trey came over, he explained that he was handpicking Beladors he could trust to transport the women, but he had to find the ones who were not already on duty with non-Beladors and give them time to access ambulances not presently in use. Trey asked Mattie questions about what had happened. Knowing him, he was also using telepathy concurrently to communicate and organize the medical support.

Evalle nudged Tzader with a shoulder.

He asked, "What?"

"Don't give up hope," she whispered. "We *will* save Brina."

He gave her a sad smile, not even trying to deny where his mind had been. "I have to break a two-thousand-year-old curse to free a dragon and take him to Treoir. I have no way to *get* the dragon to Treoir. I also have to find Lanna before Grendal leaves the country with her, and Quinn is putting himself in danger right now trying to keep Maeve and Cathbad out of our way. Looking pretty bleak."

He reached to free Mattie's arm from the leather clasp.

Light flashed and a cloud of sparkles showered in one spot. When it cleared, a six-foot-two woman with rich mocha skin, eyes sparkling like sapphires, and auburn hair blanketing her shoulders stood glaring at everyone in the room.

Her gaze landed on Tzader's hands still holding one last strap on Mattie's arm.

The Amazon beauty's frigid gaze went to Tzader's face. She announced, "You die first."

CHAPTER 32

Evalle shoved a kinetic force field in front of her, Mattie, and Tzader. In a flash, Storm and Trey showed up next to her and Tzader. Had Grendal set this as a trap, then sent someone back to the basement to wipe them all out?

The crazy sparkly woman pointed her finger and said, "Now you're just pissing me off—"

Mattie called out, still sounding drugged. "Don't harm them, Caron! They're saving me."

Evalle groaned. "Crap." Now she recognized that face as the one in the photo at Mattie's house The photo that had freakin' looked up at her.

Caron pulled back her still-loaded finger and tapped her chin. "Mattie? What *are* you doing here?"

"Having tea. What the hell does it look like?"

"Your language could use a good scrubbing," Caron muttered, then focused on Evalle and her group. "You were snooping around Mattie's house."

Caron knew? That was give-you-nightmares scary, and Evalle couldn't deny the accusation. "I was trying to find out who'd kidnapped her."

With no indication of whether she accepted that or not, Caron ordered, "Drop that ridiculous shield or I'll turn it into a head wrap for all of you."

Since they'd all heard that Caron was capable of leveling a city, Evalle lowered her shield. She asked Caron, "How'd you know she was here?"

"You talkin' to me?" Caron replied in a voice pitched with an accent straight from a New York 'hood.

Trey snapped his fingers. "De Niro in *Taxi Driver*, right?"

"I should never have encouraged you to watch my movies," Mattie grumbled. "Worst Robert De Niro impression *ever*."

Evalle's mouth dropped open. Mattie was just waking up from being obviously abused, they were surrounded by innocent women who, from the look of it, might never fully recover from the horror they'd suffered, and these two were sniping at each other about movies.

"Better than you crooning songs by that old fart, Sinatra, while you cook."

Mattie gasped. "You are so disrespectful."

"You are so right."

Caron marched over to where Mattie was sitting completely upright now, with Tzader's help. Mattie said, "Glad you're here, but I wasn't expecting you until tomorrow. What brought you in early?"

"I got a message."

Mattie studied Caron with lifted eyebrows. "Oh? From an old boyfriend?"

"From an old *slug*." Caron glanced around her. "What are you doing in this place?"

Mattie gave Caron a short version of what Grendal had done.

"He's mine," Caron declared, leaving no room for discussion.

Evalle would like to watch Grendal go up against Caron. She had a hunch Grendal had picked his last fight. But she doubted Grendal would be traveling alone. Evidently Caron believed she could take on anything. *Guess we'll find out.*

Tzader told Caron, "He has a young woman who is important to us. We need to find out what Grendal's done with her before anyone kills him."

Caron huffed. "Why is this my problem?"

Evalle started to speak, but Mattie beat her to it. "Because that young woman put her life at risk to find me, plus she's the reason I'm not dead, and now we have a chance to save Sissy."

Caron's forehead creased in confusion. "Sissy? What's wrong with her? Where is she?"

Mattie pointed to the next bed. Tzader stepped aside as Caron hurried around. Trey had found a blanket to better cover up Mattie's granddaughter, who had yet to make a sound. When Caron pulled the cover back, she sucked in a breath at the vicious bruises, dried blood, and the glassy-eyed stare.

Caron released that breath in a vicious growl.

Emotion rasping her voice, Mattie said, "Grendal raped and tortured her because I wouldn't help him find Lanna. I didn't know where she was, but even if I'd known, we don't sacrifice one life for another. What are we going to do?"

Caron tenderly stroked the young woman's forehead, then brushed her eyelids closed. "Let me clear her memories and put her into a deep sleep to allow her body to begin healing. She'll need at least a week in stasis, then we'll figure it out." Caron laid her hand back on the abused woman's forehead and murmured soft words, which Evalle doubted she would recognize even if Caron had spoken louder.

Once the Fae woman had finished, she turned to Mattie. "I need to follow this wizard while the trail is fresh. Are you safe until I return?"

"Yes, but how will you find them so quickly? From what Grendal was saying, he and his bodyguard were leaving with Lanna and heading for an airport. They were using a vehicle. No way to follow a scent."

Caron stared at her half sister for long seconds, then finally said, "Do you have anything the wizard touched?"

"Sissy's shirt. He tore it off her."

"Probably this one," Trey said as he crossed the room and lifted a pink sweatshirt spotted with blood. "It was underneath her table when we came in." He brought it to Caron, who nodded her acknowledgement and said, "I know someone who can find them with this."

Mattie's mouth fell open. "You think Deek will help?"

Caron shrugged. "If he refuses me, I'll rip his tongue out."

Evalle met Tzader's gaze. Having a centaur and Fae battle would put the cherry on this day.

"Caron," Mattie said in a tired voice.

"Oh, all right. I'll try not to kill him before I get what I need. Satisfied?"

"Yes. Please find the girl. If there's a choice between bringing Lanna back safely and killing Grendal, save the girl, because he plans something worse for her than he did to Sissy."

Tzader interrupted. "Hold on. Depending on how long it takes you to get back, we may have to leave with the women. I have three people outside, a block away, who will be exposed if any Medb show up and the cloaking fails."

Evalle ticked each threat off mentally. Queen Maeve, Cathbad, or the Scáth Force. Then there was Macha and VIPER.

"I don't have time to waste," Caron said. "You will protect these women with your life and stay here until I return."

Tzader went from understanding to fierce in two seconds. "Now wait a minute."

Caron lifted her arms and vanished.

"*Shit!*"

His outburst worried Evalle. "I'm *not* just sitting here."

Mattie warned, "Please give her a chance to find Grendal and come back. If I know Caron, she'll find them fast and return in a blink. She left Sissy and me only because I told her I trust you. As long as I'm right here with you when she returns, it will be fine. If not, well, let's just say it would be dangerous to push her when she's already on edge. She and Sissy are very close."

Evalle suggested to Tzader, "All the women are stable right now. What if Trey and I bring the other three here?"

"That's a much better idea than crossing Caron," Mattie interjected. "She acts as if ice water runs through her veins, but the truth is she's insanely protective of those she holds dear. Give her a chance to find this Grendal and your Lanna."

Tzader had little choice, which showed on his face.

It wasn't as though he could make it to Treoir without getting Tristan back up to speed anyway, and that wasn't happening any time soon.

Evalle and Trey hurried to where Adrianna, Tristan, and the grouchy dragon waited in the park at the corner.

Adrianna was starting to tire from trying different approaches with the throne while maintaining the cloaking. Tristan had fallen asleep, and the dragon started in on Evalle and Trey the minute they entered the concealed area.

Daegan ordered, "What is taking you so long? How do you people get anything done?"

Tristan shook his head and stood up, listing to one side. He shoved a hand against the wall to support himself. His words were mangled. "We reshcued you, didn't we? Why, I'm shtill not sure."

Evalle heard the slur in Tristan's speech and took a closer look.

Daegan scoffed, "Pat yourself on the back for a half-assed mission. Yes, I'm out of the tower, but locked in this form I'm a sitting target."

"Detailsh, detailsh," Tristan mumbled.

Evalle frowned at Tristan. "Can you walk a block under your own power?"

"Sure."

She turned to the witch. "Adrianna, if you'll keep us cloaked until we reach that next building, you'll get a break."

"Done."

"Trey and I are going to carry the throne."

Tristan slurred, "Not usin' ki...neticsh?"

"We're pretty wiped out and have to save what we have in case more Medb show up." However, as a Belador, and especially as an Alterant-gryphon, she was far stronger than a human.

She tilted the throne back and caught his shoulders. Trey grabbed the bottom.

Daegan grumbled, "This is absurd."

Evalle held her head back away from that fire-breathing snout. "We killed five of their elite Scáth Force, which means someone will come looking for them or the witches as soon as Cathbad and Queen Maeve leave the Tribunal meeting we set up to get them out of TÅµr Medb. One of our friends is keeping those two busy arguing a case, but there's a limit to how much time anyone can drag out one of those meetings. Unless you want to remain right here in this form forever, work with us while we get the witches set."

"Fine, but why're you wasting precious minutes on a bunch of witches when your warrior queen is running out of time and needs my help?"

The group moved quickly across the intersection even with Tristan stumbling alongside them.

Evalle said, "Because this is how we roll. No one left behind. We don't leave those in need or put our own interests first."

"Oh? You follow Macha who puts *her* interests first."

"That's not going to be part of the equation after this."

"What do you mean?"

Evalle gritted out her reply while trying to keep up her end of the throne. "Surely you can figure it out. Every Belador involved in this operation to get you out of TÅµr Medb has gone rogue. We've all broken our vows to Macha, and we all face possible death for this level of breach." Evalle shifted her hold and strained to keep walking. "You weigh a ton."

Tristan muttered, "You should try teleporthing his heavy asth."

"You should all stop speaking of me as though I'm a piece of furniture," Daegan warned.

Tristan glanced over at Evalle and sent the word *certifiable* to her telepathically.

She wasn't arguing.

Daegan said, "Don't worry about Macha. You'll be under my protection."

Right. No one home in that camp. Evalle and Storm had talked about potential consequences.

If all else failed, Storm got to implement his Plan B, which meant disappearing, but only if Evalle could take everyone else with them.

Thinking about giving up everything she'd been building with Storm hurt too much. When they reached the locked front door of the building, Evalle asked Tristan, "Can you get us in this way?"

"Eashy," he boasted. It took him longer than normal just to execute the simple task, but he managed to move the tumblers kinetically. Finally he had the door open, allowing them to enter on the street level and finally put the dragon down.

Tristan locked up behind them. "Now what?"

Adrianna found a place to sit on a set of stairs. "I'm not moving another inch until I have to."

Evalle said, "I'm going back down to help Tzader and Storm."

Trey stepped over next to her. "Me, too."

"You're going to leave me up here exposed?" Daegan complained. "You don't think the Medb can walk through that door just as easily?"

Aiming a give-me-a-break look at Daegan, Evalle said, "Fine. We're all going downstairs. You, too, Adrianna."

She made a disturbingly scary sound and stomped over to the dragon. "I hate you." Then she headed down the stairs.

Tristan opened his mouth and Evalle just knew he was going to agree. She said, "Tristan, you go down next in case we need some help stopping him if I drop my end of the throne."

"Do not toy with me," Daegan growled.

That brought a grin to Tristan's face, then he was gone.

Trey took the heavy downside end, which was fine by Evalle since the Belador brute outweighed her by a hundred pounds of muscle. When they finally found a suitable spot downstairs for the dragon, Evalle stood upright and stretched her back.

No sign of the Fae woman yet.

CHAPTER 33

Tribunal meeting, Nether Realm

"Now that Queen Maeve and Cathbad the Druid are present, what is your grievance against them, Belador?"

Quinn just managed not to roll his eyes at Loki's booming announcement.

He'd have to do his best to drag this out without Loki, Varpulis, or Ma'at losing patience ... or losing all the gryphons to this queen bitch.

That might end with bloodshed. His.

Shifting his attention to the queen and Cathbad, Quinn said, "I am the current Maistir over the North American Beladors. As such, it is my duty to protect all those the VIPER coalition serves, second only to protecting humans. But it is my moral obligation to see that no one is falsely accused of any crime. We live in chaotic times, and I wish to see the end of this conflict that has gone on too long between the Medb and the Beladors."

Loki's eyes had narrowed more with each comment, surely ready to pounce on Quinn and demand he move this along faster. That was until Quinn made noises about smoothing out relations between the Beladors and the Medb.

Queen Maeve and Cathbad eyed him with suspicion, as they should.

He certainly had no intention of making their lives any easier.

Quinn continued, expounding on how he'd personally protected a witch of the Medb coven recently and how he'd been instructing his Beladors to do the right thing.

In truth, he'd slammed on his brakes right before hitting a woman crossing the street against the light, who'd then yelled at him and threatened to report him to VIPER. He'd protected the witch from his wrath, thus making his statement true.

And he had told Beladors over and over to do the right thing, which was to always protect the tribe.

Cathbad interrupted a couple of times, trying to push Quinn to make his point, but Quinn knew how to orate and would use those opportunities to ask, "Am I the only one present who truly wishes to see peace between our peoples?"

That shut up Cathbad and drew groans from the peanut gallery on the dais.

Time often ran longer in the human world than it did here. When Quinn felt he had stretched his intro as far as he could, he said, "With all that in mind, I bring a grave situation to this Tribunal."

He heard mutters of "Finally," from all around the space.

Quinn held his pleasant composure, but turned his "concerned face" up a notch. "I'm sure by now that Queen Maeve and Cathbad have been made aware of the white witches who were recently kidnapped in Atlanta of the human world."

The fact that neither Cathbad nor the queen made a sound was damning in Quinn's eyes. He continued, "Evidence of Noirre majik has been found at the homes of the missing witches."

Loki asked, "Are you accusing Queen Maeve and Cathbad of being involved or of ordering these kidnappings?"

Quinn allowed the silence to build until he said, "I am not one to jump to conclusions. I am here to avoid more conflict. You have convicted wrongdoers on far less than the evidence I have that points to their involvement."

Cathbad erupted in a flurry of anger. "Noirre was traded to non-Medb coven witches prior to our return. Anyone could have used Noirre."

"Exactly," Quinn agreed. "You might have noted that I've yet to accuse anyone present of being behind this."

"Then what are we doin' here, Belador?"

"Meeting on neutral ground to determine just what has happened. I have agents tracking down a witness who reported that a Medb warlock was seen at Mother Mattie's house around the time of her kidnapping." That much was true, because the warlocks made a habit of touring areas where white witches lived.

Queen Maeve took a step forward. "My grievance is greater than his. I do not come here with maybes and possibilities, but absolutes that have not been addressed."

Quinn knew where she was going, and jumped in to cut her off. "I cannot speak for Macha when it comes to the gryphons, but since you've brought it up I'd like to ask the Tribunal if they might be ready to vote on the gryphon right to be a free race."

"You can't do that!" Queen Maeve froze and looked up at Loki, suddenly aware of how her words had sounded.

All three deities turned to her. Loki asked, "Do you think to come here and tell us what we may or may not do?"

She took a step back, and Quinn could tell it cost her to eat humble pie. "My apologies. I'm clearly not happy about being accused of yet another mishap. I'm allowed to transfer only a few of our coven at a time to the human world, and they enter a hostile environment. Cathbad and I were slightly delayed in our arrival here because we'd taken the time to inform VIPER of what our warlocks had learned about the missing witches. Not only are we not behind it, but we're helping VIPER find those at fault."

Bloody hell. Quinn hadn't expected that, but he wasn't done with her. He'd gain the Tribunal's vote on the gryphons. That might bring Macha, but he seriously doubted Macha cared whether or not the Tribunal ever voted on the gryphons.

Now that everyone on the dais had resumed their positions, Loki said, "Good. Sounds as though your groups are finally doing something to end this squabbling."

Classic Loki. He reduced hundreds of years of bloody battles to a pissing contest.

Queen Maeve said, "If I may, I have something to suggest that would simplify the gryphon vote."

She'd hit on the right note for Loki. "By all means, share it."

"I propose it's a waste of time to change the gryphon status, and to do so would also set a dangerous precedent."

What the hell was she up to now?

The goddess Ma'at said, "Please explain."

Smiling like someone who held all the cards, Queen Maeve did just that. "It's quite simple. Demons aren't a recognized race, wyverns aren't a recognized race, and, therefore, gryphons shouldn't be allowed to set a precedent that may start a chain of requests concerning other ... beasts."

That miserable witch. Quinn argued, "Demons and wyverns have never lived in the human world, protecting humans and nonhumans as VIPER agents. Evalle Kincaid has repeatedly proven her value in that capacity, and deserves to be given the right to live as a free person, as do the other gryphons."

Cathbad let out a *pfffft* sound. "The only difference is that gryphons can shift their form to one emulating a human."

Emulating. Quinn wanted to rip that druid's head off.

The druid was not finished. "Evalle started out as a human who could shift into a beast, then she evolved into a gryphon. Perhaps we've not seen the end of this evolution. How can you expect a Tribunal to grant any group this level of recognition when they have no idea what the final version will be? Gryphons may continue to change and regress into mindless beasts. What would we do then?"

Unbelievable. How had this turned into one new way to screw Evalle and the gryphons?

Ma'at shared her opinion. "You've made a valid point, Cathbad."

Quinn had no argument to counter the unknown. Gods and goddesses were wary of Alterants already, and this just gave them the perfect answer for how to avoid getting any more deeply involved in this issue.

Macha, damn her self-centered soul, would never stand here and fight for the gryphons. But neither would she give them up.

Quinn opened his mouth to return everyone to the original topic of missing witches, though even he had to admit pursuing that argument would be more difficult now that Queen Maeve had addressed it.

Her gaze speared Quinn, making it clear she was not finished with him. Now what?

Loki spoke up. "With nothing new to discuss, that concludes..."

Quinn said, "Wait," at the same moment Queen Maeve said, "I am not finished with addressing what is more important to me than all of this."

Snapping his mouth shut, Quinn waited for her new attack. What did she have up her sleeve?

Varpulis never missed a step, running quickly in place, and not sweating a drop. He asked, "What is your complaint?"

Loki and Ma'at looked at the skinny guy, as though surprised he had vocal chords.

Taking her own pause for dramatic effect, Queen Maeve said, "I request you bring Macha of Treoir here, as she must answer for her Maistir's role in the theft of my property."

Quinn's jaw fell slack.

They were all busted. Quinn had no way to inform Tzader, Evalle, Tristan, and Adrianna.

CHAPTER 34

Caron owed Deek for his help.

He hadn't gloated.

That worried her.

Only for Mattie and Sissy would she have gone to Deek. To his credit, he'd made it easy. Once she'd filled him in, Deek tapped one of his connections—a Greek goddess—to locate Grendal. Caron would have eventually found the wizard, but not in less than a minute the way Deek had.

She did not thank him.

A Fae would not insult someone by allowing words to diminish a favor of such magnitude. She merely said, "I'll be in touch to repay you."

Deek hadn't said a word once he'd given her the information. Why hadn't he stomped around and carried on? He hadn't even shifted into his power form as a centaur. No, he'd stood calmly outside his nightclub, dressed in black jeans and a deep red Henley, looking like some kind of dark fantasy. His gaze had drifted over her from head to toe, but he hadn't made the first arrogant comment.

Sexy irritation. Thankfully, he'd excused himself to take care of an issue inside, or she would have made a fool of herself standing there too long, staring at him.

He might have even realized she still nursed a broken heart.

When salt air teased her nose, she sharpened her focus.

She shared a bond with wind above all other elements and it came to her aid now, as it always did. She traveled swiftly toward the Atlantic

Ocean where it lapped against the coast at Charleston, and glided out over the water, an invisible assassin intent on justice. Once she located the cargo ship, she found a narrow space between stacked containers that hid her change into human form. The same form she'd shown the strangers around Mattie.

Few had ever seen her true form.

Most of those were dead.

Calm seas and gentle winds allowed the ship to glide along smoothly. She moved from shadow to shadow until she caught the odor of Grendal's disgusting majik.

What had he done to damage his majik until it smelled so putrid? If he wasn't shielding the odor, then he was either too arrogant to think anyone would catch him here or his majik was too weak. Maybe both.

She swept past crewmembers with a gentle, whispered, *don't-look-at-me* glamour, forcing them to ignore her. They passed by, oblivious to her presence. After a five-minute walk, Caron entered a quiet hallway with no crew traffic.

Grendal's stink clogged the air down here.

Striding forward with an easy gait, she came upon a woman with dark red skin. Red, as if someone had roasted her in the sun until she was medium rare on the outside. What had happened to her hair? Bald on one side and chin-length on the other side. And purple. Hard to tell her age, but she appeared close to Caron's twenty-seven, and she was equal to Caron in size.

Size would get you only so far in a fight.

Caron could tell that this woman had once been a witch. She was cut, physically, like a warrior, but no human woman, witch or otherwise, would ever be Caron's equal.

One day, Deek D'Alimonte would get that through his thick skull.

Why am I allowing him to distract me right now?

This woman could be green-skinned or covered in scales. Caron didn't care as long as she got out of the way.

What did Mattie preach? Try the easy way first. Caron ordered, "Move."

Cinnamon Girl cocked her head with a confused-dog look. Did she not understand English?

Maybe I should try a different language and address her directly. Caron said, "Bogadh ... Sai d' ai'... Movimento ... *bitch.*"

The woman finally squared her shoulders and said, "Leave."

She did understand English. *So much for the easy way, Mattie.*

Past the point of putting up with another delay, Caron took a step.

The woman dove forward, flicking a handful of wicked fingernails at Caron's throat. Caron rolled back out of the way, twisted, and yanked Sunburn Girl over her head, letting momentum take her to the floor.

When the woman flipped back to her feet, Caron clapped. "Got any other tricks? Do those fingernails double as hors d'oeuvres skewers? No? Guess I'll just have to see how far down your throat I can shove them."

Her opponent's red skin glowed and the muscles across her shoulders bulged into a hump on her back. When the woman spoke this time, it sounded as though she'd swallowed Darth Vader. "I will take you apart slowly and savor your death."

"It speaks! Okay, let's get on with it. I'm pushed for time."

When the woman charged her this time, Caron waited calmly, watching for the majik attack. Vicious words meant for cursing your worst enemy flowed from the dark lips of what had to be Grendal's guard.

Caron lifted a hand and called upon the air to spin the poisonous flow back at the woman.

All at once, her attacker jerked to a stop and on the next inhale she clawed at her throat, choking as her neck swelled thicker and thicker.

Something was growing in there.

Her face went from deep red to purple to blue until she jabbed a long fingernail straight into her own heart. She arched back, unable to scream, and dropped to the floor, twitching.

Caron glanced down at herself. "One down and not a drop of blood on me. Score."

She put her hand on the door handle, turning it slowly. As she opened the door, she heard wrenching sobs that took her breath away. The female voice reminded Caron of her great-niece.

Grendal must have put a cloaking on his red watchdog and something to hide the sound inside this room as long as the door remained shut. Caron hurried to step inside and close the door, standing in a tiny foyer created only by a short wall separating her from the rest of the room. She kept her presence hidden until she had a better idea of what she was going up against.

A wizard who could overpower Mattie and change a witch into that red abomination outside was not one to take lightly.

Caron eased up to the corner and looked around to find a blonde teenage girl hanging midair with dark shadows swirling around her. She screamed, "Noooo!"

The stink made sense now. A hideous, yellow-skinned man was busy calling up his dark spirits, which were swamping the terrified girl. Grendal hadn't heard Caron's quiet entry. He shouted at his captive, who had to be Lanna, "Give me your majik. You will make more. Look at what you've done to me, you bitch. I'm dying from the outside in. My skin is drawing tight and killing me."

The dark spirits were holding Lanna's arms straight out from her body. She screamed, "No! You will kill others."

"But you will live. Stop making this more difficult." Grendal stood up. "We'll do it another way, but it will take longer." He unzipped his pants.

Caron had seen enough. Her father would be angry if he knew she went into a fight without any idea of the power she battled, but she'd told him more than once that sometimes you just have to wing it.

First the spirits had to go, so that she faced off with only Grendal.

Calling up her majik, she revealed herself and ordered, "Spirits of darkness, release her now!"

The spirits howled and snarled, bouncing all over the room.

Why hadn't that worked?

Grendal turned around with his pants falling down around his bony knees.

Oh, please. Not even an acid wash was going to wipe that creepy image from her mind.

"Who are you?" Grendal shouted.

How often did she answer stupid questions? *Let me think on that ... never.*

Caron dissolved her human form into a crystalized state that should protect her from anything Grendal came up with, but that didn't stop him from calling up more spirits and bellowing curses at her. Caron attacked the spirits on their level, lashing out at each one with her majik. Energy clawed at her and punched her in the head. She wheeled sideways and spun around, grabbing both spirits in her hands and slinging them around and around.

Screaming and wailing filled the small room.

Caron had been trying to protect Lanna, but Lanna was in the way and was getting battered around, wailing in fear. It was time to end this. Caron called upon the wind from the north, hoping her idea would work. A frosty breeze stirred and grew, swirling through the room until it coated the frenetic spirits.

Gotcha, you little devils. With one slap of Caron's power, the spirits exploded into tiny, ice-like shards that caught the light and fell to the floor.

Sparkles. Her gaze locked on the glitter and held. Until Grendal started yelling for Leeshen while trying to pull his pants back up.

Leeshen had been the overbaked guard, huh?

Lanna shook and cried, still hanging in midair.

Caron gently wrapped her arms around Lanna and moved her down to a bed, where the girl immediately curled into a ball. Caron said, "Stay here. He won't touch you again."

Sucking in breaths between sniffles, Lanna nodded without looking up.

Caron spun around and called up her solid form again.

"What are you?" he shouted.

"The last woman you'll ever set eyes on."

He opened his mouth to call forth his dark powers.

She moved so quickly he never spit out the first word. She wrenched his head off and slammed it against the wall.

She used her thumbs and forefingers to make a square and peered through it at the carnage on the wall. "Dang. Missed my calling as an artist."

CHAPTER 35

Tzader shoved the last of the dead warlocks into a body bag and dragged it over to the side of the basement with the other four. Trey had one of their Beladors deliver the bags from a friend of theirs who ran a morgue in Chamblee. That same Belador would be back with a truck as soon as Trey gave word to pick up the bodies.

Someone had located water trickling in a stained sink, and Tzader used it to wash the blood from his hands.

When he stepped over to check on Mattie, she'd laid back and was holding her side, her breathing raspy. The burst of energy she'd had moments ago had subsided, but then again she had a few years on her. He asked gently, "How you doing, Mattie?"

She waved a thin hand around. "I'll be fine as soon as I can get Sissy and the others home where I can take care of them."

"I can have people here to move you with one phone call, but—"

"—Caron is a loose cannon when someone hurts her, but she's far worse if they touch someone she cares for. Don't blame her. It's in her blood."

What did that mean?

"Are we spending all day here?" Daegan boomed from the corner.

Mattie pushed up. "Hush. You're getting on my nerves, young man."

Tzader risked a quick look at Daegan, whose jaws opened, then snapped shut. Well, damn. That was a first.

"What is he supposed to be, anyhow?" Mattie whispered.

"Says he was a dragon cursed into being a—"

"*Throne*," Daegan supplied. "Not bloody furniture."

Tristan leaned forward where he sat on the ground next to Daegan. "Okay. What *is* a throne, if not a piece of furniture?"

"A seat of power, not a decorative bit of fluffy comfort."

Trey walked by and muttered, "Semantics."

Mattie tapped Tzader's hand. He looked down. "Yes, ma'am?"

"Has anyone tried to break the spell?"

"Yes."

"Who?"

Well, hell. Given her distaste for the Sterling witch, this would not go smoothly, but he wasn't going to lie to Mattie. Tzader explained, "Adrianna Lafontaine has tried twice, but Queen Maeve cast the spell and it seems unbreakable."

"Nothing is—"

Power surged into the room.

Everyone turned to the spot near Tzader where a shower of crystals announced Caron's return. When she came into view, she held Lanna in her arms.

Tzader took the girl. "Lanna? Are you hurt?"

She was pale and sounded weak when she said, "I will survive."

Solemn words from a girl who always had something snappy and lighthearted to say.

Evalle looked over his shoulder. "Hey, Lanna banana."

That tugged a smile from Lanna. "Hi, Evalle. I think I know why I frighten Oskar. He smelled Grendal's majik in my blood."

"Huh. That's possible."

Tzader said gently to Lanna, "I'm going to send you with Trey. He'll keep you until Quinn can come for you. Your cousin is in a Tribunal meeting right now."

Lanna made a valiant effort to sound in control, but panic had burrowed deep into her psyche, and peeked out through her eyes now. "I want to go back home to Evalle and Storm's building. I am safe now. Caron ... destroyed Grendal."

Tzader had one piece of good news to give Quinn.

Storm showed up on the other side of Tzader. His tone was smooth and consoling. "Evalle and I have to help Tzader a little longer. We'd feel better if you were with Trey until we're home, then you can come back to your apartment. Sound okay?"

"That is good. Thank you." Her eyes drifted shut.

Tzader handed Lanna off to Trey, who lifted her into his arms, waiting for instructions.

Turning to the Fae, Tzader said, "Tha—"

"*Tzader!*" Mattie ordered with the strength of a general.

"What?"

"Do not ask for favors or thank the Fae."

He knew a little about the Fae and had heard that, but wanted to know what Mattie would say. "Why not?"

"I know it won't make sense to you, but it is practically insulting. Saying thank you for something they have gone to a great deal of trouble to accomplish is almost dismissing the deed as inconsequential."

"That's ... " Tzader couldn't begin to understand such nonsense.

Caron said, "I want no debts. What do you want for saving and protecting my family and their friends?"

Tzader angled his head toward Mattie. "Now what do I say?"

"Tell her what you want. You're not asking for anything, just allowing her to clear a debt."

His gaze jumped to the dragon. "Can she break a curse?"

"No," Mattie answered before Caron could get the words out. "But I can tell you how."

Adrianna had been resting in the shadows at the far end of the room, melting into obscurity when no one had needed her services. Now she strode forward. "I've already tried using an incantation that includes the reverse of what Daegan remembers as the specific curse." She stopped at the foot of the table where Mattie was sitting.

The witches had a little stare-off for a moment, then Mattie said, "I argued against Rowan to keep you out of our council."

Adrianna said nothing.

"But after hearing of how you joined this group of lunatics who went after one of Queen Maeve's prized possessions—"

Growling rumbled from the direction of the throne, and smoke puffed from the dragon's nose.

Mattie merely tossed him a look meant to let him know she was not impressed, and finished telling Adrianna, "I might have to revise that opinion. As for the curse, I can tell you how to do it based on some very old tricks of our trade, but even with the Witchlock power, that doesn't mean you will be successful in breaking it in this realm. Some curses are bound by one realm and vulnerable in another."

Daegan had remained silent during the exchange, but now he said, "She's right. I mentioned earlier that I know of a place the reversal would have the best chance of working."

Mattie twisted toward him and her tone changed from polite to one of blasting reprimand. "Trying to break your curse anywhere else than the ideal spot is risky for everyone involved. Reversing a spell by a powerful being is a dangerous proposition to begin with."

Tzader's gaze narrowed to a sharp edge when it sliced at Daegan. "Where is this *ideal* place?"

"Does it really matter, when your gryphon can't take us anywhere?" Daegan snapped back at him. "Besides, I'm beginning to doubt Adrianna possesses enough power or skill to break the curse." He cast a surly look her way. "No insult intended."

Adrianna wheeled on him. "If I can't do it with Witchlock, then you should prepare to spend the rest of your life as furniture. No insult intended."

Daegan growled.

Caron looked at Mattie. "Is this going anywhere?"

"Patience, dear. We will leave in a moment." Then the elderly witch told Daegan, "Adrianna is correct. Witchlock is as ancient as you are." She swung her attention to Adrianna. "However, where you have power, I have experience. Come closer and I'll tell you what you need to know. This is for no one else's ears."

The room seemed to hold its collective breath as everyone waited to see what Adrianna would do.

She stepped over to the older woman and leaned down to where she was sitting. Adrianna's expression went from stiff to interested to a surprised frown as Mattie whispered to her.

Adrianna finally stepped back. "Really. That works?"

"Yes." Mattie smiled with the kind of quiet smugness due a woman of her years.

"If everyone is finished swapping curse recipes, I want to wrap this up and get these women out of here," Caron announced.

Tzader bit his tongue to keep from pointing out they had all been waiting for *her*, but the woman had saved Lanna and dealt with Grendal. He'd cut her some slack.

"Daegan," Tzader called over. "Where is this perfect location?"

"Treoir Island, of course. That's why I kept saying we have to go there."

Evalle murmured, "I thought you were saying it because we have to get to Brina."

"That's correct as well. Matters not either way, if we can't go."

A hologram began to take shape near Daegan. When it fully formed, it was Brina clutching the scale, now faded to a pale pink like a red mint that had been sucked on.

Tzader's heart started pounding. He looked at Daegan, who said, "The scale is losing its power."

Brina said, "I came to say goodbye, Tzader."

Her words filled his chest with ice water.

She looked at no one but Tzader. Could she even see anyone else? He said, "Don't give up, Brina. I'm on my way to see you." As soon as he figured out how to get there.

"It's not necessary," she said in a flat voice, as if she read her words from a script. "Macha explained how you hate life on Treoir, and that it's my duty to tell you that Allyn and I will be wed within the hour so this is goodbye. She wants me to stay safe inside the castle until I can produce a child." Brina's image wavered, vanishing.

Tzader roared, "*Brina!*"

But she was gone.

He couldn't breathe. Macha had taken Brina from him. No, this couldn't be happening. His hands fisted. Power warped inside his body. "I'm going to kill that bloody goddess with my bare hands!"

"You'll wait in line behind me!" Daegan declared. "Take me to Treoir, now!"

Tzader shouted back, "Are you *sure* we can break it there?"

"Yes. I'll tell you everything as soon as I'm freed, but we need to leave here before Queen Maeve catches up to us or Macha marries Brina to someone else. Once Brina gives her wedding vow, she cannot break it."

Tristan stood up. Dried blood still speckled around his ears and nose. "I can give it a try, but I might kill all of us."

Caron was tapping her foot. "Would someone give me the bullet points so we can wrap this up and let me leave with my family?"

Tzader felt Evalle's hand on his arm. That stalled his outburst that had been building all evening.

Evalle told Caron, "To break the curse on that dragon called Daegan, we have to take him to Treoir Island, which is hidden in another realm. Then Daegan says he can bring back the memories that our warrior queen, Brina, is losing due to a Medb Noirre attack. Tristan—" She nodded at him. "Has been teleporting us, but he wasn't born with the gift so his power to do that is limited. He's maxed out after three trips in a few hours, and his head's going to explode if he tries to take me, Tzader, Storm, Adrianna, and the dragon with him to Treoir. That simple enough?"

"That works." Caron was back to tapping her chin with her nail, thinking. She asked, "Who's going to transport these women to Mattie's home?"

Trey spoke up. "I've got three ambulances operated by Beladors standing by. They can carry two patients each. They're sitting a mile away, waiting for my call. Our warriors will keep watch over the women in transit and at Mattie's home if she'll allow that."

Bless Trey for knowing his way around witches. He aimed a questioning look at Mattie, and the elderly witch nodded her agreement. Caron looked to Tzader. "Get your group together. I'll teleport you, then my debt is paid."

"Really, you're—"

"Are we going to talk or go? If you cost me another ten seconds, I'm leaving."

Tzader turned to gather his group around Daegan, but they were already hurrying to take their places. Adrianna dropped hard onto the throne seat.

Daegan cursed in Gaelic.

Adrianna's eyes twinkled. "Careful what you suggest. I could give you the ability to do that by yourself."

Trey called out. "Ambulances are on the way, coming in with no lights or sirens. I'll have these women to Mattie's house ASAP."

Caron gave him a nod and touched Tzader's shoulder.

He got a sizzle of power that shocked the hell out of him, and he had a feeling she was holding back.

She told him, "You're driving. I'm just giving you the power to get there. Focus on exactly where you want to land. The minute we arrive, I'm out of there. I am *not* battling a Celtic goddess for any of you."

Tzader said, "Everyone make contact. We're leaving."

CHAPTER 36

Tribunal meeting, Nether Realm

Perspiration trickled down Quinn's back. He was trapped in this Tribunal meeting and Queen Maeve was the one holding the trip wire.

Why was she here if she knew about her throne being stolen? That was the only possible theft that had been committed by Beladors.

Did she see this as the perfect chance to shove Macha and the Beladors completely out of VIPER? Maybe that's the war Adrianna had been dreaming about.

Cathbad and the queen were smug in their silence, waiting to humiliate Macha. That would make the Belador goddess even more furious. Quinn prepared to face her wrath, glad he'd put his foot down to keep Lanna out of all this.

If only he had a way to warn Tzader and the rest of the team.

Were they already locked in Queen Maeve's dungeon, or was she allowing them to run, giving them the rope to hang themselves once they were caught red-handed? Hope flitted through his chest that Adrianna had been able to break the curse and free the dragon.

Quinn's freedom was a lost hope at this point, but the dragon might be able to save the others. Or buy them time to escape.

Light flashed between him and the TÅµr Medb pair, drawing everyone's attention to Macha, who had dressed to dazzle. Her hair shimmered in deep-auburn waves and the gown she'd chosen for this face-off was of a rich, green color that flowed and shone as though made of flexible lacquered paint.

Queen Maeve yawned.

Cathbad ignored her.

Macha could see everyone from where she stood. When her head swiveled to her right, she raked a merciless glare toward Quinn.

Smiling as if he found all of this entertaining, Loki said, "This is the last time I will be part of any Tribunal held to discuss the gryphons or any other conflict between the Beladors and the Medb."

Varpulis and Ma'at both agreed.

Continuing, Loki said, "Queen Maeve has asked that we address a theft of her property, and frankly, after listening to the longest opening speech ever for a Tribunal meeting by this Belador Maistir, I'm inclined to make a swift decision and end this."

Macha's lips tightened at the embarrassment Quinn had wrought on her, but with the hole he'd dug for himself, he could only go up.

Queen Maeve tilted her head at Loki. "Thank you all for your patience. I would like to point out that I've answered questions raised by Vladimir Quinn about my involvement in missing white witches. I ask only that I am given equal respect for my questions."

Quinn didn't need Macha to look his way to know she gritted her teeth. The minute she had no audience, she would demand to know how white witches were her problem and why he'd created this fiasco with a Tribunal.

He'd have no answer for her. He'd stall for as long as he could to give Tzader and company time to complete their mission. There was one positive in this. Now that Macha was here, she wouldn't be in the way when the time came to bring the dragon and Brina together.

"I expect the truth," Queen Maeve added.

Macha made a show of releasing a heavy sigh. "Oh, do get on with it, Maeve, or have you already forgotten that anyone who tells a lie here will glow like a red beacon?"

Queen Maeve's face twisted in advance of a snarl, but Cathbad calmed her with a hand on her arm and something whispered that relaxed her face. Her deadly eyes focused on Quinn. A viper prepared to strike.

She asked Quinn, "Did you entomb the Medb priestess Kizira's body in the human world?"

That's what that queen wanted? Quinn had a moment of relief that she didn't know about her throne yet, but panic smashed through his relief. Why was she asking about Kizira?

Macha had turned to stone. Oh, yes, he still had her to face.

"I don't understand the question," Quinn hedged, buying time to think.

"Is it true that you placed Kizira's body in Oakland Cemetery, in Atlanta, Georgia, of the human world?"

Quinn was shocked speechless. How could she know that?

Ma'at demanded, "Answer her, Belador."

His pulse jacked into overdrive. He swallowed, still watching Macha, who had yet to flick a second look his way. There was no way around it. He said, "Yes, Kizira's body is laid to rest in Oakland Cemetery."

Queen Maeve shouted, "I demand the return of my priestess and her body intact."

"By what right do you claim such?" Quinn argued, tossing all diplomacy to the wind. "She died during a Medb attack on Treoir. There is no law that demands we return slain enemy."

Kizira had not been his enemy, but his statement was still true.

"Are you not familiar with *Dlí Fola*? The Blood Law allows me the right to claim the body of any blood relation in my line."

"What?" Quinn searched his mind for this, but he'd never come across any such law. He looked to Macha, who met his gaze with disgust.

Loki had cocked his head in a thoughtful pose and said, "That is a viable claim." He looked at the Belador goddess. "Do you agree, Macha?"

She ignored Quinn when she said, "Yes."

A six-foot-tall candle appeared on the dais and Loki lit the wick with a touch of his finger. "We are all three in agreement that Vladimir Quinn will deliver the body—not the ashes—of Kizira to this Tribunal before the flame burns out in five cycles of Earth's revolution around the sun. The body may not be moved to a new location during that time. If the body is not handed over by the deadline, Queen Maeve is granted freedom to gain this body in any manner she chooses, and VIPER will be sent to bring in Vladimir Quinn."

Quinn couldn't breathe. How was he going to keep Kizira's body out of Queen Maeve's hands?

Lanna's warning echoed in his mind. She'd told him it was dangerous to leave Kizira's body for those who wanted to access the power, but he'd been arrogant in thinking he had it handled. He knew what Queen Maeve wanted with Kizira's body.

Necromancy.

Sen appeared next to Quinn. "Time to go."

That's when he realized everyone had left except Macha. She floated over to him. "You didn't burn the body. She will call up Kizira's soul and the enemy you protected will suffer a thousand times more in TÅµr Medb than what I would have done to her. I may send them a thank-you note. I am done with you."

Macha whipped her arms up and vanished.

Quinn didn't have it in him to care what she thought.

The minute Queen Maeve got her hands on Kizira's body, she would discover the secret Kizira had spent her adult life fighting to protect. The gift she'd trusted Quinn to find and shield with his own life.

Their daughter, Phoedra.

CHAPTER 37

Treoir Island in a hidden realm above the Irish Sea

Tzader had been teleported many times, but not this fast and in a way that felt as if they were flying.

The Fae evidently enjoyed hyperspeed. His feet touched the ground, and all sensation of the teleporting disappeared just as quickly.

Swinging around, he caught himself before he thanked Caron.

Fae rules were strange.

Evalle sent him a quick telepathic message, which he shared with Caron. "Mattie needs to know that Oskar is safe at Evalle and Storm's home. Rowan can reach Evalle when Mattie is ready to have him returned." Or Trey could get to Oskar if Tzader, Evalle, and Storm didn't survive this, but he was past the point of worst-case scenarios.

Before Caron could respond, Tzader quickly added, "Trey will take care of anything Mattie needs." He held up his hand when Caron started to argue, no doubt ready to read him the riot act over how she needed no help from those who ranked below her on the power scale. "The white witches are friends of ours and Trey is married to one. He'll have Beladors running security so that you and Mattie can take care of those ladies without dealing with any issues."

Caron's bottom lip pushed up against her top one in a thoughtful expression. "I accept the security. Good luck."

She winked out of view.

Tzader turned to take in his location. They'd landed within a sparsely wooded area just in sight of the castle. He thought he'd chosen the cleared lawn beyond the trees that ran the length of a football field to the castle.

For all her abrupt personality, Caron had clearly guided them to what she must have deemed a superior location where they wouldn't immediately be seen.

But Macha would know the minute they came into this realm.

In fact, Tzader was surprised she hadn't appeared next to him yet.

It was too much to wish that Quinn could have dragged Macha into the Tribunal, too, but Quinn had amazed Tzader with his impressive litigation skills many times in the past. Drawing Macha away from Treoir at this moment would top all his other feats combined.

Evalle asked Tzader, "Can Adrianna use her majik here? Storm was warned not to shift here without Macha's approval or he'd burst into flames."

"Ah, shit." Tzader turned to Adrianna and Daegan as she started to lift her hands. "Wait."

Daegan shouted, "What?"

Tzader repeated Evalle's question.

Daegan said, "Adrianna and I are safe from any backlash in this realm."

I hope that damn dragon is as good as his boasting. Tzader said, "Then get to it."

A circle of fire burst up from the ground, surrounding Adrianna and the dragon throne.

Evalle, Storm, and Tristan spread apart to take protective stances at the outer edges of the ten-foot-wide, blazing circle. The narrow flames rose two feet, as though they were shooting up from individual wicks stuck in the ground.

Adrianna raised her hands just as she had before and her lips moved, but Tzader couldn't hear a word she was saying.

She lowered her hands with one palm facing up. The glowing Witchlock orb started the size of a marble this time, constantly rolling in place as it grew as big as a grapefruit. Adrianna seemed to talk faster and faster and with more intensity now. Her neck muscles strained and her face showed the effort of whatever she was attempting.

She was executing Mother Mattie's instructions.

If Adrianna had a heart attack, Tzader wasn't sure any of them could cross that fire to reach her, because he was pretty sure she had the dragon throne locked inside a ward.

White light raced around and around the orb, which now hovered above her hand.

Storm watched Adrianna with a doubtful gaze when he wasn't keeping surveillance on their surroundings.

Tristan had his arms crossed, peeking at Adrianna between worried looks he cast toward the castle.

Evalle's attention was just as divided, but she had no poker face. Her eyes were shiny with hope that mirrored the gut-wrenching longing Tzader harbored in his heart.

All at once, the white light spinning around the orb lassoed Daegan. The circle of flames turned fiery red and flared higher.

The throne wobbled, jerking back and forth. Parts bulged and bent, jerking in and out in sickening ways.

Daegan opened his dragon snout and sucked in hard.

The curved outline of flames shot into the air and swept around Adrianna then into Daegan's mouth. It seemed as if that went on forever, but it took only seconds until every flame had vanished and the dragon jaws clamped shut.

Adrianna had been watching Daegan closely. Her eyes bloomed with fear. She backed up and took off running, right past Tzader as she shouted, *"Move!"*

The others scattered, and Tzader started backpedaling as the throne expanded and bulged, growing larger. The gold of the throne began to change color, turning from glowing metallic to maroon. Steam poured from it as the metal took on a leathery texture and muscles began to buckle and shift. Bones snapped with the loud crack of two-foot-thick trees breaking. The odd-shaped conglomeration curved backwards, straining and shaking with the effort to break free.

Scales formed over the leathery skin in a rapid layering pattern.

They gleamed iridescently at first, but as Daegan moved, light caught the scales, turning them all a brilliant red just like the one Brina had held.

Tzader's heart tried to claw its way to freedom.

Macha had not made an appearance, but Brina hadn't shown her face either.

If he'd lost Brina ... all the vengeance in the world wouldn't bring light back into his life.

The mangled shape at the top of the still-forming dragon had to be Daegan's head, which dropped back as he appeared to stare at the sky. His body expanded faster, straining and shaking.

His jaws opened, and fire belched fifty feet into the air, sounding like a rocket engine. With a roar that raised chills across Tzader's skin, Daegan's reptilian-looking wings whipped away from his body.

When it was all done, the dragon stood fifteen feet tall, with a wingspan capable of carrying all that weight.

"Damn." Tzader hadn't allowed himself to believe they could do this, not until this very moment.

Shouts came from the direction of the castle.

Tzader stepped around to see Belador soldiers pouring out. "They should have known the minute we arrived."

Adrianna had returned and informed him, "I kept all of this shielded until Daegan exploded it."

Seeing the castle guards running with Belador speed toward them, Tzader sighed. He wasn't done. He looked over his shoulder at the fierce dragon arched above him. "Daegan? Can you understand me in that form?"

Dipping his giant head down to eye level with Tzader, Daegan spoke in a deep baritone. "Yes. Now you shall learn the truths you've never known."

"Ceartas said that," Tzader said.

"I know."

Tzader replayed the meetings with Ceartas in his mind and said, "Why was—"

"Do you want to save Brina or not?"

A hundred soldiers flooded the trees, surrounding them. The first ten stepped into the clearing, swords drawn, all following that damn Allyn.

Tzader stepped between them and Daegan. "I am Tzader Burke, former Belador Maistir. Allyn is not your leader. This dragon is here to aid your warrior queen. Do not harm him, or you will all pay for that mistake with your lives."

In the next second, Evalle and Storm stepped up on his right. Tristan and Adrianna lined up on his left. He felt their solidarity, and was damn glad he had this hardheaded bunch on his side.

Tzader had so seldom asked anyone for anything, but Ceartas had said he couldn't win wars alone. That crazy warrior was right.

It took the support of people willing to put their lives on the line for what they believed.

These four, and Quinn, had risked everything for him. Even Trey had stuck his neck out.

And Tzader would do no less in protecting them.

Allyn stepped forward. "You are no longer a Maistir, Tzader Burke. You were banished from Treoir. Now you dare to return uninvited and bring this ... *beast* with you? You have committed treason."

Evalle quipped, "Awww, now you've gone and hurt the dragon's feelings."

Daegan snorted at that.

Tzader wanted to strangle Allyn, but getting through these soldiers to reach Brina came first above all else. He was still a Belador, and these men were doing their duty. He did not want to harm any of them.

Daegan's commanding voice filled the air. "I will not forget how the five of you put your lives at risk for mine, but now I need you to move aside. Leave these Beladors to me."

Murmurs of awe and whispered questions came from the group of castle guards when they heard Daegan speak. Tzader sighed. This was all going to blow up before they got to Brina, but he'd come this far and had no choice but to back the dragon now.

He nodded at the other four, who moved reluctantly, then he stepped aside.

Allyn raised his sword, looking like a child pointing a toothpick at a snarling Rottweiler. "I will defend this castle, my queen, and my goddess with my life."

Daegan crooked his head, eyeing Allyn like someone would consider a tasty morsel at a party. "That's an enticing offer, because I haven't taken a life for two thousand years, and find I'm in terrible need of spilling some blood," the dragon warned in a frightening voice. Anger swirled in his silver eyes. The black diamond pupils narrowed. "I will allow you one chance to redeem yourself at this slight, Allyn, and you should take it. I'm not known for showing mercy."

Tzader had been watching both of them and noticed Allyn's sword shook almost as much as his knees.

Daegan ordered, "Stand down until you have a reason to defend anyone or anything. If you make a move before I give you permission, I will destroy you. Keep in mind that my dragon fire is not precise. You'll likely kill the ten closest to you as well."

The dragon's head was probably fifty feet from Allyn, but who knew how far that torch could actually reach?

Allyn had enough sense to look confused and think a moment.

No confusion with the other guards. They shuffled backwards, putting distance between them and the dragon.

Daegan raised his head and called out, "I command you to present yourself to me, Brina of Treoir."

No one could call her that way except Macha.

Tzader started to explain so the dragon wouldn't lose his shit when she didn't show, but ... there she was, shimmering into solid form right in front of Daegan.

And wearing her finest gown. Tzader had seen a painting of her mother wearing that gown—on her wedding day.

Allyn made a move toward Brina.

Daegan growled and the ground shook.

Tzader stood frozen at Daegan's side. "Brina?"

She turned to him, her eyes glassy.

No one home.

He swallowed, refusing to accept that he was too late. *Please let the dragon bring Brina back.* Macha could strike Tzader down when she found out what he'd done, but he was not leaving Brina like this.

If this didn't work ... he'd lose any hope of ever seeing Brina again. Macha would not be so kind as to dump him back in the human realm. She'd send him somewhere he'd spend eternity alone, with only his thoughts of how he'd failed Brina.

He'd go willingly if that would save her.

Brina gazed up at the dragon, struggling with what she saw. "Who are you?"

Daegan addressed everyone, but kept his voice quiet. "I'm going to return to my human form. Those of you who think I'm vulnerable while shifting, think again. Brina and the group who stand with me are under my protection. If you dare to approach me or harm any one of my people, you'll die screaming, and death will be slow to embrace you."

In a swirl of flashing red, Daegan shrank all that mass to a six-foot-four man wearing a white shirt, leather vest, pants, and boots. A man Tzader had seen before.

Now that he looked more closely at the tattoo on Daegan's bicep, he realized it was the tail of a dragon.

Tzader struggled to force out one word. "*Ceartas?*"

Daegan's smirk said it all, but still he confirmed, "Another name I have been called in my life."

Tzader's thoughts raced around, trying to figure out where to start and where to end. He caught a glimpse of Adrianna, which knocked him back to the moment, reminding him what Daegan had to do next. He asked Daegan in a whisper, "Do you need to know the special whammy Adrianna used to break your curse for curing Brina?"

"I am only reversing a Noirre spell now, not breaking a curse placed on *me* by an immortal who has lived far longer than she deserves. I know what to do. No more talking." Daegan now stood twenty feet from Brina.

He offered his hand. "Come to me, niece."

The blood drained from Tzader's head. *Niece?*

He heard that word echoed around the clearing.

"Silence." Daegan shot everyone a look that warned consequences if anyone failed to obey.

Not even the wind dared stir after that order.

That might be because Tzader wasn't the only one holding his breath, waiting to see what happened next.

Confusion breaking through her gaze, Brina walked to Daegan and took his hand.

He said, "Queen Flaevynn of TÅµr Medb cast a spell to steal your past, your present, and your future. Close your eyes and listen to my words. Take them deep into your heart as I ask the favor of having the spell removed. To force this spell from your body, I must give you something to take its place." He leaned close to her ear and whispered nonstop for over a minute. As he continued speaking, Brina's skin turned purple.

Tzader started to step forward, but caught himself. He felt his heart clench. What was the dragon doing?

The purple wicked off Brina's body and coalesced into the shape of an empty-eyed ghoul that lifted above her, still tied to her by a smoky, black umbilical cord that touched the back of her neck.

Daegan lifted away from her face and barked an order in a strange language that sounded even older than Daegan must be. Tzader didn't recognize it, and he'd grown up around ancient languages.

The purple, undulating shape opened its jaws and howled.

Daegan roared and hit the ghoul with a short blast of fire, turning it into gray ashes that blinked away.

Daegan nodded to Tzader, and Tzader took a step toward Brina, unsure whether approaching too quickly or touching her now would startle her.

Daegan turned her around to face Tzader and kept his hands on her shoulders, steadying her.

Beautiful green eyes shimmered in a face Tzader wanted to see every day for the rest of his days, which might be fewer than he'd ever expected once Macha returned. He really did not care. Not when Brina stared at him now with the love he'd first seen when she was a young girl. *"Tzader!"*

She lunged into his arms, hugging and kissing him.

He didn't give a damn who stood in the clearing. He kissed Brina with all the feeling he'd kept bottled up during four long years waiting for her. He picked her up and swung her around, finally, hearing his group cheering for him.

Screw the rest of the guards.

Daegan chuckled, then admonished, "Take care with her condition."

Slowing, he placed her feet on the ground.

She smiled. "I don't have any uncles. Who is this man, Tzader, and what condition would he be talkin' about?" Her face turned green and she spun away, falling to her knees.

Tzader held her and kept her hair from her face as she threw up.

She grumbled, "I'm never sick."

Daegan laughed.

Brina gave him a look that threatened bodily harm as soon as she felt better.

Smiling now, Daegan said, "You're not sick, niece. You're carryin'."

Adrianna walked over. "Have we stepped back into medieval times? Carryin'?"

Daegan grinned and produced a cup of water out of thin air for Brina, who took it gladly and rinsed out her mouth.

She started shaking her head. "Pregnant?" Her hand went to her still-flat belly. "How could I be pregnant and not know?"

Tzader pulled her to him when they stood, and hugged her close to his side. "Macha's been keeping that from you, and keeping you from me." Tzader looked over at Allyn. "I realize Macha has played us all at one time or another. If Daegan can keep from killing you after you mouthed off at him, then I won't kill you either as long as you never come within a mile of my future wife ever again. Understood?"

"Yes, Maistir." Allyn became the epitome of humility.

Power whipped into the clearing. "What the devil are you doing here, you miserable dragon?"

Macha had arrived.

CHAPTER 38

Evalle stepped close to Storm and whispered, "Whatever you do, don't attack Macha here. She is all powerful in Treoir."

Storm whispered, "I don't plan to lift a finger."

His easy acceptance surprised Evalle, especially combined with the oddly calm outlook he had regarding Macha's arrival.

But Macha was ready to wave her hand and destroy everyone in the clearing.

Starting with Daegan.

Daegan crossed his arms. "Hello, Macha. Long time no see, but then you knew where I was and chose to let me rot in TÅµr Medb."

Evalle exchanged glances with Tzader, who seemed as blown away as she was.

Macha finally took note of Brina's presence and the way Tzader had her in his protective embrace. She cut her gaze back to Daegan. "What are you up to, dragon? Leave Brina alone and get off my island."

"*Your* island?" Daegan's deep voice bellowed with such intensity he blew leaves off the trees. "You've had two thousand years to lie and manipulate, but your reign of abuse and mishandling Treoir descendants is over. This is *my* island, *my* castle, and *my* family."

Silence slammed the air. Everyone stood tense, watching as a deadly goddess faced off with a furious dragon shifter.

Brina turned to Daegan. "What would you be talkin' about?"

For her, Daegan's voice softened. "You are a direct descendant of my sister, Breanna, one of two sisters I had before Macha and Maeve started warring for control of this island *and* the Beladors. She's had thousands of years to convince generation after generation that her distorted version of Treoir history is the truth."

He wheeled his furious gaze back to Macha. "Haven't you? You had Brina under your thumb, and convinced everyone she had to stay in the castle, didn't you?" He never gave Macha a chance to answer. "Treoir women are *never* told that their place is inside, waiting to be treated as brood mares. Treoir women are warriors who lead their armies into battle and live life as they choose. When they have a child, it's born of love, and not to be a power source for anyone. You have taken advantage of Treoir women for the last time."

Macha's hair blazed bright red. It literally looked to be on fire. Her eyes went from human to immortal, pissed-off-goddess red in seconds, burning brighter than anything Evalle had ever witnessed on that woman.

The goddess snarled at Evalle and Tristan. "You expect me to go to bat in a Tribunal to free you after this? If you side with him, gryphons will never be free."

Daegan laughed, but the sound rocked dark humor. "They don't need you or some spineless Tribunal to grant them the freedom that was theirs upon birth. Every gryphon here is under my protection, and anyone who dares to touch one will not like the consequences."

Tristan stepped up. "What he said."

Macha's voice turned shrill. Energy shot from her balled fists. "You can't take control of this island. You've been gone too long. I've infused power into this continually, protecting every generation of Treoirs. This island lives and dies by me. The Beladors belong to *me*." She lifted off the ground in a blaze of righteous anger. Lightning bolts sparked and shot through the clearing, barely missing bodies.

Daegan roared and opened his arms.

Oops. Never wake the bear, or, in this instance ... the dragon.

A red cloud of flame flashed in the air above him, and in the next moment he stood in all his dragon glory. His voice deepened and his eyes turned a deadly silver. "I am the son of King Gruffyn of Treoir. By his word, I am the last of my kind, and by your blood oath given, you may rule this island in agreement with his descendants and take possession *only* if his three children no longer live. As his last living child and sole son, I rule this island and you must obey *me*! The Beladors swore fealty to *my* father and *our* family. Not to any pantheon. They are under my protection. Get off my island, Macha."

Tristan quipped, "Nothing like new management."

Evalle watched in amazement at the horror filling Macha's face. There was someone above her in the food chain?

Macha opened her mouth to speak, but her body started turning translucent before their eyes, and not a word came out during her silent, panicked yelling.

When she vanished, Evalle let out her breath. She looked at Storm. "You suspected this, didn't you?"

"Sort of. Everything I sensed from Daegan said he could back up his words. More than that, he spoke not one lie in all that he just said."

Allyn's face drooped. He probably needed new underwear about now. "May, um, I apologize for ..."

Daegan made a dragon noise that Evalle translated as a sigh then he waved a massive claw tipped with talons. "Accepted. Go back to your duties and take the castle guards with you. We'll speak later, but if I were you, I'd keep my distance from Tzader. I've fought him when he thought I was a threat to Brina, and he's not one to cross."

Once Allyn and the troops hurried back to the castle, Tzader turned to Daegan. "I may owe you an apology as well."

"No, you don't. You were protecting Brina, and I would give up a hundred Treoir Islands to protect her, but this is her birthright. And now it will belong to both of you."

Brina sounded breathless when she said, "I don't know what to believe anymore, but I'm hearin' the ring of truth in what you say. Four years ago, after Da an' my brothers were killed in battle, Macha first told me I had to stay inside the castle for my safety. After I returned from vanishing durin' the Noirre spell, things became far more tense between us, and I threatened to teleport away. She said until the Treoir dynasty was rebuilt, my stayin' inside offered the strongest power for the Beladors."

"Have you ever read your family's history?"

"Yes, there's a tome I've been spendin' a lot of time goin' back through when I was tryin' to regain my memories."

Daegan grumbled. "There should be a *wall* of books. Not just one. I will tell you more when we have time. At the moment, I think Tzader would like you to himself."

"I would."

"Oh, and Brina?"

"Yes ... uh, what do I call you?"

"Daegan or Uncle or Uncle Daegan is acceptable. I meant what I said about Treoir women being warriors, but you are with your first child. I would prefer you didn't lead any armies into battle in the near future."

She smiled. "I'll be takin' good care of our bairn." The tears spilled down her face and she hugged Tzader. "We're goin' to have a baby, Tzader."

"I know, *muirnin*. I can't wait."

Daegan cleared his voice. "You're getting married right away."

Tzader kissed her, paying no attention to the dragon other than to say, "Absolutely. But I'd like a little time with just her. Something I haven't had in four years. I want to celebrate my new family." He took a breath and asked Brina, "Want to find our favorite place on the island in *this* realm?"

Brina's face lit up, then she paused and asked Daegan, "Do you have a notion if teleportin' will harm the child?"

"Not for a Treoir and not here. You're strong."

Grinning, she wrapped her arms around Tzader and they blinked out of sight just that quickly.

Evalle walked over to Daegan and had to step back to look up at him without straining her neck. "You might have noticed that we have a mess going on with the Medb in Atlanta."

"It's not going to be a mess for long."

Whew. She was glad to hear that.

Daegan added, "It's going to be a war that has been building for many years."

Ah, crap.

Swinging his huge head toward Tristan, he said, "I understand we have a gryphon pack on the island. Are you up to shifting and giving me a tour?"

"Absofuckinglutely." Tristan grinned, looking truly happy for the first time since Evalle had known him.

As Tristan stripped and started shifting, Evalle brought up one last thing with Daegan. "Thank you for what you said about the gryphons. We've lived according to the whims of every power that's wanted to use us. What's your plan for us?"

Tristan had shifted and stood to the side. He sent her a telepathic message. *Don't piss off Daegan. He may be our only hope.*

I'm not trying to piss him off. You're always on my ass about giving the gryphons a chance to go home and live the lives they want. I'm not stopping until we're all able to come and go as we please.

Daegan's voice boomed in her head. *Our gryphons are all free to do as they please. I hope they choose to spend some time to shore up the defenses here once I retrain our forces, but that will be their choice.*

Evalle said nothing, surprised at how easily Daegan had picked up their conversation.

Tristan answered in the same telepathic way, *I'll do that. If I can teleport to the human world for breaks, I'll come here as often as you need me to develop a strong defense.*

Evalle couldn't believe what she was hearing. Tristan volunteering to do anything on his own was monumental.

Daegan spoke out loud. "Good. Tristan and I are going to tour the island. It's been a long time since I've been able to stretch my wings, and even longer since I was last here."

"Wait." Evalle held up her hand. "I'll come back whenever you need help, too, but I'd like to go home now with Storm. And we need to send Adrianna back."

Daegan cocked his head at Adrianna, "I'm not much on witches—"

"I'm not much on dragons," Adrianna said, cutting him off with a smirk.

"Insolent witch," he muttered. "I find myself in your debt. You may call in that favor when you need it."

Eyes gleaming with humor, she said, "I'll keep that tucked away for a rainy day."

Smoke puffed from his nostrils, forming a cloud around Adrianna.

She swatted it away. "Irritating dragon."

Daegan chuckled then asked, "Are the three of you ready to return?"

Storm wrapped his arms around Evalle, pulling her back to his front.

She leaned into him then asked Daegan, "Do we need to touch?"

"No, that's only for deficient teleportation abilities."

Tristan snorted loudly. He was going to be just fine here.

Since gryphons couldn't talk in that form, she sent Tristan a message mind to mind, not caring if Daegan picked up on it. *Thank you for staying here for now, but I meant it when I said I'd come back. I'll take my turn and help Daegan any way I can, plus allow you a chance, finally, for a life. There's no telling what this is going to mean to our future, but we'll all face it together.*

Yep. A damn paradigm shift if I ever saw one.

Look at you using big words.

Storm hugged her close just as Treoir disappeared from her vision.

The End.

Watch for **Dragon King of Treoir** (Book 8) in Jan 2017

TO CONTACT DIANNA –

Website: www.AuthorDiannaLove.com and www.Beladors.com
Facebook – "Dianna Love Fan Page"
Twitter @DiannaLove
"**Dianna Love Street Team**" Facebook group page (Readers invited)
Newsletter (sign up on Dianna's website to stay current on all of her events)

Thank you for reading the Belador series. If you'd like to keep up with all my Belador releases, please go to authordiannalove.com and sign up for my newsletter. I often send special deals out to my readers only and you will see only a few emails from me each year.

If you have a moment, please consider leaving a review wherever you purchased this book. Reviews are a big help to every author and I very much appreciate them – no matter how short or long.

Thanks! Dianna

REVIEWS ON BELADOR BOOKS:

Belador novels are released in print, e-book and audio.

BLOOD TRINITY – Belador Book 1

Atlanta has become the battlefield between human and demon.

As an outcast among her own people, Evalle Kincaid has walked the line between human and beast her whole life as a half-blood Belador. An Alterant. Her true origins unknown, she searches to learn more about her past before it kills her, but when a demon claims a young woman in a terrifying attack and there's no one else to blame, Evalle comes under suspicion.

The one person who can help her is Storm, the sexy new agent brought in to catch her in a lie, just one of his gifts besides being a Skinwalker. On a deadly quest for her own survival, Evalle is forced to work with the mysterious stranger who has the power to unravel her world. Through the sordid underbelly of an alternate Atlanta where nothing is as it seems to the front lines of the city where former allies now hunt her, Evalle must prove her innocence or pay the ultimate price. But saving herself is the least of her problems if she doesn't stop the coming apocalypse. The clock is ticking and Atlanta is about to ignite.

"BLOOD TRINITY is an ingenious urban fantasy … Book One in the Belador series will enthrall you during every compellingly entertaining scene." **Amelia Richards, Single Titles**

"…a well written book that will take you out of your everyday life and transport you to an exciting new world…" **Heated Steve**

ALTERANT: Belador Book 2

Evalle must hunt her own kind...or die with them.

In this explosive new world of betrayals and shaky alliances, as the only Alterant not incarcerated, Evalle faces an impossible task – recapture three dangerous, escaped creatures before they slaughter more humans...or her.

When words uttered in the heat of combat are twisted against her, Evalle is blamed for the prison break of three dangerous Alterants and forced to recapture the escapees. Deals with gods and goddesses are tricky at best, and now the lives of all Beladors, and the safety of innocent humans, rides on Evalle's success. Her Skinwalker partner, Storm, is determined to plant all four of his black jaguar paws in the middle of her world, but Evalle has no time for a love life. Not present when a Tribunal sends her to the last place she wants to show her face.

The only person she can ask for help is the one man who wants to see her dead.

"There are SO many things in this series that I want to learn more about; there's no way I could list them all." **Lily, Romance Junkies Reviews**

THE CURSE: Belador book 3

Troll powered gang wars explode in cemeteries and no one in Atlanta is safe.

Demonic Svart Trolls have invaded Atlanta and Evalle suddenly has little hope of fulfilling a promise with the freedom of an entire race hanging in the balance, even if she had more than two days. She takes a leap of faith, seeking help from Isak, the Black Ops specialist who recently put Evalle in his cross hairs and has a personal vendetta against Alterants who killed his best friend.

Bloody troll led gang wars force Evalle into unwittingly exposing a secret that endangers all she holds dear, and complicates her already tumultuous love life with the mysterious Skinwalker, Storm. But it's when the entire Medb coven comes after her that Evalle is forced to make a game-changing decision with no time left on the clock.

"Evalle, continues to be one of my favorite female warriors in paranormal/urban fantasy… I loved The Curse… This was a great story from start to finish, super fun, lots of action, couples to root for, and a fantastic heroine." **Barb, The Reading Café**

RISE OF THE GRYPHON: Belador Book 4

If dying is the cost of protecting those you love… bring it.

Evalle has a chance to find out her true origin, and give all Alterants a place in the world. To do so, she'll have to take down the Belador traitor and bring home a captured friend, which means infiltrating the dangerous Medb coven. To do that, she'll have to turn her back on her vows and enter a vicious game to the death. What she does discover about Alterants is not good, especially for the Beladors.

Her best friends, Tzader and Quinn, face unthinkable choices, as relationships with the women they love grow twisted. With time ticking down on a decision that will compel allies to become deadly enemies, Evalle turns to Storm and takes a major step in their relationship, but the witchdoctor he's been hunting now stalks Evalle. Now Evalle is forced to embrace her destiny . . . but at what price?

"Longtime fans of the Belador series will have much to celebrate in the fearless Evalle Kincaid's fourth outing…with such heart and investment, each scene has an intensity that will quicken the pulse and capture the imagination..."
— RT Book Reviews

DEMON STORM: Belador book 5

We all have demons... some are more real than others.

With Treoir Island in shambles after a Medb attack that left the survival of the missing Belador warrior queen in question and Belador powers compromised, there is one hope for her return and their future – Evalle Kincaid, whose recent transformation has turned her into an even more formidable warrior. First she has to locate Storm, the Skinwalker she's bonded with who she believes can find the Belador queen, but Storm stalks the witch doctor who's threatening Evalle's life. When he finally corners the witch doctor, she throws Storm a curve that may cost him everything, including Evalle. The hunter becomes the hunted, and Evalle must face her greatest nightmare to save Storm and the Beladors or watch the future of mankind fall to deadly preternatural predators.

DEMON STORM includes a BONUS SHORT STORY - DEADLY FIXATION, from the Belador world.

"There is so much action in this book I feel like I've burned calories just reading it."
D Antonio

"...nonstop adventures overflowing with danger and heartfelt emotions. DEMON STORM leaves you breathless on countless occasions."
~Amelia Richard, Single Titles

WITCHLOCK: Belador Book 6

Witchlock vanished in the 13th century ... or did it?

If Atlanta falls, Witchlock will sweep the country in a bloodbath.
After finally earning her place among the Beladors, Evalle is navigating

the ups and downs of her new life with Storm when she's sucked into a power play between her Belador tribe and the Medb coven. Both groups claim possession of the Alterant gryphons, especially Evalle, the gryphon leader. But an influx of demons and dark witches into Atlanta threatens to unleash war between covens, pitting allies against each other as a legendary majik known as Witchlock invades the city and attacks powerful beings. Evalle has one hope for stopping the invasion, but the cost may be her sanity and having to choose which friend to save.

"Evalle and friends are back in another high energy, pulse pounding adventure...Fans of Rachel Caine's Weather Warden series will enjoy this series. I surely do." **In My Humble Opinion Blogspot**

ROGUE BELADOR: Belador Book 7

Immortals fear little ... except a secret in the wrong hands.

While searching for a way to save Brina of Treoir's failing memories, Tzader Burke discovers someone who can help her if he is willing to sneak into the heart of his enemy's stronghold—TÅµr Medb. He'll do anything to protect the woman he loves from becoming a mindless empty shell, but his decision could be the catalyst for an apocalyptic war. The deeper he digs for the truth, the more lies he uncovers that shake the very foundation of being a Belador and the future of his clan.

While battling on every front, a secret is exposed that two immortal powers have spent thousands of years keeping buried. Tzader and his team have no choice but to fight for what they believe in, because the world as they know it is never going to be the same again.

MORE BOOKS FROM DIANNA LOVE

New York Times bestselling Belador urban fantasy Series

Blood Trinity
Alterant
The Curse
Rise Of The Gryphon
Demon Storm
Witchlock
Rogue Belador
Dragon King of Treoir (Jan 2017)
*Midnight Kiss Goodbye (Belador novella) is in the Dead After Dark anthology
and runs concurrently with Blood Trinity timeline
Tristan's Escape (Belador novella) occurs between Witchlock and Rogue Belador
timelines
*Firebound (novella of how Evalle found Feenix – free at
www.AuthorDiannaLove.com)

Slye Temp romantic thriller Series

Last Chance To Run
Nowhere Safe
Honeymoon To Die For
Kiss The Enemy
Deceptive Treasures
Stolen Vengeance
Fatal Promise (June 2016)

Micah Caida young adult Trilogy

Time Trap
Time Return
Time Lock

To read excerpts, go to **http://www.MicahCaida.com**

NOTE FROM DIANNA:

Thank you for reading this series. I'd like to thank you if you posted a review. It's the easiest way to help an author and something we all appreciate … especially me!

Thanks so much!!
Dianna

ACKNOWLEDGEMENTS

Thank you for reading *Rogue Belador*. I hope you enjoyed seeing the new direction the Beladors are going. *Dragon King of Treoir* is the next Belador book (January 2017). If nothing changes my plans, I'll be in New Orleans, Louisian with Karen Marie Moning in January 2017 when she releases her next Fever urban fantasy story (keep an eye on her Facebook page). The wonderful Darynda Jones will be joining us with her Charley Davidson paranormal mystery series. I'll share the information on my Facebook page, too, once things are firmed up.

No book is possible without the support of love of my amazing husband, Karl.

Writing a book is a solitary job, but handing my readers the best version of that book depends upon my terrific team. My first read to last read is Cassondra who catches large and small issues, plus she helps me keep up with a ton of little details about the series, which is a tremendous help every time. My brain is filled with the big picture of this story, the next one and the next one so it's easy to miss something that needs to be right to make each book an enjoyable read. Joyce Ann McLaughlin jumps in on the early reads and to help with audio production. Judy Carney, Kim Huther, Steve Doyle, Kimber Mirabella and Sharon Livngston Griffiths all saw this book early as well.

I dedicated this to my Dianna Love Street Team who visit with me on our Facebook group page by that name (all readers are welcome to join us). I'm not sure what other Street Teams do, but we get together to chat during the week, I love to give away gifts and if someone wants to share information about my books I very much appreciate it. But there are no rules (I wouldn't know what to make for rules).

All that being said, here's my message to all of you on my team:

You've been amazing to me from posting reviews and blogs to sharing my Facebook posts and more. Your generosity touches me deeply and humbles me. I'm thrilled to have you as part of my life and I'm over-the-moon happy every time I get a chance to meet one of you in person. You are a tremendous support that I feel blessed to have, but more than that - you are my family of readers who see all the work and love I put into every book. You make it worth the time I spend alone for months, but you keep me company through those months and give me joy all year long by sharing your time and love. Thank you from the bottom of my heart. ☺

Dianna

AUTHOR'S BIO

New York Times bestseller Dianna Love once dangled over a hundred feet in the air to create unusual marketing projects for Fortune 500 companies. She now writes high-octane romantic thrillers, young adult and urban fantasy. Fans of the bestselling Belador urban fantasy series will have two new books soon - Witchlock (July 2015) and Rogue Belador (April 2016). Watch for a holiday Belador novella in December 2015, too. Dianna's Slye Temp romantic thriller series launched to rave reviews and more are coming soon. Look for her books in print, e-book and audio. On the rare occasions Dianna is out of her writing cave, she tours the country on her BMW motorcycle searching for new story locations. Dianna lives in the Atlanta, GA area with her husband who is a motorcycle instructor and with a tank full of unruly saltwater critters.

Dianna Love **www.authordiannalove.com** or Join her Dianna Love Street Team on Facebook and get in on the fun!

CPSIA information can be obtained
at www.ICGtesting.com
Printed in the USA
FSOW01n2002110118
43345FS